Men W Stilettos Better Part 2

P W Matthews

First Edition 2015

First Edition Ltd Cover 2020

Front cover: Leland Bobbe @ Pintrest & Pixaby

Other books from the stiletto trilogy

Men wear stilettos better Part 1
Men wear stilettos better Part 3 - Ruby's Story

'We are all part of one community
which were our rights at birth.
And it was because of those rights, that we are free'.
© Peter Matthews 2012

This book is dedicated to all of those friends; that I have made over the years. Friends passed, and friends new.

'Beauty is not all about what is shown on the outside, for it is what a person shows from within the inside. For when it is shown, it is this inner beauty which shows us the true person.'
© Peter Matthews 2012

Introduction

Robert had come a long way since those earlier days of putting his mother's clothes on as a child; and spending hours in his sister's room, helping himself to her cosmetics. Now he had secured himself a successful career, both on the cabaret circuit and in the world of runway. Robert or Bobby was just a memory, as he embraced his female side and now goes by the name of Roxy.

Were things now coming to an end, for this couple who had the world at their feet?

Having lived most of his life as she was Roxy over thinking things, when she saw Danni and Adam embrace? Could she have been mistaken, with what she had seen that day when she walked in on Danni and Adam?

Danni and Roxy never held back from each other; and they had no need too. They were as close as they could ever be, as they had no reason for secrets and lies.

They had what was thought of as a perfect relationship, from the mouths of their friends and cabaret family, with Danni getting the best of both worlds from Robert and Roxy.

Did Danni now seek pleasure elsewhere and did he really cheat on Roxy?

Had the fact that they considered sharing their bed with another, now enticed Danni to want to go it alone without her?

Had he had too much of the forbidden fruit, that this was the ultimate betrayal that he could have ever shown?

Follow the story to the next level; and see how things develop, in what Roxy things is the end to her world.

Take the journey with Roxy, through laughter and emotion. Through the heartache, as she comes to term with this dilemma she is facing.

And who was that stranger, that had spooked Roxy; and who had been watching her for the last two weeks?

Had the press finally found out where she lived; and did this result in her having a stalker?

All will be revealed in the second part of this trilogy.

Continued…

As the elevator closed, I heard Danni bang on the doors crying and shouting to me.

"Roxy, Roxy I can explain, come back babes, it is not what you think."

I did not quite listen to his words, as I was deeply hurt. All I could think about, was seeing them both together in that manly embrace… naked. I felt as if I had been betrayed, as we had promised each other that we would never be in the arms of another man, not without the other one being there. I could not get it out of my mind, the picture of them holding each other as they both had erections, with Adam being naked in the arms of my semi naked husband.

"Roxy, oh please Roxy come back let me explain." He cried, as he looked at me like a little lost boy standing in the doorway, not making a move to walk down the hallway to the elevator.

I had never heard Danni cry like this, in all the time I had been with him; and I did want to hear his explanation, but my pride would not let me. I thought to myself if he had not done anything wrong, then why is he standing in the doorway; and not running to me like he should do? The elevator door then closed, as I heard Danni shouting once again to me.

"ROXY, Miss Roxy please come back." He shouted, as he banged on the elevator door

I could not go back into the apartment, because I was hurt, and I just felt I needed to get out of there. I kept asking myself why, why would he do such a thing? Why would my husband; and someone that I classed as my little brother, be holding each other in such a way that they needed to be naked?

Why would they do this to me?

As I got the basement, I looked in my purse and realised I had no house keys or car keys.

"Bollocks, fuck, fuck. Now what am I going too fuckin do?" I cursed.

I was not going to go back upstairs, even though I knew it was the right thing to do logically. I should have at least heard him out, but the thought of them both being in that grip with each other; and also seeing them both with erections just played on my mind which outweighed the logic. I opened the main doors and exited the building. Instead of walking to the main gates, I used the trade entrance at the side, as this way I was not seen from the apartment. With my shoes and dress in my hand, I walked up the side street where I then hailed a cab.

"*Where to miss*?" Said the cab driver.

I gave him Ruby's address; and after a while I realised that would be the first place he would look, so I could not go there; neither could I go to his father's apartment as I had not picked up my keys. My phone then rang; and looking at the display I saw that it was Danni, so I just switched it off as I did not want to talk to him, because I needed time to think, think what I must do about what I had seen.
Halfway through the journey, I asked the driver to take me to the Grand Metropole at The Strand, as I have since changed my mind. He turned the cab around and without any hesitation drove me directly to the hotel. I then noticed the driver once or twice look at me, as he saw me place my handkerchief to my eyes, which had become very red by now, and the fact I cried from time to time.

"*You ok miss, is everything ok*?" He asked.
"*Yes driver, please just get me to the hotel as quickly as you can.*" I told him, as again I wiped my tears.
"*Not nice this time of year is it Miss? What with all the pollen about. My daughter is exactly the same and has to take anti histamines daily.*" He said, trying to make conversation.
"*True and it plays havoc with your sinuses, as does cheating husbands. And it definitely ruins your eye makeup.*" I replied.

"*Cheating* husbands? Your husband cheating on you Miss? He asked.

"*Yes… No… I don't know I just saw.*" I said, as I stopped halfway through the sentence.

"*Just get me to the hotel, as quickly as you can please honey.*" I begged, as I began to think about the situation again.
"*Nearly there Miss, we will not be long now.*" He said, now in a very nice calming voice.

When we arrived at the hotel, I checked my purse for the fare, and found that I only had a fifty pound note on me.

"*Sorry honey, I only have a fifty, so better keep the change.*" I said, as I just wanted to get into the hotel and lock myself away.
"*Thank you Miss that is very kind of you.*" He replied, as he had a shocked look on his face; at the thought of being given a large tip.
"*You are welcome honey; and if anyone asks please do not let them know I am at this hotel.*" I asked, now getting a little distraught.
"*Sure thing Miss, you take care of yourself.*" He replied.

I had never given anyone such a large tip before, but I just wanted to get out of the cab and go somewhere where I could get my head together in peace.
I got to reception and asked for a suite, I was being given singles or doubles rooms and not what I asked for.

"If I wanted a God damn double room, I would have asked you, I asked for a suite. Now do you have a suite or not?" I yelled, now becoming angrier.

"The suites have been taken Miss, and the one that is available is only for one night, and you have stated you would like a room for longer than that." He said sarcastically, as he looked at me rolling his eyes.
"Yes, I know what I stated, and I come here regular you know, and I don't need to hear your judgmental attitude either." I screamed, as I then used something, that I detest any celebrity saying, as it is just complete rudeness. *"Do you know who I am?"*

"No Miss I do not." He replied, again sarcastically.
"Then I suggest instead of giving customers a hard time, you should educate yourself a little more instead of giving attitude. Start reading newspapers or watch the news" I shouted.

With all the commotion the manager suddenly came over and asked if everything was ok, as he looked at me and he noticed I was in such a state. Standing there in his tracks, he looked at me and said.

"Roxy, Roxy Garcia, I mean Svenningsen is that you?"
"Yes, it is Roxy; and who are you may I ask? I just want a suite; and I am being given all sorts of attitude here. Do I look as though I am in need of a single room? I knew I should have gone to the Dorchester." I said, now with my eyes beginning to tear up.

The manager looked at the receptionist and told him that it would be ok, that he would take me into the office and get this sorted out. He asked me to escort him to his office, where we could talk in private; and as he opened the door, like a gentleman he allowed me to go in first where he then followed behind shutting the door behind us.

"Now Miss Roxy, what's all this about? And I am surprised you do not know me, it is I Giles, you know … hotel manager, bodyguard to one of your few escapades from the paparazzi." He asked.

I looked up and sobbing I replied.

"Giles please forgive me as my mind is all over the place at the moment; I thought you were just another interfering manager. I just want a suite, to lock myself away for a little while."

With tears once again rolling down my face, he came around to me and placed his hand on my shoulder. Then from his inside pocket he reached inside; and offered me his handkerchief.

"What on earth is going on Miss Roxy? Could I get you a drink? Maybe I could get you a brandy or something less alcoholic?" He asked.
"Please Giles; and I think a brandy would be very welcoming at this precise moment." I replied.

With his handkerchief I dried my eyes; and noticed that my mascara had marked the lovely thing. I apologised to him and told him I would get it cleaned as soon as I could, but I really did need to go and get some quiet time and somewhere that I would not be disturbed.

After a little bit more of a chat, Giles went onto his computer and searched for the rooms he knew would be suited to my liking; and to what I may have had in the past. It was not as though I was a snob, I had money and I thought why not enjoy spending it, besides as I had stayed there before, he knew just what rooms I liked.

"I am afraid we have no suites available for another four days or so Miss Roxy, but we do have the penthouse, which I see has only just become available because of a cancellation. I can let you have that if you would like to, it is up to you." He said, reassuring me everything would be ok

"I will Giles; and thank you. You will have to let me know how much I owe you, once I get settled and sorted." I cried.

"Leave it with me; we will sort this out later. I just need to type something on the screen so that reception and booking agents know it is now unavailable until further notice. That way you will not get anyone booking in and disturbing you. Do you have any luggage Miss Roxy or is that all you have?" He asked.

"This is all I have at the moment, I am afraid. I will need to sort out an arrangement for some other clothes to be brought in later, so please just let me get to my room, I need to lie down." I replied.

Giles opened the door for me, where he escorted me out of his office. He then went over to the reception and spoke to the young man there, then came back over to me with the penthouse key. We then both got inside the elevator, all the time Giles was comforting me, telling me that things will be alright once I have a good night's sleep which would enable me to think things through more clearly.

As we got to the sixth floor, Giles opened the doors to the penthouse as I walked inside. Once inside he asked if everything was to my liking, in which I told him that it was simply perfect, then looked at him and placed my arms around him giving him a kiss on the cheek, where I kept telling him thank you for all he had done. Before he left, I asked him if he could get room service to fix me up with a bottle of champagne and a bucket of ice. Giles nodded to me and told me he would do it straight away; and that he would bring it up to me himself.

About fifteen minutes later there was a knock on the door; and as I was on the balcony, I did not have time to get to the door, so Giles just walked in and placed the champagne on the table.

"Thank you Giles." I said, as I made my way indoors.
"You are most welcome Miss Roxy." He replied, placing the champagne and bucket on the side lamp table
"Thank you. And Giles if anyone asks, I am not here ok. I do not want to be disturbed." I told him, now fully composed.
"What about Danni Miss Roxy?" He replied.

13

"No one Giles, do not let anyone at all know that I am here, I am begging you; and that includes Danni." I again said, as I welled up again.

"Do not worry about anything; I will make sure I update the computer to let the relevant departments know not to disturb you. And I promise you, I will not let anyone else know you are here" He said, as again he tried to comfort me.

I then thanked him again, as I then removed the sign from behind the door, placing it on the handle letting people know not to disturb me. I opened the bottle of champagne; and poured myself a glass and went back to sit on the balcony.

The day's events kept going through my head, as I could not control my thoughts. I still felt betrayed, not just by Adam but by my Danni too. I was thankful I had got home when I did, as I had horrible thoughts of what would I have done if I actually had seen them both in the bed together, as I am not sure I would have been able to cope with such a sight, even though the three of us had shared a bed together.

Or had they already been in the bed?

God the more I thought of it, the more I got upset.

I now began to question myself, wondering if Danni had now got fed up of Roxy; and wanted Bobby to resurface more. But surely if he did, then he would have told me; was the thought rushing around my head.

It also did not help that I was slightly under the weather; and tired from continuous work; and I was sure that I was coming down with a chill. I knew that you have to plod on, as you cannot phone up and ask for a day off like if you were in a normal job, as you have commitments that you still must make even with a cold. I did have my moments as Bobby, so I guess I was just clutching at straws trying to sort out everything; and just getting deeper and deeper in letting my mind go into horrible thoughts that did not make sense.

Before long, I had drunk the whole bottle of champagne; and now being a little tipsy and tired I went to bed.

It was so strange just lying there in an empty bed, just waiting for Danni to appear, pulling the pillows from Danni's side towards me as I just hugged them.

That following day, I just lay in bed crying, pondering over things that I had seen, as well as thoughts that were still laying heavy on my mind. Every time I put the radio on, it was playing love songs about break up's which made me feel worse. I felt sick and had to keep rushing to the bathroom; and I could not believe I had let myself get into such a state. I then went back to bed and threw the covers over me.

When I woke up again, I was still a little bit out of it; and just wondered where the hell I was, when the bombshell hit me. I again began to feel upset; and did not know what the best thing was for me to do, so I stayed all day and night in bed, not switching my phone on, as I wanted to be alone.

The following morning, I called down to reception to see if Giles was still on duty; and asked them if he could come up to the penthouse. I was lucky, as he was just about finishing up from the night shift; and signing over to the day manager. About twenty minutes later I had Giles at my door, where I asked him if he could do me a favour. I told him I had no ladies' clothes; and definitely had no men's clothes, so I asked him if he would buy me some jeans and a few t-shirts; and a good pair of shoes as I did not want to laze about in a dressing robe all day. I told him once I had them, then I could go to the bank and get him his money, as well as go and do a little bit of shopping. I knew I did not have my bag with my cards in, but the bank manager knew me; and so I knew he would be able to access my account for me. He agreed to this, which I was so grateful for as I apologised for now being in guy mode, as I know he had only ever seen me as Roxy, but I think that was more my concern than his as it did not seem to bother him.

"Please don't worry your pretty little head over that right now Miss Roxy, I have seen lots of different things in this hotel, so please do not worry about me seeing you in guy mode. You are a friend and always will be." He told me.

"Thank you honey, now what shall we do about the booking reference? I need to make sure that this bill is under my male name and not female name. Can you please sort that out for me please?" I asked.

"Miss Roxy, please do not worry about the bill, I have taken the room off the booking sheet; and I have marked it down as having a special guest using it. I have not given your name; and I have made sure they speak to me before anything is done, like housekeeping; so please don't worry about the bill as there isn't one. As for room service, anything you order is being emailed to me so

again please do not worry. Just enjoy your stay and try and get over what has happened." He said, trying to reassure me that things would be fine.

I just looked at him, and with a face that was like a panda, as I had been crying all night, I must have looked rough. I looked at him and placed my arms around him, where again I thanked him for all he was doing for me.

"*Thank you Giles. I will be ok. And thank you for all you are doing for me.*" I said, knowing he was a man of his word; and I would be safe in his hands.
"*You are welcome Miss Roxy, anything for a star.*" He replied with a wink.

I then went back inside and ordered breakfast, where I then thought I must get in touch with Ruby and Johnny. It was the least I could do, and I must let them know I am ok. I switched on my phone to a bombardment of bleeps, which accumulated to around thirty missed calls, ten voice messages and around forty texts. Most of which were from Danni, and Adam, as well as a few business ones. I scrolled down the messages and answered those which were not from Danni, and then I composed myself before even attempting to read all of his texts. By now breakfast had arrived, and I was not the least bit interested in it. I thought I must call Johnny and let him know I am fine, so putting the breakfast on the table I dialled his number.
Once Johnny answered his phone, I could not retain my emotions, as again I broke down

"Johnny." I cried, now a blubbering fool

"Roxy, sweetheart, where are you? Danni has been frantic all afternoon and night. He has not stopped texting you or calling you and is so worried. Where are you sweetie?" He asked, as I could see that he was very worried and concerned.

"Johnny, I am ok. I just need to be on my own." I cried.

"Where are you Roxy?" He again asked.

"It does not matter where I am, what matters Johnny is I am ok." I told him.

"Yeah, it sounds like it, you sound pretty damn dandy to me baby girl; and I can sense it in your voice that you really are not ok." He said, as he showed concern in a strict sort of way

"There is no need to be sarcastic Johnny, if your so called friend told you what had happened then you would understand." I said back, now in a bit of a temper by thinking Johnny had taken Danni's side.

"He has told me; and has said that you have got everything wrong Roxy, what you saw was not what it looked like. You have him wrong, please call him Roxy and put his mind at ease. Danni would never hurt you sweetie, surely you know that? Call him Roxy, It's the least you can do babe, please let him know you are ok." He said, now comforting me and begging me to phone Danni.

"The least I could do, that is charming I must say. You were not there Johnny, I walked in and Adam and Danni were hugging, Adam was naked with the pair of them rock hard. What am I to believe? I am going now Johnny as I need to think, I will not be in this week, and so could

you ask Ruby or Dixie to do the comparing on Saturday. Bye Johnny." I said, as I then ended the call abruptly.

I put the phone down on Johnny, as I was just starting to text Danni, when just before I got to the end of the text the phone rang. I could not answer it, as I needed to send a message first; and I knew that if I heard his voice I would have simply broke down, so for me the best thing was to send a text. Once the phone stopped ringing, I then sent him the message that I had finished writing which read.

'*Danni what was I meant to think? I came in from shopping and I saw you hugging Adam, and he was stark naked. You left nothing to the imagination, both of you standing there with erections. I am ok, so please do not worry, I am hurt; and I need time to get my head around things. I love you Danni, I love you more than anything in this world, but right now I feel so lost and lonely that I need to be on my own.*'
I then pressed the send button; and switched off my phone. Moving to the dining table, I started to try and eat the breakfast that had been left for me; but I simply could not face it, let alone eat it all. I managed to have only the croissants and marmalade; and that was a struggle, so I got the tray and placed it outside where I again made sure I put the do not disturb sign on the door, just in case housekeeping was on the floor. I ran a bath, dropped the dressing gown on the bedroom floor and started to put the bubbles into the water. Once I got inside, I just lay there soaking up the bubbles, where I began to relax. Having a little bit of music on in the

background, seemed to ease my senses as I began to relax, so much so, that I did not hear the doorbell to the penthouse ring. All of a sudden, the bathroom door opened, and it gave me quite a scare, when I dried my eyes to find that there was a man peering his face at me. Giles had come in to see if I were around as I did not answer, and when he came into the bathroom he was as shocked as I was as he politely apologised.

"I am sorry Miss Roxy to barge in, I just heard the music and had no answer. I was worried in case something had happened, in case you had gone and done something silly." He said, with a panic stricken face.
"Oh thank you I must say. I may be a dizzy bitch at times, but I am not a psycho. Giles I would never contemplate that, because life is too short to take such drastic measures. I just needed to chill out and relax; and look at you, seeing me in all my glory. Now that's a first I think, and what a state I look too." I said, as I hid my modesty, by covering myself with the bubbles
"You look just as nice as a guy Miss Roxy, but not being rude, you are something special as a woman." He replied.
"You will make me blush in a moment Giles." I told him, as I pushed some bubbles over me to cover my modesty

I was submerged in the bath, with the bubbles covering my dignity. Giles sat there for a while and he told me that he had brought some clothes over, and that they were in the lounge next to the couch. We then started to chat, where I told him what had happened.

"I am so sorry to hear that Miss Roxy, but please put it this way. It could have been innocent, or yes, there could have been something going on. What the eye sometimes sees, is not always what the mind thinks, as there could well be an explanation for which you should find out sooner rather than later. I know how much Danni loves you; and do you really think he would jeopardise your relationship?" He said, as he made sense when he explained things to me.

"I don't know, but what I saw." I said, as I was interrupted.

"Roxy, what you saw was Danni holding Adam; and it was not how you would have expected to see either of them that day. So, Adam was naked, so what, he may have just got out of the shower. The thing is you did not catch them in bed with one another; and you did not catch them doing anything, you know… giving each other head, or even fuckin. Danni may have just been comforting him, I don't know I was not there, but you do have to look at it both ways Miss Roxy. God Andrew and I have had things like this happen to us before; and it was all a misunderstanding. Besides if I caught Andrew in bed with another man, I would cut his fuckin dick off." He said, trying to make me smile, as he ranted on

"But… But." I replied.

"But nothing Miss Roxy, you do need to though, at some point call Danni. I am sure all of this is just a simple misunderstanding. Well, I do hope so anyway for his sake; and not for yours." He told me, apologising for being upfront

"Oh, and why is that Giles?"
"Because I would not like to be the person on the other end of your tongue, I have seen your television interviews; and you say it as it is. Pity is the man who crosses our Miss Roxy, for that will be the time he will be reduced to tears." Giles said, now with eyebrows raised

"Oh yes my little outbursts, they are becoming quite a talking point now." I laughed.

"Well, Miss Roxy, do enjoy your bath; and you can stay here as long as you wish, but please, for me, give Danni a call sometime. Think about it miss Roxy, never have I seen such love than the love you and Danni have. Most people would die to have that kind of love; and you know don't you... you know that he would never ever hurt you or betray you. Now if there's anything else you need you have my phone number, call me or Andrew come to that. I will be back on duty this evening, if you need to talk" He said now making me question my antics

"Thank you Giles. I will not forget how kind you have been to me. Thank you." I replied.

"And Danni?" He said, putting his hand like a phone to his ear.

"Yes, I promise Giles, now out with you before I wrinkle up." I said, as he began to leave

When he left, and again I doubted myself, as I wondered if I acted too rational, if I had acted like a bit of a drama queen. But I could not get out of my head what I saw, and it was that which hurt me. I just thought that he could have text me whilst I was out shopping, just to let me know what was going on, as surely that would have been the best thing to do? I just thought I can't handle this right now, that I would have to deal with it later. I climbed out of the bath and dried myself, then put on the dressing gown where I just chilled out. I then thought that I had better call Ruby; and let her know what had happened and that I was fine.

Switching my phone on, I again was bombarded with texts and miss calls. I just thought I would read them later, as I wanted to call Ruby. Once I had phoned her, we were on the phone almost half an hour, when I had to cut it short due to my battery being low. She told me that she had heard what had happened; and that Danni was in a right state. She told me that I had got the wrong end of what I had seen; and it was all innocent. She had contacted Adam as she then told me a few more things about him, as it came out that he and Stuart had a big argument a few days ago.

Adam had since locked himself in his little flat; and had locked everything and everyone out, it was only when he came to visit me, did he venture out, but I was not there. Everything began falling into place; and I felt like a proper idiot, a proper drama queen. But I also thought were they just saying this to make me feel better?

I was confused but also part of me was happy that I may have got everything wrong. I then thought but why were they naked? Why was Adam standing there naked if he only went to see Danni or me?

Whilst we were talking, Ruby asked me a few times where I was staying; and not thinking clearly I just told her that I was at The Grand Metropole at The Strand. She told me to take the rest of the week off; and if I did not want to compare on Saturday, then she would do it.

She was working at the pub anyway, so it would not
have mattered to her.

"*Just call Danni dearie, as he is going out of his mind
with worry. You know he would never hurt you, you
know that don't you? You and Danni were meant to be,
and he has no eyes or feelings for anyone else. Call him
dear, for Ruby.*" She said, in her gentle mothering sort of
way
"*Ok Ruby, I will give him a phone call later. Now I have
to get dressed and I am in guy mode, and what an utter
mess I look.*" I said laughing.

I then read Danni's text; and it was sweet and short
saying sorry, but nothing happened. That he was still
sorry to have hurt me, as he continued to say that he
would never do anything like that to me, as he thought
we had a special bond. I then decided to give him a call,
where I was nervous at first, as I did not know what sort
of reaction I would get. As I got his name up on my
phone, I pressed the dial button still feeling very nervous;
as I thought well there is no going back now, because his
phone only rang twice before Danni picked up.

"*Roxy, is that you? Are you alright babe?*" He asked,
showing concern as well as tears
"*I don't have much time, as I have just a little juice on
my phone Danni.*" I replied.
"*Oh Roxy, I have missed you. Nothing happened babe, it
was all innocent. Please believe me.*" He cried, as I
could hear how distressed he was

24

"What do you expect me to think Danni? I came in and you were in the bedroom holding Adam. It was not as though he had a dressing gown or a towel on Danni, he was stark naked; and you left nothing to the imagination with only having your boxers on and a hard on. What am I to think?" I asked, as my words were high pitched due to being upset

"It was all innocent Roxy; Adam came for you for comfort. You were not here; and he looked a mess, all scruffy and unkempt so I told him to take a shower as you would go mad at him. He went into the bedroom to get undressed to take a shower when he just broke down." He said, as by now I had lost power to my phone.

I just managed to hear the part where Adam had got to take a shower; and then my phone died on me. I just sat down and asked myself, what was Danni going to say? I could not ring him back as I was now in a flood of tears. Just hearing his voice was enough to upset me; and I could not ring him back, for fear of him telling me that he was now seeing Adam. I did not want to use the phone in the penthouse, as I knew he would come rushing over; and by now I was in such a state I decided to go back to bed, where I just threw the covers over me again and blocked everything from my mind.
It was now 11am, and usually this time of day I would be out shopping, or just chilling at home.
After another hour in bed, I decided to get up and get changed. As I had no women's clothes but for the dress I wore as I checked in; and I did not like being in guy mode, however, under the circumstances I did not care about Roxy, still thinking that Danni had gone off that

side of me. I also had to go to the bank for Giles and pay him back for his kindness, so I got dressed and left the hotel. Being a man, Giles brought men's clothes and not women's, but I did understand as he was after all a man. It was not long before I got into the city and visited my favourite shops. I was fortunate in some of the shops as they had seen me in guy mode, though not for a long time. I was in no mood for ignorance, as I would have certainly ripped their heads off if they had said anything; and I just wanted to get back to the hotel, where I was away from people looking at me strangely.

Once I had finished in the city, I made my way back to the hotel, where I went to the bar and just ordered a latte, as I needed to gather my thoughts again now realising, I may just well have been over thinking things.

I thought I would call Danni when I got back to the penthouse; and I would find out how he was doing, as I would let him know where I was staying.

Just as I was about to go to the elevator, Giles came out of his office, where he caught my attention; and then said

"Miss Roxy nice to see you, I hope everything is sorting itself out?"
"Yes, thank you Giles; and I have something for you if you can give me a minute." I replied
"Oh, thank you Roxy and Miss Roxy there is someone." He replied, as I interrupted him.
"I will catch you later Giles, I need to go and relax with this latte in my room." I replied.
"But Miss Roxy." He said, trying to make conversation.

Cutting off his conversation, I went into the elevator and pressed the button to the penthouse. I looked in the mirror as I normally did; and thought was a mess I was, as I said to myself, what a wreck I look.

As I got inside the penthouse, there was an enormous and beautiful bouquet of flowers on the table. They were my favourite, which were lily and roses and looked just like my wedding bouquet.

"What the!!" I said.

I dropped my bags, as whilst I was out, I got a pair of men's jeans that were more my style; and shut the door behind me using my heel to close it. I then walked over to the bouquet of flowers; and as I cupped my hands over the roses, I got the smell of the sweet Old English aroma these roses offer; and then I saw the message, so taking the card out of the bouquet I read the message.

'To my beautiful Roxy, I do not blame you for the actions that made you leave. It was not what you thought; and I would never hurt you. I love you more than anything in this world. You are my life Miss Roxy, my life and my world. Yours Always .... Danni.'

I now had tears once again streaming down my face; and it was a good job I didn't have my face painted or I would have looked like a right raccoon.

"Oh Danni, I love you too." I cried.

I then turned around; and there, standing in the bedroom doorway was Danni.

"*Hey, how are you doing babe?*" He said, in his softest of voices

Well again Danni surprised me, as I jumped out of my skin.

"*Christ Danni, you gave me a shock there. Don't creep up on me.*" I said, as I jumped out of my skin.
"*Sorry babe.*" He replied, as I noticed he had been crying
"*How on earth did you get here? I told no one where I was.*" I asked, trying to hold back my tears.
"*Ruby told me where you were staying, so I got dressed and rushed over here; and then I persuaded Giles to let me in. Come here babes, come here Roxy and give your Danni a hug.*" He said, holding his arms out for me

I just turned around; and looking at the flowers I burst into tears. Danni came up behind me, and with his arms on my shoulders he kissed my neck. He turned me around so that I was facing him, where he held me by the waist. I had my hands clenched in a fist, where I started hitting him on his chest. Not violently, but lightly as I began crying.

"*I am sorry Roxy, truly I am. I should not have let you walk out the door in the manner that you did. I should not have let go into the elevator alone, I should have come after you there and then.*" He said
"*No No No No.*" I replied, as I hit my hands on his chest.

"You could have phoned me, you could have told me Adam was coming over, or you could have text me Danni." I cried

"Yes, I know and I am sorry." He said, wiping the tears from my face

"You could have told me he looked rough; and he was taking a shower. And you could have been dressed Danni." I replied.

"I know Miss Roxy, I am sorry, I just never thought" He said.

Now crying my eyes out, and tears falling onto my arms I said to him.

"What was I to think Danni? What was I to think?"
"Oh Roxy, you know I would never hurt you, that would be the last thing on my mind. It was all innocent Roxy; he came for you for comfort. You were not there; and he looked a mess, so I told him to take a shower, then as he came out of the bathroom, he was about to put his dirty clothes on when he broke down. It all happened so fast, next thing I knew you were coming through the door. Roxy I am sorry; and I would not and will not hurt you."
He said, as he began to get emotional himself

I was in a right state, and I could not stop my emotions; even though I was finally pleased that Danni was there.

"Come here babes; come on give me a hug." He said, as he slowly took my hands and kissed them.

I then placed my hands around his back and placed my head on his shoulder, crying on him as he comforted me.

"I know I can be a bit of a drama queen Danni, but I thought you were having an affair. And to top it all, I thought it was with our Adam."

"I don't blame you Roxy, I would have felt the same if I had seen you half dressed; and in the arms of a naked man. I do promise you Roxy, nothing happened between us. I promise you with the love I have for you and for Jake and Sophie, that nothing happened between Adam and me. I would never do that to you, because you are the only person that I want; that I love, that I want to be with." He replied, as he saw it from my side; and understood why I reacted the way I did.
"I am sorry Danni, I am such a fool, such a drama queen." I cried, now holding him tight.
"No, it is I who is sorry Miss Roxy." He said, as he picked me up and took me to the bedroom.

We lay on the bed, Danni with his arms around me as I nestled into his body. The sweet smell of his cologne brought those senses back to me that I had missed; and his warm tender touch filled me with comfort and a knowing I was safe. I slowly finished crying, as we just lay there with Danni talking to me softly as he comforted me. I raised my hand to his face; and with my hand holding his cheek I placed my lips on to his and kissed him.

"I love you Danni, I really do love you." I said in a
croaking voice
*"I know Miss Roxy; and I love you too. I always have
and I always will."* He replied

With my head now on his chest, he started to tell me
what had truly happened when I had walked in.

*"You had gone out; and as you know I hadn't got
dressed as it was pointless when we were home together.
As I was finishing my work, I heard the bell ring and I
thought you had left your keys. Once I got to the
intercom, I just pressed release; and then once I realised
it was Adam, I just let him in not thinking about anything
else. I only had time to put on my boxers before he was
knocking at the door, so once I opened the front door, I
then took one look at him; and knew he had been feeling
a little rough for a few days."* He said, as I now
understood his situation; and realized that I had indeed
acted like a drama queen.
*"Yes, he phoned the bar to say he needed time off,
something about a bug or the flu."* I replied.
*"It was more than that Roxy; I can tell you. I took one
look at him and told him he looked rough and scruffy;
and he should take a shower before you got home. I told
him you would not be happy to see him like that; and you
would have only told him the same as I told him. So as
he went into the bedroom, I went to grab my trousers
from the wardrobe when he began crying, I went over to
him too find out what was really wrong. It was there that
he told me that he and Stuart had had an argument; and
not even thinking that he was naked I just put my arms*

31

*around him. It was then that you walked in, and well . . .
the rest is history."* He told me.
*"I am so sorry Danni; I feel such a fool. Please forgive
me honey. I have not been feeling right for a few days,
and my imagination went into over drive."* I told him,
now realising I had been a drama queen

*"There is nothing to forgive Roxy; I would most likely
have done the same. I just wished you had let me explain
before going out. I have been so worried about you; and
have not slept all night."* He said, as he held onto me for
dear life.
*"There is Danni. I walked out for no reason, because my
mind could not see that it was all harmless. I put you
through that, because of my stupidity not to stay and
listen to you and Adam. I am sorry for putting you
through unnecessary worry, just because I have an over
imaginative mind. So, I again say, please forgive me
Danni, because I forgot about trust; and I know you
would never hurt me because I trust you."* I said, as I
came to realise, I had put him through hell.
*"Ok you are forgiven, but there was no need honey. I am
just glad you are ok, for I wouldn't know what I would
have done if I had lost you."* He said, now with a lump in
his throat.
*"You would never have lost me Danni, I just needed to
sort my head out. I didn't know what to think, and yes, I
should have let you explain. I really did act like a stupid
drama queen, and for that I am really sorry."* I answered.
*"Well, it is all over with now Miss Roxy, and I have my
wife here in my arms, even if she is in drab mode."* He
laughed.

"I know, I could not believe that I only walked out with an evening dress and a pair of shoes. I had no makeup, or any other sort of clothing. And worse of all Danni; I had no clean knickers." I laughed.

"Shoes and no knickers… disgusting? A proper Essex girl then Miss Roxy." He said.
"I am not an Essex girl you cheeky boy, I am a Kentish girl." I replied, now with the colour back in my cheeks and a smile on my face.

Danni turned to me; and then placed a big kiss on my lips. He then wrapped his arms around me, as he touched me gently, placing his mouth over my exposed neck, ready for him to kiss me. We both undressed each other, and for the next two hours Danni made love to me time and time again. I thought he was going to wear me out, as he did not falter one bit, as he paid attention to detail; and made love to me just as much as if I had been in Roxy mode. I knew being Bobby, was not a problem for him as he embraced both my roles equally, as he often told me he liked the feminine side of me, still keeping my male crown jewels as that was why he was so attracted to me. I was beyond being called a cock in a frock, like most guys would call you, because he knew as a woman, I was convincing to take that part; and as a man I never disappointed him. Knowing all of that should have made me realise that there was nothing going on, but I just did not think straight with all of the work I had been doing over the last months non-stop. We stayed in the penthouse all night, just talking and cuddling up to each other. He then asked me if I wanted to go out to eat, where I just told him that I would rather stay here for the night with him. Danni phoned Giles; and asked if he could get some food sent up with a bottle of champagne too, as Danni then text Johnny to let him know all was ok; and that we were both taking some time out for a few days.

That night we ate in the penthouse as we sipped champagne, before both taking a bath and again making love all night. I then fell asleep in Danni's arms, and again I felt safe and comfortable.

We spent another day in the hotel, before Danni and I headed home. Just before leaving he had a word with Giles, which later I believe was to thank him and to pay for the bill. As we were leaving, I saw the receptionist who I was a little rude to, so I went up to him and apologised. He was fine about it; and he told me that he did not realise who I was at first; and it was not a thing I used to say or use by using the words do you know who I am? I was one of those celebrities, who never used their fame to get what they wanted, because I thought that was disgraceful. I knew that I was rude to this guy, so therefore I apologised accordingly. He was taken back mind you, as I had entered the hotel as a woman; and I was leaving as a man.

Before leaving Danni had phoned Marcus to come and pick us up; and he was now waiting for us outside. Looking at me dressed as a guy, he still greeted me as Miss Roxy; and then opened the door as though nothing was any different with me. As we got home Danni brought all my bags inside, closing the door behind him, as he then made his way towards the kitchen as he asked me if I wanted a coffee.

"*Home at last.*" He said.

"*It is nice to be home at last, and yes please Danni, a coffee would go down a treat.*" I replied.

It was only when I had gone into our bedroom, I realised how this had affected Danni. His clothes were scattered everywhere; and the bed looked as though a herd of elephants had slept there. Walking into the bathroom I could see he had not cleaned up after himself, which was unusual for Danni, as he was so tidy and proper.

The towels were still on the floor, instead of them being put right into the laundry bin. Going back towards the bedroom, I noticed a photo frame was sticking out from under his pillow. It was our wedding photograph from out of the lounge; and with that I knew just how much all of this had upset him. I then came out of the bedroom; and running down the stairs to where I saw Danni sitting on the couch. I ran up to him and threw my arms around him, holding him very tight.

"*I am so sorry I put you through this, you must think me a right cold bitch.*" I said, now realising what I had put him through.

"*Not at all Roxy, I just couldn't sleep and to be honest I couldn't care about the state of the room, I just was concerned about you. I will clean it up later.*" He said, now holding me around the waist as he looked into my eyes

"*We will both do it, as Pip is not due here till tomorrow, and I can live with it till then. Let's just sit down and have coffee, then we will clear the mess up. I am sorry though; and I promise I will never put you through anything this again.*" I told him.

"*I know you will not Miss Roxy, let's forget it now. It is just nice to have you home, as the place was not the same without you.*" He said, as he held me once again.

"*I am such a drama queen Danni.*" I said, as I had a cheeky smile on my face

"*Yeah, you are, and I still love you.*" He replied, now with a big smile which again made me melt

We then sat down, and as I took my shoes off, Danni reached for the stool so I could put my feet up.
He then went into the kitchen and brought in the coffee's, placing them on the coffee table.
We just sat there chatting, when Danni had a call which reminded me that I had not charged my phone.
Whilst Danni was on the phone, I went into my bag and reached for my phone, where I then scurried into the kitchen and placed it on charge. Coming back into the lounge I heard Danni say, '*she is fine, and she is home now.*'
He was talking to Johnny, who seemed to be relieved about the situation. He told Johnny that I could not phone or answer texts, as my phone was dead.
Once he had finished, Danni told me that they were concerned, but were pleased I was back home.

"*Give Ruby a call later babes, she is still a little worried about you.*" He told me.
"*Yes, I will do honey; I will give her a call her later this afternoon to let her know all is ok.*" I replied.

We both just sat down on the couch again, Danni having his arms over the back cushions with his hand touching my shoulder; and with my head reaching towards his neck. I just rested it there, as Danni moved his arm so that it now embraced me. We stayed like that for a good hour, chatting and kissing, when I thought it was time to make a start by cleaning up. I picked up the bags that Danni had brought in, and then made my way up to the bedroom. Having sorted out the male clothes I brought, I placed them in the wardrobe without even hanging them up, then with the other bags, I made my way to my shoe room; and I placed my shoes in my shoe room, where being silly, I told them that I had missed them.

They were like my little children; and now they had a few more pairs to join them, except that is for the men's pair of shoes that I had got. I was so pleased to be home, around all my nice things, and my clothes and shoes.

I could not believe I did not think straight; and I just walked out with no thought about what I would wear the next day, as well as just staying where I was so I got a true explanation.

When I got back to the lounge, Danni had already arranged my flowers by my side of the couch, on my lamp table. They were still very beautiful; and had such a beautiful intoxicating aroma. I showed Danni the dress in which I had brought for his father's function, and he thought it looked beautiful.

"You do have good taste Roxy; father is going to love that dress." He said, looking at the price tag.

"Is that all, I would have thought it would have been a lot more than that babe. They must have liked you, as you have an eye for a bargain?" He replied.
"There was some discount, but I think two and a half thousand pounds was pretty awesome for such a beautiful dress." I replied

"It was, and you will look simply stunning in it Roxy. Father was going to go up to a few thousand for a complete outfit, so he will be pleased." He laughed, seeing my expression about spending two grand on a dress
"Really Danni? I think you will have to take me back as they had a matching bag as well." I laughed
"Ok Roxy, we can go later today." He told me, smiling and happy to see I was back to my normal dizzy self.
"No that's ok, I was only joking. I really do have enough handbags I think, and I have a nice vintage purse I have not yet used." I replied.
"Oh, ok Roxy, but if you change your mind let me know. I don't mind taking you in to the city later." He said.

We just sat down and with my arm under his, I firmly gripped his arm where I then looked at him and gave him a kiss. Later that day, I finally called Ruby to let her know that everything was ok, and that she needn't worry anymore. That I was ok and back home with Danni, spending some quality time together. Ruby was pleased about this; and told me she would have a chat with me on Saturday if I were coming into the bar.
Once I had finished speaking to Ruby, Danni looked at me where he just smiled.

"*Everything ok Roxy? I bet she is thankful that you are now safely home?*" He asked.

"*Yes, I think she was pleased I was back home, and not worrying myself in some lonely hotel room. No matter how splendid the penthouse was Danni, there is nothing like your own home.*" I replied, now back to my normal self, if somewhat a bit dizzy

"*I agree with you, and I am just going to tidy up the bedroom, so stay there. Maybe you would like to go out tonight for a meal.*" He said, as we had now got back into what was the norm.

"*Oh yes that would be lovely Danni, it seems like ages since we ate out.*" I replied.

"Well, I will let you decide where you would like to go to eat, and you can let me know once I have cleaned up." He told me, as he made his way to the kitchen to put away the coffee pot he had been using.

"*Ok honey, I will do.*" I replied.

He also suggested that we go away real soon, he wanted to take me to his homeland and show me the village in which he was born. Danni was born in a little village called 'Hyggen' which was near Drammen, overlooking the Hyggenvika Fjord. I told him that it sounded wonderful; and I agreed that next time I get some time off, I would really like to see where he was born. Putting my mind back to eating out, I then thought of a few places, and then realised there was a lovely new Chinese restaurant opened in the West End. Apart from the eat as much as you like buffet downstairs, upstairs was more for their refined cliental, and it had a stage where they often put on their own shows.

"How about a Chinese honey, we could try that new one that has opened in the West End." I shouted.

Danni came into the lounge, and with the dirty towels in his hand he looked at me and said.

"You mean The Blue Dragon?"
"Yes, honey that's the one, how about it?" I asked.
"Sure, if that's what you want babe, I told you it's your call Roxy. I will book wherever you want to." He replied.
"Well, we seem to have a lot of Italian and Greek, so be nice to try something different. And we could go upstairs and see if there is a show being performed, as I do not fancy that eat all you want rubbish. I prefer to order a meal and be served properly." I told him.
"I know what you mean, some people are so damn rude and are like gannets. Had a few of those buffets during work lunches, and I could not believe the number of times people went up to the buffet to choose something to eat; only to throw half of what they put on their plate away. Such a waste, I think. If you are not sure about the Hungarian restaurant down the road from the Apollo in Victoria, that's supposed to be excellent." He replied.
"We can go to the Chinese first, and if it is not what we like then we could go to Victoria. Not too far to nip home then should my feet hurt, as I am braking in another pair of shoes." I said with a little laugh.

"You and your bloody shoes Roxy, it looks like I will have to knock through to the little room soon and extend." He said laughing.
"That is a dangerous move honey, extend means more shoes Danni; and more shoes means lots more shopping." I said, thinking about what I should go for next, as there were a few more good designers now who have new collections coming out.

"You get worse Roxy, but lovely with it." He said, as he threw a towel at me.
"Hey, watch the hair. It took me an hour this morning to get it right." I said as I stood up and threw it back at him.

That was it; he threw the towel back, and then got the other washing and threw it at me. Then he got his boxers, and as they were in his hand I screamed.

"No Danni, don't you bloody dare. They need washing you dirty swine, don't you dare I warn you." I screamed.
"Oh, don't dare me Miss Roxy, as I follow a dare through to the end." He said, as he now came walking into the lounge.
"No Danni put them away." I said, as he then threw them at me.
"Right, you are in for it now, just wait till I get my flipping hands on you." I said, as I ran to him.

I got up and left the lounge, then scurried up the stairs to our bedroom. As I got into the bedroom he wasn't there, so I knew he was hiding.

"I know you are in here Danni; you just wait till I get my hands on you. I am going to throttle you, throwing your dirty boxers at me." I shouted.

I looked around the room and he was not there, so I crept into the bathroom only to find he also was not there also. Surely, he could not have gone onto the balcony, I thought. Then as I came back into the bedroom and was about to go out the door, he came from behind it making me scream like I had never screamed before.

"You idiot, you will give me a heart attack one of these days." I said, as I screamed at the top of my voice.

He could not keep his composure, and kept laughing, so I got my hand and slapped him across the ass, where he was now making rude gestures. He just grabbed hold of me and threw me on the bed; and then he came towards me and lay on top of me, where we played like kids for a few minutes. I began to hit him with the pillow; and tried to wriggle away from him, but he had me pinned down good and proper. He then tried to kiss me, but I kept moving my face out of the way, as he reached down and failed each time. When I did let him kiss me, he had let his guard down and I managed too free myself, where I rolled him over and where I was now straddling him.

"Oh, I do love it when you are dominant Roxy, you are such a temptress." He said, now seeing he had best give up.

As I leaned forward to kiss him, he again took over and got me on my back, where this time he was able to place a kiss on my lips. This went on for about ten minutes, before we slowly undressed each other, where Danni then made love to me. Towards the early evening, we got out of bed, and then put the laundry in the basket. Danni then fetched clean towels, where we both showered together; and as we both got dressed and got ourselves ready, when Danni tidied the bed before we then left to go and eat.

As we got to the Chinese it was very busy and very noisy, so we decided we would go to the Hungarian restaurant in which we had a beautiful meal, with a lovely atmosphere, and of course a bottle of wine for me, as Danni had bourbon. We stayed at the restaurant for around two and a half hours, and once Danni had settled the bill, we caught a cab and went to the bar. Being the gentleman Danni was, he made sure I got into the cab first, and that I was the last one out as he waited by the car door, always having his hand there ready for me to take; and would always have either his arm waiting for me, or his hand reaching for mine.

We got to the bar, and once inside I noticed Adam was at the bar. He looked at me and his head dropped, as he went to serve a couple at the end of the bar.

Johnny put his arms around me and told me that it was lovely to see us both, as Ruby waved and blew me a kiss.

"*Is it the usual drinks?*" Said Johnny

Danni looked at me, when he asked if I wanted wine or champers.

"A bottle of champagne would be nice honey, as you know me and my expensive taste." I replied

"Then it is a bottle of your finest champagne, please Johnny; and I will have my usual double bourbon." Danni asked.

"Coming right up Danni." Johnny said, as he looked over to Adam.

I then tapped Johnny on his hand to get his attention; and when he turned around, I asked him if I could have a word with Adam, as I knew I had miss read things and got things in the wrong context, so I needed to make my apologies known. Johnny then asked me if it was private, or would I prefer to go to the royal box out of the way of wandering ears. In response, I told Johnny that I would have a word with him in my dressing room, as I was sure Adam would appreciate that more than being in the royal box, as I knew he could get emotional at times; and being in the dressing room he would not show his emotions in public, for fear of everyone looking at him. Johnny looked at me and nodded his head as to give me permission, and then started talking to Danni as I went up to Adam; and as I placed my hand on his shoulder, I put my head to his ear and softly said.

"Hiya Adam, can I kindly have a word with you please honey?"

"Sure Miss Roxy." He replied, with a sheepish look on his face.

"Right Adam, I am going to be in my dressing room, so I will see you up there as soon as you finish serving that guy." I told him.
"Yes Miss Roxy." He replied.

I went over to Ruby, where I gave her a kiss on each cheek, and told her I would be down shortly.

"Need to have a word with Adam, and don't want to do it in public. I have got to grovel enough as it is." I said quietly.

"Ok dear, come and sit with me in the royal box when you finish." She said, patting the sofa seat cushion.

I then made my way up to my dressing room; and as I walked in, I saw a present on my dressing table. It was a square box about twelve inches in diameter, and I was puzzled as to what it was. As I opened it, I removed all the pink tissue paper, only to find a gold star with the name Roxy engraved on it.
There was a little message in the box too which read.
'*Dear Roxy you have certainly deserved this, and it is a long time coming. I have listened to all the reviews, and you certainly have captured the essence of this bar.*
You have got your own little following; and you have become a lovely little performer. You are a star; and now you can place this on your door, as you are no longer the understudy Roxy, as you have shone into a real first class performer.
Love & Kisses Ruby and Johnny xxx'

I had a little lump in my throat, when suddenly there was a knock on the door.

"Come in." I said, as I coughed to try and clear my throat.

"Are you ok Miss Roxy? Do you want me to fetch Danni?" Adam said, as he began to worry about me crying.

I picked up the star and showed it to Adam, with my hand by my mouth to cover the surprise Adam said.

"Well done Miss Roxy, you have worked hard to get that."
"Right honey, sit down. I think we have things to talk about." I said rather sternly.
"Yes Miss Roxy, I am really sorry." Adam said, as I interrupted him.

I placed my arms around him; and gave him a big hug as I told him I was sorry; followed by a kiss on the cheek as we then sat down.

"Why oh, why, could you not have text me Adam? Why on earth, did you not tell me that you and Stuart had had an argument? Yes, I was horrified with what I saw; and I will be honest, I did think you were sleeping with my Danni behind my back, but that was only my stupid imagination. You never text or called me to let me know what had gone on, don't you know you are like a little brother to me Adam? I love you so much; and it hurts

that you could not have text me to let me know what was going on." I told him, as I placed my hand onto his knee

Adam then put his face in his hands and started to cry.

"*I am so sorry Miss Roxy; I didn't know what to do or where to go. When I did find the courage to come and see you, you were out. Danni told me I looked a mess and that I should shower, because you would be displeased at how I looked.*"
"*Yes, I know Adam; Danni has told me.*" I replied

"*It was not what you thought Miss Roxy, I just needed a shoulder. I would never hurt you Miss Roxy; I am so sorry, honest.*" He replied, now in a real fit of crying.

As we were both on the chaise lounge, I turned more towards him so that I was face on, which then ended with my knees hitting his, and with my hand I lifted his face up.

"*Hey Adam, it is ok. Danni has told me everything, so please come on stop those tears. Do not ever do anything like this again though Adam; if anything happens with you and Stuart or anyone else for that matter, you must phone both Danni and I straight away. Don't ever lock yourself away again, you silly boy. That's what we are here for honey. You know we would drop everything and pick you up, as we would not want you to feel you were alone. You mean just as much to Danni, as you do me, so please promise us in future you will always contact one of us first.*" I said, now comforting him. I then placed my arms around him and brought him close to me, putting his head on my breast. I comforted him for a while until he let it all out, when at that moment Danni came into the dressing room with a glass of champagne for me.

"*Is everything now ok with you two?*" He asked.
"*Yes Danni, come and sit down next to us.*" I asked him, as Danni sat next to Adam. I then looked at Danni, and then with my eyes made signs for him to put his arms around him and to give Adam a hug. Danni then took over, as I stood up and dried my jacket.   I looked at Adam and said to him as I was grinning cheekily.

"*We are both here for you Adam, please always remember that. Next time you want a hug from my Danni, make sure you keep your clothes on, as I don't want to see my little brother's big cock; and cute ass on show all the time.*"

He started to smile, and with Danni soon got into a laughing mood.

"*So, you think my ass is cute Miss Roxy?*" He asked.

"*Of course I do, but you shouldn't be showing it me all the time. I have seen it once, now that's enough for the time being.*" I replied laughing.

He then looked at Danni and smiled as he said. "*She thinks I have a cute ass.*"

Danni also smiled as he agreed; and also agreed about his large endowment. I then looked at Adam and said.

"Less of the SHE. You, cheeky swine Adam." I said, as I took a sip of my champagne, and then offered it to Adam to have a sip.
"Here honey take a sip, you will feel better." I told him.

He took a sip and still being comforted by Danni, I told him to wash his face.

"If you put some water into your eyes, it will take away the redness honey, I will go downstairs and see Johnny and clear it with him about you being up here. Have yourself a twenty minute break, to compose yourself and I will let Johnny know." I said.
"Yes Miss Roxy." He replied.
"Danni you could stay with him for a while if you wanted, you know give him a man to man shoulder. I cannot as I am still waiting for this one to dry." I told him

I then made my way out of the dressing room; and went downstairs to see Johnny and Ruby. I explained to Johnny, that Adam is having a break due to his tears; and that I would give him a hand if he wanted.
As he didn't need me, he told me to go and sit with Ruby, as he could cover the bar now that it was beginning to quieten down. I walked over towards Ruby where I thanked her for my present; and as I hugged her, she whispered in my ear that I deserved it. It was not long before Adam and Danni came back into the bar; and

Danni had his arm over his shoulder, as Adam had his arm around his waist.

"Oh that's nice Ruby, the family has made up. I cannot actually believe I acted like I did, but still you know what I am like." I said, now smiling to see Danni and Adam back too normal.

"Yeah I do, you drama queen. Well it's done and dusted now dearie, you got your boys back so that must be a relief. And you got a posh apartment for a break, so can't be too bad." Ruby said.
"It is nice to see them back, and sorry I disappeared upstairs; I just needed to make sure Adam was ok as he has man trouble." I told her.
"Oh not the dreaded man trouble, what are we going to do? We can't live with them, and we can't live without them." Ruby said in her dry sarcastic voice.
"That's true, boys will be boys; and if anything, and I mean anything, should ever upset them you know who they always come running too? To Miss Ruby and Miss Roxy that's who." I laughed.
"What are you two laughing at? I dread to think what you are up to, when you both get together." Danni asked.
"Well, that's for us to know, and for you to find out honey." I shouted back.

Danni brought the champagne bottle over and placed it on the table, he then gave me a kiss on the cheek and told me he was going to have a chat with Johnny.

"Oh, I see we are not good enough for you then?" I asked.
"You stick to your fisher wife tales, and I will have a proper chat with my mate." He replied.
"Fisher wife, you had best be careful Danni or I will give you a slap." I told him.
"Mmmmmm I love it when you talk dirty, and don't preach what you can't follow through." He replied with a cheeky grin. As I told him that I was a woman of my word; and that I often practice what I preach.
I looked at Ruby and told her that it was ok, as I would deal with him later. We then started catching up on the subject of her operation; and how she feels now that's it is all done and dusted. I guess we were like a couple of washer women, as we always had something to say or discuss. It was then that she asked me if I wanted to do a little turn on the Saturday, not a full show but maybe a twenty minute spot, so that she could go backstage and concentrate on her show. She wanted me to take the reins of compare, as she thought it would be a nice change.

"I have a new dress, and it is going to take me at least five minutes to get into it, especially as I will be changing my shoes and jewellery. You are such a bad influence Roxy, not being seen in the same shoes and bling for each number." She said, as she nodded her head rolling her eyes
"I am an old pro at it now." I laughed.
"Well, I wouldn't call you old dear." She said
"Oh! And what about the pro?" I asked.

51

"Well, I will let you sort that one out, but as the saying goes, if the cap fits..." She told me, as she laughed and then patted my hand.

Once the pub had closed, we were thinking of going to the club, but Ruby was still not quite herself. She was getting there, but still needed time. I asked Adam what he was up to, and he just told me that he had nothing planned. As he just shrugged his shoulders as if to say nothing, I looked at Danni and told him that it was back to ours. Then looking at Adam and telling him that his room is still made up, so he may as well come back with us. Adam thanked me, telling me that he would like that. We left the bar, and as Johnny and Ruby went on their way, we all gave each other a hug, and then hailed a cab to take us home. When we got home, I was a little tiddly, but not too serious; and as we got upstairs, we made our way to the lounge. Adam went directly to the kitchen, and then asked if we wanted tea or coffee.

"Oh no honey, I think I will finish the night off with a Brandy and Babycham please." I said, as Adam shouted ok as he walked back into the kitchen. Just at that point Danni asked him if he could pour him a bourbon, as he had a bottle of JD in the cabinet, then telling him to help himself to what he wanted.

I stood by the kitchen door, and as Adam was coming out to go into the drinks suite' I reminded him about the Miss Roxy subject...

"Honey, please remember when you are not at work it is just Roxy." I told him.
"Ok Roxy, I am sorry I keep forgetting." He said, as he smiled.

He made me my drink and brought one over for Danni, as he then poured himself a glass of wine; and then came and sat down on the couch next to me. I placed my hand on his knee; and asked if he was ok. To which he told me he was and that he was safe and settled. Danni then sat next to me; and placed his hand over my neck. I turned around and gently lay on him, as I put my feet up and placed them on Adam's lap.

"Oh, this is the life, got my two boys with me. All I need now is a bunch of grapes, and I will feel like the Queen of Sheba." I said.
"Well, I don't know about Sheba Roxy, but you are definitely a queen." Adam said.
"Now Now, no need for any cheek you young rascal, you are not too old to be put over my knee." I said to him.
"Oooohhhh, kinky." He said laughing.
"Come here Adam, let's have a group hug." I asked

I lay on my side with my head in Danni's chest, as Danni had his arm over me. Then Adam lay down on me; and as he did, I had my hand over his neck where I gently rubbed his chest. Danni then had his arm spread over the back of the couch, with our heads resting on his arm as his hand held Adam's shoulder.

"That's better, a proper family hug." I said.

"Nice and cosy Roxy." Danni replied.

After a while we all got up, as I could feel Danni slowly dropping off, as every now and then he would jolt and scare the life out of me as he tried to stay awake.
Adam was also almost asleep, as he softly started snoring, although it was nothing like the heavy snoring I heard, when in one of the hotel rooms I were in on my cabaret tours; and having to put up with the room next door. Adam's snore was more like a soft intake of breath.

"Come on boys, time for bed." I shouted.

We all slowly got up off the couch, for which we had so got comfortable. Danni kissed me on the cheek and told me that he would see me when I got to bed. I kissed him back and told him to get my side warm, and then Danni went to Adam and gave him a hug and a kiss on the cheek.

"Come on honey, let's get you to bed. You look as though you have had a very hard day." I said to Adam
"A very hard couple of days Roxy, I haven't heard from Stuart in six days; and I don't know what I have done to him." He replied.
"Well, we can talk about it tomorrow honey, come on give your Roxy a hug." I said

We gave each other a hug, and as Adam pressed himself against me, I gently pushed him away.

"*Adam is that what I think it is.*" I said, pointing to his crotch.

"*You have a bloody hard on, you horny thing.*" I laughed, as I grabbed hold of it.

"*I have just woken up Miss Roxy, it is natural.*" He replied, going a little red at what I had said to him.

"*You horny devil, I can see you are not a little boy either; Stuart would be foolish not to want you.*" I told him, as I still stared at his package.

Adam withdrew and pulled himself away, now very red and embarrassed. I then slapped him on the ass; and gave him a kiss on the cheek and told him to try and get a good night's sleep. I then made my way up to our bedroom and noticed Danni was now fast asleep, with my side of the bed pulled back. I undressed and climbed into bed, put my arms around Danni, and kissed him on the neck; where I fell asleep holding onto him, and I stayed there until we both woke up the next day.

A couple of weeks had since past, and we had decided to take a well-earned break in Hove. We had made plans to go to Norway in the next few months, as Danni still had a few meetings he needed to attend and could easily make the journey if we were in Hove. As Adam also had the weekend off, we asked him along, as he still had not heard from his Stuart; and we thought the break from London and the scene would do him the world of good. We set off that morning; and arrived in Hove just in time to go out and have lunch. We dropped off the bags, and Adam was amazed that I did not use the flat that much, as he thought it was beautiful. He told me that I have privacy and a nice garden, with lots of nice nooks and crannies to relax in. when I told him that it was lovely; and when the sun is out, just at the bottom of the garden, there is a place that you can nudie bathe without anyone seeing you. Adams eyes lit up; and he had a big smile on his face.

"So do you and Danni nude sunbathe then, or do you wear a bikini?" Adam asked.

"No Adam, I do not wear a bikini, if I am having a chill out day I will be in guy mode and sunbathe nude. Rub a bit of oil into Danni's back; and when he is a little relaxed, I massage it into his ass and have a little play with his ass cheeks." I said laughing, as he asked me if I would let him join us sometime, that is if it was ok to suggest such a thing. I just smiled at him, then telling him that he could help me rub oil into Danni's back and front. Adam went as red as a beetroot, as Danni looked at me and said.

"Oh yes, and do I not have a say in this. You two rubbing me down would certainly get me into trouble."

I told Danni that he would love it, as he always did when I rubbed him down; and having this much attention he would be in heaven. He totally agreed with me; and with that we made our way out to the seafront, to find somewhere to have lunch. On the way, I pointed out to Adam all the nice places that Danni and I would go. How we would walk along the seafront up to Shoreham; and then walk back again to Brighton pier, which certainly did us a world of good as we were shattered at the end of the walk.

"*A killer if you had stilettos on honey, so a smaller heel is more logical.*" I said, as Adam told me that he loved it down here; and he thought that he could easily live here. That he was getting fed up with London now, with guys messing you around. Danni then asked him if he had heard from… What's his name? when I interrupted and told him that it was Stuart. Looking a little lost, he told us that he had not heard anything from Stuart, that it felt as though he did not ever exist; and that hurt. He told us that he had text him, but that he does not return his texts, so he is not going to bother to text him again. That if he wants to get in touch, then he had his number; and that he was not going to wait around for ever; and that he is certainly not going to run after him, let alone any other guy. I told him that I did not blame him, as I would not do the same. But I was sure there was some deep underlining reason why Stuart has been distant. I don't know what it is, I just had this inkling that something was amiss, this was so out of character for Stuart. However, if he was being plain and simple awkward and selfish by not getting in touch with him, then he was a prize idiot, because Adam was the loveliest boy you could wish to meet, next to Danni and Johnny of course.

"*There must be a reason honey, maybe he is busy with work and study.*" I told him.
"*Yeah right, or maybe he hasn't got the balls to tell me he doesn't want to be with me.*" Adam replied, rather bitchy but understandable.

He told me that he once asked about moving in with him, but he got funny towards him. Adam didn't want him moving in with him, as he only had a small flat; and there was not enough room to swing a cat. But Stuart had a much bigger place and thought that was the better option. He told me that he thought if they both lived together, then it would have saved on rent and bills, as they both seemed to be paying out on two sets of utilities. That way they could have saved harder for their own place, but he didn't seem interested. I grabbed hold of him and gave him a hug. I then told him to leave it with me; and I would find out what was going on. That he should forget it now; and pick what he wanted to eat, as he could have anything he liked as we were paying. Danni looked at me and then said.

"We, don't you mean me babe?"
"Oh yes, silly me. Danni is paying for this Adam; it is his treat." I said laughing.
"Ok cool, but I do have money if you want some." Adam replied
"No that's alright honey, and Adam you poor thing, do not worry I am sure things will work out." I told him
"Now come on and choose what you want, and I think a nice bottle of wine wouldn't go amiss Danni." I said, suggesting either a nice Australian white, or a New Zealand red
"Yes Miss Roxy, would that be your usual?" He asked
"Oh yes honey, Pinot Grecio cooled." I said, as I placed my hand on his knee.

We all ordered lunch, and as we would be out that evening I decided to go for a tomato and Mozzarella salad with a basil and olive oil dressing. I could not believe what the boys had ordered, or where they would put it all. Both had a 12oz steak with all the trimmings; and just looking at it made me put on a stone.

"Looks like you both will need to walk that off later, all those calories. I know I said Danni was going to treat us, but I never thought I would see a whole cow on the table. Those steaks were huge. I don't know where you boys put it all." I said now laughing, as Danni told me that they were both growing boys and that they needed it.

I placed my hand on Danni's knee, and moved it up towards his thigh. Looking at him directly in the eyes, I told him that he was not growing yet, when Danni told me to behave myself, calling me minx; and suggesting that I could work it off later. Just then Adam again went red, as I looked over at him and smiled. I told him that I was sorry, but that we were always like it. That I didn't mean to embarrass him, as I placed my hand on his thigh which made him jump and squeal.

After the initial shock of me placing my hand on his thigh; and with him trying to hide his embarrassment, he told us that he knew we were, and it was so nice to see such foolery and laughter in a relationship. That that's was how he thought it should be like it a relationship. That he and Stuart had times like that as well which was so nice; and now wondering if he had done something wrong to stop him texting him. He apologised for going bright red, letting us know that he was still a little shy. I told him that he was a sweet boy, and not to worry, as I told him to enjoy himself as he was on holiday. Then I told him that he may even find himself a nice Brighton lad, someone who would bring him out of his shell, when he then dropped a bombshell, making me go bright red.

"I think I would stand more of a chance with you and Danni, because you are the only ones who really treat me right." He said, not knowing what thoughts had just gone through our mind

I then looked at Danni, and we both had a little sparkle in our eyes. I then placed my hand on Adams knee again and told him that he worries too much. We just sat there eating our meal, chatting about everything, as we watched the trade go by as we kept nudging Adam to check it out; and seeing his face either get excited or become disappointed. It was so funny people watching and teasing Adam, but I think it took his mind of certain things; and hopefully made him relax a little more.
Once we had finished, I told Danni we would need to get a few provisions, as all we had in the apartment were a case or two of wine. Danni then looked at Adam, where he asked him if he would escort me home whilst he went to the supermarket. That I would need escorting after having that lunchtime drink, because I cannot take alcohol in the afternoon because it goes right to my head, and especially with my age. Adam agreed, when the penny dropped. Giving him an evil look, I asked him what he meant about my age, calling him a cheeky queen,

then asking him what he meant about me not being able to take it, as he had never complained before.

"Told you Adam… the wine lol." Danni said.

I told them both that I must have had a blonde moment, and I as I told Danni to get some pain killers as I had a throbbing headache, what with this sun and the wine, it has gone straight to my head. Danni asked for the bill and paid it, as Adam stood up and took my arm; and like a gentleman he held his arm out for me, in which I placed it under his. He gave us both a kiss on the cheek as he went into town, as Adam escorted me the short journey to the apartment. When we got there, I got my keys out and just handed them to Adam, as I was having trouble. When we got inside the apartment, he asked me if I wanted as glass of water, in which I told him I thought a coffee without milk was a better idea.

*"Honey you are going to have to excuse me, but I need to take my face off and wet my hair. All I can say it was a good job I was not wearing a wig otherwise I would have melted, what with this heatwave we are having. The emersion heater should have got the water hot by now, so I thin*k I am going to have a warm bath, as I need to chill." I told Adam, as I walked out of the lounge.
"Ok Roxy, I will bring it in for you when you are ready." He replied, being concerned about how I was.
"You are a darling Adam, thank you so much. Just give me ten minutes to take off my face and get in the bath, and if Danni asks where I am just let him know." I said, stumbling down the hallway.

"I will do Roxy." He replied.
"And if you want to chat with me, you are welcome to come and sit on the chair in bathroom, don't sit in the lounge on your own." I told Adam, now getting to the bathroom and stumbling through the door.

I started to run a bath, then went into the bedroom to get my wipes and makeup towel. I then began to get undressed placing my clothes neatly on the bed, as I then went back into the bathroom. Once I took off my makeup, I put a little bit of bubble bath into the bath; and started to put in the cold water. I never ever used both taps at the same time as I loved a hot bath. However, today as it was quite hot anyway, so I decided to use more cold water. I then climbed into the bath and slowly eased my way in, soaking up the bubbles and just lying there. Shortly after Adam came in, and again he apologised as he saw me naked. Yes, he was a shy guy, but we were trying to bring his better side out, even though it was sweet to see. Adam placed my coffee on the side of the bath, and he then went and sat on the chair. He did not look at me at first as he tried avoiding me, and I could tell he was very shy. I told him that he should know me by now, so there was no need to stare at the wall. If he wanted to talk to me, then he should look directly at me ok, as I placed some of the bubbles over my naked body, so as not to completely embarrass him. He said ok, and that he had never seen me naked in the bath before, let alone anywhere else, when I looked at him; and grabbing my coffee, I told him that at the end of the day, we are all the same. That I have a cock just like him; and that my only difference is I dress more like a lady than a guy. But we are still the same underneath. Adam smiled at me and agreed, as he asked me still to forgive him, because he still has him shy moments. That did make me smile, because I was once Adam many years ago, so I could understand. I looked at him and told him that I was not going to get out of the bath and pounce on him; and that he should know me better than that; and besides I was rather tiddly anyway.

"I know you and Danni wouldn't do that Roxy, and besides chance would be a fine thing." He replied, as I felt a sense of suggestion from his part.

"ADAM!!! Are you flirting with Roxy?" I asked him, as he once again went bright red; and at that moment we heard the front door open.

"It's Danni, I had best get out of here." He said, as he quickly got up ready to dash out of the door.

"Don't you dare, we are having a chat and Danni will know that." I replied.

Danni came into the bathroom where he seen Adam sitting on the chair chatting to me, he gave me the painkillers in which I opened the jar and took two straight away. Jokingly Danni asked what the pair of us was up to, when Adam got a little scared and told Danni that we were only chatting. That he was a little concerned about me being tipsy and in a bath of hot water, which could have become dangerous. Danni put him at ease, when he told him that he was only joking, that he was just teasing him. Then he put his hand on his shoulder and told him that it was just a figure of speech. Then telling us both that he was going to put the shopping away; and was going to have a nice cup of coffee. Just as Adam got comfortable again, he shouted to me about going into the garden later. He then poked his head back around the door, and I told him that I may go outside, but was he coming into the bath with me, as I moved a few of the bubbles, so that he could see his prize. Seeing what I had on offer, he licked his lips as he told he that he was going to have his coffee first; and then he would come back into the bathroom and join me in the bath. Adam became shy again and suggested that he leave us alone; and let me bathe in peace. I told him not to be silly and to go into the kitchen with Danni and fix himself a drink, then to come back into the bathroom and we can all have a chat.

"Are you sure Roxy? I mean it is personal when you bathe with someone." He said, as he had now become red with shyness
"Of course I am sure, we will not mind. I am not having you sit on your own, so you can come and chat with us if you want to?" I told him
"Ok Roxy." He answered.

He then left the bathroom when I heard him ask Danni if it was ok to chat with us in the bathroom. I knew Danni would tell him all would be fine, as we had nothing to hide; and we did not want him to start feeling uncomfortable and alone in the lounge. The more he spoke to us, the less he would have his mind on Stuart we thought, as we knew he must be finding it very hard to cope with not knowing what was going on, or even why Stuart just made no attempt to contact him.
Shortly after going into the kitchen, Adam came back

into the bathroom when I told him to open the window, as it was getting a bit misty. He sat back down on the chair when we began chatting again, when all of a sudden Danni walked in stark naked. Adam nearly died in shock, as I just laughed at him.

"Oh well Adam, Danni got to see you, so now you get to see my Danni. And Danni shame on you for embarrassing the boy." I said with a little giggle.

Danni then stepped into the bath behind me; and wrapped his arms around me as he kissed my neck.

"You really do have the water a little bit too hot Roxy; now wonder you always look like a lobster when you finally get out of the bath." He told me.

I told him to put in a little bit more cold water, because it may be a little too hot for him. As the taps were on the side of the bath, it made it so easy to lie down as no one ever had the taps digging in their backs. I then looked over at Adam and told him that if he felt uncomfortable, then by all means please go into the lounge. But I assured him that there was nothing to worry about, we are only chatting; and Danni and I would not make out in front of him.

"That's ok Roxy; it was just a bit of a shock really. I am ok with it now and if I may say so Danni, you do have a lovely fit body; and god you have a massive cock."
Adam said.

"Thank you Adam, but alas I feel am beginning to lose my six-pack and put on a few pounds, need to go back to the gym at some point." Danni answered.

"Well Danni your body looks better than mine, you are nice and hairy and very muscular where I am just skinny." Adam replied

"You look nice as you are Adam, so have no worries. And you do not need to have lots of hair, or a six-pack anyway to look sexy." Danni said.

"I agree Danni, Adam you are lovely as you are and never forget that. The beauty of a person is not what you see on the outside, but what you give from the inside. And listen to me talking like an agony aunt. You are lovely and sexy as you are honey; and you are very handsome; and so damn hot." I told Adam, when Adam told me that he did not think I felt that way about him.

"You know you are sexy Adam, now stop fishing for compliments or you will get a slap." I said sarcastically.
"We both think you are sexy Adam, and you need to believe in yourself more. You have had one guy who you got on with, who has turned out to be a prat; and who could have text you by the way. There will be others trust me, Roxy and I both think you are a very good looking young man." Danni said.

"Thank you both, I think you two are a very sexy couple too; and you are like family to me which I have never had before. But please, come on Danni. Look at your cock it is a monster. Mine is not as big as that, though I must admit, Stuart has a nice big cock." He said.

"Now now Adam; no getting upset, or we will just have to get out of the bath and hug you; and trust me I am not a pretty sight now I am wrinkly." I said, also telling him that I do not have a big cock, but it is not the size that matters, that it is what you do with it that counts.

Adam laughed, and told us how he is enjoying himself, but we must excuse his quiet moments. I then went all out, which I know was the drink talking. I looked at Adam and asked him if he cared to join us. Adam's face was a picture of joy, although as he looked at us it became a picture a of sheer horror, not realising what I was about to say as he interrupted Danni and said.

"Join you, you mean in the bath?"
"Let me finish, do you want to join us outside in the garden when we get out of here?" Danni again asked Adam. *"Unless you want to join us in the bath first?"*
"Yes sure, I would like that. Err I mean I would like to join you outside. Would you like me to make some drinks to take out?" He asked, now stuttering at what Danni had said and how he got it wrong. Or did he, was he hoping we had asked him to join us in the bath, we will never know.
"No honey, we will bring some out with us. Right you boys will have to excuse me as I am getting out of the bath." I said to them both.
"Me too honey, I have had enough today, need to get a few more sun rays before tonight." Danni said, as we both stood up, giving Adam a clear view of both of us naked. He then placed his hand over his eyes and told us that he was not looking; and proceeded to run out of the

bathroom as quick as lightening. We both made our way to the bedroom, as Adam went into the kitchen. Whilst we were drying ourselves, I gave Danni a kiss on the lips and told him I loved him.

"*I love you too babes, you know that.*" He replied, as he started to dry off.
"*Yes, I know you do, and honey I do not mind if you oil both me and Adam down. I think he needs a bit of love at the moment. I will kill that Stuart when I see him, the fuckin idiot playing with our boy's head.*" I said, now suggestion something exciting and erotic to Danni.
"*Don't jump too quickly to judge him Roxy, there may be a genuine reason why Stuart has not got in touch with Adam. Just give it time; and it will all reveal itself in the end.*" Danni replied.
"*There had best be, I do not like seeing our Adam the way he is.*" I said, as Danni hugged me.
"*He will be fine, as he does at least have us babe. So, you don't mind me rubbing him down then honey, are you really sure?*" Danni asked, unsure of what I had said.
"*Yes, I am sure, after all I am there; and you can do me as well. Besides I think Adam needs a manly figure around him, not a womanly figure. He really likes you honey; and looks up to you, so maybe you can take him to one side at some point and have a chat with him.*" I replied, not showing any jealousy or misgivings.
"*Sure Roxy, I am sure I can sort that out.*" He replied.

Just then, Adam came into the bedroom and asked if there was anything he could do. I told him to get out of his clothes and put on the blue dressing gown behind the bathroom door, then to take the blanket that was folded on the bed outside. Seeing both Danni and I naked, now did not seem to worry Adam; and I think he was slowly beginning to relax with Danni and me. Adam took the dressing gown and placed it on the bed, then started to undress, so not as to embarrass him too much; Danni and I made our way into the garden. Danni and I went into the back garden; and with our blanket we spread them on the floor, where we removed our dressing gowns and lay on our fronts. We started to chat for a while, mainly about Adam and how we both liked him, as well as him being a very special person to us. Danni told me that he would like to take him under his wing, that he would like to be like a big brother/father figure to him, as he knows he has had a rough time; and anything he could do to help, then he would. I thought that was a lovely thing to suggest; and I told Danni that I too thought about that some time ago, that I would have liked to be a sister mother kind of person to him, that I too wanted to look after him and show him the nicer things that are out there. That I knew Adam deserved to see a nicer thing to the gay scene, but to also see us more than just friends. I suggested that we put it too him later on if the conversation ever led that way.

As we were laying there, Danni surprised me with the next bit of chat, as he asked me about a conversation that we had months ago, a conversation about a threesome. I told him that I do remember that conversation as though it were only yesterday. Then Danni suggested Adam, that what did I think of asking Adam, after all we both liked him; and he was very special to us; and god was he cute, he was so fuckin young and cute. I stopped for a

moment to think, then I told Danni that if Adam agreed, then I would be up for it, as he would be a very good choice. That I would prefer it to be Adam because he is a private lad, and he would keep things to himself and not spread it on the gay scene. I also told Danni, that if Adam agreed, then I would not want anyone else with regards a threesome. Danni agreed; and suggested that if it worked then maybe it could become a regular thing. Regular but not as in every day, or every week, because we could become bored. I just smiled telling him that I didn't know about being bored, that I would be in heaven playing with my two boys. Danni then moved over to me and kissed me on my back, as he placed his leg over my ass cheeks.
He then placed his face by my ear where he whispered.

"You little minx, you had this planned all along didn't you, you saucy minx?"

I told him that it was he who suggested it not me, but it would be nice to see him being spit roasted by his wife and lover. He kissed me on my ear, and playfully slapped my ass, when all of a sudden Adam came into the garden. He apologised for coming into the garden too soon, especially as we were being frisky. I assured him that we were not being frisky, that it is just Danni being kinky by slapping my ass. I then patted the ground for him to come and join us, telling him that Danni would move his towel over to make some room.

"Yes Miss Roxy." Danni said as he too moved over to make some room for Adam.

Adam placed his towel on the airbed and came in between us. He was still very shy as he kept his boxers on, but we never minded as we did not like to pressure people. We had a very large airbed so it easily fitted the three of us. Adam then put his towel in the middle; and lay on his tummy, he then looking at me he thanked me again for letting him come away with us, as this was something he needed. He also told us that he was having a really nice time; and didn't want it to end. I told him that he had another two days left on his holiday; and to enjoy himself. Then without warning, I asked him if he would like Danni to rub some oil into his beautiful body. He perked up, as he told me that he would like that very much, and that was of course, if Danni did not object. And so, Adam asked Danni if he would rub oil into his back, and Danni did just that; and obliged. Danni then came over to me and started to do my shoulders and back, as I felt something rather hard touching my ass. I put on my aunty Roxy voice, as I then asked him, if that was what I thought it was, then he can move, as it was rather too early for me to be poked by a throbbing cock. Jokingly Danni again pressed his cock into my ass, as he rubbed my shoulders and back. He knew this would either get me horny, in which we would end up having a little play, or would annoy me, in which I would just end up going indoors. I looked at him and told him that maybe later, he could most likely have me later, as I then told him to go and massage Adam, as I needed to get some sun and some colour, as I was lacking in my vitamin D. Danni asked me how I was fairing, especially with having that afternoon drink. In which I told him I was ok, but I thought that it was more the bath and the lunch that had got to me; and that I now needed to lie on my back, asking him to pass me the spare pillows so that I could sit up a little. Danni passed me the pillows so that my head was not flat on the bed. I then had a sigh of relief, as Danni oiled my legs. With a bit of the oil, he placed in my hands, I started to oil my front. I could see now that Danni was rock hard, and he had got me the same way. I still wanted to get a bit of sun, and sex was not really on the cards for me as of yet. I asked Danni again to give Adam a massage, and to just let me settle for a while. I told him that I needed five minutes as well as a glass of water, as by now I started to be dehydrated. Danni then moved over to Adam, where he first of all sat by his side and rubbed his shoulders. Worried that he may get oil over his boxers, Danni asked Adam to take them off, giving him the reason why. Adam being Adam, asked Danni if it was ok to do so, as he did not want to embarrass anybody, least of all himself; and I knew that he may already have done so, because I noticed that he had a bit of a boner in his boxers, to which I thought that omg, does anyone ever sunbathe and not get a fuckin boner. Adam removed his boxers; and Danni resumed his position. Adam seemed to love every minute of it as he slowly moaned with contentment, flinching a few times when Danni had discovered as knot or tight muscle in his back, slowly using his techniques to make him unstressed. As he moved down his body, you could see that Adam was now totally relaxed. Danni then straddled him as he started to work his back and sides, and as he did so his cock was also pressing against Adams ass crack. The further he massaged his back, the further his cock slid up and down Adams crack; and the more Adam enjoyed it. Adam then turned his head towards me, and looked directly at me, when he said.

"Can I hold your hand Roxy; as this is scary and so intense?"
"Of course, you can honey, but why is it scary?" I replied, as I offered him my hand.
"I have never done anything like this before, and I certainly have never had such a massive cock anywhere near me. He told me.
"Oh, don't worry about that honey, I was scared for a while when I first met Danni; and it is not as though he is just gonna thrust it right inside you. Try and relax and just enjoy your massage, as Danni also told him to relax; and that he would never push him to do anything he did not want to do.

I also noticed that he did not just look at my face when we chatted, but also looked down my body towards my cock. Being a little sarcastic I asked him if he liked what he saw, because the view does not get any better. Going bright red, Adam then told me that he did indeed like what he saw; and that he felt privileged to be spending a weekend with his two-favourite people, as I told him to behave as he would get me blushing soon. I then told him that it was our pleasure, because we both liked him, and we liked him more than a friend, because we considered him family.
As Danni massaged him harder, and touched some of his weak spots, he squeezed on my hand a little harder. When Danni's cock slid through his ass cheeks, I did

hear Adam making a whimpering sound; and so I held his hand tight. Danni then worked his way down his legs, going in between his thighs and making sure he had not missed any bits. Then with his hands coming back up his legs he would massage his ass; and gently press his thumbs into his ass crack.

Before long, Danni asked Adam to turn over so that he could oil his front. I knew Adam was shy, because he asked me if he had too; and so, I just came out with it, as I teased him because he had a hard on. This time he did not go as red, but instead just came out with it, telling me that yes, he did have a hard on, and that he did not care anymore. I then told him to look at both Danni and me, as it was not as though we were flaccid; and it did not bother us in the slightest.

"But you haven't seen me hard before, and I don't want to embarrass you." Adam said.
"Well, I have seen you Adam, I may have caught a little glimpse of you back in London when I hugged you; and it takes a lot to embarrass her I can tell you." Danni said.

Adam turned around, and he was no small lad either. He had the cutest of hair on his chest which was just in the centre; which was a lovely light ginger; that glistened in the sun when it caught his body right. He was still a young man and had time to fill out, so looking at him he was lovely and slender, if not too white as I feel he was not really a sun worshiper. He did though have big balls and masses of pubic hair, with that lovely flight path line going from navel to cock, and a cock that was easily eight inches long as well as being thick and cut. He kept

74

his pubic area trimmed, even though he still had masses of hair down there, but he did have his balls shaved which was a godsend.

"*See that didn't hurt did it?*" I asked
"*No, I guess not, but I am feeling more relaxed with you both. I know my shyness will eventually go, but I also know it will take time.*" He said now with his legs wide open, as Danni sat in between them.

Danni then gently massaged his chest and shoulders, as Adam once again reached for my hand. As Danni moved further down his body, I could see him raise his ass enticing Danni's cock to go closer towards him, as he began to get even more excited with Danni giving him a massage; and feeling his cock touching his body.
Adam held my hand tighter, as Danni now began to massage his thighs and groin, his cock bobbing up and down, as he thrust his legs in the air now with his cock oozing pre cum, as he exposed his hot firm ass. I heard Adam tell Danni that he was good at what he was doing, but he had to slow down as he was going a little too fast, and it was intense. Danni then moved into Adams groin, as he pulled him towards him, his legs now over his shoulders as Danni's cock touched his ass and balls. Leaning into Adam he massaged him again, as Danni's cock just hit the tip of his hole. It was then that Adam surprised me, as he asked me if he could have a kiss. I thought that so sweet; and so I turned on my side, and as Adams hand slipped from mine he grabbed hold of my cock. I then started to kiss him, as Danni rubbed his body and massaged his cock, placing his own cock

between Adam's ass and without thrusting inside him. He was such a beautiful kisser, so gentle, yet so very passionate. Danni then released his legs and let them lie at the side of him, as Danni then moved in between Adams legs and took his cock in his mouth.

"Oh, no Danni, stop for a minute please. Please stop." He said

Danni released his mouth from Adams cock, as he once again lifted his legs over his shoulders as he began sucking his balls and rimmed his ass. Adam was now thrusting and gyrating with excitement, as he kissed me passionately and told me that he wanted us both to make love to him. I looked at him and got my hand and cupped it over his sweet face, then told him that we could do that later, that we could spend all night doing what he had just asked me if it pleased him, but for now, he should just enjoy the moment. Panting heavily, he told me that if Danni continued, then he was going to shoot his load; and that was unusual for him because he was a long stayer, and never was a quick cummer. I told him to relax; and if it was a case that he shot his load, then he should let it happen, as Danni also told him that it was fine by him as he would take all of him. Kissing me again; and now stroking my cock, Adam asked Danni to keep licking his balls and ass for a while. Danni being obliging as he was, told Adam not to fret, as he began sucking Adams balls, and sliding his tongue up and down his shaft, as he fingered his ass and rimmed him much to Adam's willingness.

"*I don't think I can hold on much longer Roxy.*" Adam said, now moaning and asking permission to let go of his load.
"*That's ok my little firecracker; do you want Danni to suck your cock again?*" I asked him
"*Oh yes please, Danni I am ready, will you please take my cock?*" He asked

I often called Adam my little firecracker; and it was not a disrespectful gesture because he had the most gorgeous ginger hair. It was because he was quiet at first; and when he warmed up, the intensity he had inside just exploded like that of a firework.
Danni again dropped his legs, as he laid them by his side. He then took Adams cock into his mouth, as he pulled on his balls; when Adam then began kissing me passionately, as he began to rub my cock harder.

"*Easy tiger before you pull the fuckin thing off, you horny bitch.*" I told him
"*Oh yes Miss Roxy, I am yours and Danni's horny slut, your fuck buddy.*" He replied

I looked at Danni and smiled, then looked over at Adam and said, with a slight laugh.

"*You have been watching too much porn, fuck buddy indeed.*"
"*Yes Miss Roxy, but this is better, better than any old porno you may want to watch.*" He answered, and then looked at Danni and said to him.

"Danni, Sir will you please take me, I want to feel you inside me, and I want you to feel all of me?"

"You will get my cock when I am ready Adam; and not minute sooner. I am going to milk you, now lay back and just relax. Hold on to Miss Roxy's cock and play with her, until I am ready for you to take mine." Danni said, now being in complete control
"Yes Sir, whatever you say Sir." He replied.

Danni then placed his cock onto Adams and gently teased him, as he grabbed my ass and fingered me whilst I was kissing Adam. Both Danni and I kissed Adam, and then Danni began kissing me. Adam was switching from one to the other, as he now had my cock in one hand and Danni's in the other. Danni then sat up, and as he did, then held his cock in his hand; and thrust it towards Adam, as he also placed his cock onto Adams and began rubbing them both together. He then looked at Adam again, and then told Adam to suck his cock.

"Come on Adam, suck that big dick. You know you want to; and I want you to take all of it." Danni said, waving his cock around in the sun; teasing Adam more as he pulled away when he got close to him.
"I haven't sucked a cock that big before Sir, please let me go slow." Adam replied
"Just suck my dick boy, whilst I suck off Miss Roxy to completion." He replied, as he placed his hard cock over Adam's face.
"Yes Sir, sorry Sir." He replied.

Adam started to suck Danni's cock, which gave himself time to relax and not just shoot his load. Danni started sucking my cock; and coming up to my face where he would kiss me passionately. Before long I told Danni that I was cumming, and I could not stop.

Danni worked on me and milked my cock, taking every last drop as I shot down his throat. He then took his cock from Adams mouth, which by now Adam had managed to take all of Danni's cock down his throat.

Danni made his way back between Adams legs, as he took Adam's cock into his mouth, pulling again on his balls. He took Adam deep inside him; and started to suck him hard. Adam pressed his lips against mine as he kissed me, and kept saying thank you Miss, and thank you Sir, as the pair of us pleasured this hot horny young man. Adam could no longer hang on, as he told Danni that he was cumming, apologising to us both that he could no longer hold on and that he was about to shoot his load. He screamed, as he began to wriggle and moan as he was ready to orgasm

Danni held tight onto Adam, as he thrust his cock back inside his mouth. Adam then couldn't stop himself, as he thrust his body into Danni and thrust his cock deep inside his throat, emptying all what his cock had.

"Stop please Sir, I am so sensitive. Please stop." He said as he tried to get Danni off him.

This only made Danni worse, as he began to torment Adam in a playful way, as he licked the tip of his cock until Adam was shaking. It was then that Danni stopped, as he knew I used to get like that. He then thanked us both in turn, telling us how amazing that was and how he was grateful that it was all over. Danni then looked at him; and told him that who mentioned that we had finished, that it was now his turn; and that he was going to take all of his load. Now sounding a little nervous, Adam told Danni that he did not swallow, that he had not quite tried it because he was scared too; and whatever Danni had planned, he still must take things slow. Knowing how he was nervous, Danni just told him that all was ok; and that he could rim his ass as he jerks over him; and once he shoots his load, then he could taste a little bit of it. Adam agreed to that, thanking him for not forcing him to undertake something he did not want to do. Danni then straddled Adams face, as I told Danni I needed to go and fetch some more water. I left Danni and Adam to get on with it; and once I got back, Danni had just shot over Adams stomach and cock, as Adam was now taking the remainder of Danni's wet cock in his mouth.

"Oh god that was good, I have never had sex like that before. Thank you." Said Adam
"That's ok honey, there is plenty more where that came from. Well until you find a boyfriend that is, or Stuart gets back to you." I told him, as I just lay back down and relaxed for a while.

We just lay there for a few more hours, before going indoors to shower and get ready for the evening that we had planned. Adam asked me if the three of us ever made love again, would I still be as Roxy; or would I be in guy mode. I knew he liked me as both, but somehow,

I think he wanted to experience a night with the proper Roxy. I asked him if he was sure, telling him that once you have had a night with Roxy, you will never go back to wanting a normal night. Adam then told us yes, that he would with both of our decisions and permission, like to experience a night with us both again, but with me being dressed as Roxy and not being in drab mode. I just thought he has already had a little taster, and now he cannot get enough of us; and that we cannot spoil him too much too quickly. As I got ready, Adam looked in his bag and found he had not packed any really nice clothes to go out, just jeans and t shirts. I looked at him and told him to go into my wardrobe. There I told him that if he were to go to the far right hand side, that he would find my men's clothes; and as I no longer wear them, he could take his pick, that they were years old, and when I was as slim as he was, so I was sure he would find something suitable. He walked towards the wardrobes, and after sliding a few summer outfits out of the way, he stopped and gasped. Picking a suit out of the wardrobe, he looked at me; and just like an excited child, he told me that he could not wear such magnificent clothes as they were top end designer, saying that he thought them to be a little too posh for him. I told him that they had never been worn, and to help himself. There were suits as well as trousers, jumpers and tops, as well as there being jeans and t-shirts. That he should just help himself, because in all honesty, it would be nice to see them getting used. He saw what we were both wearing; and dressed himself accordingly. Danni was rarely in casual attire if we went out, as he did like his suits and ties. It was only when we were at home alone together that he would wear a t-shirt and jeans, or joggers. Sometimes he would only wear lounging pants, depending on what time he got home. Tonight though was of no exception, and with his Armani suit, and yellow stripe shirt he looked absolutely stunning.

Adam went a little more casual with a nice pair of Calvin Klein trousers, a nice polo shirt and shoes, with a jumper wrapped around his shoulders. I on the other hand dressed to impress, with a figure-hugging knee length dress and matching jacket, accompanied with my favourite diamond necklace, earrings and bracelet; that Danni had brought me; and off course I would not be dressed without my black suede stiletto heels.

Danni ordered a cab, as we had a glass of wine whilst we waited; and I made sure I had everything I needed. I never went anywhere without my lipstick, small handbag mirror and powder, amongst everything else, such as purse, handkerchief, keys and phone. Standing in the doorway, I looked at my two boys and asked if I would do, as they were in awe with what I was wearing, telling me that I looked stunning. Danni came up towards me and moved my hair slightly. As he placed a kiss on my cheek, telling me that I never let him down. I thought the same as he had told me, that he never lets me down; and now looking at my boys, both dressed immaculately made me smile. They were dressed perfectly, with Danni looking like the father, as his boy dressed smart and casual. Oh yes, I was very pleased how my boys had turned out; and told myself that I was a very lucky lady indeed.

As the cab arrived, I asked Danni to do the honours of locking up; and then we made our way down the drive towards the cab, where we climbed in, with the boys giving way to me first. Then Danni told the driver to take us to The Lanes, where we just walked and window shopped, until we walked in to one of our favourite Italian restaurants. Everyone looked around and sent their gaze towards us. I did not care whether their stares were of the fact they knew who I was, or if they were jealous of the fact, I had just walked into the restaurant with two very handsome smartly dressed men. Yes, the way Adam was dressed, now sent him into another league. He was no longer that ordinary boy I knew from the rainbow, but instead, like a phoenix, he had emerged from our bedroom a man.

We were given the best table in the house as always, as a bottle of champagne was placed on the table, ten with the manager coming over to us and greeting us by shaking our hands. He then asked the boys what they cared to drink, in which he then ordered his barman to take the order. It was only now that whispers were roaming around the restaurant, however, it did not matter how much they whispered, we were truly looked after by the manager.

After having a lovely meal, and me being in the company of my boys, we decided to go a few gay bars. I know I often called Danni and Adam my favourite boys, but I did in fact have five very special boys, which were Danni, Johnny, Adam, Stuart and my little prince Jake. Even though Stuart was being a pain, he was still one of my boys; and I was lucky enough to have three special ladies, being Ruby, Ellie and Sophie my little princess. Wherever I went, there always seemed to be cameras flashing, and I was now bringing Adam into a world of photographers, and reporters. Tonight, was no different, as it did not take long for some paparazzi to recognise me, as they then started taking pictures, which then got people looking around as you heard them point and often ask each other who we were. Luckily the restaurants we use knew us, and always gave us a table out of the prying eyes of the lens, however, when leaving the restaurant, you could not help but get recognised.

I was also often surrounded by what we called fag hags too; women just wanting to have a chat and catch a photograph and autograph, as they get their five minutes of fame. I did not mind that much, as after all I had a very big following from a lot of everyday women, which I was very thankful for, which had now followed me to the Brighton scene; and it still made me laugh when they asked if I had my cock snipped off, or where did I put it as it never showed in what I was wearing.

We again hailed a cab, where Danni then asked the driver to take us to St James Street, where we exited and made our way through some back streets, to get to one of the nice bars we used when we visited the gay scene.

It was quite funny that when I first worked down here, I was simply a nobody. I was just a guy who worked in a bar, where no one would talk to me, but now that I was a well-known celebrity and had a huge following, everyone wanted to know me.

We had gone into 'The Brighton Belle' cabaret bar, where there was a show on that evening; and of all people to perform it was our friend Totty. Once Danni had ordered the drinks, I asked for a bottle of bubbly; and then asked if I could go backstage to see her.

The manager walked me through the bar to get away

from the crowd; and took me backstage. I greeted Totty; who was now overwhelmed to see me, as we gave each other a drag kiss.

"Roxy, Oh my word. What the fuck, what are you doing here Roxy? Thought you would be in London?" She said, as she turned around to take a better look at me.
"Charming that is, not even a wow nice to see you Roxy." I laughed.
"It is nice to see you Roxy, but I didn't even know you were down here." She replied.

"Had to run and hide dear, what with all the paparazzi after me. I am staying at the Hove apartment with Danni and Adam honey, thought we would just come in here by chance. I am so glad I did now, it has been an age since I saw you; and oh my, you are looking fabulous as ever."
I said, pleased that I had seen another of my friends.

"The Hove Apartment? Oh, I say. I feel I am hobnobbing with royalty sweetie. Nice to see you too babe, what you want to drink?" She asked, as she stood up and gave me a hug.
"Don't worry about that, I got a bottle of champers coming, so we can have a little drink ourselves." I told her.
"Oh god lovely, hope I don't get pissed, I don't want to end up being blue on stage." She laughed.
"You do not need to be sober honey to be blue. Whether you have had a drink or not your mouth is like a fuckin gutter tramp." I said as I laughed with her.

"Aint that true Roxy. You know me so well. Oh I am so glad you have come, as I am not sure about this crowd." She told me, now showing a few nerves, which was not her.

I told her that the crowd in this bar, was one of the friendliest crowds in Brighton, but warned her that you do get some mouthy queens come in, the ones who are very clicky, so expect some abuse from them, but they are nothing honey, they are just tacky drag queens.

I then began to tell her, about how strange it is, how times change when you least expect it. That when I started, I was a young gay man doing a bit of drag and collecting glasses; and no one ever wanted to know me. Now look at me, a big star like her; and then all of a sudden, I have friends coming out of the woodwork.

She agreed and told me people were so fuckin fickle, as she too had the same experience; and now that she has a name on the drag circuit, those so called people she tells them to fuck off, as they didn't want to know her then and she doesn't want to know them now.

"You know who you friends are honey, trust me, those who stay close to you through thick and thin. All the others are just fuckin hangers on. Still if you can get a fuckin shag out of them it's a bonus; and I haven't had a fuckin shag in weeks." she said.

"Weeks Totty? Yeah right, knowing you it would have been more like last night." I said, teasing her the way we used to do with one another

"Oh ok, well at least twenty four hours, and it was the first time I had a chicken love. Never gone for a young guy before as I find them too inexperienced. But let me

86

tell you something. For a seventeen year old, he taught me a few things, and omg, my ass is so sore after being rode by his ten incher. Got I squealed like a little drag queen." she said, laughing.

"*You dirty slapper, could never imagine you with a seventeen year old. But they do say once you have tasted youth, you never want to go back to a leathery older man. There is just something about young gay cock, that makes you want more. Right honey, better get back to the hubby, he will wonder what has happened. Snap a lash honey; and see you afterwards.*" I said, as I kissed her on the cheek.
"*Yeah, too right honey, says a queen who has everything fall at her feet. I will see you after the show.*" She replied, as she gave me a wink.

She asked me where we would be standing, so I told her that it may be behind the bar, or just as she gets onto the stage. I left the dressing room; and headed back to the bar. I stood at the edge of the bar and stage, when Malcolm and James stood by me, as they started reminiscing about my old days in Brighton; and how the queens brushed me off, apart for them, as they did take me under their wing; and was so sorry to see me leave as they had missed me so much. I told them that I did miss it down in Brighton; and that I was a different person now, so very different from that ever so young naive 16 year old. We then agreed how fickle some people can be, and how clicky some groups get, when they told me I should not leave it as long next time, as I should come and visit the wonderful City by the seaside a lot more than I do. We then got onto the subject of them trading in their guest house for this wonderful attraction, when they told me that a change is as good as a rest. They had made the right move, because the hotel industry is so up and down, with some weeks not even having guests. Yet they purchased this bar when it was on its last legs, and pulled it out of the past, and brought it back into the present, with it being the most famous bar in Brighton, going from a twenty percent yield to now one being that every night surprises them, as they are always full to the brim. That they thought their investment would take about twenty years to complete, but they completed it within four years and were now mortgage free. It was then we got off the subject of business, and looking around, seeing the clicky groups gather together, Malcolm told me that there was nothing bitchier than the drag crowd in Brighton, but once in their circle you do become one of them. Yes that was true, but it took so long to get into the circle as outsiders were considered a no no. their group only grew because they were friends of the group in the first place. For an outsider to be accepted, meant a lot of grovelling; and I aint was not the kind of queen to go sticking my head up some fuddy duddy drag queen's ass. James laughed and told me that I don't need to, that they will soon want to be accepted by me. I then pondered a little as I looked at them; and told them that I would love to give them a piece of my tongue, because there was no need for rudeness. I then got hold of Danni, and gave his ass a squeeze, as I gave Adam a peck on the cheek. A few members of the crowd kept looking over at me, then a few actually braved the walk over to tell me that I looked fab, as well as tell me that they had missed me on the scene.

Then it was time for Totty to come on stage, so as the spotlight came on, Malcolm got on stage and introduced her. It was really funny as some had already seen Totty's show, so they moved away, except for those in which this would have been their first time, they were in for a shock. She entered the stage as fabulous as a drag queen could be, with auburn hair almost as high as the ceiling, and her eyes as drag like as you could get; which protruded just below her forehead; making her look like a 'Divine' lookalike. She was well into her number as she weighed up the crowd; and then that was it...

She began to rip the hell out of everyone.

She had changed since I last saw her, as then she was tamer. Now she didn't give a fuck, whom she picked on or upset, as she had since become very blue; and no one got away from her as she bitch slapped everyone, well except for Danni and me of course. I think she took a liking to Adam, but Adam was so scared of her, that he hid behind Danni, Totty just laughed and asked if he was a little fuck buddy. Adam went as red as a beetroot, as I looked at Totty and replied.

"Every queen needs a fuck buddy honey, what are you going to do when the husband is at work and you feel horny?"

It went down a storm, and I was just waiting for her to reply bitchy, but instead put her thumbs up and carried on. She was absolutely brilliant; and now wonder she could not confirm a booking with us that often, as she had a year's booking ahead of her throughout the UK.

I think she was going to be performing at the Rainbow late November, which we were very excited about, because she was family, and one act we thoroughly enjoyed whenever we saw her.

As soon as her show started, it did not seem long before she had finished. How times fly when you are enjoying yourself. With a standing ovation she left the stage, only to be called back on again; and like all drag queens, we always had a spare number to perform. She looked at me and placed her hand out for me to take it, ready to be led on the stage. I of course declined as it was her night, and then all of a sudden, the crowd went wild.

This would be the first time I would have been on this stage, the first time since I performed in a talent show; and the first time with Totty.

"Hold on a minute honey, I am going to change the track" She said, as she went up to the DJ and spoke to him. She put on *'Oh I remember it well'* from Gigi; then she introduced me to the crowd, which by now the penny seemed to have dropped about who I was. I was a lot different from my television appearances as I had mellowed by not wearing wigs when I went out. I had since begun to wear my own hair, so often had stares from the public just like the ones I had prior to entering the bar. Just before the track played, she looked at me and in her microphone she said.

"If only your friends could see you now Roxy."
"What friends are you talking about, oh the queens of the south you mean, the ones who have brown noses?" I replied, very sarcastically as I looked them in the eye

"*Yes Roxy, they say you can only count your friends on one hand.*" She replied.

"*Oh that is so true honey, they do say the only friends you can count on are on your hand; and that's not counting the times they have pissed you off, and you end up fisting the bitches.*" I said, as I looked around the room at those who knew I was talking about them.

Well, the crowd roared; and looking over at Danni he nearly choked. I looked at him and said.

"*Honey how long we been together now? And you are still having problems swallowing.*"

He just looked at me and mouthed the words '*bitch*' and then seeing Adam laugh, I looked at him and just told him I would get him later.

"*Well, you are certainly fisting them now Roxy, look where you are now; and do not think about where you began, because these bitches will never get the limelight that we have. And I have just the song for you.*" She said, as she had now found the track that she wanted to use

I noticed Adam hanging on to Danni for dear life as he had his arms around him, and I just looked and told him it's ok. Thing is I wouldn't pick on family on purpose, I may be sarcastic now and then, but family is a no go area, unless of course it is just for a bit of camp.

The music played and Totty told me that she would do the male lead, but it didn't matter what we did as we didn't sing the words. We used our own words, which we just made up as we went along. The crowd were pissing themselves as we tried to compose ourselves, as we started to bitch each other and took the piss out of one another.

When it had ended, I had never seen so many people in a small area with tears strolling down their face; and laughing like a pack of hyenas. That was all but the stale crusty old queens that we had slated. No, it was too much for them that they decided to sit there and keep quiet, all but a few who walked out in being embarrassed. We took our bows a few times; and as I exited the stage to be by Danni and Adam, Totty went back into the dressing room where she said she would see us soon. About twenty minutes later she came out; and came and stood by the boys and me. The crowd were still buzzing, as they came around to congratulate her, as well as them coming up to compliment me apologising for not recognising me. As always Totty was now in guy mode, as she never stayed in her make up if she didn't have a follow up booking. I then introduced her to Adam, with whom she thought he was lovely, as she kept stroking his hair and telling me when we had finished with him, she would have him. Again, Adam went red and kept moving around by Danni, holding him tightly because he was worried about her. I told Totty, that Adam was our adopted son, and I was his drag mother when dressed as Roxy. That he was very nervous, but he was becoming more confident as each day goes by.

"Give him to me, a few hours and I will fuck the shyness out of him." She said, as she went to brush his hair once again..

92

That was it, he pressed his body into Danni's and got his arms to shelter him. Seeing how nervous he was, Totty told him that she was only joking, calling him a dizzy queen and how he must have led a sheltered life. Then telling him that she had the utmost respect for both Danni and me; and that he was in good hands. Just as Adam began to move a little closer to us, Totty told him that it was so sweet, because most guys, despite age, would jump at the fact of being with a drag queen; and would be so happy to be fucked senseless by them, as she then took hold of Adam's hand and kissed him on the cheek telling him to relax as he was safe.

I looked at both Danni and Adam and winked at them, thinking if only you knew.

As soon as Totty had been paid and picked up her contract, she bid her goodbyes as she had to travel back to London. We gave her a hug, even Adam once Danni coaxed him a little, then we started chatting to Malcolm and James again.

It was then that Malcolm asked me if I would be interested in a booking there; and James, almost begging me, that I thought he was going to get on his knees and beg. I agreed but told them I would have to consult my diary and look for dates, as it was back at home.

We stayed in the bar till closing, and the boys asked us if we were going to the club. Looking at my boys, we all nodded and agreed we would go there for a little while. Malcolm told me to hold on, as he would phone Adrian the owner and he would reserve a table for us; and as I was something of a local celebrity, we would not have to queue up. We made our way to the club which was near the pier called Zeros, and I thought nothing had changed, still got the same bar staff, and big windows.

The décor was still the same as when I left, although it was still very modern, with the bar holding stage by being in the centre of the room, with seating all around which also had a VIP seating area; and had the cabaret lounge downstairs. I was indeed treated as a celebrity when I arrived, with the manager coming up to me and greeting me and my boys, giving us the VIP table at the far end away from everyone, and a bringing over the complimentary drinks. We even had our own security guy, making sure no one interrupted us, or pestered us unnecessarily.

By now I had drunk more than a little champagne, but I was still no way unladylike to be out of my head; and falling all over the place like most drunken people.

I knew how to spread my drinks; and most the time a bottle served the three of us. We spent the next couple of hours with the boys; and caught up with all the latest gossip. One or two of the queens from my past came in and recognised me but would not come over as they saw I was with company; and besides I never gave them that much attention.

I did not mean to snub them, but it was something they deserved for doing the same to me in those early years that I was in Brighton. A part of me wanted them to come over and say something, just so I could remind them that they had short memories, but then decided not to because I did not want to enter into a drag war.

I think we left the club about 3am, as we were all very tired by now; not to mention a little worse for wear. Malcolm called his friend who lived just up the road, who was a private cabbie who had just finished his shift, so he came into the club to collect us and then he drove us back home. As Danni went to pay for the cab home, he was told that the boys had sorted it, so Danni gave him a good tip. Adam opened the door, and asked if we wanted a night cap. He then proceeded to make us a coffee, and then sat on the sofa in between us, he turned around and gave Danni a kiss on the lips and thanked him, then did the same to me.

"*Oh, you daft sod Adam, I am just glad you enjoyed yourself.*" I said, hugging him
"*I did until Totty came out; and then I was nervous. I have seen you a few times on stage Miss Roxy; and got scared when you got into your routine, so imagine what it was like with Totty. She is so intimidating just looking at her.*" He said, now feeling relaxed that he was home.
"*You will get used to it Adam, you just need to come out with Roxy and me more*." Danni said. "*You will soon come out of that shell; and it will make you more confident buddy. Most drag queen are harmless, it is just who they are, so always remember, it is only an act; and if it is not* you, they are picking on, then it will be some other queen.*"

Danni then pulled the coffee table closer, as he then put his arm around Adam, which also touched my neck. We then had our usual group hug, and again gave each other kisses. Shortly after we had settled, we all had a hug and then went off to bed. Danni and I in the master bedroom; and Adam further down the hallway facing the front garden. Our bedroom I liked more, as it had its own patio doors to walk out into the garden; and many times Danni and I have walked out in the summer nights and made out on the sun loungers.

During the morning as I rolled over, I happened to wake up to find that Danni was not there, so I got up out of bed still with my lingerie on and a dressing gown, where I walked out of the bedroom into the hallway. I heard Adam stirring, so I walked down to his room and poked my head around. I asked if he was having a hard time with sleeping; and would he like a nice herbal tea. He told me he thought it was because he had had too much to drink; and that he had a bit of a headache that was keeping him awake. It was then I thought about something really funny. I thought about getting my own back on Danni again.

"Hey Adam come with me. I think Danni is in the kitchen. I am going get the fucker back Adam for scaring me a while back." I said to him, quietly as I put my finger to my lips.

Adam got out of bed; and god did he look horny in his white tight boxers. I looked down at him and told him how yummy he looked. He then placed his hand on his cock and thrust it at me, telling me it was all mine. I then grabbed his hand; and led him through the hallway.

"When I count to three, I want you to say what are you doing?" I said to him.

"Ok Roxy, this is fun. He is going to kill us." He said, as he got a little excited at pulling a prank on Danni.

Once again as I took hold of his hand, we crept by the kitchen door, where Danni seemed to be making himself a cappuccino. He was naked and was reading a magazine, so I looked at Adam and mimed one, two, three. At the same time, and whilst we were standing in the doorway unawares to Danni that we were there, we shouted

"WHAT ARE YOU DOING?"

Well jump out of your skin was an understatement, he nearly piddled himself as he jumped for his life, dropping the magazine that he was reading; and as he spilled his coffee, he looked around and said.

"WHAT THE!!! You pair of bitches; you nearly gave me a god damn heart attack."

We just looked at him and couldn't stop laughing, as we held each other.

"You just wait you little fuckers." He said, as he got a cloth to wipe up the spillage, he had made by spilling his cup.

He then turned around and gave us the eye.

"Run for it Adam, quick run." I shouted.

We turned around and ran out of the kitchen into the lounge. Danni came right after us shouting and cursing, as we just kept going; and when we got into the hallway Adam was about to go to his bedroom.

"No Adam come on in here honey, quick open the patio doors." I told him.

Danni first of all must have gone into Adams room, as I heard him shout bollocks as he was mooching around. Adam had just opened the patio doors, as Danni came into the bedroom. I told Adam to be quick; and to get into the garden. I was too late however, to get through the doors, as Danni had caught me. He picked me up and threw me on the bed.

"You bitch Roxy, you frightened the fucking life out of me." He said, as he began grappling with me
"Serves you right Danni, you have caught me out a few times." I replied, as I then told him it was payback time.

Danni started to tickle me and hit me with the pillow. It was then that I saw Adam just peering through the door, so I signalled to him to get him, so Adam came in the bedroom quietly and jumped on top of Danni.

"Get off her you animal, leave her alone." He said, as he had his hands around his neck and his legs straddling his waist.
"Oh, I see it gang up on Danni is it? Well, I can play like that as well." Danni said.

He managed to get Adam off his back and pin him down on the top of me. I was now well and truly trapped. Danni started to slap Adams ass, as he started to squeal. Adam told Danni to stop, calling him a brute; and to

98

leave his ass alone. Danni now being in full flow told Adam to be warned, as he called him a cheeky fucker; and that he was going to rip those pants off him and he was going to give him a good spanking. Adam laughed at Danni, as he told him that he would not dare, that he would get me to help pin him down and slap his ass. Danni then lay on both of us, and I was screaming that I couldn't breathe. Danni quickly removed Adams boxers and gave him a slap across the ass in which even I felt his body quiver.

"Ouch you bully that fuckin hurt." Adam yelped.
"Danni please get off I can't breathe honey." I said, as I was gasping for breath. Or was I?

Danni got of us both, and then pinned Adam down as he straddled him. Danni was now sitting over his waist with Adams cock touching Danni's ass. He asked if I was ok, telling me that he was sorry. I told him that I was ok; and to give me five minutes to get my breath. I then walked behind him; and caught Adams eye. I told him to push Danni towards my side of the bed. As Adam did this I jumped on Danni; and between the two of us we both had him pinned down. Adam was now straddling Danni, as I lay over his chest.

"You cunning little minx Roxy, and there was me thinking you couldn't breathe, telling you that I was sorry." Danni said, as he gave me daggers
"I could not breathe honey, and I did need to get my breath, honest. It was just quicker than normal getting it back." I replied, as I winked at him.

99

Pinning him down, I just kissed him on the lips and asked him what it felt like. He just laughed at me as he told me that I had got him, and that we had got him back good and proper. By now Danni and Adam were fully erect, and as I got up off Danni, he held his arm out for me to lie down. I placed my body in his arms and turned to him, as I felt him stroke my back. Adam started to gyrate up and down on Danni's cock, as he bent down to kiss him.

"*So, you little fucker you, do you think you can take my big cock then?*" Danni said, looking at Adam as he gave him the eye.
"*I will try Sir, please let me try.*" He answered, all excited as well as being very hot and bothered
"*You will have to earn it first Adam, I think you should get off me and play with Miss Roxy.*" Danni said.
"*Yes Sir, anything you say.*" He replied

He got off from Danni's waist and straddled me, as Danni got up over the bed and stood before me.
With my head slightly to one side, Danni offered me his cock and ass; and with Adam straddling me, Danni started to slide his cock down my throat, as I heard him tell Adam to raise my legs over his shoulders; and then bring himself forward so that he could kiss him. Having Danni inside my mouth; and Adam's cock pushing against my ass; Danni told Adam to take his cock and thrust it deep inside me, and for him to please me by making love to me. Well, everything had gone out of the window, as I always said no one would ever go near my

ass but Danni. I was hot and very horny; and just thought what the hell it's my boy anyway; and god this was horny being spit roasted by my boys. Harder Danni thrust down my throat nearly choking me, as he saw Adam now penetrating his Roxy. This really got him going, as he thrust in my mouth and withdrew so I could lick off his precum. Danni then got up as he kissed Adam, as he then exposed his ass for my tongue to explore. With my hands parting his cheeks I slid my tongue into his ass, as he pulled Adam towards him kissing him passionately.

"*Yeah Adam, take her* tight hole. Give Miss Roxy your young thick hard cock." He said, now egging him on to take me.

It did not take Adam long before he shot his load into me, but it was long enough, as he was thrusting away panting until he got out of breath. He certainly knew how to fuck his Miss Roxy; and make her feel exhausted from the number of times he pumped himself into me, just like a man on heat. Once he had fucked me; and he saw Danni was still in my throat, he removed his cock and went between my legs rimming my hot moist ass.
I was in boy toy heaven, as never before had I been thrilled both ends; and this would be something that I would want more. Danni then looked at me, and then told me that he thought that it was our turn; and that we should break our boy in. I got off the bed; and waited for Danni to tell Adam what to do. Danni ordered me on my back, where he told Adam to straddle me in the sixty-nine position. He told Adam that he wanted him to suck

my cock; and to rim my ass, as he took his tight ginger virgin ass. Adam did not make complaint, as he told Danni that his ass was all his. Adam straddled me and took my cock in his mouth, as Danni slowly placed his cock between his cheeks. I had never seen a view like this before; and it made me very moist as I dripped precum into Adams mouth. Slowly Danni had his cock in Adams ass, as Adam screamed with pain.

"Gentle please Sir, please be gentle." Adam said, as he flinched at the feel of Danni behind him.

Once Danni had lubed Adam's ass with his precum and Adam relaxed, like a good trooper he took every inch of Danni's cock much to his delight. I had Adams cock down my throat, as I pulled on Danni balls, he penetrated Adam deep and hard. I felt Adam gag a few times on my cock; and as Danni thrust into him, we both heard his little outbursts of pain, as Danni went too far. Danni took it slower, until he got used to his ten inch cock. I was so horny as I saw Danni's cock penetrate his ass, as I was sucking on his cock. I told him to fuck him harder, as I called Adam our little firecracker. Danni then said that he wanted to see me as he exploded into Adam, so he told Adam to sit upright and to let me go, speaking rather dominantly. Adam sat up so that I could turn around and lay on the bed, as he was now facing my head. As I lay there, Adam was in doggy position, where he went from my cock to my mouth, making both very sensual with the way he worked his mouth. Pushing full on Danni's cock, Danni began playing with Adams nipples as he thrust himself into Adam ass, making him squeal a little from time to time. After a while I got up, now with a cock stiff and soaking with the juices of my young boy, as well as glistening with my own precum. Danni then ordered me to stand at the edge of the bed, as he positioned Adam on the corner.

"*Adam, now take Miss Roxy again in your mouth, and I now want you to swallow her, you have tasted enough to know how sweet she is.*" Danni ordered Adam.
"*Yes Sir.*" He replied.

Adam took my cock again in his mouth, as he was again placed in the doggy position. Danni again thrust deep inside his ass, as he grabbed me and kissed me.

"*I love you Miss Roxy, GOD do I fuckin love you.*" Danni said.
"*I love you too honey, thank you.*" I replied.

After a period of kissing Adam, and having him work my cock hard, I was about to shoot my load, in which I could not hold back I could not hold back if I tried. I shouted to both of them that I was about to come; and I could not control it, when Danni ordered Adam to work my cock with his hands, and then to take me in his mouth and swallow all of my juices for him. Adam did not make a sound, he just pulled on my balls as I was ready to shoot in his throat. I held onto the side of his head as my knees began to tremble; and I could feel my hot load coming to the surface.

"Oooohhhh god yes boys, I am cumming fuck me, Adam take that load." I shouted

Danni got all worked up at the sound of Adam gagging on my cock, as he then swallowing my warm thick juices, which I shot deep inside him. Adam began gagging and moaning as he took my cock, coming up for air as he screamed.

"Oh god yeah Sir, fuck my ass. Oh, Miss Roxy you taste so sweet. Fuck me Sir."

Adam then went back towards my cock, ready to take the last bits of my warm juices, as Danni held onto his waist and thrust deeper into him. Danni was now moaning with complete pleasure as he fucked his boy; and as he withdrew his cock, he was still losing his load. I put my hand over the tip of his head and shaft rubbing the droplets of cum over it, then opened Adams ass and told Danni to thrust again.
Again, Danni thrust into Adam, as Adam screamed and sucked on my cock, Danni now becoming uncontrollable as he neared completion.

"OH MY GOD. I am cumming, Mmmmmm, Yes Yes Yes." He cried, as he thrust and shot his load into Adam's ass.

We then just collapsed on the bed. Adam being in the middle, as both Danni and I wrapped our arms around him.

"Thank you Danni, thank you Roxy." Adam said. *"I really enjoyed that, even though you hurt at first Danni, but I never thought I would ever take all of you inside my ass."*

"It's all about relaxing Adam, lube and relaxation that is the key. You really did well; in fact, you did very well." Danni told him as he placed a kiss on his warm sexed face, saying that he could still taste the pair of us. I then had a strange question asked by Adam, as he asked me why I kept my stilettos on, whilst engaging in sex. I told him that a girl is never properly dressed without her heels; and it is sacrilege to have sex in stocking feet. It is the duty of the woman to wear them, for it is her way of letting you know that she is 100% in control, not only of her appearance, but also in the art of seduction. That a woman who has sex in full make-up and stocking feet shows she has no class, yet a woman in full make-up and heels, shows that she is a proper woman. He thanked me for explaining; and hoped I did not mind asking; and hoped I did not sound rude. I told him that it was ok, he needn't apologise. However, he would at least know now if he ever got to fuck a girl without shoes, that she would be nothing but a slut and not a woman. He just laughed as he said there was no chance that he would ever fuck another woman, as I was the only woman with a cock he would ever have intimacy with. He then asked me if that was the same as a hetro woman, when I told him that it only applied to the gay scene, although it is still a carnal sin to engage in sex and not have your shoes on, whether woman with a cock or vagina. We then just collapsed on the bed; and said to each other that we should have a few more hours sleep.

Danni slept in the middle and placed his arms around me, as he then cuddled up to me, as Adam snuggled up all comfortably into Danni. We must have dozed off for more than a few hours, as by now the people with who deliver the free papers made a clanging sound at the door. Adam got up to see what it was, and then must have gone into the lounge. Next thing I knew, he came to my side of the bed and nudged me to tell me he had brought me a coffee; and then he did the same too Danni.
He then asked if we wanted some breakfast, which I thought was a very good idea; to which Adam asked.

"How do you like your eggs Roxy?"
"The same as always Adam, Unfertilized and not smelling of cum." I said, with a wink and a smile.

He then asked if he could take a shower first, as he was wide awake and ready to hit the town to do some shopping. Both Danni and I together told him to feel free; and that he should not have to ask us when he wants to do certain things, as he should treat our home as it is his own. Whilst Adam was taking a shower, I cuddled up to Danni where we embraced and kissed each other good morning as we often did. I then suggested to Danni about Adam coming to stay with us for a while. He was surprised I asked that; and then asked me if I was sure, as he asked me about our privacy. I smiled as I told him that you could not be more private than how we are now. If he is in his bedroom and we are in ours, then we have all the privacy we need, besides I did not invite him to stay where he would be in our bed all the time. I just wanted to look after him, and I know Danni wanted the same. We wanted to make sure he was ok; and that was not an invite to be with us all the time in our bed. He agreed with me, when he then asked about the three of us; and what do we do now, now that we have invited him into a threesome, wondering where we go from here.

"Well, it is not as though he hasn't seen us naked honey, and as for the three of us, well I would prefer it to only be the three should this ever happen again. And not ever doing it separately or abuse the fact he may eventually find a guy. If that were to happen then we would knock it on the head altogether, but it would not stop us from caring about him and letting him live with us." I replied.
"You mean stay loyal to each other, but should we want a bit of fun then it is only us together as a couple with, let's say Adam for argument sake?" He asked.
"Yes, honey for the time being anyway. I do not want an open relationship, as I have no need to see guys on my own. But should we fancy a little bit of other fun, then it has to be you and me as a couple. And yes, I am loyal and faithful to you; and you will always be my priority." I again said, resting my head on Danni's chest
"I know that babes, I just wanted to make sure, because I do not really want to sleep with anyone else but you. Last night was fun; and it was very special with our boy. I am not into going to bars to find guys for a threesome, I like you, have no need to; and like you I would not like it every single day, as I feel it would become tediously boring. You are enough for me Roxy. As for Adam moving in, it is up to you babes, I will go along with what you both agree." He replied, as he almost squeezed the life out of me

107

"Thing is Danni, it is a grotty little place he has, you cannot swing a cat around in it. For what he pays for that, he may as well come here for a while, then he can save his money a little more, until he has enough for a better place." I said, now started to be broody.

"Then tell him, if he agrees that it is on a trial period, as we may not be comfortable with him being here full time; and he may not like it either. Besides when you are at the bar and I am on my own here, I am always naked, as it seems pointless in getting dressed. Also, we often sit around the house naked, so he has to know about that, and that is not a ploy to have sex, it is just us chilling. Us being naked is never a sign we want sex, because as you well know, you and I do not engage in intimacy every day." He replied, as he always seemed to find the right things to say.

I agreed with him and told him that I would have a word with Adam when I got the chance. Adam then got out of the shower and now not even thinking about his shyness, he walked into the bedroom naked and went to the wardrobe where he picked out some clothes.

"Are you sure Miss Roxy that I can wear these clothes, I mean they are brand new and fab." He asked, marvelling at the amount of clothes he had to choose from. He had never had so many clothes to his name before.
"Honey they are yours, like I said I never wear them. At least when you come down again you will know that you have a wardrobe of clothes, so there is no need to bring a suitcase." I replied.

"Yeah; and all you need do is throw them in the machine Adam; and then iron them. You can do ours at the same time too." Danni said.

"Of course, I have a load of washing to do as it is, so once we come back from town, I will put a load on. And just for the record Danni and Roxy. I love ironing, as it is so therapeutical." He replied.

"That's a good boy we will have to train you properly, as there is no need to just lie around the house looking pretty all day Adam." I laughed.

"Now you are teasing me Roxy, aren't you?" He asked.

"Ermm, yes just a bit honey." I replied. *"It's just harmless fun; and I pray for the day you tease me and Danni. The time will come I know.*

"And what if I want to just chill out, will you mind if it is just boxers, or if I am in the garden to just be nude?" He asked.

"Adam you can chill out just as you feel comfy, I am hardly in boxers when I am at home, so just be yourself and relax as you want to. I mean most days I am home alone, I am naked, as I feel there is no rush to get dressed." Danni said, hoping to start the subject on him moving in with us, but I needed time to tell him. I was thinking how to approach, no matter how many cue lines Danni threw at me.

"Stick a fucking dildo up your ass if you like, but as long as you are comfy do what you please." I said, rather sarcastically, in which Adam looked at me and uttered the words *'oh yeah...cool.'*

He then got himself dressed; and prepared some breakfast for us. He was quite the little handy houseboy;

and I was beginning to get very paternal and protective towards him, just as Danni was.

That weekend we did a lot of shopping; and walked a lot along the beach where we then would have lunch and dinner, depending on our mood. We then went back to the apartment where we just chilled and watched a few movies, as we constantly chatted to each other, fooling around like little kids. Also, that weekend, all three of us continued to play with each other, making love until the early hours of the morning, satisfying all as we played, had fun and had some good hot wicked sex.

When we had got back to London, I decided to call Paul to find out is he knew anything about Stuart, as we had not seen him now for nearly two weeks. I found out that he was on compassionate leave, as his mother was in the hospital having had major surgery. As soon as I put the phone down, I thought the only thing I could do was give him a call, as Paul did give me his number. I could not even begin to imagine what he was going through, as I had never been in that situation, but thought if he knew we were there for him it would ease the pressure.

"Stuart, is that you?" I asked.
"Yes, this is Stuart, may I ask who is calling." He replied.
"Yes honey, it is Roxy, you know from the Rainbow. Please don't hang up let me speak." I begged.
"Oh, ok Roxy, but I do not have long as I have to check on mother." He replied.

I began to tell him that I was sorry to hear about what was happening; and that if he ever needed to speak to anyone then I would be there. We must have spoken for about ten minutes, when I then asked how his feelings were towards Adam. He told me that he loves Adam so much it hurts, but at the moment he needed to be with his mother. That the one day a week that he has arranged for himself, he just sits and chills by the Thames, because the rest of the week he is not available due to being at the hospital. He continued to tell me that there was never a day that goes by that he does not think of Adam, and he knew he had blown things, as he was sure Adam had moved on. I felt so sad for him and the ordeal he was in, as I told him that I was so sorry, but not in a sympathetic way because I know he would have hated that. I asked him to do me a favour, in which he asked me what it was. I asked him that if he got a minute to spare, to just text him. To text him and to tell him that you need time, as you need to be with your mother. I told him if he wished, I would bring him up to date with what has happened with his mother, but I think he should speak to him because he is going crazy not knowing what has happened; and that he misses him so much. He then began to cry as he told me it is hard; and that he has to cry himself to sleep just to try and forget about his mother being poorly; and how so much a waste of space his sister and stepdad were. How we wished Adam was there or even Danni and me, which shocked me.

"You and Danni have been very kind to me Roxy; and you have never judged me or pointed the finger. You have accepted me into your family and introduced me to Adam, no one has been as kind to me as you and Danni, but I need time. I do not know what to do; and seeing my

mother like she is every single day is so emotionally draining, but I know I have to be strong, not just for me but for her too." He said crying.

"You know where I live Stuart; and here's my number. Should you want to pop in and have a chat, or simply meet up for coffee then just call; and we will have a little get together just you and me." I replied.

"Really Roxy, you would really do that?" He asked.

"Yes honey, you are family. But you still must text or call Adam. He loves you so much Stuart, so please text him." I said, now understanding everything that had been going on.

"Ok Roxy I will do; and I have a couple of hours to myself Tuesday afternoon, if you would like to join me for a coffee." He replied.

We then made a date, and I told him that Danni may be here if he is working from home, otherwise we would be here together alone and could have a nice chat. He did not mind that; and I think the relief of speaking to someone really helped him with his state of mind.

I then told him I would see him Tuesday as he said goodbye to me crying, which I just wanted to go over there and give him a hug.

When Danni came into the lounge, I explained what had happened with Stuart; and that I would be meeting him Tuesday for a coffee. I told him that he would be coming to our home; and if he were here no to worry as we would not disturb him. I also told him the sweet thing that Stuart had said, which also touched Danni, as I mentioned to Danni that I think we should not have a threesome anymore with Adam, as it seems unfair now knowing the truth of Stuart's predicament.

He understood what I was saying, and then told me that we first need to speak to Adam and let him know what we think. All of a sudden, the phone began to ring again; and just as though he had been a fly on the wall listening to us, it was Adam on the other end of the line. He sounded so excited at the fact Stuart had got in touch, as he told me he was now so very relieved. I then went on to explain that I had spoken to Stuart; and told Adam about the situation with his mother. I told him to give Stuart time, but I know things will be fine. Then I sat him down and told him that I have something else to tell him. He asked if he should be worried, when I told him that he shouldn't. I told him that I have asked Stuart over for a coffee and a chat; and that I did not want him to worry; and that I will make sure he texts or phones you more often. I told him that I thought he needed his Aunty Roxy's shoulder. Adam told me that it was ok, that he was just happy that had contacted him, that now he can sleep easy at night. He then asked me if he would tell him that he loved him, when I told him he could tell him himself, because I was sure he would be getting another call soon. I did smile, because Adam was so excited, he was now like a little schoolboy who had just been given a gold star. I then thought well why not go all out on surprises, so just before I put the phone down, I told him that we need to have a little chat soon anyway; and not to worry, because it was not anything to worry about, so he should not spend all day thinking about it. I then gave him a kiss down the phone, telling him that I was so pleased to hear his news; and I knew Danni would feel the same. I went on with my daily duties, and as routine visiting my shoe room to see and marvel in my little babies, thinking about what colour to get next, or what style. I often went in there when I had time to spare, just to try them on and walk up my catwalk. It passed the time of day; and sitting on the lounger admiring my shoes was definitely heaven.

The next day I prepared a little lunch; and tried to use some of my baking skills that mother once taught me. I made a nice Victoria sponge, but it was nowhere as big as the ones in the local supermarket, when all of a sudden, the intercom buzzed which startled me, as I was being naughty by licking the spoon of whipped cream which ended up landing on my nose. Once I answered the buzzer and realized that it was Stuart, I pressed the release button to let him in in. He was very sweet as once he arrived at the door, in his hand was a lovely little bouquet of lilies; and a very cheeky boyish grin as he pointed towards my nose which still had a bit of cream on the sides. He kissed me on the cheek; and then I told him to make himself comfy on the couch, as I then brought the tray of coffee in; and of course, the usual biscuits and cake which made his eyes light up.

I sat next to him and told him that he could spoil me; and that he could pour the coffee and be mother. I sat back and slightly turned to him, placed my hand on his thigh and told him he could tell me anything. He just broke down, as he started to tell me how hard it was at home, how his stepfather did not want to know; and his sister was a waste of space, as everything had been left to him to sort out; and you could see the strain on his face.

I put my arms around his neck and pulled him towards

me, offering him my shoulder as he rested his head on me just crying nonstop.

"That's it honey, let it out, you poor thing you. God you must have been bottling all this up for such a long-time sweetheart." I said, as I comforted him.

After about five minutes of Stuart crying on my shoulder, I told him that I would get some tissue as my shoulder was beginning to get rather wet.
It was so good to see that he trusted me enough to confide in me; and want to talk to me, in such a way that I just wanted to hug him and take away all of his pain.
I walked into the kitchen, and as I was just about to wipe myself down, he came in and again tried to speak but was too overwhelmed by his distress. I asked him to sit down on the stool, because he was much taller than I was; and I did not want a crick in my neck. With a glimmer of ease, I managed to get a little smile out of him, although he still had a rather heart felt flushed look about him. His mother's health had taken its toll on him, and he looked so rugged and one who looked as though he had not had much sleep. I got some tissue and started to wipe his eyes, as I then told him that Danni and I would always be here for him. Looking directly at him, I opened his legs and moved towards him, as I now had his head on my shoulder when again he began crying. With his arms around my waist, I had one hand stroking the back of his head as my other hand was around his waist, telling him again to just let it out and not to be afraid to show me how he has been feeling these past few weeks, every now and then getting up to wipe his eyes, and to give

him a kiss on the cheek. I told him that Adam was very worried and concerned, as were we, as he just seemed to have disappeared from the radar.

"Never feel that you are on your own Stuart, as you have a man who loves you, and you have Danni and me who loves you as well, as well as caring for you. If you ever have a moment to yourself just send a text saying you are ok, even if you are not. Just do not go days without saying anything, as a reply often lifts the spirits. I don't know, what am I going to do with my boys? You know Roxy is always here don't you?" I said, as I held him in my arms
"Yes Roxy, I know you are there it's just I don't like asking." He replied.
"Don't be silly honey, you can ask me anything." I told him.

I then again gave him a hug as he pulled me towards him; and as he did my hand rested on his thigh.
I gave him a hug and then pulled away, telling him we should get our coffee, not showing him that I was slightly blushing. I got the tissues and put them in the bin turning away from him, as we both made our way into the lounge where we continued to chat, as Stuart began telling me his story.

"I do not know where to begin Roxy, so you will have to forgive me if I get muddled up." He said, as he made himself comfortable.

"You take your time Stuart; I am here to listen to you honey no matter how long it takes you." I replied, taking a sip of my coffee.

He then composed himself, took a sip of coffee and began his story.

"My mother has always been a poorly lady, what with her constant tummy troubles. She has had so many tests over the years; and so many doctors prodding her about like she was a pin cushion. What has upset me the most Roxy, is that I had come home from my shift; and like always, I then went right upstairs to get changed out of my uniform. Before I got to my bedroom, I noticed the bathroom door was open, but there was no movement; and as I got closer, I saw my mother lying on the floor not moving. I panicked as I thought she was dead." He said, now getting a little emotional.
"Oh My God Stuart, that must have been awful to witness." I asked
"It was Roxy; and that so called man of a stepfather was a waste of bleeding time. I called down to him to call an ambulance but got no reply. I then ran downstairs only to find him still engrossed in the television, so I told him what I thought of him. He just told me that she is my mother; and I should do it myself. He never really liked me, but to be honest the feeling was mutual." He replied, now getting a little angry, as I slowly calmed him down.
"And what about your real father Stuart, where is he now?" I asked him.

"My father died when I was four years old, as like me he was a police officer. He died on the job in a robbery that went wrong, and subsequently he got shot. My sister is my half-sister; and she is my stepdad's daughter. We do not get on as she is a spoiled brat." He said, with a bit of anger in his voice.

"She sounds it honey, but I cannot understand your stepdad actions, because she is his wife." I told him.

"Oh, he is a waste of fucking space Roxy. Don't get me wrong, he was ok at first; and then as mom got more involved with him, she began starting to sign things over to him, like the insurance policies, as well as putting his name on the deeds to the house. Only thing she did not sign over was her pension she gets from the police force from dad, but it would not surprise me if he has not tried to do so, because he is money orientated." He said, now getting a little annoyed again.

He again began getting a little wound up, where I told him to relax and have a drink of his coffee. He then looked at me and apologised, to which I called him silly as he then continued his story.

"The pair of them do nothing at all for my mother, except just sit on their bloody arses all day. I went upstairs and found mother collapsed; and it was me who ended up calling the ambulance. They asked me if she was breathing and what colour she was, as I explained she was breathing and she looked very yellow. It was not long before the ambulance arrived and we made our way to the hospital, whilst that pair of inbreds were still in

118

the lounge watching television. I have often asked my mother to leave that son of a bitch; and for just the two of us to move somewhere else. But all she says is that she cannot leave him, because she would lose too much; and she married for better or worse and for sickness and health." He continued to say.

"*It was a good job you got home when you did honey.*" I replied, as I placed my hand on his hand for comfort.

"*Upon arriving to hospital, they admitted her immediately for tests; and as I was in still in my uniform, I went through instead of waiting in the waiting room. They asked me a few questions; and told me that she may have yellow jaundice, or it could be her liver and kidneys shutting down. They took so much blood off her to test; and then after an hour they put her on a ward. They then connected her up to a drip in both arms giving her fluids and God knows what. I can't lose my mom Roxy; she is all I have.*" He said, as he now cried.

Again, I held him as he placed his head on my shoulder, as I told him that she is in the right place. That she will get the best help, as I know St Mary's is a very good hospital. Stuart then told me, that Adam had asked that they moved in together.

"*I could not move into his flat Roxy, because you couldn't swing a cat in there; and I know it is not Adam fault, but the flat is damp. I did think about him moving in with me, but if I was to be on split shifts then I would disturb him; and I only have a one-bedroom flat. That is why mother could not move in with me.*" He said, explaining his reasons to me

"Is that why the saving was mentioned, so you could both afford something better? And you just said you went to change at your moms." I replied, now understanding the whole situation
"Yes Miss Roxy; and it would then feel like our place and not his or mine. It would be a place that we both could put our stamp on; and not be afraid to make changes. I still have my bedroom at my mother's house; and still have a few clothes there. Because of the situation with my stepdad, I promised my mother that I would stay over two or three times a week to help her out. And heavens forbid, I could never let Adam stay at mother's house, not with how toxic the atmosphere is with him and his daughter." He told me.

I looked at Stuart and told him to trust me; and to leave everything with me and I will see what I could sort out. I then told him that he was a good lad, with a kind heart; and that he should never forget that. He was so sweet as he told me that he did trust me, and he thanked me for the kind words; and for our chat which he so needed. Shortly after our little talk he told me that he would have to make a move, as we had been chatting nearly two hours and his mother would wonder where he was. He thanked me for listening to him, and for offering him a shoulder. Just as he was leaving, I again gave him a hug; and told him that I needed bigger heels as I always got a stiff neck reaching up to him.

"You are just like Danni, Stuart; and think I will need bigger heels, or you will have to bend down to me." I told him.
"And stop you getting a stiff neck, well I have to apologise Miss Roxy, as you did get me a little stiff. It is something about you, as you make people so relaxed, but really I do apologise." He replied, now becoming a little embarrassed.

I told him not to worry about it, as I had that effect on men, when he laughed and told me that I certainly did have that effect on men, and me being married too. I just smiled at him and then winked at him, as I told him to have a safe journey back. I then told him not to worry and to remember, that Danni and I were just a phone call or text away, as he told me he knew; and he will text us more often now.
Over the next few weeks, the private parties went well; and now they became a regular Wednesday evening. Adam was beginning to make himself a bit of extra cash in his tips; and I still gave him a generous percentage of what was given to me. The group was becoming much bigger, with even more piers and the likes of the rich and famous, which spilt out into my gift being that of a much larger monetary amount. Even being given perfume and jewellery by the judge, just for making him over each time he came to the venue. It was these nights that took my mind off things that were going on within my family circle, as at times it could be too overwhelming with Stuart's mother; not in the fact that I objected, it was more that I was able to put certain things to one side and concentrate on other things; but it did not mean I did not

dismiss either Stuart or his mother, I still needed me time, even though my family were always in the forefront of my mind.

Johnny and Ruby were about to take their annual holidays, when she asked me to look after the bar with Ellie. She always knew I would stand in for her, as many times I did just that. She knew that Ellie and I got on and we were a good team, besides Danni would always come in to check up on us both when he had finished work. Dixie helped out when she could too, but did have a lot of bookings; so, between the three of us we managed pretty well.

The next day I decided to go to the Rainbow a little early, as Ellie was a little short staffed. I text Danni to tell him that I would not be home, but instead, for him to come and pick me up from the bar; and we would go for something to eat, and then have an early night.

Danni was working a little late as he had a few meetings to sort out, as there was a big job on the cards, so it just meant pain stakingly meeting after meeting and large arguments and bids of some sort. I never knew that much about the business, apart from they had gone in a new direction from renovating houses, to now having a portfolio of taking old office buildings and making them into apartments. Danni and Steve had already hit most of Europe; and were now fighting to win a contract in the USA, which would have tied both his and Steve's company with that of his fathers, so they had a lot riding on the bids and contracts. I knew it was a lot to take on, because some nights Danni was so exhausted that he just fell asleep on the couch, with me ending up throwing a

122

duvet over him. I arrived at the Rainbow nice and early, around 5pm, did my usual routine of greeting Ellie, and then hanging my coat up in the office. The first few hours were quite as they usually were, and then the crowd started to come in. Dave the doorman had arrived; and he first said hello to us before as we chatted for a while before he started his shift. Not long after Dave started his duty, there was a bit of a rumpus outside, in which Dave got it sorted, but for some unknown reason someone rushed into the bar shouting abuse.

"*You fuckin' faggot bastards, hope you all die of fucking aids*." This guy shouted.

I looked at Ellie and told her to stay where she is; and I then casually walked over to him, to try and defuse the situation, as I had dealt with bar brawls before; and thought I could somehow defuse this altercation. Calmly, I told him that there was no need for him to be offensive; and to leave as I did not want that sort of behaviour in the bar. That I do not take abusive language from my regulars, so I will not tolerate it from him. Dave was still tackling a few guys outside; and then the one I was talking too pushed me, which had us both falling back in the bar when he then came at me at full force. Well apart from him hitting me in the face, I gave him a good left hook myself, hurting my fist in the process; and losing a few Swarovski crystals out of my dress ring. I tried to keep my expensive jewellery just for best, except of course for my wedding and engagement ring. So, having a bit of classy Swarovski on my other hand, completed my wedding hand.

Somehow in the confusion of me giving this guy a left hook; and him coming after me with brute force, we got into a tight hold as we were grappling with each other; and I then felt a rather sharp stabbing pain to my side, as though he had punched me in my kidneys. By this time, one of the customers came to my rescue; and with his help we managed to throw him out of the bar, as I thanked him and told him to tell Ellie to give him a complimentary drink. Now what seemed like a few minutes, was in fact a good twenty minutes of spoken words and grappling, and by now the police had since arrived; and he and his gang of thugs had scarpered, all but for the one that Dave was left grappling with. I then went back inside and looked at Ellie, as I was now all hot and bothered with a bit of a bloody nose.

I sat down and looked at her; and asked her if I could have a drink, as I needed it after that kerfuffle. She smiled and asked me if I would like a glass of white. Shaking like a leaf and with a tissue one of the boys handed to me, I nodded and said yes. Ellie asked me if I wanted her to call Danni; and explain to him what had happened. I told her that it was ok and best not bother him, that I knew he would be in a meeting. I knew that it was only a bloody nose, telling her that I am sure that he had come of worse, as I was sure I heard his jaw crack. Just then Dave came back into the bar and asked if I were ok, then looking at my face, he patted me on the shoulder and told me that I can't half give a good punch. That he thought I had busted his jaw. He was so sweet, as he then told me for a girly guy, I don't half have some force behind that fist of mine; and he thought that I should be in charge of the door with him. He made his way outside, when the commotion had died down a bit, and after about twenty minutes he came back into the bar letting me know that the police have caught the guy who assaulted me; and that he was making a complaint against for for grievous bodily harm with intent, when they just laughed at him and told him to try.

Just then two police officers came in to see us, first speaking with Dave to get the ins and outs of the altercation; and then coming over to me to get my story of events. One of the police officers was a very young guy; and you could see he had not long come out of training as a cadet. As he was talking to me, I kept feeling a slight pain in my side; and I felt as though I was going to pass out. Again, I asked Ellie for a drink, but this time for her to fetch me a glass of water, as I had not even touched the glass of wine that she had poured for me. She asked me if I was ok, as all of a sudden, I had gone white as a sheet. I told her that I do feel strange, but I guess it's the adrenalin now wearing off, as I asked her for a bar towel to put on my forehead.

She came behind me and placed the damp towel on my head, trying to cool me down in the process. As I started telling the police officer what had happened, I placed my hand to my side to hold it, as I tried to massage out the pain. It was then that the police offer looked down at me; and saw that my dress was covered in blood. He asked me if I was ok; and was I injured, as I had a heavy blood stain on your side. I told the police officer that he hit me in the face; and I gave just as good back, so let him complain. When I went to see what the police officer was going on about. He then looked over to his buddy and called him over, but by then it was too late. I had removed my hand to see it saturated in blood, as I looked at my side. I then looked at the policemen and Ellie in disbelief.

"Ellie, oh Ellie I can't stop bleeding." I said, panicking and now hyperventilating.

Ellie came rushing over, but by then I had collapsed. All I can remember was laying on the floor, with Ellie kneeling beside me, telling me that the ambulance was on its way. She told me that I had been stabbed, as she informed the police officers that there was a slash mark at the side of my dress. I kept asking Ellie if Danni was here yet, as I was going in and out of consciousness. The young police officer was holding my hand, as he told Ellie to make sure she keeps pressure on the wound, as Ellie told me that she has called him, but that his phone was switched off, so she has left a voicemail for him. She told me not to worry and that everything would be ok, that I am just to relax and wait for the ambulance. I heard the police officer's radio going off; and them heard him telling the station that it is now a malicious wounding with intent and an attempted murder that he should be charged with; but as I was going in and out of consciousness, everything was distant and a blur. Even Ellie's voice sounded as though I was in a tunnel, as I heard it close and then fade into the distance.

"Danni is on his way Roxy, please don't worry, he will not be long; and the ambulance has just arrived. Stay with us Aunty Roxy, come on everything is going to be

fine" She said, all calm but with tears flooding down her face.

I do not remember anything at all, that is until I woke up in the hospital recovery unit in intensive care, when I then realised it had to be pretty bad. As I woke, there by my side was Danni and Ellie.

"*Hey babe, how are you doing?*" He asked.

I told him that I have had better day's; and I bet I looked a right mess? Then making a joke of the situation I asked him how many times have I told him, that he should never wake me up until the hairdresser shows. He smiled a little bit, telling me that it was nice to see that I still got some humour inside me; and that I gave them quite a scare. Ellie came towards my left side of the bed, and with tears that had been there, but now dried up but still glistening, she told me that she did not know what was going on, first I was talking to her and the police officers, when all of a sudden, I fell off the stool, and it was only because of the young policemans reflex's, that he was able to catch me, when they both then laid me down on the floor lay you down. Danni held my hand and told me I was very brave; and thought it best now to double the door staff, as there had been an increase of gay bashings in the city. Trying to make light of the conversation, Danni told me that he heard that I gave him a good left hook, as he had been making a complaint against me, but the police have told him that he is in more trouble than that of making a complaint towards the victim. However, they do have to take these things serious and not show prejudice, so there still may be a complaint brought against me. I did not care, as I told them both that I hoped they threw the book at him. Danni told me to relax, as I had tried to get up a little, but the pain was intense. He told me to lay back down for a while, and not to do anything too soon, not until I get to see the doctor anyway.

Losing all track of things, I asked what the time was, when Ellie told me that it was midnight; and that I had been at the hospital since 7 or 8pm. I then asked for my handbag and coat, as I had my keys and money in them; and that I cannot get home without them, as now I wanted to go home, which made me cry. Ellie then informed me that she had my bag with her, and that her coat is in the office still, back at the bar. I looked at Danni and asked him to take me home, I did not like being in this bed; and I hated hospitals like the plague. I then became a little more tearful, as I asked Danni to take me home, but he told me that we had to wait for the doctor to come round to see her. We had to wait to see what he had to say, and that I must be a little more patient, even though I too wanted to take her home.

It was a further hour before the doctor came around to check on how I was; and as I was still drowsy I heard only little bits. He spoke to Danni letting him know all that had gone on; and how lucky I had been.

"It is a deep flesh wound Mr Svenningsen; and it will heal up nicely in time. She has been lucky though, as the knife only just missed her vital organs. With a couple of week's rest, I think she will be fine, but we would like to keep her in overnight for observation."

That's the only thing I really heard, was to keep me in. I begged the doctor to let me go home, that I did not like hospitals at the best of times. With Ellie holding my hand crying with relief, and as Danni was speaking to the doctor. I heard Danni tell the doctor he wanted me transferring to a private ward right away; and he asked if his friend Geoff was on duty.

"Geoff, Mr Svenningsen?" He asked.
"You Know, Geoffrey." Danni replied, as he was interrupted.
"Do you mean Sir Geoffrey Charles, Mr Svenningsen?" The doctor asked.
"Yes doctor, is he on duty tonight?" Danni asked.
"No, he has gone home, what do you need to see him for?" The doctor asked.
"I want Roxy moving to a private ward now; and as Geoff is a colleague of ours, I will ask him to take care of it." Danni said.
"I can get that done for you, but really I would say not tonight, as I think Mrs Svenningsen needs to rest." The doctor replied.

Danni thought the conversation was getting nowhere, as he told the doctor it was not good enough; and with that he pulled his phone from his pocket and continued to call our friend Geoff. I was moved to a private ward, within the hour of Danni asking for me to be moved; and for his friend to be called. Sir Geoffrey had stopped what he was doing; and had made his way into the hospital to come and see us. He was talking to the doctor for a while;

and then came over to us to explain that the doctor did only have my best interests at heart. Feeling a little better, Geoff told me that the other doctor was only doing his job; and that he is a very good doctor. He just did not know who I was; and that I always go private should I visit such establishments. He told me that it was all settled now; and that I should get some rest, as he told me that he would call in on me in the morning.

Again, I asked if I could go home, as I did not want to be in the hospital any longer. I was told adamantly that I had to stay in, as they wanted to monitor me. That the injury was not a scratch, but a deep wound which missed some vital organs. That I would be monitored throughout the night so they can make sure everything is all right, and not to move too much, as I would disturb the stiches, as the knife wound left me with around eight stitches to bare with. Then another doctor picked something up from the staff nurse, as he then told me that he apologised for any confusion I may have; and that he was there should I require anything. Then placing the injection into my arm, he told me that it will make me a little drowsy and give me time to rest. I placed my hand on his arm and told him thank you, but I still wanted to go home. Danni then said he would come and see me in the morning; and he would bring me a case of fresh clothes and toiletries. He waited with me until the drug the doctor gave me, had begun to take its effect on me where I had started to become drowsy and was now falling asleep. Before being totally knocked out I heard him say that he loved me; and I muttered to him that I loved him back.

Next morning, I was woken by one of the private nurses,

who pulled back the curtains and brought in some breakfast for me. I could not believe I had been woken up so early; and I was still slightly thick headed from the drug they had given me. The time was now 7am, and in walked Danni with Geoff. Normally there were no visitors at that time of morning, but with this being a private hospital; and of course, with Danni having some influence with Geoff, he informed the hospital of Danni's arrival.

"Good morning Roxy; and how are we feeling today?" They asked.
"Morning babe, I hope you had a good night's sleep. How are you feeling today?" Danni asked
"I am fine, just wondering when I am going home. I am just taking up space here; and I would be better off in my own bed." I replied.

It did no matter what I said, I stayed in that hospital for two more days; and I had to put up with it, even though I knew I could heal just as quick back in my own home and bed. I had loads of flowers sent; and I was never short of visitors which did pass the time away. However, I just hated being in that bed all on my own, as I was used to my Danni next to me. Ellie had packed my makeup as Danni hadn't a clue; and I had just the basics which I needed to still remain feminine. But it was when Danni came to take me home, that I was most overjoyed, as I knew I had been looked after very well by the doctors and nurses. I just wanted to go home, as I did not stress so much with my natural surroundings.
I was finally told I could go home on the third day; and

that I would have to come back in a weeks' time to have the stitches removed, and then come and see the doctor in about a months' time.

It was an uncomfortable journey going home, what with my side hurting from the surgery. I just lay in Danni's arms, as he held me next to him, as he told me he was glad I was safe. He also asked me if I wanted to go away on holiday with him, as he hadn't seen the little ones for a while; and he thought that a holiday to the USA may cheer me up. I jumped at the offer, as I too had missed little Jake and Sophie. I had all manner of things going through my head with regards Jake and Sophie, planning all the places to go and things to do and see, when I then had thoughts about their mother, would she not have anything to say about this, about me having her children whilst being over there, as we really did not like each other in the slightest. To me she was jealous of what I had. I had money, as did Danni and her ex-husband. She was nothing but a troll, a gold digging bitch of a troll. Danni then told me that his dad has already had a word with her; and he has told her that we will be looking after them. It cost him though, as he has just paid for her to go on a four week cruise around the Bahamas.

That made my blood boil.

It was as though she was using her children to get what she wanted; and that was the lowest and dirtiest thing you could ever do. Children are not objects that you put a monitory value on, they should be allowed to have access to all who are important to them. I apologised to Danni as I called her a parasite; and a bloody gold digger, where everything has a price and love has no meaning at all. Smiling at me, he agreed, saying that she never once

132

showed him any love. That he had his father, who was both mother and father to him; and that he was so grateful for that. That she was either out for what she could get or lying flat on her back screwing the next millionaire.

We spent a few more days at home, whilst with Johnny's permission I handed over my role to Adam. Adam then told me, that he and Stuart are getting on much better again; and that he has asked him to come and meet his mother. I thought that was wonderful news; and I was so pleased they were back on track; and I did tell him we needed to have a little chat still, as I needed to clear a few things up. A few days later, I had a visit from Paul, who told me that the guy who stabbed me had made a complaint against me. That he had to see it through and could not brush it to one side, because his solicitor had since got involved. He told me not to worry though, as he had a strong feeling that my brief and the judge, would throw it out of court, should the CPS actually go ahead with trying to counter charge me. He again told me that it would most likely be a case of self-defence, when I looked at Paul and told him that in all honesty, I could not give a damn about the charge set against me. That he came at me; and it is obvious that he had intent to injure a member of the gay community, as he had come prepared by having on his person an offensive weapon. My argument would be, that it was self-defence, which it was. He hit out at me first; and I retaliated in defence of being hit even more without just cause. Paul then told me that I should be a copper, or a solicitor, as I had a good argument, when I told him I do not need to be either, because I have good friends in both fields who could have the task of fighting for my corner.

I then asked Paul, if he had any insight to why this group of guys came to the bar to cause trouble. That we were not directly in the gay community, where most of the gay bashings were becoming quite common, that we were in London Bridge and not Soho, so I could not understand their actions, as if anyone should have caused a scene, then surely it would have been locals?

Paul then told me that they had planned to go to Soho, as one member of the gang had a magazine showing the names and addresses of the local gay bars; and that it was clearly a pre-meditated plan to cause harm towards the gay community. He further went on to say, that the gang of youths had only stopped at London Bridge to fuel the fire with alcohol, and it was there that they noticed the Rainbow; where they browsed the magazine they were holding, only to find that it was indeed a gay if not gay friendly establishment.

"I guess really it was the old saying Roxy. Wrong place at the wrong time. If they had not got off the tube in London Bridge, they would have made their way to Soho as intended." Paul explained.

In told Paul, that I thought it may have been something like that, because we at the Rainbow have never experienced such volatile behaviour before; that the most we have experienced was that of a bar brawl.

When the time was ready, I had my stitches out and was cleared by the doctor to be able to fly. He was not over struck on me going, but as it was more of a deep flesh wound, he could see no problem. Danni then called his father letting him know what had happened; and that we would be over to see him that following Friday.

I had cancelled all appointments I had for that month; and I had let Johnny and Ruby know, as I made plans to spend a bit of time with Rik and the little ones.

Danni had booked first class seats with British Airways, and we started to pack a few things for a journey.

I did not take as much with me, as I knew I could have some fun shopping in New York, so I would bring more back with me, as it was obvious a shopping trip was on the horizon. Stuart came to see me before we went away; and he explained that his mother is making good progress. That some of her lower bowels were not working properly and they had to be removed; and much to her relief she did not have to have a colostomy bag. I told him that I was pleased for her; and then told him to tell his mother I would go and see her when I returned from my holiday.

When we arrived at John Kennedy airport, Rik was already waiting for us there in his private car. We did not have long to wait in customs, as Danni had an American passport, as well as his British and Norwegian; and by now my application for dual passports had been successfully approved; and it was nice just walking through the barriers, instead of staying in the long queue that we saw before us. Once through the gates, Rik greeted me carefully, so as not to put pressure to my side; and told me that the little ones would not be arriving until the next day, when he had to go and collect them. Rik asked me if I was ok, as he could only assume that it must have been pretty harrowing for me, as he then praised me for fighting back, although some may have said it was foolish to do so. I told him that I was fine, although somewhat sore. Then laughing slightly, I told him that I too was not sure about fighting back, as I never expected any of this to happen, never in a month of Sunday's. he told me that none of us expected it, as he helped Danni with the suitcases. As the cases had been loaded, I looked at Rik, and told him that he was looking well. That the new image he has suits him, as I then asked him what made him make the change. He told me that he decided that he would no longer colour the grey hair that he has; and instead, he decided to just let it grow out naturally, as people told him that he looked fine and distinguished, and more handsome, as he smiled and then laughed.

Oh, he really did look like everything he had been told. I thought that white hair with streaks of grey, was so very sexy, which in my eyes made him even more handsome than before. Rik just smiled at me and told me that flattery would get me everywhere, now with a smile and a glint in his eye. He opened the door for me, as Danni put the last of the cases in the boot. We then left the airport and made our way to his apartment, which really did have beautiful views over-looking Central Park. Once indoors I was made a nice cup of coffee, as I sat outside admiring the view as Danni and his father were chatting about work and of course me and the incident that had happened. We stayed in that night, with Danni and his father making dinner. It was so lovely to see them working together; and they really did complement each other. When the children did arrive, they came running up to me as both Rik and Danni told them to be careful, as I had just come out of hospital. They were, however, still very excited and ran into my arms, where they placed their heads on my shoulders.

"My little prince and princess, I have missed you both so much." I cried
"I love you mommy Roxy." They both said, as again they hugged me.
"Come on children leave Roxy alone now, she has been poorly." Rik said.

They asked me what was wrong, so I just lifted up my blouse and shown them the large gauze plaster that was on my side.

"A naughty man came into the bar and had a go at me, he hurt me with a knife. So, remember little ones do not play around with knives ok?" I told them, now hugging them for dear life
"Yes Roxy, we do not play around with knives or guns anyway, as they are too dangerous." They said, as they told me about a few shootings that had happened not far from them.

That month was the best month of my life, going shopping with the children, then going out in the evening to have a meal and having them call me mommy, as people stared and smiled saying nice sweet children, as they tried to guess which one was the father.
They were very well behaved, but with me I encouraged them to be children and not little adults, as I thought there was nothing more lovely sounding than the laughter of children's voices. We had lots of fun going to

the park, and taking day trips out, with Jake forever holding my hand and staying by my side, as Sophie was all Danni and Rik.

I guess opposites attract as they say, although Sophie loved me just as much; and we played as big sister and little sister, she also loved her big brother just as much. She often used to say she did not think of him as a brother, but more of a daddy; and how nice it was to have a real mommy and two daddies.

Neither of the children liked their mother; and they often said she kept her distance from them. The money that Rik had put into a trust fund for them, which was for them to go to college, was not enough for his ex-wife, as she kept asking her children to sign their money over to her; and she would sort college out for them. But Rik had made sure that their trust funds were tightly sealed, with only him being able to release the money early, by giving his consent by signature. There was nothing that she would not try and do, to get her greedy hands on their money, even resorting to blackmail when she told him that he could not see the little ones.

Rik had since won his parental rights in a family court; and was given his rights as a parent to be allowed to see his children on a regular basis, thus awarding him every other weekend; and longer in the school breaks which infuriated their mother to the core.

No, that month was a very special month for me, having my Danni with me all the time; and my little prince and princess; and of course, not forgetting Rik.

I felt very blessed, that I had such a lovely family, but often wondered about my sisters and why they did not contact me. I wrote to them every month, letting them know what was happening in my life, telling them how much I love them and miss them. I was advised a long time ago, that it would be in my interest to send any such correspondence to Rik's, as their mother would have only destroyed anything that I sent to them at their own address. I even sent numerous letters to my own mother, as well as flowers every month, thinking that she would come around and see how I was doing, however, I still did not have any reply from any of them.

When the month had ended, I found it was very hard to leave, as they both cried for hours when it was time for us to go, with Jake sitting on my lap as he sobbed his little heart out crying; and Sophie going over to Danni.

"Please do not go mommy Roxy, please stay here with Sophie and me; and look after us." He said, sobbing his little heart out.

And whilst Sophie was sitting next to me on Danni's lap, holding on to my arm she stroked Jakes head, telling me just the same as her brother; and begging me to stay.

It was a very upsetting moment for all of us, but with Rik and Danni we managed to eventually sort things out, as I told them I would visit them very soon; and to think of all the fun we would have on my next visit.

On the flight home I was very quiet as was Danni; and it was not until Danni told me his reason for being so quiet, did I fully understand. It was not just the fact he missed his brother and sister, or indeed his father. Danni told me that the American contract had fallen through, as someone had pipped them to the post. I placed my hand on his, as I gave him a kiss on the cheek, then told him that there would be other deals to have. Some of which he would most likely win; and some he would for sure lose, as I then told him to trust me, to trust me when I say that he would most definitely. He knew I was right, as he told me that this was a special deal, as it would have got both him and his father that important foot in the door; and we ourselves could have considered relocating to the USA. The thought of relocating was such a nice thought to have, because I knew I would see the little ones more often. I told Danni that there would be another day, and another and so forth; and that we could still relocate if it meant that much to him, placing my arm underneath his and resting my head on his shoulder. We had a very quiet journey back home, holding each other as we watched a few movies and had a few drinks. We were both glad when we got back to our apartment, as we reflected on those last few weeks together in America, and with the little ones. I could see now how important Danni's family was to him; and he could see how I was when I was parted from my little prince and princess. We all had such a special bond; and it was that bond which brought us closer together as a family.

A few days later I went back to the bar, where I was greeted by Johnny and Ruby, who asked how I was. Ruby was doing a show that night; and as always on her last number she called me up on stage. The crowd then whistled and jeered as I walked on stage; and as I took the microphone, I Thanked them all for their support, with flowers and cards that they had left for me. It was so nice to have such a big family think of you in that way. I then told them that there was an old saying, that you can't keep a good bitch down; and no well no fuckin gay basher would get the better of me or think they could come and harass anyone from our community. Much to the applause, I continued to tell them that I am not one for violence, however, let them come here and try and kick the fuck out of us; and I will tell you that you will fail, for I will always stand tall and stand amongst my community. And with that I would like to sing a classic song by Elton John, titled '*The Bitch Is Back*' with an uproar of applause, as Ruby left the stage and let me do my comeback song. Once my number had finished, I had a standing ovation, and finished the show with Ruby with yet another classic song '*That's what friends are for.*' Johnny had now increased the door security, with two guys and a girl, whilst bag checks were enforced, not just for weapons, but for alcohol as some people were bringing their own in before going to the club, which of course meant they only brought soft drinks, as they tried to use their alcohol to top it up.

It was about another month before I had my little chat with Adam; and I had asked if he wanted to move in with us on a temporary basis until we could get his flat sorted. He jumped at the offer, but I still had to tell him not to give his place up, as I still had a few strings in which I could pull. That week he decided to go over and grab a few things to bring to ours, as we loaded the car. He was text daily by Stuart; and bless him, even I got a text letting me know how things were. Stuart had his ups and downs, but it was only natural for someone in his position, but he knew that we were there for him should he ever need a shoulder; and a friendly face to gaze upon Adam made himself very comfortable in the big bedroom downstairs; and loved his view as well as his little balcony. It was then I mentioned that we no longer have a threesome together, as it would be unfair on Stuart, plus, I felt guilty knowing they had not split up; and we had engaged in some sexual activity with him. Adam understood; and he thanked me for thinking about them, as he would not know what to do if Stuart found out, or indeed if Stuart finished with him, because of our intimate sessions.

That Wednesday when we put on the now elite party that it was becoming, I took Jason to one side and asked if he could help the situation with regards Adams living arrangements; and apparently, I was told that where he lived was due to be pulled down, so he would have a chance to move. I asked him however, if he could find something in his ward, as where Adam lived was now being brought up by private developers; and people buying their own council homes, in turn the local authorities were only keeping a few properties; and I could not see anything going in Adam's favour because of that, despite the heavy damp in his property.

Jason told me to leave it with him, and he would get back to me as soon as he could, he then put his face by mine and told me I looked beautiful as he gave me a peck on the cheek. As I placed my hand on his chest, I thanked him for what he was about to do; and thanked him for all the support he had given me over the years.

It was about a week later when Jason got in touch with me; and then asked me to inform Adam, that he had to

142

be at a certain housing office at a certain time.

Jason had certainly pulled a few strings; and he did exactly as he said he would do. Adam could now give notice where he was living, as Jason had got him a nice big two-bedroom apartment in the District of London Bridge, overlooking the Thames which was not that far from Johnny and Ruby's. Adam was delighted; and although the apartment was still being refurbished, this gave him enough time to gather his things together and start packing. It was about a further three months later when Adam moved into his apartment; and it was at that time that I received a call from Stuart who was having a somewhat unexpected breakdown, due to all what had happened with his mother and stepfather. He was so pleased that she was on the mend, but he too needed that little bit extra looking after. I suggested that we all go to Hove real soon, as all I needed to do was clear it with Johnny and Ruby. I had no shows on the agenda; and any television appearance that I had, I felt I could travel to and from Hove if and when needed; and as Ruby had now taken over the Wednesdays venue looking after our special guests, I just needed to see if they could let Adam go for a while, as I was sure this would have also helped Stuart. I arranged everything for us to go down on the Thursday, as Stuart was still on compassionate leave for another week, when Ruby then gave me the all clear, about Adam taking a much needed break so that he could sort things out with his new accommodation.

His apartment was simply beautiful, with high end appliances and furniture. His kitchen was simply divine; and instead of it being separate, it was an open plan living and kitchen area. His two bedrooms were absolutely gorgeous and very spacious; and the best feature was him having a very large balcony that wrapped around his apartment. He had the view of the Thames from both his lounge and two bedrooms, so if he wanted, he could have had breakfast on the balcony. The master bedroom had patio doors that let onto the balcony, whilst the other bedroom had French doors. All in all, he had certainly landed on his feet.

When Danni had got home, he told me that he would not be able to make the Thursday, however, he would be with me in Hove on the Friday night. Adam, however, could only make it on the Saturday and Sunday, so it was arranged for Stuart to come to our apartment and I would take him with me to Hove on the Thursday morning.

I told Stuart we would go by train, as Danni would bring the car down with him the next day with all the bags. We just needed a small case for a change of clothes for the next day, and of course a change for the evening. Adam came over to take us to the station before going to work, as they were a member of staff down; and Ruby really did need him to do that shift, so Adam being Adam did not complain and just said he would be there. It gave him and Stuart some time together as my phone bleeped, Danni text to ask me to let him know when we arrived; and he would be with us most likely early Friday morning, or if it he finished ahead of time, he would drive down Thursday night. After about half an hour, Adam and Stuart came out of the bedroom as I was just finishing coffee. Adam asked if I were ready to go; and after telling him that I was, he got my overnight bag as Stuart reached for his bag and we all headed towards Victoria Station. We made our way through the barriers, as we were herded like cattle through one gate that was open, instead of the usual three gates; all the time having yet more delay as the ticket inspectors and guards made sure you had the right ticket for travel on that day.

Adam then gave us both one last wave, as Stuart now took hold of my arm and escorted me to the awaiting train, as it was not long before it would set off.

When we had found a seat on the train, I text Danni to let him know we were on our way, also letting him know I had a large suitcase to bring down, as I needed some clothes at Hove now it was becoming a regular thing.

On the journey down to Hove, Stuart and I chatted about everything and nothing, all the time with my arm firmly underneath his. I think this also comforted him, as it took his mind off things, even though we did have a little discussion about his mother. It was not in depth, as I did not want to upset him any more than he had been of late. Being a gentleman, he sat on the outside by the aisle, as he let me have a window seat; and there with my arm underneath his, I sometimes dropped my hand so that it was on his thigh. I was like a little schoolgirl having my handsome young policeman as my escort, as we looked like a couple very much in love, laughing and making light conversation about things less trivial than we usually conversed about, making flirtatious remarks which got heads turning, as we looked again at each other and smiled at one another. Once we arrived at Hove, we got a cab to the apartment and we just dropped the bags inside. I told Stuart that I would need to go and get a few provisions; and whilst we were out, we could have a spot of lunch.

As we left to go shopping, he once again offered me his

arm and asked if he could have mine under his. It was a lovely feeling having this tall muscular policeman give me all the attention I loved, which did sometimes show in his trouser department. I kept thinking again, how so blessed I am with my family, amongst all the bitchiness and hurt from some people, this however made up for it. I made sure I only had nice people around me; and my ever so growing family was increasing. I just thought that it was going to be a very expensive this Christmas, as all my family had good taste. We decided to eat first; and as we were in town we went into this lovely bistro and cake shop. Stuart pulled out the chair for me, sliding it under me as I sat down, then he sat opposite me as we looked at the menu; and then once we were comfortably seated, we ordered coffee and whatever else caught our eye on the menu. I then suggested to him, that if he liked, we could go out for a meal that evening, so I would be eating really light. Making light of the conversation, I told him that I had to think of my figure, as I did not want to put a great deal of weight on, now flirting with him. He told me that I have a gorgeous figure; and a very sexy one at that, as he placed his hand over mine. Telling me that he had seen more fat on a French fry, than he had seen on me; and that I ate like a sparrow. I agreed with him; and told him that I was such a fussy eater, but no matter what I eat, I get full so quickly. That once I could eat like a horse; and where I would have my plate loaded with food and it would not matter one bit. But now, for some reason no matter what I eat, I fill up to quickly, that is why I only ever have child portions, because I can just about manage them.

We spent about an hour in the bistro, before going to the supermarket to get groceries. When we got back home, I just had to take my shoes off and relax; and I know it was not ladylike, but one cannot look glamorous all the time. I then apologised, as I told him I needed to kick off my shoes, because they were killing me, as he asked me if I would like him to make a pot of tea or coffee. I told him that I would love a cup coffee, and that I would be in the garden if he cared to join me. Stuart joined me in the garden where I was sitting in a shady nook, with the jasmine hanging over the pagoda. This was Danni and my favourite place when we came into the garden; and when were not nude sunbathing. Stuart sat down next to me where again we began to chat, getting to know each other more and more as he opened up to me. After a while Stuart was getting a little jittery; and then asked me if he could put his arm around me. I was taken back with his suggestion, then told him that it would be nice; and even nicer if it got him to chill out as well. The surprises did not stop there, because as he had his arm over my neck, with my head close to his chest, he told me that he knew I have Danni; and he was with Adam, but I really did make him feel at ease. That he has enjoyed today, even if he was a little bit nervous to start with. But having me hold his arm on the train; and as I let him escort me into town made him feel really special. He then told me that I was one classy lady and one very sexy lady. That it has been a pleasure spending the afternoon with me; and taking me into town. I thought that that was so sweet of him to say; and that I could only be who I really am. I told him I hoped he knew that he too was a part of our family; and that I will always be there for him, just as much as the others. I told him that he was a sweet guy; and that he had gone through a lot lately; and how I wished he would have spoken to me sooner about things, but not to worry, because he could talk to me about anything in the future, as I brushed his cheek with my hand

"You shouldn't have said that Roxy, as there is a lot I could talk about, but do not want to ruin what you have given me." He told me.
"Oh really, I am very much intrigued by that response Stuart; and you should never ever keep a lady guessing." I replied, now being quite curious.

Putting his arm over my shoulder, he looked at me and whispered in my ear that he could easily fall in love with me.

"I do love Adam; and I love him very much. But I also find myself attracted to your Danni; and strangely enough I find you very intoxicating in which I could, if not already have, fall in love with you both." He softly said.
"Stuart I am overwhelmed with what you have just said, as I find an attraction to you as well. Whatever you said would never spoil what we have together; and it certainly would not upset or change Danni's views about you. But I do hope you realise that under all this beauty and make up, I am still a man and I have a cock; and please do not let your feelings get mixed up between love and lust." I told him, now feeling a little hot under the collar, so to speak

"That's the thing I like about you Roxy, you are a beautiful woman with a cock. I like the fact you have not changed your body, which you do not need to do by the way; and feels like she wants to go down the road like Ruby has. A transgirl looking as beautiful as you; and having a cock is such a turn on." He replied.
"Are you flirting with me Stuart? Now you are making me blush." I laughed, as I went red.

With his arm over my shoulder, he gently squeezed my shoulder as he placed a kiss on my face.

"Now behave Stuart, because I can see something stirring; and I am sure you would not like to get embarrassed?" I said, as I gripped his thigh.
"I will never ever do anything, to spoil what we have; and I will not do anything behind Danni's back, as we made a promise a long time ago about such times as these." I ensured him

We stayed in the garden for a few hours just chatting, before I suggested we go inside and relax before going out.

"Honey on the lamp table is my address book, would you find the number for Giuseppe's and make a booking for tonight at around 8.30? Tell them it is for Roxy; and I want the usual on ice." I asked him.

"Sure Roxy, I will do that now." He replied.

I made my way into the bedroom and sorted a few things out for that evening. I was slightly nervous myself, as this was the first night out, that I would not be with Danni; and having this handsome guy take his place was every girl's dream. A taste of the forbidden fruit, even though temptation stayed in my mind and would not go any further, as I would never play that sort of game with my Danni, because I knew what the situation of me seeing Adam and Danni together; and I would never put Danni in that position. I then had a text from Danni to say he had managed to finish earlier than he thought; and he would be driving down to Hove around 6 pm, that I should go ahead as planned as he would eat before he left, and that I should enjoy myself. I text back and told him to take it easy; and to drive safely as I let him know that Stuart and I were going for a meal; and then we would come back home as we both did not want to make a late night of it. So, I had a shower and started to get myself ready, as I heard Stuart in the spare room moving about, then he came to my bedroom door and asked if it was ok for him to shower. I popped my head around the door; and then told him he did not need my permission. I explained to him where the linen cupboard was; and that the water was very hot, so to be careful when stepping in the shower.

As the restaurant was not too far away, there was no need to rush, as we would get there in plenty of time in a cab. Stuart looked absolutely gorgeous in his designer suit, and so very handsome. I was so lucky to have such handsome men in my life, both on the inside as well as the outside; but my Danni was still my number one, and always would be.

Stuart locked up for me and escorted me to the cab, where like a gentleman, he opened doors for me and offered me his arm. He passed compliments to me telling me that I looked absolutely beautiful, that I was very elegant and classy, then saying that he hoped he had scrubbed up well enough for me; and that I did not let me down in any, now coming across all bashful. Being flirtatious, I told him that he had indeed scrubbed up well; and that he could have been standing there in just his boxers; and he would have still been handsome. He then made a jest about maybe he will do it when he gets back to the apartment, and just stand there with his boxers on. I laughed at him as I told him to stop flirting with me; and to behave himself. He was such a sweet guy, but so was Adam and the rest of my boys. He told me that he was not flirting with me, though heaven forbid he had often thought about it, but that he was just trying to make me smile, because he knew that I too had had a rough time these last few weeks. The thing was it was working. Having Stuart there with me made me feel safe; and it was not because he was a copper, or indeed taller; and musclier than I was. It was with the likes of Danni, Johnny and now Stuart, I felt protected more. Adam was kind of on my level, and although I felt safe with Adam, we really were just two dizzy queens when we were together, though I would not underestimate him being a queen, as I know he can look after himself too. Thing is nothing was ever too serious, yes I flirted and so did Stuart, as well as Danni and everyone else. It was just a little harmless fun; and no matter what, they were always gentlemen who would not take liberties.

Stuart and I got to the restaurant where the owners were

pleased to see us; and then escorted us to our seats. There was already a bottle of champagne on ice at our table; and as Stuart seated me, he then went to his seat where we were offered the menus.

"*Do not worry what's on the menu or the price honey, this is my treat.*" I told him.
"*I don't think so Roxy, I am paying for this meal. It is a pleasure to come out with you; and to be alone with you for once as I get to know you more, especially away from London and the drag circuit, as I get to know what Roxy is really like. I am so proud and excited; and I could not think of a nicer lady to come out with. I now know why Danni loves you so much; and how much you mean to Adam, as he constantly talks about you both and praises you always.*" He replied, adamant I was not to get my purse out, otherwise he would become annoyed.
I told him that I did notice a few people give you him a look of jealousy or was that look towards me. I mean, I was usually with Danni; and the staff had already given us a few looks already. As Stuart told me that it was their problem; as he then said that he was going to give them something else to talk about, as he called for my ear, but instead placed a kiss on my lips.

"*You naughty boy Stuart, they are going to think I am a tart.*" I replied.
"*Never in a million years will you be a tart, you are too classy Miss Roxy.*" He said, now with a big grin on his face.

I wanted so much to tell him about Adam and us; but did not know how to approach it. I knew this was not the right time, but I really did have to somehow clear the air as I wanted no hard feelings. We both ordered from the menu, and although Stuart was not much of a champagne drinker, he did have one glass with me before going onto his lager. It was a pleasant evening with a trip down memory lane; and a laugh or two along the way, when he picked up on the incident that happened at the bar; and told me that if he had been on duty, then he would have killed the fucker. He told me that Paul and his squad were besides themselves with worry, as he unofficially told me that they gave him hell in the cells. I thanked him for his concern; and knew that he would have indeed killed the fucker. I told Stuart, that I was fortunate enough to have friends in high places; and it is nice that they think of me in a way that they do by worrying about. I can tell you though, once I saw the blood oozing from me, I thought I was going to die; and if it were not for that young police officer catching me, I don't know what would have happened. Then Stuart told me his name. it was an officer called Douggie. That his name was Ian Douglas, but as there was another Ian Douglas in the squad, they decided to call him Douggie. I told Stuart, that I was going to somehow, thank him for what he did for me that day, as I still had not had the time to do so, which I thought was awful of me. When Stuart then took my hand; and told me not to worry about it, that Paul and the Commander gave him a commendation. That he was out of boot camp less than a week; and the force was mighty proud of the youngster, as you could see that he too was proud of the young copper. Stuart then asked me

153

how I met Danni, and I told him of that night in the dressing room which really got him going. By the end of the evening, we had both got to know each other a little better; and I got to find out a little bit more about Stuart and his background. He was indeed a very genuine guy and a loving guy; and I was so proud and privileged to have him come into my family. His hard exterior as a policeman, was nothing like the real him, as underneath all that he showed as a stern police officer, he was a big soft pussycat underneath. His passion towards his mother was a joy to hear; and I felt sad about him losing his father at such a young age. I told him that his father would be very proud of him, especially as he is following him in his footsteps. I also told him that I am so pleased that he has come into our lives, as well as making it up with my little firecracker. Just then I got the attention of the waiter for the bill, Stuart looked at me and then said.

"Roxy, I am paying for the meal. Please it has been such an honour tonight; and you have made me feel so very special."
"Honestly it is ok Stuart, you can do it another time, if you like?" I replied, as I placed my credit card on the saucer with the bill.
"Remember I am a policeman; and if you do not abide by the law, I may have to use handcuffs." He said, as he caught me off guard.

I nearly choked on my champagne as we both laughed; and I was not going to argue with that. Stuart picked up my credit card and slipped it inside my purse which was

154

open and next to my glass of champagne. He then placed his own card there; and called for the waiter as he paid the bill. We then left the restaurant, as I kissed the owners on the cheek; and asked to book a table for the next night too, letting them know it will be for three of us. Stuart held the door open for me as we made our way outside; and as he was about to hail a cab, I suggested to him that we would walk.

It was a lovely summers evening; and a stroll along the seafront would be so nice I thought. He gladly offered me his arm as I put mine underneath his; and happily, we made our way to the sea front, walking like the night just belonged to us. Our eyes fixed to each other as we were chatting as we regularly stopped to hear the waves; and as we looked up to see the moonlit sky, as well as gathering my composure, because of the champagne I had drunk which made me a little unsteady on my feet. I told him that this was one of the many walks that Danni and I made; and how romantic it was then and is still. He was overwhelmed that I honoured him with the same presence that I gave Danni; and he told me that I was a very romantic person, especially in the way I described things.

"Roxy may I do something; and hope that it will not spoil things for us?" he asked.
"Do what Stuart?" I replied, rather intrigued
"May I thank you with a kiss? I have had such a wonderful night with a beautiful lady; and cannot think of anything nicer but to end it with a kiss." He said, as he told me it would just make the whole night end on a high.

"Honey I am flattered." I replied.

I looked at him; and as I went to move my cheek to his face, he kissed me right on the lips.

"Stuart." I said, shocked but pleasantly happy.
"Sorry Roxy, please forgive me. It just made my night; and I thought you would not have minded, after all we kissed in the restaurant." He said apologetically.
"I was not expecting that honey, you just surprised me that's all. Thank you it was a lovely surprise; and as for the restaurant, you took advantage of me you naughty boy." I replied, with a cheeky grin.
"I am hurt, deeply hurt." He said, now starting to laugh.

With my hand under his arm, he put his other hand on my hand and told me again thank you, as he also thanked me for not being mad at him.
By the time we had walked along the seafront, we headed back to the apartment to now chill out. I kept thinking about that kiss; and how shocked he was at me for being surprised, but I also thought how wonderful it was; and I had wished he had never stopped when he did. I wanted to stop and give him a kiss, just to let him know it was ok; and there was no harm in it, because we were both adults; and truth be known if I did not want it to happen, then it wouldn't have. We got back home; and I made my way to the lounge, where I went through to the kitchen and got a bottle of wine out of the fridge, rather than make tea or coffee. I poured Stuart a vodka and coke, as we never had any lager in the drinks cabinet; and brought both glasses through to the lounge. We sat

on the couch as we chatted, listening to music in the background whilst we chatted lightly.

Stuart was seated next to me; and just like Danni, he held his arm out as I lay into his chest, his arm embracing me as my back fell firmly into his front, hearing his heart pound softly fluttering here and there; and his warm breath on my neck sending chills down my spine.

It was a lovely evening; and one I could not have wished to go any better, as we were chatting like old friends, and Stuart never ever pushed for anything more. I think he was glad of the company; and glad he had someone to talk to on his own level. Yes, Adam was good for Stuart, but sometimes he could be a dizzy queen and not understand how he is feeling. He was engrossed in his relationship; and like a proud peacock that he was dating a copper, that any such in depth conversations were too hard for Adam to contemplate. I hated to admit it, but at times I thought it was all about Adam; and fuck anyone else if they needed a shoulder; and not blowing my own trumpet, I knew how to approach people and just listen. Even though we were having a lovely evening, when we were talking about his family and then mine, I still missed my Danni, and wished he was here with us.

It was then that my phone bleeped; and a text came through. '*Just leaving London now, will be with you in a few hours. If you are in bed, I will try not to disturb you.*'

I didn't think I would be able to stay up, as I was quite tired by now; and after having a busy day and a wonderful night, the time soon caught up with me. I told Stuart that it was now midnight; and would he mind if I retired to my bedroom. He told me that he did not mind at all, as he thought that he too should get some sleep, as it has been quite a day today, now stretching and yawning himself. I then told him that if he heard a noise in the night, not to worry as it would be Danni, as he is on his way down here; and it was why I did not lock up. I got up off the couch; and took the glasses into the kitchen. Coming back into the lounge Stuart had already gone to his bedroom, so I decided to walk in to bid him goodnight. I went as red as a beetroot when I walked in the room, as even though I had knocked on the door, he stood there with just a nice tight pair of black boxers on; and something that really left nothing to the imagination. He did not bulge as big as Danni, but it made a clear impression through those boxers, that he was more adequate than most in the cock department.

"I am sorry Stuart, I did knock. I just wanted to say goodnight." I said, as he told me that he did not hear me, what with his mind being all over the place. *"You ok honey."* I asked him, now looking at him as I felt sorry for him, knowing he was still holding a lot back.
"Yes Roxy, I will be fine; and thank you again for a wonderful night, you really are very special to me." He said, with a little glimmer in his eye and a voice starting to tear up.
"Come here honey, give me a hug." I told him, as I held out my arms for him to come into my embrace.

Like a little boy he came towards me; and as I held him his head rested on my shoulder. He held me tight and just started to cry, thanking me as he apologised for talking about being upset; and hoping he had not ruined the evening. I knew this was about his mother, so assured him I would be there for him, as would Danni.

"*It will be ok honey, you have gone through a lot lately, but remember we are here. Come on let it all out honey, do not go to bed in a crying fit. You never know what lies around the corner, where your mother is concerned*" I said, as I comforted him
"*Thank you Roxy. Just being with you cheers me up, I can assure you. You have not mentioned anything that has gone on, but instead you have helped put my mind on other things, to take my mind off mom.*" He cried, as he held me tight and sobbed his heart out.

He may have been a copper, and a big boy at that. In height as well as girth, but he was still my boy. I looked him directly in the eyes as I told him that I could see that he loved his mother very much; and I was so proud of him, that he had so much love for her and was not afraid to show it, but at times he did need to let everything out; and not store it inside where it builds up and just gets worse. That it plays with your heart and your mind, and that is not a good thing to have spinning through your thought as you cannot think straight. I told him to remember, that he has a group of special people around him; and now he has Adam back in his life, who also loves him very much, as I stroked his hand gently.
He told me that he wished Adam could have made it, but he does understand. I then picked his head up and looked in his eyes, when I then put my lips to his mouth and kissed him, my hand pressing firmly against his cheek as I held his face.

"You are so loving and gentle Roxy, you are really very special, whether Roxy the male, or Roxy the female, you are indeed special and one in a million." He told me, feeling a little better that he had opened up to me. I told him that he was very sweet; and to try and get some sleep, as I would see him in the morning.

Just as I was going to bed my phone rang and it was Danni, so I answered it straight away. He asked how things were and I told him not good. I told him that I was worried about him, that he was a complete wreck just crying in his bedroom; and that was not Stuart because he was normally a strong guy; and I did not like to see him in that way, as I tried my best to whisper and not let him hear.

"Not good honey, is he really that upset?" He asked.
"Yes honey, and I did try and take his mind off things when we were out which seemed to work. But as we got home and we chatted he just broke down, and I hate leaving him like that." I replied.
"Well babe, I will not be long now, I just pulled over before joining the M23." He replied.
"Ok honey, I will see you soon; and get off the damn phone if you are driving. You know it worries me Danni." I replied, as I did not hear him clearly, when he mentioned he had pulled over.

Danni put the phone down, and I went back into Stuart's room to tell him Danni would be here in an hour or so; and that I was going to go to bed. But as I got to his

160

room it seemed as though he was already asleep, so either the crying or the drink had finally relaxed him. I then made my way to the bathroom and freshened up, then got dressed into my sexy black lingerie where I placed my dressing gown around me; and with my shoes walked into the lounge to wait for Danni. The excitement of knowing he was not that far now, had made me wake up a little bit more; and I waited impatiently, until he walked through the door. Just as I was finishing a glass of wine, I heard the key in the door; and then rushing to the hallway, I opened the door for him and ran into his arms. He told me that he had missed me so much, as I told him that I had missed him too. Then he asked if Stuart was alright; and was he now settled. Then changing the subject by asking if we had a lovely night out. I told him that he now seems to be asleep, as I then continued to tell him about our night; and how lovely and relaxing it was. Then telling him that I was sure that he was my lover, as they were used to me and him going to the restaurant, but it did not half get people staring and whispering behind their menu cards. Danni was not surprised, as he too accepted the fact that Stuart was a good looking guy; and a very handsome policeman in his uniform, and he betted that I was in heaven, going out with a policeman in civvies. I looked at him and then just told him that I do love a man in uniform, but I also love a man in a business suit; and he knew that without asking. I then told him that I had best shut the door and lock up for the night; and we had best be a little quiet, for I did not want us to wake him. Danni had left all of the bags in the car, as we knew they would be ok, as the car was safely on the drive and we were in a respectful area of Hove where the only crime we had in twenty years, was some old dear's milk being stolen from her doorstep; and so, unlike some of the houses and side streets in Hove that was a haven for street crime. He told me that it was also best, as there were a few suitcases; and he did not want to clunk and clank around the apartment, so would be best just leaving them in the boot. We walked into the lounge; and then right into the kitchen where I went to make Danni his much needed mug of coffee, when he told me that he would much prefer a glass of bourbon. I poured myself a glass of wine; and then poured him a bourbon on the rocks, we made our way back into the lounge, as we caught up on what had been happening. He told me he tried to get Adam off work, but they were really stretched for staff. Danni told me that Adam would be down tomorrow; and that he said he is going to text us when he is leaving. I lay in Danni's arms with my head on his chest; and my feet on the couch whilst wearing my fluffy slippers, as I had since taken off my shoes. Just then Stuart came through the door; and saw us and hoped he wasn't disturbing us. He was startled at first, as he told us that he did not realise that we were still up; and that he had come in for a glass of water. I asked him if it was us that had woken him; and were we a little too noisy, when he told us no, it was just a fact that he could not sleep, so getting up and getting some water he thought would help. Danni asked him if he was ok; and did he enjoy his night out with his Roxy, when he told Danni he did, that his wife was truly amazing. How I made him feel so comfortable; and he had had a very good night that he didn't want it to end, as he began to tear up. I looked at

Danni and asked him to go and see if he was alright, as I thought he needed the male touch rather than just me fussing over him with worry. Danni got off the couch and walked into the kitchen, where I then heard Stuart crying again. He then began to gently comfort Stuart with warming words, telling him exactly as I did earlier, to let it all out as he offered his shoulder for support. I finished off my glass of wine, and then walked into the kitchen. Seeing my boys embrace each other, as Stuart looked up at me and again said sorry; and still in Danni's embrace, I went over to Stuart and kissed him softly on the lips. Danni then held his arm open for me; and I embraced both my boys, as Stuart dropped his head onto my neck, and then kissed me softly on the neck, telling me that he loved us both.

"See I told you I am not as tall without having my heels on, that's why you need to reach down to me, because I would get a nosebleed." I said, with a bit of a laugh.

I then looked at Danni and gave him a kiss, where I told him I loved him. Danni saw something in my eye which he knew what to do, so as I gave him a second kiss, I told him I was going to bed and that I would see them there. Danni shouted that he would see me shortly, and for me to get the warm, which I told him he was being too cheeky.
Shortly after going to bed, the boys came in, where Stuart seemed a little nervous. I told Stuart to come over by me; and that he could sleep in the middle and then he would have us both next to him. That he can't sleep alone tonight, because I thought he just needed a cuddle

163

as Adam wasn't here to snuggle up next to him I told him. He made his way over towards me; and there he clambered over the bed until he got to the middle, there getting underneath the duvet. He told us that he hoped he was not intruding, although he knew Danni had said it was ok and that in fairness, he did not want to be alone. Just as Stuart got himself comfortable, he noticed Danni remove his boxers. This made him go a little red, as he had never seen anyone naked other than Adam. Feeling awkward he looked at Danni and asked him if he would you like him to remove his boxers too, or would I prefer him to keep them on. Danni looked at me in which I smiled at them both.

"There's your answer Stuart, Roxy smiling tells you to take them off. She does like her boys to be natural." He said, walking towards his side of the bed.
"And would you mind if I slept on the edge Roxy? Nothing against you or Danni, I just don't sleep in the middle so well." He asked
"Whatever you like honey, but if you find me straddling you in the night it is because I need to get up." I replied.
"What about straddling Danni to get up, would that not be easier?" He asked, feeling a little calmer.
"If I straddle Danni, I assure you that I would not be getting up. Chances are he would grab hold of me and be naughty." I replied.
"Oh, ok then, looks like Roxy will straddle me for safety then Danni." He laughed.

Stuart had since got out of bed to take off his boxers and placed them on my dressing room stool, I caught a

164

glimpse of his semi hard cock. Like Danni he was blonde, but a very soft blonde; and he did not have that much body hair as it was trimmed, but what he did have was lovely; and his hair followed his body right down to a beautiful thick seven inch cock.

Having now returned from the bathroom, I got into bed and made my way towards the middle which I thought would be better, as that way if Stuart wanted to go back into his bedroom, then he did not have to clamber over me or Danni. when Danni and Stuart climbed in next to me. Both Danni and Stuart put their arms under my pillows where they then touched each other's shoulders. Then they lay on their sides and came towards me, as they leaned over me and kissed each other.

I then kissed them both, to which I replied.

"Come on I think it is time to get some sleep, it has been a very long day for all of us; and I am in need of my beauty sleep." In which, they both then laughed at me.

The invite to share our bed with us, was not with a hidden agenda to have sex. I for one wanted him with us so that if he did want some reassurance, then we were there, although it was nice having naughty thoughts about the two of them. We had a big enough bed, as it was a superking; and could fit four people, so we all had room beside us, and we were not tight and on top of each other. It was not long before we were all asleep, with my boy's arms around me; and where somehow in the night my hands ended up by my side, where I found myself holding onto both of their cocks, as I was sprawled on my back.

That morning I awoke; and I had turned over to face Stuart, I had my arms around him; and Danni had turned around to face me, with his arm over me and Stuart. We were just like the three wise monkeys. I had my arm around Stuart, with my hand holding on to his cock, which by now as he was waking because he was becoming aroused. Danni had his aroused cock pressing against my ass and thighs, where he gently positioned it into my ass crease. Then Danni placed his hand on my breast, as Stuart turned onto his back and placed his over me and Danni, fondling his ass. Danni then began kissing me on the lips as Stuart kissed my breasts, as he stroked my legs and started moving his hand towards my panties. With me now being on my back, Stuart placed his hand inside my panties as I raised my body so he could remove them; and slowly he did as he moved down the bed to take them off my feet. Stuart then stayed at the bottom of the bed and straddled both Danni's and my legs, as in turn he took each of our cocks into his mouth. Danni now getting rather hot started kissing me passionately, as I stroked his chest hair whilst feeling his tongue slip into my mouth and mingle with mine. I told them both they had to stop, as I needed to go to the bathroom; and so, I looked at them both and told them to have a bit of fun until I get back, as it would be nice to see them both playing with one another. I went to the bathroom just to freshen up; and then made my way to my wardrobe where I got my black stilettos out, carefully placing them on my feet as I did the ankle straps up. As Danni and Stuart, were now in the sixty nine position; and I had Stuarts ass facing me, so I just got onto my knees and began to rim him ass.

"Oh god Roxy that's good, Christ I have never had that before, please don't stop." He told me.
"Don't worry I won't, and don't you boys ever learn not to speak with your mouths full." I chuckled.

As I slid my tongue deeper into his ass, I made sure he was moist ready for a finger or two. I gently slid my finger at the base of his hole and teased it, before inserting inside him. He was moaning with so much pleasure, and I could see he was very tight. Danni could see what I was doing; and as he was sucking Stuarts cock, he played with mine and played with my ass, when I stood up and straddled his head. Getting back on my knees I kissed Stuarts ass, as I again gently inserted another finger into him, making him take two fingers. Whilst doing this, I was looking at Danni and kissing him on the forehead, as I seen him take all of Stuarts cock down his throat, as he lifted up his balls to gently play with them. I heard Stuart gagging a little bit on Danni's cock; and at that point I got Danni's hand and told him to take over as I had finished making sure he takes a few more fingers to stretch his hole. I then went around the other side of the bed to see Stuart; and as I knelt on the bed, I raised his head slightly so that he could take my cock in his mouth. Once again Stuart went from Danni's cock to my cock, never disappointing as he took all of mine easily in his mouth, but still struggled with Danni's. I lifted him up and just kissed him on the lips, where I told him he had done well to get all of Danni's cock inside his mouth, all but the remaining two inches.

167

Next thing I knew Danni had tapped Stuart on the ass and told him to get off him; and then got to his knees as he told me to get on all fours. He asked me to get in the doggy position; and to take Stuarts cock. He wanted to see me suck him whilst he fucked me. So, I got on all fours and began sucking Stuarts cock, as Danni slid his wet hard cock inside me. Stuart had now got even harder; and had started to leak pre cum from the sight of seeing me being fucked, and I know it had excited him as he thrust deeper into my mouth. This really turned Stuart on, as he told Danni, that he wouldn't mind a piece of my ass, as it looked so hot and good. Then to my amazement, Danni told him to be his guest if he wanted a piece of my ass. So, Danni removed his cock from my ass, as Stuart got behind me and started to finger my hole, before inserting his cock into me. As he gave me his cock inch by inch, I could feel him tense up as he savoured the moment. He began telling me how hot he thought this was; and how tight I was that he would have to be careful in case he shot his load as it was that intense.

"Have you ever had a double fuck Stuart?" I asked him.
"A what Roxy?" He replied.
"A double fuck Stuart, you know as you are fucking me, then Danni will get behind you and start to fuck you. Like a sandwich; and you being the one in the middle as the filling." I said, with a cheeky laugh.
"No never, remember I am a gay virgin so to say, only thing I have had is a blow job." He answered

"Do you want to try Stuart? I will be very gentle with you and if you say stop I will." Said Danni

168

"Sure Danni, but please do be very careful, at the moment I do not know if I am a top, bottom or versatile, as I have only ever penetrated Adam which was great, as for the rest I am unsure." He replied.

Stuart just left his cock inside me, as Danni prepared his ass with a bit of lube. He then got the tip of his cock inside Stuart's ass, where he told him that he would have to push down slightly on him to take the head.
Stuart started moaning in both pleasure and pain, as he took inch by inch, but not all of it right away, as he then held onto my waist and pulled me towards him fucking me harder as he took Danni's cock. He told us that it was blowing his mind, but it felt so good. He then said that it hurts a little, having Danni's ten incher trying to go all the way, but it was so horny. Then saying that I had a lovely tight ass, and he knew that he liked to be top, however he had to stop for fear of cumming too soon. That turned Danni on, as he then told Stuart, that if he was going to shoot his load, that he would need to see it. He then told me to get on my back and to throw my legs over Stuart's shoulders.

"Yes Danni, Stuart will you please stand up at the end of the bed and pull me towards you so that my ass is just hanging off the edge." I said, as Stuart had now removed himself from me, and as I was now positioning myself on my back.

Stuart did as he was told and pulled me towards him, sliding his cock back inside my ass. Danni then straddled my head giving me his balls and ass to lick. With my hands pulling his ass cheeks apart; and my tongue sliding inside his ass, Danni reached for Stuart and kissed him and then told him to fuck me. Stuart did this; and after about a further five minutes he told Danni he was going to cum.

"Cum Stuart; and when you do fully withdraw and thrust it back harder into her ass." He told him.

Stuart did just that, as he shot his first load inside me and then he withdrew and spilt some of his warm juice over my balls, before thrusting it back inside me to give me every last drop. Stuart was now breathing frantically as he could not stop pumping my ass, which in turn got Danni off even more. Danni then told Stuart to lie on the bed just like I did, and with that he told me to straddle his face and make him take my cock until I shot my load. I straddled Stuarts face and gave him my very wet cock, as Danni once again took his ass. By now Stuart had taken all of Danni's cock; and had mine all the way down his throat, as he played with my balls and ass.

"Oh god Danni, that's so good please don't stop. Fuck that ass hard. Roxy, I want to taste your cum, let me know when you are ready; and you can empty it down my throat." He asked, begging me to cream his throat.

He pulled harder on my balls as he slid his finger up my ass; and took my cock deeper into his throat as he slid his tongue over my slit as he came up for air.
I told both Danni and Stuart that I was not far off cumming; and as I held onto Stuarts chest pulling on his

nipples, I couldn't help myself, as I thrust a few more times shooting my hot creamy cum down his throat, removing it to show Danni, as I dripped cum on his lips. Danni got hold of Stuart's hard cock again as he was rock hard; and as he too was ready to cum for the second time, so Danni jerked his cock until Stuart shot over his tummy; and Danni filled his virgin ass with his cum. We lay there for just a few seconds, before getting up and cleaning off. I removed my lingerie and went into the bathroom to take off my makeup, which once again got Danni hard.

"Are you always hard Danni? Don't you ever stay soft? And Roxy you are fucking gorgeous, do you think I may have the chance with you two again as guys?" said Stuart. *"I cannot see why not honey. I just need to let my face breath tonight."* I replied. *"I am going to have to be honest with Adam though, I do not want to have any secrets from him."* Stuart said.

I then just told him that I understood; and I am sure that Adam would not mind what had happened. I now felt guilty for the second time, but this just seemed to happen without warning; and no one objected. I looked at Stuart and told him, if I were to confide in him would he keep it a secret until the right time? He told me that he would, so I began telling him about us and Adam, when he was here with us last. He was shocked at first, but understandably said it was ok, as he was sure Adam thought they had split up; and besides he had just engaged in pleasure with both Danni and I, and therefore he would in time let Adam know when the time was right, and if we would not say anything until he had approached him, in which we both agreed we would not say anything. We were all now so pretty much done in, so suggested we have another hour in bed. I then told Danni to jump in the middle; and with that I kissed them both on the lips and turned around. Danni lay on his side with his arm above my head and his hand stroking my ass and back, sending me to sleep. With his cock pressing firmly between my legs, as I felt a second hand come over me and stroke my cock, which by now I had realised that it was Stuarts.

"Thank you for everything you have done for me, both of you thank you." He told us

I then turned around, almost kneeing Danni in the balls, gave him a kiss on the lips, and told Danni to turn around as well so that I could cuddle him. Next thing I knew, I was being woken up by Stuart with an orange juice and some toast. He greeted me by saying morning, which he later corrected to afternoon; and told me that Danni had told him to bring me some breakfast. I thanked him, as I then asked for the time, rubbing my eyes and focusing on Stuart just in his boxers. Stuart informed me that it was eleven; and that they were both in the garden, as it was a beautiful sunny day.
"Blimey I had best get up; and that's a cheek calling it afternoon when it's still morning Stuart. Are you ok honey?" I asked, as Stuart looked a little different.
"Yes Roxy, still buzzing from yesterday; and of course, what happened earlier this morning. Your Danni is one horny guy, twice through the morning his cock was rock

hard and touching my ass. I hope you did not mind me telling you, as I am still thinking about it now as we speak. I just hope you don't think me a tart?" He replied, now getting semi hard.

"No, I don't mind, wait till I fuck you and spit roast you again." I replied, picking up a piece of toast as though I had not uttered a word.

Stuart placed the breakfast tray on the bedside table, bent over and kissed me on the lips, as he slid his hand under the bed to reach for my cock. He got to his knees and took my cock in his mouth, again thanking me and letting me know that he could not wait for another session. He then got back up and told me he would be in the garden with Danni; and he would see me when I joined them. I ate my breakfast, and then went into the bathroom and removed my make-up, where I then slipped on my dressing gown; and with my glass of orange juice, I walked into the garden. Stuart was surprised I came out as a guy; and I told him that as we are just having a lazy day, then there is no need to get dolled up to lounge around in the garden, in which Stuart told me that I was just as handsome in guy mode as I was sexy as Roxy. Once again not keeping track on time, I heard the doorbell go, so leaving the boys to themselves I went indoors.

When I finally arrived at the front door and opened it, there before me was Adam. He ran into my arms and gave me a hug; and then asked if Stuart was here or had he gone into town?

"You should have phoned us Adam, not just turned up, Danni was going to come and collect you, and yes the boys are in the garden, but cover your eyes as they are in their boxers." I laughed

"Well, I have seen it all before Roxy." He said as he gave me another hug, this time putting his hand inside my dressing gown and reaching for my cock.

"Later young man, you can have it later." I suggested to him

"What all four of us Roxy, or just you and me?" He asked, as he had a twinkle in his eye.

"All four of us if you wish, the more the merrier, but I think you had better speak to Stuart later. Anyway, Adam please forgive me for being blonde, but it is not Saturday is it?" I asked a little confused.

"No Roxy it is Friday and..." He replied, as I interrupted him

"Then what are you doing here then, you should not be arriving until tomorrow?" I told him

"I was told it may only be Thursday night I was needed, but I may have to work Friday too, as nothing was guaranteed. Johnny let me go early, as he had enough staff to cover, so I thought I would just surprise you all." He replied, now excited at the fact he was back in his beloved Hove; and was excited to see us all.

"Well, you have certainly done that now haven't you? So why don't you go and surprise the boys." I said, as I hugged him and slapped his ass like a naughty boy.

He went into the garden and certainly did that, Stuart opened his arms and Adam ran into them, as he reached

174

over and kissed Danni. Then as I got into a pair of jogging shorts and a t-shirt, Adam started to chat, which I guess was to let them know why he was a day early. We just all sat there chatting and having breakfast, when I suggested we go into town together; so, we decided to get changed and have a trip into Brighton. As it was a sunny day, we decided to walk; and I then reminded Danni to phone the restaurant to let them know there would now be four of us eating. Once I had got myself changed, I brushed my hair and I swept it back off my face and clipped it at the sides. It reminded me that I would soon have to dye it again, as some roots were beginning to show, so again asked Danni to remind me to get a hair dye.

I stayed as Bobby that afternoon, just for a change, which delighted all three boys, as they got to see, that even as Bobby my personality stayed the same.

When we went into town, I decided again to do a bit of shoe shopping; and of course, my boys looking through the window laughing at me as they tutted. I guess they liked shopping with me but hated going around every shoe shop with me. I did call Danni in to see what he thought, as I valued his opinion as well as ignoring it sometimes. I then told him to go to the little bistro by the jewellers; and I would meet them there as I had one last job to do.

"Ok babes, what do you fancy for lunch?" He asked.
"Well, you know me honey, I will have a green salad as usual, but I think I will also have a ham and avocado sandwich." I replied
"Ok Roxy, don't be long." He said, as he left the shop.

I purchased the shoes and a matching handbag, when I then went into Debenhams to look for something for my boys. I knew they all wore boxers, so I got each of them CK and Armani tight boxers. I then made my way to the perfume counter and brought them all some cologne. Adam was very much into his Givenchy Gentlemen, Stuart liked his Au Savage, and of course I got my man the latest bottle of Calvin Klein. I then made my way around to the bistro, where I already had lunch waiting and as I was quick, a latte that was still hot. I waited until we got home before handing out the presents, much to the delight and surprise of my boys.

"Wow Miss Roxy, you shouldn't have done that, you have spoilt us as it is." Stuart said.
"No Miss Roxy, if anything we should have brought you something." Adam replied.

Taking hold of my Danni, I looked at them and said.
"Well, a lady can look after her boys if she wants to, as it says in my book, why does a man always have to buy gifts for his girl?"

They all came over to me and gave me a big hug and a kiss, as again they said thank you. I then told them that there were conditions for the gifts; and that was that they had to do something for me. Stuart asked me what conditions, with that certain look about him, when he was in cheeky mode. I looked at Danni with a smile, and then looked at the boys as a whole, as I told them that before they go out this evening, I wanted them to stand in front of me, just in their boxers, so that I may examine them. Stuart and Adam looked towards one another, then said it was because of the uniform issue, that it had since gone to my head; and that I wanted to line them up on parade.

"*Are you sure you were not a drill sergeant in your previous life Miss Roxy? Because it sure sounds like it*" Stuart asked.
"*She is just kinky guys; and I am surprised she hasn't asked us to stand naked in front of her first, and then watched as we put on the boxers.*" Danni replied
"*You have that the wrong way around honey, because I will see you in your boxers first; and if they do not fit you right, then I will adjust them.*" I said sarcastically.

Well straight away Danni and Stuart got a hard on; and it was not long before Adam followed suit. I made my way back into the bedroom; and picked out a dress for the evening. I decided to go short but not tarty, as I always seemed to wear outfits just below the knee, so by wearing something just above the knee, I knew would get the boys going. The dress was a figure hugging one which, came just above the knee, and the neckline showed off my cleavage; and the colour was cream with black bead work on the bust.
After chilling out for a few hours, I told the boys that I was going to have a shower first. If there was enough room in the bath, I would have invited them all in to bathe with me, but four would be a bit of a squeeze.

"But it would be interesting and fun Roxy; maybe we should get a Jacuzzi outside and have a bit of fun there sometime." Danni said, now suggesting all manner of things we could do.

"Oh yes that would be fun, all four of us in the Jacuzzi together, and I would get to see my boy's bits bobbing about." I replied.

I took my shower and once inside, Danni came in to join me. He washed my back and front as I did his; and then we told the boys that the bathroom was free for them. Whilst I was getting ready, Danni just sat in the lounge in a towel as he brought me a coffee through.

Once I had put my face on, I got into my cream Basque; and gently placed my stockings on asking Danni to do the backs for me. Danni then looked at me and asked if I was ready to inspect him. I told him that I was ready; and that I wanted the three of them in the lounge standing next to one another, but not quite touching each other. Danni went over and told Adam and Stuart; and then called me when they were ready. Once I heard Danni's voice, I walked into the lounge and dropped my dressing gown, revealing myself just in my lingerie. Well, the boys all of a sudden got erect, and started to adjust themselves.

"Excuse me boys, who gave you permission to touch your cocks?" I asked, as I put my finger to the corner of my mouth.

"Sorry Miss Roxy." They all replied.

178

They dropped their hands by their side as I walked up and down the line, firstly walking behind them as I checked to see if their asses looked nice. Firstly, looking over at Adam and saying to him 'very nice' as I stroked his ass; and then moving onto Stuart and finally Danni, even though with Danni I did slide my hand down the back of his boxers to give him a bit of a taster. I then moved to the front of them and I could see clearly that they were fully erect. Danni then placed his hand on his crotch, where he was about to move his cock into a more comfortable position.

"Don't you dare young man; I have not given you permission." I told him.
"Sorry Miss Roxy, but it is uncomfortable, as you well know, I dress to the left, not the right." He replied.
"For that you can put your hands on your head; and leave you fuckin cock alone until I am ready." I ordered him.
"YES Miss Roxy." He answered, now seeing I was in Dom mode.

I then went straight to Adam and looked at his bulge, then placing my hand over it, as I felt him tweak his cock in my hand.

"Your boxers fit you quite well, Adam; and they show off your bulge very nicely." I told him.
"Thank you, Miss Roxy, but I also need to move my cock around as like Danni it is uncomfortable." He replied.

I then placed my body right into his, as I placed my mouth to his ear and softly said to him.

"So, you would like Miss Roxy to adjust your bulge for you then Adam?"
"Oh yes Miss Roxy, very much so." He replied.

As my head was on his neck, I gently kissed his ear; and then I placed my hand inside his boxers and pulled his cock upwards, so it could rest better than it was before.

"There you go, it is all tucked away nicely, so it is not sticking right out. And my handsome Adam, you are dribbling honey, so I suggest you go to the bathroom and clean up." I told him, as I licked the pre cum off my fingers.

I dismissed him and he rushed to the bathroom, as I then went on to Stuart. As Stuart was slightly taller, I looked at him; and with my finger I suggested that he come to me. He did as I ordered willingly; and then again getting his ear by my mouth I whispered to him.

"So, I guess you want me to do the same to you then don't you? Would you like Miss Roxy to adjust your bulge?"

"Yes, please Miss Roxy; and you can do anything you like as well." He replied
"If I want to do more to you than move your cock, then I will young man, I don't need your permission Stuart." I told him.

"Yes Miss Roxy, I am sorry." He replied.

Again, I brushed up against him as I placed my hands in his boxers; and then moved his cock into a more suitable position, as I gently placed the tip of my finger over the opening of his cock. I heard him take a sharp breath, as he moaned slightly.

"You too need to go to the bathroom and clean up, as you are also oozing pre cum; and may I make a suggestion and get your man to lick it all off first." I told him.
"Yes Miss Roxy, I will do that." He replied.

Stuart then rushed to the bathroom, where I heard him ask Adam to take him in his mouth. I then moved to Danni and looked him in the eye, as I then said to him.

"What am I going to do with you Danni?"
"What do you mean Miss Roxy?" He replied, looking at me in a seductive manner, rather than that of a naughty boy manner, which brought a smile to my face without breaking my role position.
"What I mean is. What am I going to do with you? I gave you an order not to play with yourself; and there you were ready to do just that. I told you that I would inspect you; and if things were not right it would be my place not yours to adjust." I said, now getting into the swing of being the mistress.

"I am sorry Miss Roxy; I will never disobey you again." He replied, now as he got back into character

"That's good, so you think you would like Miss Roxy to adjust your cock?" I asked

"Oh yes please Miss Roxy." He replied, all excited

"Well, it is tough, I want you to keep your hands on your head and get on your knees." I told him.

"Yes Miss Roxy." He replied, as he dropped his head.

He got down on his knees as I teased him by thrusting my groin into his face, as I told him he could not use his hands or indeed his mouth. This was agony for him, but he did as I told him. Placing my hands on the side of his face, I reached down where I then placed a kiss on his lips. I gradually got to my knees and threw my arms around him, as I then asked him to put his arms around me. As my character went back to Roxy, I told Danni that I can only keep up this charade for a little longer, that I was not really a dominant person as he well knew; and that I do forget at times what I should say and how I should say it. I told him to just hold me; and to take over for me, for him to be the dominant one. He then told me that I was doing ok, and that I need a little bit of practice. He also told me that I should most likely read a few books about the subject in question or watch a bit of porn to get an idea. I just told him I would see, as I did prefer him being the one who took the leading role.

I told Danni that I did not mind doing it with the two of us, but it gets a little confusing with other people. He again told me with practice I will get the hang of it, as he then told me not to worry my pretty head about it, as I was doing ok until I let it get to me. That we should forget about it now; and we should get ready to go out.

I then shouted to the boys to see if they were ok, but I got no answer. I got up to see where they were, and I heard them in the bedroom talking, so I came out and left them for a while. As I got into the lounge, I told Danni that they were talking, and that we should give them a bit of time. He asked if I wanted a drink, to which I asked for the usual. Lying in Danni's arms, I started to tell him that I hoped all was ok; and hope we had not caused any problems with the boys. I told him that I did feel guilty, as now we had kind of taken advantage twice on two occasions. He then told me not to worry, as if they did not want it to happen then they would not have participated.

"Thing is Roxy; I think you worry too much. I am sure things are fine, besides, I cannot hear them screaming or fighting, can you?" He replied.
"Not exactly, but they have been in there for some time Danni." I answered, worried that something may have happened.
"You did tell Stuart to go into the bathroom to Adam and suck his precum, so maybe they are having a play." He said, as he comforted me; and told me that we should have done the same.

I knew he was right, and I did hope that we did not cause any problems with them; especially as they were both so special to Danni and me.
About another twenty minutes, they came out of the bedroom, looked at me and smiled. I asked if everything was ok, and they book looked at me and said that it was. I then got up and gave them a hug, as Stuart whispered

in my ear that he had told Adam, and all was fine.

I was so relieved, that I hugged him tight then went into the bedroom to pick up my bag and a light jacket.

Adam came into the bedroom and just told me that he had told Stuart about what had happened, and Stuart had told him what had also gone on with Stuart and us that morning. I apologised for being so forward, and taking advantage, to which Adam said that it was ok, as they could have said no. I got up, and put my arms around Adam, as we made our way back into the lounge, where we then left to go and eat.

I know that Adam was not really into drag queens, but he often told me that as he knew me as both male and female, and that he only ever thought of me as Roxy. That although he did not fancy drag queens, he was relaxed with me and knew that I was a guy underneath whatever I wore; that some drag queens referred to their private parts as feminine, as that of a pussy, where I always referred to my genitals as what it was… a cock. He went on to say, that I would be the only guy he would go with who had two roles, because he was fortunate enough to have been introduced to both, and although he had seen other pretty drag queens, he was not attracted to them in a way that he was to me, which I thought was the biggest compliment anyone could give.

He often made me laugh when he described himself as a typical gay male full of testosterone, and only had feelings for real men; and that I was an exception.

It made me laugh, because I am sure he was last in the queue when testosterone was handed out, as he was as camp as Christmas, but so sweet.

The evening went very well, as we chatted like we had only met for the first time. Danni and Stuart getting closer as they both opened up, as Adam and I chatted about the bar, Ruby and Johnny, and his new apartment. We then walked home via the seafront, with my arm around Danni, and Stuart and Adam holding hands.
As we got home, Stuart had taken over and brought in refreshments, as we all engaged in chat whilst we had a bit of music on in the background. I had by now updated the lounge; and had purchased a three seater and two seater sofa. Stuart and Adam; were lounging about on the two seater, as I lay in Danni's arms on the three seater. It was not long before the conversation went on the day's events, especially towards me being a drill sergeant. I could see them all getting aroused, and looking at Danni for approval, I got up and made my excuses to go to the bathroom. I had in fact gone to the bedroom and stripped down to just my lingerie. I made my way back to the lounge, startling Adam and Stuart then ordered them to stand in a line. They did as I had asked them to do, as I then asked them to remove their clothes but for their boxers.
I had never seen anyone get undressed so quickly and untidily, as they just dropped their clothes on the floor. Now standing in front of me with bulges showing through their boxers, I inspected them removing their cocks as I went from one to the other, now having their erect cocks pointing out of their boxers towards my face. I looked at Danni and ordered him to get on his knees, as he watched me take Adam's and Stuarts cock in my mouth. Then I ordered Adam to also get down on his knees and to start kissing Danni.

185

I held Stuart in my arms as I stroked his chest and cock, and as he bent down to kiss me on the neck. Shortly afterwards I told Stuart to kneel down next to Danni and Adam. As they were kneeling down and cocks standing to attention; I stood in front of them and one by one offered them my hard cock. I suggested we go into the bedroom, and like three excited little boys, they got off their knees and hurried into our bedroom. Still keeping in role, I told Adam to get on the bed, as I looked at Stuart and Danni to stand by the side of the bed.

As Adam was lying down, I straddled him as I got on all fours; ordering Stuart to get behind me and place his cock in my ass, as I started to suck Adam's cock.

I kept looking over at Danni, and I could see how turned on he was, but how obedient he was also by not doing anything as I had ordered. I looked at him with my seductive eyes, and I am sure he almost shot his load there and then. Stuart was now deep inside my ass fucking me hard, as I took Adam down my throat. I then decided to put Danni out of his misery.

"Danni remove your boxers; and come and lay down by Adam." I ordered.
"Yes Miss Roxy." He replied, with a sigh of relief.

Danni removed his boxers; and then lay next to Adam, as I then ordered Adam to get up and give Danni a sixty nine. For a short time, I decided that I would let Stuart still take me from behind, as I saw Danni give me the odd glare of approval, if not somewhat jealous. I mimed the words to him that I loved him, and he just had that beautiful sparkle in his gorgeous blue eyes.

186

I then told Stuart to remove himself from me, when I just turned around and gave him a kiss on the lips and held him tight.

"*Right boys, time to change position, Danni I want you to get up and wait for me to compose myself, where I then would like you to come and lay on top of me; and then start to make love to me.*" I told them
"*Yes Miss Roxy.*" He replied.
"*Stuart, you get behind Danni and start to fuck his ass once he is inside me, and Adam I want you sitting up so that I can have your cock and balls.*" I said, as they listened and began to get into position.

They waited for me to get comfortable, when Danni came towards me and pulled me on to his cock. Adam had sat up so that my mouth was over his cock and balls, and then Stuart took my Danni from behind. I could hear Danni moaning with pleasure as he was being fucked; and was fucking me at the same time. I was sucking Adams cock, as Danni was stroking my back and kissing me on the neck, as I reached underneath me and played with his balls.
It was not long before Stuart told me he was going to shoot, and Adam was very close too. I told Stuart to fuck Danni's ass to completion, as he shot inside his hot horny ass, as I told Danni to ride Stuart with all his might. They all did as they were told, and I heard both Stuart and Adam moan with pleasure as they both climaxed at the same time.
Once they had finished, they asked to be excused so they could both take a breather, in which I gave permission.

Danni turned me around so that I was on my back, with my legs over his shoulders and started fucking me again until he was ready to cum, knowing I was almost there he waited for me. He took me in his mouth and emptied me, once again returning to my ass to fill me up as he thrust his hot wet cock back inside me.

Whilst Danni was making love to me, the boys were on the couch in the bedroom watching and kissing each other. Danni was now holding onto me as he thrust deep inside me, hitting me that hard I just shot my load; with Danni following shortly after, as I saw all three boys with a big smile on their faces like they were the cat who got the cream.

We had a most enjoyable evening, with my hand every now and then sliding onto Danni's thigh, as well as teasing Stuarts; and with my foot stretching it under the table till it rested in Adam's groin.

Once again big smiles were had when we were eating, and little suggestive comments were made as well as the usual banter we chatted about. We then decided to finish the night off by going back into the lounge to finish our drinks, the three boys just sitting there naked, as I was still in lingerie but for missing my panties.

Shortly afterwards I went into the bathroom, where I removed all my make-up and clothes and just put my dressing gown on returning to the lounge.

That night we again went into our bedroom and had a one on one, a two-way spit roast, me riding Danni and Stuart riding Adam, as we both kissed. There was nothing we did not try, and that weekend was full of sex and alcohol, romantic walks together from Hove to the harbour, fish and chips and just an easy afternoon sitting on the beach chatting and laughing. On the Sunday night Danni took Adam back with him to London and hoped that we had another few days of fun and relaxation. Danni whispered in my ear that he did not mind if I slept with Stuart, even though he knew I wouldn't; and I replied to him to take Adam home and he could do the same.

"*If anything does happen between us honey, I will tell you as I will not hide anything away from you. But just to fall asleep with nothing happening would be just as nice, as you know I would feel guilty with it not being you; and I do not like hidden agendas.*" I told him.
"*I trust you Roxy, I always trust you. If you just want to sleep with him and fall asleep then that is fine by me as well. Just hurry up and come home.*" He replied.
"*Do you want us to come back with you now? Honestly, I don't mind; and I am sure Stuart wouldn't mind either. So, shall we come back with you…Yes or No?*" I told him, not really being concerned if we stayed in Hove or not

"*No, that's ok honey, have another day or so; and I will see you when you get home, as I am a little busy this week anyway and wouldn't be home till late.*" He said, now standing on the other side of the doorway, ready to set off.

I gave him a kiss and a hug, as Stuart did the same with Adam; and then we waved them goodbye and went back into the lounge, sitting together and thinking how quiet it was without them.

We both went out for another meal that night, and then on to a few gay bars to finish the evening. Stuart was a gentleman and although temptation was there, he gave me a kiss on the lips as he made his way to his bedroom. The next morning, he surprised me by bringing in breakfast, and whilst sitting on the bed next to me, we ate breakfast and chatted, then after a quick tidy up, we just picked up a few things, as Danni and Adam had taken most of the things back in the car.

I stayed as Bobby during that day, as we both travelled back to London, minus the arm under Stuart's.

Once we got back to our apartment, Stuart told me he would have to go as he wanted to check on his mother. I hugged him and thanked his for a lovely long weekend; and asked him to text me to let me know if his mom is alright. I also asked him if she would mind if I went over to visit her, and to take her some flowers; to which he told me he thought it would be a lovely idea, but to let him put it too her first. I told him I did not mind being either Bobby or Roxy, as I would respect her wishes; to which he hugged me and told me I was amazing.

Stuart had left, and I for a change made a pot of tea, as I looked through my diary to see that Ruby and I were going to be busy for the next few months, with cabaret bookings of our own, plus a few modelling jobs and TV interviews. A few days later Stuart phoned me to say he has spoken to his mother, as he then said to me that she does not mind seeing me as Roxy, as she has heard so much about me. I took a deep breath and then said to Stuart, that I hoped she has not heard everything about me, especially when Roxy had been a little naughty. That made him cough, as I could have sworn he almost choked on something. Getting his voice back, he told me that he was not that open with his mother, no matter how much he loved her. That she would have thought of him as a sex starved tart if ever she got wind of it. Then being cheeky, he told me that as I was the older woman, she would have assumed that I had taken advantage of a nice young policeman

"*You cheeky bitch, just wait till I get my hands on you. Older woman indeed, I am deeply hurt.*" I told him, with him giving such a remark that made me gasp.
"*Awwww, you I will make it up to you.*" He replied, as I heard him again giggle.
"Yes Stuart, you will, with a nice bouquet of flowers and a box of chocolates." I replied.

We just chatted for a while, where Stuart had told me that his mother has met Adam and she approves. I was so pleased, pleased that she accepted Adam and that it did not make a difference to her home situation. That if Stuart wanted to take Adam back to her home, she told him that he was welcomed and to excuse the ignorance should anything be said to them, as her husband was an ignorant homophobic, which bred the same ignorance to his daughter.
I told Stuart to let his mother know, that I would visit her on Thursday as I had an appointment at the hairdressers, which was Kyle's salon. Stuart then suggested we meet at 'The old coffee pot' which was a lovely English bistro near Leicester Square, where I agreed, and told him what time I would roughly be there. It was arranged for 1pm, giving me an hour to spare after my hair appointment.

Danni had a few late nights, due to work commitments, so I chilled out at home going to bed before he came in. Through the day I went to see Ruby, to get the agenda for our forthcoming booking, as we were going to be doing a London tour straight for four weeks. Adam had settled nicely into his apartment, and had it looking very clean and posh, with white walls and the odd framed pop poster here and there. Stuart spent a few nights a week with him at his, then Adam would spend a few nights at Stuarts; unless of course Stuart was on night shift where they stayed at their own places.

I went to see Kyle on the Thursday, who coloured and styled my hair, as we caught up with the latest modelling gossip from runway to photoshoots. Usually there was a long waiting list for anyone to be style by Kyle, but he always made room for me and a few of his other favourite people. After I had finished with Kyle, I caught a cab and asked him to take me to Covent Garden to the flower market and to wait for me; before going to Leicester Square. I thought it was nice of Stuart to think of my travelling, although I would not have objected going to Chelsea where his mother lived.

As I arrived at the coffee shop, Stuart was already there with his mother, and as I was struggling as I attempted to get out of the cab, Stuart ran to the kerb and held the door open for me. I paid the cabbie, as I was escorted to the outside table. He held the chair out for me, as he then introduced me to his mother.

"*Very nice to meet you Roxy, I have heard so much about you.*" She said, as she got up and gave me a kiss on the cheek.

"So very nice to meet you too, and I hope it's not all bad news you have heard." I replied, happy but still a little nervous.

"Oh, nothing bad at all Roxy, it's all nice. And thank you for looking after my boy." She said, as she looked at us both and smiled

As Stuart held the back of the chair for me, until he seated me. We all then sat down. I handed the bouquet of flowers to his mother, where she just told me how beautiful they were.

"You are worth it Mrs Kennedy; you are so welcome." I told her.

She then had a little giggle with Stuart, and I looked puzzled. Stuart then looked at me and told me that I should not worry, that it had been a long time since his mother had been called Mrs Kennedy. I then realised what I had said. I had called her Stuarts surname not thinking about her new surname. I told his mother that I was so sorry, that I was… as I was then interrupted by her. She told me that I should call her by her first name, being that of Margaret. That she had to admit, that it had been so long since she had been called Mrs Kennedy; and that I had brought a few nice memories to her. We then sat down for some lunch, I had the usual as both Stuart and his mother had pastries. Margaret was never really a coffee person; and had a pot of tea instead, as Stuart and I had lattes. Then after a nice long chat getting to know one another, she dropped a bombshell which took Stuart by surprise; so much so that he ended up in tears.

"Please forgive me Roxy, but I have something I need to say to Stuart; and I could not say it whilst we were near home." She said, now preparing herself.

I told her that it was ok, and if she wanted me to leave I would, when she just put her hand on my hand and told me it was ok. Stuart then looked at her, and now quite pale he asked what the matter was.

"It has been a long-time coming son, but I cannot go on anymore. I am prepared to lose the house and money, but I can no longer let my health suffer." She explained, as Stuart asked again what was going on. *"I have decided to file for divorce; however, I have no idea where I go from there."* She said, as calmly as you could in such a situation.

There was no emotion of sadness, but I could see that she felt relieved. She explained that since her surgery, things had got worse and she cannot take anymore; and as much as she hated to admit it, she said that her so called stepdaughter Helen was a waste of space; and sided with her dad all the time. That she was not in the least bit concerned about her condition; as she was now sixteen and did the hell she pleased and thought of just herself, just like her father.
After Stuart's mother comforted him, and he gained his composure, he told us both how pleased he was.
She knew she was in for a long battle but told us she had

won bigger battles in her life, and this one was no different. Stuart was over the moon; and told his mother that she could go and live with him at his apartment if she needed have some peace. She then told him that she had survived the war, and she would survive this. That he and his daughter are living in her house, as his dad paid for most of it; and that he had only been contributing for the last two years; and that she was sure that he had no hold over the property, as his contributions were for daily living only.

I told her that I had a friend who could help her if she allowed me to get involved, as he owed me a favour and I was sure he could give her all the information she needed. She told me that she would really like that, as she was unsure how to go forward.

Stuart told his mother that he would move back in for a while to make sure his stepdad behaves, but his mother told him that it was alright. She then made me laugh in her next statement, as it reminded me of me and how I felt towards Stuart.

"I do not give a hoot about your stepdad; I have got you and Adam, my two special boys. And when you introduced me to Adam, you were in the kitchen making a cup of tea, so I told him to take very good care of you as you are my world; and I wished I had more children, so that you were not the only one. I am, however, so glad that I have you Stuart, because I could not have wished for a better child that I did having you." She said, as she gave him a kiss on the cheek

Stuart had a lump in his throat, as a tear appeared in his eyes, as his mother, now putting his head into her neck, held him and then said.

"I should have listened to you a long time ago son, I just thought that things would have sorted itself out, but your stepdad is money orientated and thinks little of me, let alone of my illness. My biggest mistake was signing things into his name, and he took advantage of me because of me being heavily medicated. Your dad would be so very proud of you son; you are so like him in many ways, in so… so… many ways son."

I then placed my hand into Stuart's hand, and told him he would be alright, and that his mother would be alright too. I told him that I would phone my lawyer friend later today, as I did not want to do it through office hours. He left his mother's embrace, where he reached towards me and thanked me. He told me that he had told his mother how special I was, and how both Danni and I look after him. He then told me that he loved me, and that I was a very special person. After the tears, we sat back and with our coffee's and Margaret's cup of tea, we toasted the future. I then looked at Margaret and told her that I hoped she did not mind, but she looked so much like Joan Collins. Again, she told me to call her Margaret, as she thanked me for the kind remarks, then saying that I had a touch Stephanie Powers about me, when I blushed but also thanked her for her remarks. I apologised about calling her Mrs Kennedy, then telling her that I could not help it as it was my upbringing.

"Margaret is my proper name, so please from now on call me Margaret. And we must do this on a regular basis, go out together again sometime." She said, as she welcomed having a new friend.

"That would be wonderful Margaret, to have someone to go shopping with who is not afraid to go into a shoe shop for a browse. You must also come to my apartment; and come and meet my other half, my special Viking, Danni." I told her, as I explained he was Norwegian.

"Oh, that would be lovely, the two of us shopping together. I always wanted a daughter to go shopping with, but I am afraid going shopping for skinny jeans and skirts the size of a handkerchief is not my kind of shopping." She said to me, as she told me that she cannot wait to meet Danni, as she placed her hand onto mine.

We then finished up, as I told Stuart I must go. So, he hailed a cab, and said he would drop me off first.

I asked Margaret if she had a phone, and she gave me her landline number. I asked if she had a mobile phone, to which she told me she did not, as she could not get on with them. She did make me laugh, but I was the same at first. She then told me that she had only just got used to a VCR, and had just about got around recording a programme, as for anything else, it is far too technical for her. I then told her that I would give Stuart a call or a text, when I have sorted things out. In which she gave me a hug and told me that I was a very special kind of person.

I had made a really nice friend that day, and it was not a gay friend, but a woman I soon became to trust and respect. She was absolutely lovely, and from the first time she saw me, she accepted me without question. When I got back home, I sat down and just thought what a lovely day today has been; only to find I did not even have time to put the kettle on before my phone buzzed. Stuart had messaged me to say thank you, and how much his mother likes me. That night I gave my friend Judge David Bellows a call, as I explained everything to him in regards Margaret's situation. He told me that he knew exactly who could help her, as he was one of the best divorce lawyers in London. His name was Anthony Brentwood, who was a Chelsea Barrister which was handy for where Margaret was. He also told me that I had met him once at one of the parties we had, but I had no recollection. He then told me that we should catch up again soon, to which I told him that it would be nice as I have not been to the Wednesday gatherings for a few weeks. After I had finished speaking to David, I had a few minutes to finish my drink when I phoned Anthony. After explaining to him who I was and where I got his number from; we started to chat as though we had known each other for years. He agreed to see Margaret and arranged an appointment for the following Monday. I then thanked him and told him I would see him soon, as I then text Stuart and gave him the news.

I did not see Stuart for nearly two months, due to our cabaret commitments, and the fact he was on late shifts. I was so glad when the two months were up, as both Ruby and I worked non-stop for just over sixty two days. I had a handbag full of money for which I needed to bank, as well as give Ruby my half towards agent fees.

Those two months were fun, but I felt that Ruby was now changing, as she became a little distant at times. Well, she was no longer a drag queen that's for sure, but she started to withdraw from me, and sometimes acted like she was my mother. I hardly got to spend time with Danni, as by the time I got back it was very late and he had gone to bed. I had the odd kiss and cuddle from him as that's all I could manage. Sex had gone out of the window, because by now we were both working late. Danni had managed to get the deal he and his father were after in America. It was not as big as the first one, but it would give their company a well-respected portfolio; as well as a sixty percent boost to their company's status showing flexibility in what they offered and were willing to take on as a global company. At the end of those two months, I had a well-earned rest, only doing the comparing at the Rainbow standing in for Ruby when she either took a night off or was comparing for Felicia. I got to see Stuart who told me his stepdad had taken the news of divorce bad, as he knew the money pot had run out; and that he, unknown to him, had been sponging off his mother for years.

Thankfully her police pension was put into her savings account and not her bank account, where records clearly showed him taking large amounts of money out of the account and putting into a separate account in just his name. He also told me that the lawyer had since had his account frozen, until he could further prove that he was entitled to the money; and it was not a matter of deception or money laundering.

His stepdad also went out and got drunk, then came back and trashed the house, so his mother called him; and with his colleagues they went around and arrested him. He told me that his mother took out an injunction against him; and he could go nowhere near her as the injunction stated he had to stay at least twenty miles from her; and subsequently she was given the rights to stay in the house. Helen had since moved out of his mother's house; and got a council flat in Tower Hamlets; and that his stepdad was asking for half of the house as well as all of her other assets. His mother is still in constant contact with her lawyer Anthony; and it seems like he is not entitled to half, as he has not been jointly paying the last of the mortgage. It came too light, that his mother was still paying the mortgage; and that his stepfather had another bank account with his monies going into that account, as well as the other account he held in which he withdrew from his mother's account. The judge told him that he had abused his wife's account; and had abused his access to internet banking by transferring large amounts from his mother's account, thus freezing all of his assets until he could prove that the monies were indeed his. He then told me that there is a settlement on the table, in which Anthony has advised Margaret to remove him from the deeds, in which the courts would adhere to and rule in her favour. He has been told that if he does not take it, then she is going to counterclaim for emotional distress; and it could lead to him not getting a penny, as he would have all the court costs to pay, as his mother has a very tight and closed case.

I could not believe it, all of this going on like a scene from crown court, and me swanning around London doing cabaret; and missing all the juicy gossip.

I was so pleased to hear the news though, and glad to

hear that Margaret still has her home. I told him to tell his mother that I would see her soon, as we needed to catch up and have lunch.

I had lunch with Margaret; and had lots more lunches to come. I began opening up to her the more I got to know her, and in one conversation I went on to explain about my circumstances; where she told me that she knew I had a male side, and it made no difference to her.

She accepted me as Roxy, and for the good friend I was to Stuart. She could not believe my mother had never contacted me, or my sisters come to that, as she would love me as a daughter. Yes, our bond was becoming very strong, and what I seemed to be losing with Ruby was being gained with Margaret. Many times, we would go to Harrods and visit the food department, before shopping and going to their restaurant.

Margaret became a regular visitor to our home, and simply adored Danni. She often said what a lovely family she has, now having three sons and a daughter. I thought it was really nice and sweet of her, as she had become the mother and friend I had so longed for. Sometimes she would come into the bar, escorted by either Stuart or Adam, and on the rare occasion both of them. She so loved the cabaret scene; but did not like the acts who were very rude and swore too many times.

Yes, I really had a nice friend in Margaret, and it was lovely now having a shopping companion who was as bad as me, although not for shoes, more the dresses where Margaret was concerned; and very much a bargain hunter, as she often told me to wait a week or so before buying as they often reduce their items; which saved me lots of money to have more days of lunching with her.

Margaret taught me a lot about shopping, and I soon became at eagle eyed as her, that was unless I saw something which I simply had to buy there and then.

Five years had since past, and by now I was not doing the cabaret so much. Apart from being a solo artiste the last five years, 'Foxy Ladies' was only performing a few times a month now, and we both knew it would not be long before we wound the act up. I still had television, radio and modelling work, which kept me busy and I still made time for my nights out with Danni and the boys where we headed towards Rainbows, where catching up with Ruby and Johnny was always the highlight of the week; even though it was mostly Johnny now.
Margaret finally got her divorce and she got to keep her house, which she was overjoyed with. Her ex-husband could not prove that the monies withdrawn from her account, in which he then put into his, were indeed his; and subsequently the courts awarded his mother all of the money he had withdrawn including the interest. Instead of reverting back to her maiden name, she reverted back to Mrs Kennedy, as those were the years that were her most memorable happy years.
The small settlement she made to her ex-husband, her boys paid, as they gave her all of their savings, so she did not have to re mortgage her house; and I recall Stuart saying he was only awarded ten grand, from a possible four hundred grand; as it was proved he had manipulated her because of her medical condition; and she was not in her right mind when she signed things over to him. It was because of Margaret that he got a settlement, because the court ruled in her favour; and ruled against

him getting anything, but to stop a further trial, she offered him the ten grand, to wave his rights of appeal, because she did not want to see him out of pocket.

What made me smile, is that Anthony had really proved how skilled he was, as if her ex did not comply, he could have easily been sent to prison for up to seven years with a charge of confidence fraud, if Margaret wished to file such a charge against him. With such a thought of prison looming over his head, he decided to take the ten grand pay-off where he waived his rights of appeal.

Stuart was still with Adam, and what we began five years ago, soon dwindled out as our friendship was more important. We would still have a few stop overs, and occasionally have a little bit of fun, but it was few and far between. Stuart then approached me and told me that he was relocating with work; and that he had applied to the Brighton and Hove constabulary for a position that had become available. After a long chat with them both, I decided to give them the keys to our Hove apartment and told them to take their time looking for their own place, as I knew our apartment was in safe hands.

I was just beginning to celebrate my twenty sixth birthday, and eight years of being with Danni. I told them both they couldn't do anything until after those celebrations. As it was not a significant celebration I only wanted a quiet celebration, and not the lavish parties that had been thrown before. But no, Danni got together with Johnny and threw me a big party in the bar. The following week Stuart had had his application accepted, and he told me that he would be moving into the Hove apartment in about one months' time, if the offer was still available. Adam decided to keep his flat on for the time being, as he needed to find a job before moving down; and had to give suitable notice to Johnny and Ruby. Each weekend that he went to visit Hove, he applied to the bars and clubs. Nothing came through except for a job he forgot about, and that was in a menswear store, which he thought was better than nothing. He then gave his notice to quit his job at the Rainbow to Johnny; and the month after Stuart moved down, Adam followed him.

That was at the beginning of 1989, and both Danni and I did miss them, so we made regular visits to Hove just to see if they both were ok.

Dannie's business had also really taken off now; and he and Steve were working all the hours that were in the day, as they were moving buildings to accommodate the new work loads, taking on a few more staff and building a gallery to show off their work projects as well as his joint business with his father. I finally got to go to Norway to visit Danni's family, and to see where he was born. The first time I went as Bobby, and slowly introduced them to Roxy which had mixed feelings. Some of his family were ok about it, where others kind of put up with it but did not like it.

In the summer of 1989 Ruby asked me if I would like to do one more UK tour with her; and to finally say goodbye to those people who put us where we were today. She had by now had enough of the cabaret circuit; and wanted to concentrate on the bar, and to look for another venture to occupy her mind. I thought long and hard about what she had said, as by now I too was tiring a little, then I agreed with her, that the time was now right for us to say goodbye to our double act, as we had both since walked different paths; and so Ruby along with the agent, sorted out a tour programme for us. After three months of organising, we were given a six month tour programme from the tip of Scotland, to our home town and of course the South of England.

We would be on the road day after day, with only one day a week to ourselves; and so, we braced ourselves for lots of driving, and lots of overnight stays in hotels, which as they were our choice were far nicer than the choice the agents gave us.

In the early years of cabaret, you have to put up with some right shit holes, but luckily, we had money and status in which we used. Each time we were away, we would have both Johnny and Danni constantly phoning us to see if we were ok, and then joining us on the odd weekend. Ruby thought she had over done this venture as it was a strain on here, but the closer we got to home the nearer she knew it was to completion. Each night we would head back to the hotel, once we had had a few drinks and laughs. I would go straight to bed and text Danni; and then relax with a book and the television. There were quite a few nights that I could not sleep, as I heard Ruby's television still being on, with a moderate volume, though when you can't sleep, the volume seemed to be annoying, so would go and knock on her door, but there was never an answer so I thought she must have dropped off; and I did not want to disturb her, though her television was disturbing me.

That last month though, was the longest month of our lives. We were so thankful for the Christmas week of

1989, as we were back home performing our very last show together. Six months of living out of a suitcase; and carting those suitcases of shoes around with you was not very flattering at all, and I think we both had lost weight. With each venue we did we thanked all the audience for their kind support; and wished everyone a safe and happy future.

Finally, it was our very last show, which was a double show as we played our own venue, as well as making one final appearance at the club Diamonds. Usually, we would perform for thirty to forty minutes, but I think that night, as it was the last night, we prepared a show of the all-time greats, and we were on stage roughly just over an hour and a half. We had now finished the tour and our very last show was where it all began.

Back at the legendary Rainbow…

I was asked by Ruby, to be lead drag queen, as it was now, that she that wanted to stay more in the wings than be on stage. We started the show where I came on stage first, before I brought on Ruby, so she could do her number giving me plenty of time to get changed.

It was now going to be the last number I did solo in our double act, and once finished I went into a bit of banter; so that Ruby could compose herself. I stood there on stage; and looking at the DJ I asked him to put the house lights on; and then started to go into my routine.

"I see they have let in royalty tonight folks. I can see you have got dolled up especially for us tonight love." I said pointing down to two of the girls in drag

"You should not have bothered, its only Ruby and little ole' me." I said, when they began to shout at me.
"What... what... you even had special hair do's oh I see. Where have you drag queens come from?" I asked them.
"What. What.... Dover. I am surprised you were not stopped by passport control to see if you were hiding stowaways in your bee-hives." I said, as the crowd roared with laughter
"What... speak up honey ... Oh you are going to a 60s party afterwards, that explains it." I said sarcastically
"Do I want to go? No honey, I have got a wooden leg, and if you get me on the dancefloor doing all that spinning around; chances are you will screw me to the floor." I said as the crowd went wild; and as they laughed themselves like good sports.

I then noticed that Ruby was ready, and I looked at the audience and with my hand waving I told them to simmer down. I then looked at the DJ to let him know that we would be ready for the last number.
Then looking at the audience, I made the final announcement.

"Ladies and gentlemen, well it had finally come to the end of the road. Foxy Ladies started their career on this stage, and tonight we finish out show here. This stage has seen many acts come and go, as they have taken their pride and place within the Rainbow family, some being legends of the Rainbow stage. I hope that you can see what a wonderful exceptional person Ruby is, as it has been such a pleasure to be her understudy, and her best friend. For the very last time tonight, I give to you

the other partner in crime. I give you the one; and the only one, Miss Ruby Passion."

I then waited for the intro of the song, and then walked out to a tremendous applause and a standing ovation, as I then announced Miss Ruby. She was overwhelmed with how the crowd reacted; and felt very honoured that she had such a following; and had such love from them. They had to start the song twice because she could not compose herself, then on the third time, as the crowd began to quieten down Ruby and I closed the show. Again, when it had finished, the crowd jeered and applauded, again giving us a standing ovation, where all of a sudden two of the bar staff came to the stage with the biggest of bouquets for Ruby and me.
I just thanked them, and as Ruby could not speak for the fact, she was so emotional, she looked to me and told me that she needed to get out of there. I then left the stage with Ruby, as the bastard DJ called us back three more times. On the third curtain call, I looked at him; and with my hand making a signal as though I was cutting my throat, he got the message that that was it, to cut it and to turn off the stage lights. That was finally the end of Foxy Ladies, and a part of me was so very sad to see it now end. I placed my flowers in the dressing room; and then I went in to see Ruby and asked her if she was alright. She was in a flood of tears, when she then came over to me and put her arms around me, thanking me for the years I had given her and Foxy Ladies. I congratulated her on the show; and then wiping her tears I said calmly to her.

"It just proves that your followers love you Ruby, you are going to be truly missed. You are a Rainbow legend, always remember that."

We both gave a performance of a lifetime, which would remain in the hearts of our fellow artistes and friends for many years to come. We both then took a well deserving Christmas rest, with Ellie looking after the bar, whilst Johnny and Ruby chilled out with Danni and me. They spent Christmas morning with us, and then with us staying with them on Boxing Day, as well as our other friends and family which by now had again grown. Shortly in the New Year of 1990, Johnny and Ruby announced that they were handing the bar over to Ellie, as they were seriously thinking about taking a big leap; and had decided they wanted to move to Gran Canaria, where they were considering buying a villa and a gated complex of apartments to rent out, as well as Johnny buying another bar. Ruby told me that it was something they needed to do before they got too old; and they may as well do it now, as she made a passing glance to Johnny. I was amazed that they thought of relocating; and told her that it was such a big step; and that we would not get to see them that often. She scoffed at me, as she told me that they were only four hours away by air; and if I was fortunate to have a private jet, then it most likely would be quicker. Then saying that London holds nothing for them anymore; and that they will visit, just not that often. Both Johnny and Danni could see I was wound up with her remark, as I gave her daggers at how she had spoken to me. But I held it in my stride as I bit my lip; and then with Danni, we both gave them a hug and wished them well for whatever venture they were setting about at. As I hugged Johnny, he hugged me like he had never hugged me before; and something told me this was not at all his idea, as I knew he was being pushed into it, but could not understand why he did not say anything. At the end of the day Rainbows was Johnny's and not Ruby's, so he could have stayed but I could not get involved.

It was the summer of 1990, when Ruby and Johnny finally left London to start a new life, and the tears were running from our eyes like an over running stream that had burst its banks. Well, mine and my boys were anyway. Ruby was like a stone-faced cold bitch; and just kept on reminding us again and again that it was only four hours away by plane, so it was not a big deal. As they went through the barriers amongst the waves and banners that their friends held up, I looked at Danni and burst into tears as I cried the words, *Johnny, Ruby our friends have gone, what am I to do now?* He was so sweet, as he held me, telling me that I still have him and my boys, reminding me that they were not that far away, when he then dried my tears. He took my hand, and once they had gone from sight, we all looked at each other when Ellie shouted.

"Come on you guys, back to work. There is nothing more to see here."

She then come up to me and held my arm, where she told me they would be fine. I still could not believe they had gone, as I thought they loved London, because Ruby on numerous occasions told me that she would never leave the city she so loved. Getting emotional, I told Ellie that it had been ten or eleven years that Ruby and I had been drag sisters; and Johnny was like a brother to me. I told her that I needed more than one phone call from her every now and then. Understanding, because she was feeling it too with it being her brother that was going, when she told me I would be fine. That I still had the bar; and my family there for support. We then all made our own ways, as Danni told me he would take me to lunch and a bit of shopping to cheer me up. I gave Ellie a hug and told her I would see her later, and then waved her off with Danni blowing her a kiss. We got into the car and left Gatwick, where he drove into the city; there we went for lunch which I was only picking at my food, so he then decided that he would take me shopping.

"*You really do miss them don't you babe?*" Danni asked, as he held my hand.
"*Yes, I do honey, sorry if I am being a miserable cow.*" I replied
"*I miss them too Roxy, but I know I still have you and the boys, and little Ellie. We can still get the photos and videos out and together take a trip down memory lane.*" He said, hoping it would cheer me up slightly.

"*Yes, I guess so.*" I replied
"*I know it is upsetting because of all the shops we have gone by, not once have you stopped to look at shoes.*" He said smiling.
"*I am sorry Danni; can we please go home?*" I asked.

"Sure Roxy, lets go back to the car and go home." He
replied, knowing it had really affected me, because to go
past a shop full of shoes and not stop, was insane from
my point of view.

We made our way back to the car and headed straight
back home, as neither of us was in the mood to go to the
bar, or go shopping, which usually was therapeutical to
me. I got in and took my shoes off, where I lay on the
couch, Danni then brought me a coffee over and sat next
to me, as he rested my head on his lap placing his hand
over my body to gently stroke my hips; and just held me
close to him. It was not much longer that I found myself
falling asleep, where Danni picked me up and took me to
bed, climbing in next to me as he cuddled me until I fell
asleep.
It took me a further few days to finally get back to my
old self, but Danni was so sweet in comforting me.
When we made love, it was very gentle and passionate,
always with him thinking of my needs holding me
tightly as he kissed me, letting me take my time to settle
down. Even the time he came in the bedroom stark
naked with a rose in his mouth, asking me which one did
I prefer; and with my answer being, to come to bed and
cuddle me did not upset him.
Yes, he knew I was feeling it, as I also could see that he
too was missing Johnny as they had grown closer
together; and were really like brothers. I too comforted
him, but soon as a few days went by we both got on with
things and looked forward to our phone calls.
It was Johnny who made most of the calls, as he also text
Danni every day, always asking about how I was and

how we were both doing. Stuart and Adam would call us every few days to see how we were, and to let us know how they were doing; and we still had the bar and our friends and family, which was still nice. Instead of Ruby being the queen bee, it was me who had now taken the role; and I had soon got into it. We had a fresh batch of drag queens coming up who were popular with our crowd, and we made a few changes to the bar.

Ellie had lots of ideas, and always ran them past me first. She had shown me her plans for modernisation, and the colour scheme which was very Greek and Aphrodite looking. The colour scheme and the layout, I thought was very girly and stylish, with that touch of Greek class. I just told her that I would go along with anything she did, as she did not need my input as she had a good eye herself, and Johnny had signed the bar over to her not me. I reminded her that I was a member of her staff, to which she told me I was more than that; and she appreciated everything I had to say and had done for her.

The stage area, which was very predominant and so in your face, would now be ripped out; and along with the kitchen backstage, she was going to move the stage right to the very end of the kitchen once she knocked it through. This gave the pub twice if not three times the space, which I could see her logic as it would bring more people in. Upstairs she wanted to make into a living area, and stay there herself, as there was plenty of room to make it into a two bedroom flat with kitchen and bathroom, and still have enough room to put a dressing room downstairs for the cabaret.

I just looked at her and jokingly in shock I screamed.

"Oh no, I have to find a home for my clothes."
"You drama queen Aunty Roxy, you can store your clothes in the second bedroom when it is finished. I just need to sort out the planning Roxy, then I feel once accepted I can change this into my place." She said, looking forward to the renovation.
"Once you got the plans sorted honey, give them to me and I will see what I can do." I replied
"Don't worry Roxy, I am not losing the atmosphere and the legends that were Roxy and Ruby, you will be portrayed throughout the bar. I just need to update it and bring it into my world." She told me.
"Were, you mean I am sacked?" I told her, joking.
"Stop it I am trying to be serious." She replied, now with a head teacher look about her.

I took her by the arm and told her sorry, then I told her that I had every trust and confidence in her and her plans. Ellie got her plans sorted, and as I now had a few names I could drop, I placed the plans into the hands of one of my very dear friends in the planning office, with the seal of approval from the local police, courts, and MP, just for good measure. It was no surprise that the plans were accepted, but I had to pretend I was, as I did not want Ellie knowing I had pulled a few strings, as like Johnny she was very proud.
Ellie shut the bar through the daytimes so work could start out the back; and then would open up for the evening, just so there were some sort of takings going into the pot. Cabaret was fun, with everything up in the air, however, we all got used to it as we avoided the obstacles by not breaking our necks, as we carefully

manoeuvred backstage like that of a builder's site.

By the New Year of 1991 the bar was finished, and she gave a grand opening where the drinks flowed freely, for the first two hours for special guests before opening to the public. It was so nice to see her happy; and see what she had achieved. It was also nice to see the gathering of the clan, to see Stuart and Adam, some of our newer family, and the support from the community.

That night I compared as Dixie and Totty were leading the show and were superb, even if they did drag me on stage to end their show with yet another camp comedy song. I of course had my first heckler in a long time, and after putting up with a lot of stick, I began putting him in his place before Totty and Dixie ripped into him.

Since taking over the Rainbow and becoming successful herself, it was nice to see that Ellie had had a lady friend for a while. I did recognise her face, but I could not think where from. It was only when Ellie came up to me and introduced her to me, that the penny dropped.

"Roxy this is Dianne or Di as she likes to be called."
"Hello Di, how are you? Please don't think me rude but your face; I have seen you before, haven't I?" I asked.
"Yes Roxy, but it was nearly five years ago since we chatted. We met at one of Pauls parties if you remember?" She told me, as my mind wandered back five years.
"Ah yes that's right, you were with Stuart to start with, and a few other guys and gals. If I remember you were the pretty blonde, who kind of scouted the bar with eyes like a hawk." I replied.
"Yes, got it in one." She answered

I then looked at Ellie and with my finger swaggering between the two of them, when she looked at me and told me that they were an item. That they had been seeing each other for the past two years, but wanted to keep it a secret, until they were ready to announce that they were a couple. She went on to tell me that her school love had cheated on her when she was at university; and when she went to visit her, they were living and sleeping together, so she just walked away and was told never to go back again to see her.

She never told anyone as she did not want to cause a stir, then last year something happened with Di and herself; and they just hit it off. She told me that they had been friends ever since one of the parties I hosted, and when I took over more, they would just go to the cinema or go for a meal and their friendship grew. Di was also just coming out of a relationship, and Ellie did not want to rush her.

I just gave her a hug and told her to be happy. Then squeezing Ellie's hand, I told her that life was too short not to take chances; and we must grasp at any sign of happiness with every opportunity we can. That at the end of the day, it is our happiness which keeps us going; and the strength of our love which keeps us together.

Di then asked if she could give me a hug, as she had heard so much about me from Ellie, and I was like an aunt to her. I opened my arms and gave her a hug, looked at Danni and told them both that we would be there for them whenever we needed it. She then whispered in my ear, that she does not normally hug men, but I was different, that I was really an amazing woman, as most gay guys and drag queens do not like us lesbians, yet I have time for everyone.

"It is not for me to judge who you are; or to cast any doubt Di. Gay does not mean just men sucking cock, as I believe it means different, diverse, to stand up and be counted, to be totally free with who we are. You are a lady in love with my Ellie; and you are just you, being you; and finding love where your heart pulls you, besides labels should be left to clothing and bigoted idiots. Gay means same sex, not just man, but also woman" I said, as I then reached for my glass to toast them.

"Too right Roxy and I think you should be a politician as you speak your mind and speak for how you feel." Said Di

"No honey, don't think I could live in number 10 now, the Palace maybe." I giggled.

"You would have thought Johnny and Ruby were still here Roxy, as I think you and Danni have taken over so well being at the end of the bar and head of the royal box. You always looked lovely together and seeing Johnny and Ruby in the bar has not changed because they are no longer here; you have taken the place in your own rights so well." Said Ellie

"Who would have thought Ellie, that all those years ago I stood in that corner with Ruby, starting a career in cabaret where I then met Danni. And now here in 2001 it is Danni and I who seem to have taken over Johnny and Ruby's place, it feels so strange as I still miss them very dearly." I said, as I had a tear for in my eye.

217

"We all do Roxy; everyone still asks about her." She replied, as she put her hand on mine.

That night I had made my little Ellie happy, and had made another friend. Both Ellie and Di would often come and visit us through the week when we were not working and on a Sunday for dinner if Di was not at the station. You could see that Ellie was very much in love; and was so proud of her Di. Di was climbing up in the ranks herself now, taking the position as detective in the CID; and no matter how many jibes she got from her co-workers, it just spurred her on even more to work even harder in her training, excelling to being number one in her class. It did still feel strange going to the bar and not seeing Johnny and Ruby, one just seemed to expect them to be there. From what was once a bar with an older view, was now fresh and modernised with an up to date feel, which brought in the regular customers and new ones, which was such a refreshing change, as the bar now had its regulars who were lesbian; and who loved the drag shows, especially those who did not mock women; as they did not like the over the top drag acts that much.

It was now Friday morning, and I got up with Danni, who asked me if I wanted to go out that night for a meal. I looked at him and told him that I would cook something that night. That I would make him one of my special roasts, and that we could have a nice quiet night in for a change; and then put our feet up and watch a few movies. I told him that Dixie was in charge of the cabaret that night, so they do not need me. He told me that the idea of a roast sounded absolutely wonderful;

and he could not wait to finish work; and finally have a nice quiet night in with the woman he loved.

I helped him with his suit jacket, as he pulled me towards him and gave me a kiss on the lips. As I lightly tied the Windsor knot in his tie, Danni told me that he loved me, calling me his sexy wife. He then told me that he always looked forward coming home, knowing that his beautiful wife would be waiting for him, unless of course she had had a shopping trip in town, then he would have to wait before he laid his eyes on me, either way, he classed himself as one lucky man with an extremely beautiful wife. In reply, I also told him that I loved him; and that it would make a change for me to cook dinner, as I did have a bit of culinary skills underneath all of my beauty and charm

He then again kissed me on the lips, where he then proceeded to leave the lounge, where I stood at the door waiting for him to go into the elevator.

"Love you honey, have a nice day." I shouted, as I blew him a kiss.

"Love you too Roxy, be good." He replied, as he blew one back, and then being rude placed his hand by his crotch.

As I had previously said, usually on a Friday we would have gone out to eat, but today I decided to cook Danni one of his favourite meals. Well, it was the only meal that I had learnt from my cookbook, as I never got to cook that often due to us eating out. I had this cookbook gifted me, from one of the past Christmas's and only used it for this meal; which was Italian slow pot roast lamb; and I promised that I would one day pick out another recipe and build on my skills of surprise by cooking something completely different. I came out of the bedroom as I had just tidied it up; and then took a shower before going to the local shops. I dressed as Bobby whilst I went to the local deli, making sure I got every ingredient that I needed.

Once I got back home, I chilled out and listened to a bit of music as Margaret phoned me to see if I was ok. I enjoyed her phone calls, as we also promised each other we would phone each other every couple of days, just to check on each other and to make sure we were both alright; and of course, catch up on any gossip which we had to tell each other. I then went back to just chilling out as I chose a dress for that evening. I thought back to one of our first nights, and chose the little black number, with suede peep toes and a diamante encrusted bow; and the diamonds that Danni had brought me.

I then prepared the meal as I always did, taking care when I trimmed off some of the fat as I decorated the leg joint with bacon and rosemary.

The preparation was the longest, taking things in stages until it went into the oven. Once finished I went into the dining room and laid the table, placing the best china and cutlery onto the table, as well as our Royal Doulton glasses; and making sure the flowers were still fresh, otherwise I would have to take another trip into town to buy fresh ones. It was not as though it was a special occasion, which called for a special meal, it was just the fact I wanted to cook a nice meal; and it made a change from pasta or eating out all the time.

Whilst the lamb was in the oven, I made myself a coffee and just put up my feet as I watched a little bit more television. I was very much into the animal and wildlife programmes; and very often had tissues by the side of me with the sad stories they often showed.

It was now 8pm and still no Danni, it was strange that he had not phoned or text me as he was rarely late.

I went in to check the dinner which by now was very well done, that the lamb fell off the bone, so I switched everything off and called his mobile phone, only for it to go to answer machine.

"What the hell, where is he?" I asked myself.

Pacing up and down the apartment, I was becoming quite irate and worried, wondering what on earth was taking him so long, when I then thought that I bet he has ended up going to a meeting that may have been a surprise for him, as some of his meetings were last minute. I just sat down and poured myself a glass of wine, then went to the balcony windows to see if I could see him coming down the road, when all of a sudden, I had chills down the back of my neck all the way to my lower back, just as though someone had walked over my grave.

"Something's not right, he is never late. Where the hell are you Danni?" I asked myself.

I called Steve, and when he answered he told me that Danni had left around 5pm as he needed to go into the city to pick something up for me. Although slightly relieved, I was still really panicking; and this was felt by

Steve who asked if I wanted him to come over. I told him I should be ok; and that I may phone the bar as he may have popped in there just to check all was ok, so I phoned the bar and spoke to Ellie, also showing my concern about Danni being late.

He had not been there either, and Ellie was now concerned and asked if I wanted her to come and wait with me. She told me that she did not think that there was ever a good explanation in those circumstances, they she knew he was never late; and that maybe he had just lost track of time. She then put her hand on my hand; and told me that maybe he was out buying me a special gift, as he used to do that quite often, where on the odd occasion, he did lose all track of time, or maybe it was the fact that this is London, and he was most likely stuck in traffic. I looked at her all negative, as I proceeded to tell her that there were a lot of maybe scenarios, as sarcastically I told her that maybe; and just maybe, he had lost his memory, or had forgotten how to text. I then told her I had to go just in case he was trying to phone the home number, and then put the phone down on her sharply. I finished off my glass of wine; and just walked up and down the lounge pacing frantically, then walking towards the window to take a look and catch a glimpse of him, even going on to the patio to see if I could get a better view. In the far distance I saw a lot of blue flashing lights, which was nothing unusual for London at that time of night, when I then said to myself, that someone was most likely being stupid again, most likely joy riders or something; and knowing my luck he was stuck behind all the traffic that it has caused.

I looked towards the other end of the balcony, to see the blues and twos again; and just thought yes, it was definitely the weekend, what with the police out in force, when just in front of me, a cyclist had been pushed off his bike, by a ford fiesta driving down the road like a loony. I then went back indoors; and poured myself another large glass of wine, as I looked on my phone to see that I still had no messages. I then told myself that I bet it was a full moon that evening, as normally when you have a full moon it brings out all the damn stupid people. I ten cursed as I looked at the clock, where I saw that it was 9pm, and that I would be drunk by the time he got home. I was all dressed up in my best, looking like a fucking lemon standing there. Telling myself that I was going to kill him when he gets home, now getting upset with worry.

Staring at the clock I was getting more and more concerned, pacing around the apartment and looking out over the patio. Then my mobile phone rang; and I just thought 'Thank God'; and without checking who was ringing I just picked it up and answered with a rather worrying rant.

"*Danni where the hell are you, I have been waiting all night for...*" I said, as I was interrupted.
"*Roxy its Ellie, I was just phoning to see if he had arrived home yet?*" she replied.

I told Ellie, that he had still not arrived yet; and that it was past a joke now, as I was not impressed to say the least, now getting rather emotional at this stage. Ellie then told me not to get upset, otherwise I would make myself worse with worry; and she thought that maybe Danni had got delayed with the London traffic, or had indeed gone into the city to find me something special, as she knew every now and then he would do something like that just to surprise me.

Still being upset, Ellie told me to leave the wine alone and to make myself a pot of tea. She told me that hearing me crying made her feel upset; and she hated seeing or even hearing me cry, as it always started her off. I told her that I was dressed all glamorous, looking like a lemon; and the dinner is now ruined. That I have had a few glasses of wine so I could not drive; and that I had already phoned Steve, in which he told me that Danni had left at around 5pm to go into the city. Crying, I then asked her where on earth was he. She told me that didn't know; and she could not understand why he was so late. Also worrying; and knowing my concern grew, she asked me if I wanted her to come over; and give me some support until he gets home. I did not want her to come over, as I knew she would have had a busy night, so I told her that I was fine, but I was not amused at all at what he was putting me through; and that I would not be impressed at all if he had gone to one of his last minute meetings, or indeed brought me a gift, knowing that by now I would ne worried sick, especially in the light he had sent no text to explain. Just then I heard her phone ring, in which she told me that she had to go, as it was Di and she had best answer it. I just told her that I would speak to her later, that I would text her when he finally shows up, maybe as drunk as a skunk no doubt, then put the phone down. I do not know why I said that, but my anger was clearly showing by now. Danni had never come home drunk; and had only ever been late once in all the years we had been together. Danni also detested drivers who drink and drive; and often said that they should never be allowed to drive again.

The only time that he came home late that I recalled, was when we were going to go to his father's function, as something came up at the last minute and he could not put it off. He ended up going on site as someone had broken into the building; and they had stolen all the copper and boilers. He left his phone in the car by mistake, so could not let me know until he had sorted the site out, finally having to cancel with his father and apologise to me. I sat down and looked at the clock again, and just cried to myself, thinking maybe something like that has happened again. Suddenly the intercom buzzed, and I thought thank God for that, the stupid idiot has lost his keys; and without asking who it was, I just pressed the release button and heard the outside door open and close. I then went into the kitchen to see if I could salvage the dinner, but the vegetables were ruined; and I would not reheat them. I just thought all I can do is carve up the meat and prepare some rice or something, saying to myself, what a bloody night because I am slightly tipsy, dinner is ruined; and what else could go wrong?

Then the doorbell rang…

Just before opening the door, I shouted '*Forgot your keys as well then*? But alas no one answered me.

When I then opened the door, I saw that it was Paul and Di, so I invited them in and then put my head around the door to see if Danni was out there.

"No Danni Paul? I thought he would have come up with you, he is so late; and I am not amused. Just wait till he gets home, because he will get the sharp end of my tongue for sure." I cursed, as Paul asked me to sit down placing his hand on my shoulder
"Sit down, sit down you are having a laugh aren't you. I have been slaving over a stove all night, preparing a nice meal for us; and he has not had the decency to even text me Paul." I shouted, as I started to go off on one, when Di came and coaxed me to sit down, where she placed her hands on mine and told me to stay calm.

"Roxy, please sit down. I am afraid we have some bad news I am afraid, please stay calm. It's Danni…" She said, as I quickly interrupted.
"Yes… its Danni, he has never done anything like this before Di; and I am worried sick." I replied
"ROXY" She shouted.

I just looked at her in shock, as she has never raised her voice to me. I sat there trembling as she held my hand.

"It's Danni he has been in an accident." She said, as her voice trembled slightly
"An accident! don't be silly, he is just late for dinner. An accident! Paul what's going on?" I asked confusingly
"Roxy there has been a road accident just two miles from here; and I am afraid Danni is involved." He told me in a calm voice.
"No… you are joking Paul, he can't have, he will be here in a minute you just wait and see. You must have it

all wrong. Stop scaring me Paul it's not nice." I replied, shaking and crying.

"*There had been an attempted bank robbery; and as they made their escape, they drove straight into Danni's side of the road hitting him head on.*" He told me, trying to explain without giving me too much concern, especially as my mind was all over the place by then.

"*Paul - Di what where, where is he now? Is he ok?*" I said as I started to shake.

"*They have taken him to the Saint Mary's.*" He said as I interrupted, now beginning to lose it as I broke down in tears as I collapsed.

When I came around, Paul had been into the kitchen and had placed a cold cloth on my head. I then looked at them both, and as I was crying again, I looked up at them and told them that I need to go and see him; and would they please take me to see him, as I kept whispering 'oh my poor Danni, my poor… poor Danni.

Di then grabbed hold of my hand and told me to get a coat; and they would take me down to see him. I rushed up the stairs to the bedroom and looked for a short jacket, then rushed back down as I told them that I was now ready. Still a bundle of nerves; and still sobbing my heart out whilst I was being comforted by Di, Paul took hold of my keys and locked up for me, and then escorted me into his car and drove me to the hospital.

Whilst in the car Paul kept on looking over his shoulder to see if I were ok; and kept telling me not to worry.

I had my head on the window with flashbacks going through my head, by now my phone was ringing like crazy but I just ignored it. Di suggested for the time being to turn off the phone, as I was in no fit state to talk to anyone. We then got to the hospital in quick time, as they had put on the blues and twos; and when we were outside, he parked in the police bay, and with my arm under Pauls, we went to reception to find out where Danni was. They informed us that he had been taken to the ICU ward, so with Paul and Di we went straight to ICU without any hesitation, which I think was also because they still had on their uniforms.

Upon arriving at the front desk Paul spoke for me, and then the nurse told me which bay he was in. the staff nurse who was overseeing his admission then told me to brace myself, to brace myself and to be strong, as it was not a pretty sight, what with all the wires that are attached over his body. I held my head high and took a deep breath, then held onto Paul as we walked down the bays in the ward, then getting to Danni I could not retain my composure, almost collapsing and having Paul and Di support me.

I then rushed to his bedside.

"Oh, my baby oh Danni I am here now your Roxy is here; and I am going nowhere." I cried, as I sat down and placed my hand on his.

The nurse told me he has been unconscious since he arrived, and that he was holding steady. He was in a right state, but they had covered him up, just so we never got to see the full extent of the injuries to his body.

He had wires and pipes everywhere, and he was so battered and bruised that he was hardly recognisable; but for his blonde hair and goatee, still with some remnants of blood that they were unable to remove fully. I just held his hand so tightly speaking to him and crying on his pillow, hearing the feint bleep of his monitor as the nurses came in and out to check on him, looking at me and asking if I needed anything. Paul was standing behind me, as he placed his hand gently onto my shoulder, when Di then asked me if I wanted a cup of tea, or maybe a coffee, but under the circumstances I really did not want anything, as my concern was with Danni; and so I looked at Di, and as I cried I told her

"Who could do such a thing like this? Who could harm my Danni? He has never done any wrong to anyone Paul, why is this happening?" I cried.
"Don't worry about all that now Roxy, you are with Danni and I am sure he knows it too. We have got two of the bank robbers under police guard here at the hospital, and there is a search for the others." He replied, comforting me as I sat by Danni's side.

"WHERE? Let me get my hands on the lowlife scum, where are they?" I screamed, as both Di and Paul had to hold me back and calm me down. *"But why us and why my Danni?"*
"It's one of those things Roxy, he was in the wrong place at the wrong time. Any earlier or later and everything would have been ok, the robbers panicked." Di said.

Then my phone rang again as I forgot to turn it off, so I gave it to Paul and asked if he could deal with it.
Paul went outside leaving me with Di, as he kindly

229

answered my missed calls. Di was lovely and I could not have wished for anyone better to be sitting with me, she sat by me holding my hand, comforting me and telling me to be strong for Danni.

After what seemed like hours of waiting, the doctor finally came in and briefed me on what had happened. I could not understand all of his jargon, so I just asked him outright, as I said.

"Is he going to be ok doctor, is my Danni going to be ok? And please do not mess with me, be honest."
"It is now up to Danni, as he has had a very traumatic experience. He is stable, but it is down to him and his will to overcome his injuries. But if you are asking for a medical decision, I would say he has a sixty five percent chance." He replied.
"I want him moving to a private ward doctor, I don't care what it costs I want him on a private ward of the hospital." I told him.

"I cannot do it tonight, however, I will see what I can do tomorrow. Let him get more stable first." He replied.
"No doctor you are not listening to me; I order you to place him onto a private ward with around the clock care. It would have been his wish as well as mine, so you will sort this out now and not tomorrow." I shouted, as I became hysterical.
"It's ok Roxy, the doctor will do it, but for now he just needs time to sort things out. Give him time Roxy, you are very upset and in shock. Danni needs to get stable, and there are still tests going on. He is in the right place Roxy, you know that. For the time being it would be

unwise to move him from ICU, until he is at a suitable level of stability." Di said, now trying to calm me down in the process.

Just then, Paul came into the room and told me he had sorted out my calls, as most were just asking how Danni and I were. He told me that he had informed Ellie; and that she would be over shortly. He then told me that he had been able to get hold of Johnny, where he would be flying over in a few days, as he needed to organise a flight; and that Ruby sends her love and told me that I should be brave, as she was sure things would be ok; and at least I was at Danni's side where I had family and friends around me. I thanked Paul and Di for all they had done. Telling them that Danni would be grateful for them looking after me, once he was awake up. Paul then said that they had to go back to the station, but would be in touch real soon, as Di then asked if I would be ok on my own. I told her that I would be fine, that I was with my Danni; and I wanted to be there when he awakes. An hour later a nurse came to me and said that Ellie was here, so I asked her to show her through. I ran into her arms and cried my eyes out, hysterically asking her why. We placed our heads on each other's shoulders, just crying and comforting each other. She told me that she had phoned Johnny and that he would be going to the airport tomorrow to book a flight, now in a flood of tears as she looked at Danni. I already knew this, as Paul had to answer my phone for me as I was too… well crying too much.

"Have you called the boys to tell them, and what about Danni's dad, have you called him?" She asked.
"No as Paul said, he will be contacting him as he is still in America." I replied.

Ellie stayed with me for a few hours, and then said she had to go home to get some rest, as she was on an early shift the next day. She asked me if I was going to go home, but I told her I would rather stay with Danni, as I wanted to be there when he woke up; and I would never forgive myself if I was not there, and he woke up asking for me. I stayed with Danni the rest of the night and morning, and it was not until Stuart arrived, that I got to see someone else other than the nurses coming over to check on Danni, and to bring me a cup of tea.
Stuart gently tapped me on the shoulder as I had fallen asleep; and looking at him I fell into his arms once again crying and not knowing when to stop, as he seen the mess Danni was in, with all the pipes and tubes and machines surrounding him. He told me that I needed to go home with me him, to get changed and then come back again later that day, as he too cried but tried to be strong for me. I told him that I could not at the moment, that I needed to be with Danni, just in case he wakes up and asks for me

"I am sure he is not going to miss you for an hour or so Roxy and the nurses have your number if he does wake up. Come on let's take you home so you can freshen up."
He told me, seeing that I needed to freshen up, especially in the makeup department.

By now the doctor had come in and heard what Stuart had said and told me it was a good idea. He had sorted a private room out and they were getting it ready, and it would not be until later that afternoon they could transfer him, depending on his stability.

"There is no point staying here Mrs Svenningsen, go home and have something to eat before coming back, it will do you the world of good. We will inform you of any changes that may occur."* He told me, now along with Stuart, they had persuaded me to leave.

I agreed, and then asked the doctor to promise me, that he would call me if there were any change. The doctor then told me that he would phone me himself, when he then called me by my full name, being Svenningsen; and just for protocol, he asked me what his religion was.

"We have no religion, but we do have a friend who is a member of the clergy. WHY?" I asked.
"It's just protocol; and may be a good idea to inform him or her so they can offer you spiritual help too." He replied.
"Thank you doctor, I will get someone to contact him for me later." I answered.

The doctor then placed his hand on my shoulder and told me to take care, and not to worry. With my eyes looking like a panda and red raw from all of the crying, I was escorted out of the hospital by Stuart, once we had found out where Danni was going to be moved to.
As I was being comforted by Stuart, we then hailed a cab,

where Stuart held me in his arms until we got home.
He sat me on the couch and let me lay down, as he went
in the kitchen to make me a coffee. He then went into the
downstairs bathroom and ran a bath for me, as he
thought it would be easier for me, than keep going up
and down the stairs to the bathroom up there. He told me
that he had run me a bath, and to go and have a nice soak,
as he would go upstairs to get a dressing gown and
slippers, so that I could just relax a little bit. I did have
my phone in my pocket, in which Stuart placed on the
bathroom stool next to the bath; and that I should not
worry, as he would sort everything out.
He walked me into the bathroom and told me I would be
fine, just as I then started crying again. He held me close
to him, stroking my back as he comforted me; removing
my jacket and placing it on the chair, helping me undress
as I was a nervous wreck as well as hysterically crying.
Once he helped me out of my clothes, he held my hand
as I stepped into the bath, and then he left saying he will
be back in shortly to see if I was ok.
I just lay there with all sorts of things running through
my mind, as I stared at the wall and had short bursts of
crying moments in my hands.
Shortly afterwards Stuart came back into the bathroom,
bringing me a cup of coffee and one himself. He pulled
the chair closer to the bath as he sat down and told me to
reach forward, as he would wash my back. In doing so I
pulled my knees up tight and placed my arms around
them nesting my head in position as I again started to cry
as I covered up my modesty, as Stuart gently washed my
back and soothed me, telling me to let go of everything.

234

It was then that my phone rang, and as Stuart had since moved the phone; and placed it on his person, he quickly jumped back, as he reached into his pocket to answer it. He told me it was Johnny, and he had to wait a further two days before he could get a flight. I held onto Stuart's hands and told him '*thank you.*'

Stuart then got up and reached for my towel opening it up for me to step into, joking about me wrinkling like a prune if I stay in the bath any longer.

Being in a comatose state, I stood up and let him place the towel around me, when he then lifted me out of the bath, and carried into the lounge so that I could lay me on the couch for a while. Stuart started making calls letting them know I was bearing up, and that they were moving Danni to a private room. He got my family address book out of the hallway dresser, and began ringing everyone from the home phone, and kept coming in to check on me.

Shortly after he had finished calling everyone, I asked if he had managed to get hold of Rik, to which he told me he had left a message with his office to give you a call as soon as he got in as it was an emergency.

He told me to put my face on, and then when I was ready, we would head back to the hospital.

Upon arriving and having to wait at the front desk, due to there being a mix up of where Danni was, we finally were given the room he was located to. The private part of the hospital was towards the back, overlooking Buckingham Palace and the Hyde Park.

Arriving at his room, there was a nurse inside with the doctor just doing a few tests, we were then allowed to go

in and sit with him again. Again, I held his hand, as
Stuart sat next to me holding mine.

*"Look at him Stuart, he is so banged up and what with
all those wires and that machine. My poor Danni, my
poor sweet Danni."* I said crying again.
*"Don't upset yourself Roxy, he is in the best place now;
and they are doing the best they can for him."* He replied,
getting even more choked up at seeing him there.

He dropped his head into my neck, and with a little kiss
on my neck he had a cry. I turned around and with one
hand still holding Danni's I fell into Stuart's body and
together we both cried and comforted each other.
All that day we had friends phoning us to find out how
he was doing, in which Stuart had to keep going out of
the room as well as my drag family calling in.
There was Ellie and Di, Steven and his wife and all those
who were dear to us, but also giving me privacy so they
did not stay long, as they just offered support and
brought flowers.
That afternoon Rik arrived, and as soon as he got to
Danni's room, he walked over to me and gave me a hug.
Paul managed to get hold of him yesterday, and he
managed to get a seat last minute the night before.
Seeing his son all laid out was too much for him and he
too broke down in a flood of tears, when Stuart said that
he would leave us too it; and go and have a coffee and so
he could go and call Adam. Rik stayed with me for about
two hours and then had to go as he needed to take a few
hour's nap from his flight. He asked me to keep him
informed, and when he awoke, he knew he would rather

see my face than any others. He embraced me and told me to be strong, and that he loved me; and we should all catch up soon. I then sat down when he had gone; and started to talk to Danni. It was all I could think of as it did not seem logical to just sit there and say nothing. I began talking about our first encounter, and some of the funny stories I had got into, then Stuart came in the room and told me I should eat, as I had not eaten since yesterday, but I had no appetite, I just wanted to be here should anything happen, and besides I had water so I could make sure I was not thirsty.

I stayed by Danni's side for a further four days, only going home when Stuart told me that I needed to freshen up and get a good shower and change my clothing.

It was now 11am, on the Monday morning when Johnny finally arrived at the hospital. As he walked into the room, he saw me holding Danni's hand, brushing his head and talking to him, oblivious to the fact that Johnny was standing there in the doorway. I then heard a voice that whispered softly; and as I looked up, I was so happy to find that it was Johnny.

"Roxy, Miss Roxy, hello sweetheart."
"Johnny, is that really you?" I asked, as he had seemed to have changed in his appearance, since the last time I saw him.
"It sure is baby girl, how you doing? Sorry I couldn't get here sooner." He replied, as he walked over towards me and placed his hands on my shoulders.

"Oh Johnny, my Danni… look at him, no matter what I do he will not wake up." I said, as I then stood up and walked into his arms crying, with Johnny holding me tight as he comforted me. Stroking my back and apologising for not being here sooner. With his voice now being croaky, he asked me if I was at the hospital alone, when I told him that Stuart was with me; and that he had gone out to get me a cup of coffee. I sat back down as Johnny leant over the bed to see his best friend.

"Oh, my dear bro, what on earth have you been up to? I am here now my friend, so please do not worry, Johnny is here Danni." He said, as he stroked his face.

I then looked at him and told him that I loved him, that everything would be fine now that Johnny was here. Wiping a tear from my eye, I continued to tell him that Johnny and I were not going anywhere; and to please come back to us soon, finally telling him that I loved him so much. I then looked at Danni and saw a tear fall from the side of his eye, as I felt him gently squeeze my hand. Then for a moment it went silent, as I heard a slight intake of breath from him; and then all the alarms on the machine began to bleep and send out an alarm. I did not know what was happening, as I called out to Danni, then placing my arms over Danni, asking him what I must do, calling out in a moment of hysteria.
Just then the doctors and nurses came in, looked at Johnny and told him to get me out of the room. I was screaming to Danni, to not leave me, as Johnny had taken hold of me.

"Roxy come on; let the doctors do their thing. We are in their way, come on sweetheart." He told me.
"Johnny my Danni, I need to be here." I cried

Just at that precise moment of being panic stricken, Stuart walked into the room and saw Johnny trying to get me out, as he asked what was wrong.

"Get her out of here now." The doctor shouted to them.
"Stuart, please give me a hand, we need to get her out of here pronto." Johnny said, as he supported me with his arms.
"What's wrong Johnny, what's happening?" He asked, as he looked over to see the doctors trying to revive Danni.

They both escorted me out of the room and into a private room that a nurse had pointed out for me to be taken too. I got into the room where Stuart had brought me a carton of water, as he had left the coffee's on the side table in Danni's room. Johnny at this time was comforting me, telling me that things would be fine, just as Stuart sat next to me, with his hand holding mine he too comforted me and offered me support.
I was a nervous wreck, crying, shaking and shouting. I kept asking Johnny, what on earth was going on, as I thought they were taking too long. He just calmly told me, that they must still be attending me; and that he was sure that it would not be long now before we got some news, brushing my hair out of my eyes, as he held my hand softly.

"Oh Johnny; my poor Danni. What on earth is going on? This cannot be happening; oh god, it really can't be happening." I cried.

"Calm down Roxy, you will only make yourself worse, come on honey try not to get upset." Stuart said, as he now sat the other end of me.

Thirty minutes later the doctor came into the waiting room, where as soon as he opened the door I knew, I just knew I had lost my Danni. I knew he had lost the fight; and that he had left me.

"I am sorry Mrs Svenningsen, it was just too much for him. We got him back twice, however, he just let go, we could not bring him back again. I am really sorry." He told us, in a very sympathetic way.

I just looked at the boys and cried, falling to my knees calling out his name.

"No, No, No, my Danni, I cannot lose him Johnny I cannot lose my Danni. Oh, Stuart what am I to do, he has left me?"

"Come on Roxy, let's get you home." Johnny said, now getting choked up himself.

"I want to see my Danni, Johnny. Stuart, please take me too him." I begged them, noticing the tears running down Stuart and Johnny's face.

They both escorted me to his room, where by now the wires were out of him and the machine taken away. The nurses had pulled the blanket up to his chest, still keeping his dignity and injuries away from sight, but for the bruised top half we saw. I sat down with my head on his chest; and my hand stroking his face as I just broke down in tears. I cried; and then told him that he promised that he would never leave me; and I wanted him to come back to me because I could not go on without him.

I also noticed that it was difficult for the boys too, as they had now composed themselves for my sake as they still tried to hold back their tears.

Johnny was the other side of me as he held onto Danni's hand, crying and saying how sorry he had moved away and left him. Stuart was by my side as he placed his hand on my hand which was on Danni's hand and a hand on my shoulder as he too could not contain his tears.

The nurses gave us a bit of time alone, as they dropped the blinds and closed the door behind them.

After twenty minutes, they came back into the room, and told us we would have to go as preparations had to be made. Stuart then thanked them for all they had done, and told him to contact either him or Johnny for any other arrangements. Johnny in the meantime had managed to get a message to Rik, but it did not get to him on time as he never managed to get to the hospital whilst we were there. We all left the hospital where a cab was hailed, and I just fell into Johnny's arms.

Just then Stuart could not contain himself as he had a call from Adam; and hearing him cry when he told him he had just passed away, brought my mothering instincts out. I sat up and looked at Stuart, where I placed his head on my shoulder and told him not to cry, that everything would be ok.

We then finally got home and after getting upstairs to the apartment, I put the kettle on and made them a drink. I poured myself a stronger one as I needed to calm down and try and think straight. Stuart had to get back to Brighton the next day, as he had taken what absence he could, and he needed Adam for his support. Johnny stayed with me to look after me, and to make all the necessary arrangements for me. He contacted Rik to let him know that we were now back at the apartment; and that I was resting on the couch with a throw over me, where he also made sure no one called me, without him first intercepting the phone to stop further distress.

That week I went into my own little world, I was oblivious to who was with me and who was around me. I did my daily chores; and just thought Johnny was there for a holiday. I did not go out at all, as I just sat and watched television or listened to the radio, telling Johnny I needed to go to bed and could not wait up any longer for Danni. It was not until the following Monday, that everything had hit home. Johnny had been given the phone call about the body being released; and Danni was now with the funeral directors.

The funeral was arranged for the following Thursday morning; and he thought it was better for me to say my goodbyes privately rather than at the chapel.

I was disappointed that Ruby never came over with Johnny, but he did remind me a few times that she was busy with her business and with his bar; and that she would come over to see me as soon as she could.

I was all over the place those first few days; and this one day that I was in the kitchen preparing dinner, when Johnny came in to see me was no exception. He asked me if I was ok, when I told him that I was and I was just cooking dinner, as I began setting the table. Johnny noticed that the table was kind of over-dressed, when he asked me who the other plate was for, because I had set three plates out, then thinking that it must be for Rik, or Stuart. I looked at him and tutted, as I told him that he was so forgetful. Tat the other plate was for Danni, as although he is not home yet, he does sometimes have to work a little later than normal. Now being in a strange world than being in the world of reality. Johnny walked over to me, where he placed his arms around my waist; and then as calm as you can be, he softly spoke, telling me that Danni had gone, that he is no longer with us, asking me if I remembered what had happened.

"Don't be daft Johnny, he will be here soon. It's five o'clock and he gets here just after that." I said, still placing things onto the table, then checking dinner.

"Roxy listen... please listen to me. Danni has gone. Don't you understand? You need to be prepared to see him tomorrow at the funeral directors." He told me. "Now don't be stupid Johnny, Danni is at work and he will be home soon. Stop talking like that." I replied, as I started to get angry.

Johnny then looked at me as he grabbed hold of my shoulders.

"Roxy Danni is DEAD, remember the car accident. He is dead sweetheart, he has gone." He said, as he shook me.

I then just looked at him and broke down, putting my hands to my face as I screamed and cried. My head knew that Danni had passed away, but my heart would not let go, as I expected him to walk through the door; and then and only then would things be alright.

"I am so sorry my sweet Roxy; I am so so very sorry." Johnny said, as he too began to fill up with emotion *"My poor Danni what am I to do? He can't have just gone Johnny, he can't leave me, because he said he would never leave me. He can't leave me Johnny, not like this"* I cried, now beginning to babble and not make sense of things.
"Come here sweetheart, I am here for you Roxy, I have lost him too, but I promise I will not lose you." He replied, as he gripped me and began stroking my hair as he comforted me.

"Oh Johnny what am I to do, my Danni my beautiful Danni." I wept.

"It will be fine my sweet Roxy; it will all be fine I promise you. Come here." He said, as he now pulled me towards him. *"I will stay with you for as long as you want me too sweetie. Ruby will be here tomorrow, so you will have some sisterly support."*

I could not stop crying, so he thought it was best he put me to bed and call his doctor friend. He walked me into the bedroom; and then helped me into bed as he used the phone by the bedside table to call the doctor; sitting with me for a while until it looked as though I was going to drop off, as we chatted and chatted.

Just then the intercom rang, and I woke up like a deer in headlights. All I could think of, was it Danni. Johnny told me that it was not Danni, that it was the doctor, come to check up on me. He told me to stay where I was, as he would let him in. Johnny, along with my boys and Ellie, thought I was in a bad place; and that it was only right to get our doctor to come and visit me.

Shortly after the doctor came in to see me; and having heard what had gone on, as well as the state I was in, he gave me a tranquiliser there and then; and a prescription for a further week's supply. Within the hour I was away with the fairies; and never knew anymore until Johnny came in to wake me up.

"*Good morning Roxy, I hope you slept well.*" He said, as he sat on the corner of the bed until I had come around.

"*My head, what on earth did that fucking doctor give me?*" I asked, now holding onto my head, as I looked like I had been dragged through a hedge backwards.

"*Nice to see the old Roxy back, are you ready for today? It is going to be hard Roxy, but I am here for you.*" He told me.

"*Not so much the old Roxy, as I am feeling like I have been hit over the head with a sledgehammer. Please just promise me Johnny you will not let me go; and you will hold me at all times.*" I replied, now taking a sip of the aromatic coffee that he had placed before me

"*You know I will sweetie, I am downstairs so I will wait for you to get dressed and come down. Then we can have breakfast if you like?*" He said, as he kissed me on the forehead; and then made his way to the lounge. I told him that I would see him soon, and that my head bloody hurt, and would he find me some painkillers. I then got showered and dressed, applying fresh makeup as by now I looked awful then made my way downstairs. Johnny was sitting at the breakfast table in the kitchen, much like Danni used to, and with a slip of the tongue I just said.

"Morning Danni my handsome hunk, oh I am so sorry Johnny morning Johnny."
"Hey, it's ok, don't worry about it sweetie, now no getting upset. Don't forget you also have to take one of your pills, I have been to the chemist for you." He said, as he placed my medicine on the table in front of me.
"Ok thank you honey." I replied.

I sat down at the table, and with a glass of orange I took one of my pills. After breakfast in which I could only manage half a croissant, we made our way to the funeral directors, where they had prepared Danni for my final goodbye. Looking at him lying there, I placed my hand on his hand; and then stroked his head as I told him I loved him. I kissed him first on his forehead, and then on the lips. Then the reality really kicked in, like a lead weight just dropping on top of me. I had lost my one true love; and there was nothing I could do to bring him back.

"Goodbye Danni my love, I miss you and I love you so much. I will love you always and forever my darling, please sleep well." I said to him, trying to hold back my tears and to compose myself, as I knew Danni would not want to see as me emotional as I was.

I again kissed him on the lips, looked at Johnny and told him I would be outside as I knew he wanted a moment alone with him. I could not help myself, I needed to leave as I was now a blubbering wreck again. Johnny thanked me, as he told me he would not be too long, as again he asked if I was ok. I placed my hand on his, looked at him and told him that I was fine, as I whispered to him to say goodbye to his brother. I walked out of the room and outside to the car, where I waited for Johnny to come out and join me.

As he got into the car, I noticed he too had been crying, so I placed my hand on his knee and told him that it is a sad day, for we had both lost someone very special, but we still have each other; and I would be there for him as much as he wanted me to be, and I wanted him to remember that.

"*And thank you for being there for me Johnny; I do not know what I would have done without my boys*"

"*I know Roxy; and thank you. I too will always be here for you.*" He said, in a voice that was holding back his emotions.

I kept my hand on his knee gently stroking him until we got home, with intervals that he would take his hand off the steering wheel and place it on top of mine comforting me. When we got home, Johnny switched his phone on, and once it had gone through the start up as most phones do; a few messages bleeped, so he scrolled down a few of them and as he read them, he just shouted. 'FUCK.'

"What's wrong honey?" I asked

"Ruby can't make it, there is some sort of problem with the bar. She has asked if you mind her not being there and accept her apologies. She has also invited you to come and stay with us for a while, that is of course if you want to?" He said, as he sounded rather disappointed with her.

I was gutted, as this is the first time Ruby had ever let me down, but I also understood she had a business to run and it was not always easy to get away. However, I still thought that if she wanted to, she would have found a way to come over, even if it were only to pay her last respects to Danni.

"Yes honey that is fine, let Ruby know I am ok and that I miss her." I said in a disgruntled voice.

That night Johnny asked if I wanted to go out to eat, as I had been cooped up now for well over a week. I told him I was ok, but he just said it may do me the world of good, so I agreed to go out and try and let Johnny take my mind of things. I got myself ready and chose a nice flared dress to go out in, it was black with a little blue and black corsage on the side hip. Johnny complimented me, saying I looked beautiful, in which I complimented him, telling he still scrubbed up well, then asking him if he minded if we only went to the restaurant, as I was not up to visiting the bar later that night, to be asked questions, and to be given sympathy by well-wishers.

He was ok with that, saying that it may be the best thing considering how I was still feeling. That he was thankful that I was going out in the first place, but then said that we still need to eat no matter how hard it would be.

We went downstairs, where Johnny hailed a cab; and we made our way into the city.

Having spent two hours there making conversation; and picking at my food he thought that it was time to leave. He could see that I was not hungry, and that my eyes were sparkling with tears that were surfacing. That I was a million miles away; and he told me that he should have realized that I was not ready for this yet. So once again we got a cab and made our way home, where again Johnny held me close to him offering me his shoulder.

When we got home, he asked me if I wanted coffee; and I told him I would have something stronger like a brandy. He brought me a brandy, and this was the first time I had seen Johnny relaxing and drinking.

Johnny joined me as he poured himself a scotch on the rocks; and brought a small bottle of coke in for me as I could not drink brandy alone. He then sat on the couch and with his arm over the couch he called me over, holding me close to him, so that I could hear his feint heartbeat as he comforted me.

We spoke about the old days, and the fun we had, how he had slowly grown fond of Danni; and soon how they became good buddies. How he thought we were a most suited couple, where the love between us each day was the same if not stronger. Holding onto me as he told me he was very lucky to have met us both, and that he had promised Danni he would always look after me.

The time was getting late now, and I had forgotten to

take my pill. I told Johnny that it was probably best I didn't take one as I had been drinking, in which he agreed. I then looked at him and said.

"Johnny please do not take this the wrong way, but I do not want to be alone. Will you please come and stay with me tonight? Will you please come and share the bed and hold me and cuddle up to me?"

"Yes sweetie if that is what you want? I told you I am not going anywhere; and I will be here for you whatever you want or ask of me." He replied.
"Just sleep next to me Johnny, just hold me and let me fall asleep with you. I really do not want to be alone tonight Johnny." I asked

"Come on then sweetie, let's lock up and take you to bed. You do look rather tired, and it has been a very long week for you." He replied.

Johnny then went to the hallway to make sure the doors were locked securely, and then he turned everything off downstairs, apart from a side lamp in which I always left on. He then came upstairs, where, by this time I had already got into bed, so looking at me, he again asked me if I was sure that I wanted this arrangement, as he could easily sleep in either of the other bedrooms.
I told him that I was sure, as I again asked him to stay with me. That I would feel much better and much safer having someone stay over with me. So, he slowly undressed, in which I noticed for the first time, how fit he still was, with just the slightest of chest hair. He did

not have a six pack, but his abs were still quite defined, where you could see he once had a six pack, or he was just getting them. He stripped down to his nice white Aussiebum boxers, and just slipped into the bed next to me. He lay down next to me; and with his hand over my pillow, he asked me to come towards him where he held me and cuddled me.

For a while I just lay there with my head on his chest, and my hand on his tummy. Thanking him for what he had done; and how grateful and honoured I was for all what my friends had done for me. I also thanked him for staying with me, as I knew he could have easily said no, but was pleased that he didn't. I then turned around, as I felt Johnny do the same but then placing his arms around me, pressing me into his front as he kept hold of me like he was protecting me. My pills were once again beginning to kick in; and this time they were kicking in much quicker, due to having pills in my system.

Just before going to sleep I faintly heard him say '*I love you Roxy, you will be safe I promise*.' I felt very safe, all the time Johnny stayed with me; and that night he did not pursue anything, which I was so grateful for. Just to be able to have someone next to you, in your bed comforting you, looking over you and making sure you are protected and without agenda, was all that I could have wished for

I had seen Rik every day since he had flown over; and he told me he was going to stay until the funeral, but then he must leave shortly afterwards as he needed to get back to America. He told me Jake and Sophie would not be over as it would be too much for them, but they did send me their love and they are going to both write me a letter. I was pleased that he told me that, and I knew that funerals could be traumatic for children, so although disappointed that I would not see them, I understood he did what he knew was the best for my prince and princess; and it would only be a matter of time before we all spoke to one another again.

It was then the day of the funeral; and it seemed to creep up on you like it was only yesterday that the accident had occurred.

How fast things go by when you least expect it.

Everyone who was invited came to the apartment where they were let in by Johnny; and then they came over to me and gave me a hug and then passed on their best wishes. Shortly before 11am Johnny announced that the cars were here, and that we should all go downstairs.

It was only a short drive to the church and the crematorium; and as I got downstairs, I had never seen so many flower tributes in my life. The gateway was brimming with camera's, as they started flashing as soon as I came out of the building, where I stopped to have a look at some of the tributes. I had not lifted a finger to arrange anything, it was all done by my boys and Rik.

On the coffin lay a beautiful rose and lily spray which represented our wedding flowers, in which the florist had got everything down to a tee, it was just perfect.

Arriving at the church it was packed to the brim with his work colleagues and friends, as well as my close celebrity friend's. I was led into the church, where I went to the front where my dad and Rik were sitting.

I never wanted the service to be separated by family and friends, but more for everyone to mingle as I looked upon our life as having a larger family.

My dad and Rik hugged me and told me to be strong, as they made a space for me inbetween them. Rik had invited my family to the funeral, but only my father responded. He was putting my father up at his apartment, so that he did not have to worry about hotels. This was a surprise to me, which was a very nice surprise having my dad there, but I wished he had asked me if he could have stayed with me as I would have loved his company and support. Having had a space made for me inbetween my dad and Rik, I looked at my father and told him that it was ok, I would have Johnny by me as well. That he has been my rock all this week; and I did not want him to be annoyed with me and the arrangements.

My father didn't mind, but Johnny then told me he would sit on the end so I could be with my two dads.

The music then played as they brought in my Danni, it was his wish that he would arrive when everyone else had been properly seated.

The bearers then carried him down the aisle, where they then placed his coffin down by the altar, where our friend Alan was the vicar and who was taking service, as they then played a piece of music which was a folksong from his Nordic heritage.

The service was a beautiful serene service, with a few people speaking with poems and other tributes with regards Danni. Once the vicar had made his tribute, he introduced Johnny, where Johnny addressed us all as he said.

"Good afternoon everyone; I would like to thank you all for turning up today in memory of my Danni, Son, husband, brother and friend. I have been asked to read

this letter from Roxy, as she is not in a condition to do so today, so I hope you will excuse her and allow me to take her place? Roxy wrote this letter as a tribute to how she feels about Danni; and would like to share it with you all."

'My dearest Danni, from the first time I saw you I knew you were someone special, but it was not until that funny moment backstage that I knew we were meant to be. When you looked me in the eyes and I saw that sparkle, and that smile and how we laughed when Ruby caught us in that uncompromising position.
The look on her face still haunts me today, as I still visualise my poor Danni running out of the dressing room because of sheer embarrassment.
How you supported me and protected me on my first stage appearance, holding me tight as I was to face my audience. Danni the support you gave me when I gave my first television appearance, as I spoke out to all who tried to put me down; and put those people down who were in the same boat as we were. You never ever judged me, but stood by me through thick and thin, and through good times and bad times. You gave me the strength to carry on, when I felt only the will to give it all up. You also gave me a family; and a love that I had not had for such a long time; and thought that I would never see again. You put up with me on my many shopping trips, taking you around shoe shop after shoe shop, giving you even more bags to carry as I did not know when to stop, giving me that look as to say oh not more shoes, but you never tried to change me. I have many fond moments of us together, sharing all of the good times and laughter,

*as we walked alone along the seafront of our beloved
Hove before going to lunch and then back out for the
evening.*
*Making me your wife was the happiest moment of my life,
knowing our love was cemented by the bond we had
created and the love we both shared for one another.*
*I love you Danni my beloved husband, my friend and my
soul mate. I love you and I will never stop loving you, as
I look back at our past together; and how I will always
be proud that I met you; and even proud to know that
because of you I became a Svenningsen.*
*Goodbye my dearest Danni, sleep well my love till we
meet and walk together again. Goodbye my sweet
Danni.'*

"*I think we all know how special the love between Danni
and Roxy was, and still is; and Roxy, thank you so much
for sharing that with us.*" Johnny said, as he coughed a
few times to clear his voice.

He brought tears to my eyes, and as he sat down, I
placed my arms around him and told him thank you.
By now there were tears flooding throughout the
congregation, with even the vicar wiping his eyes.
Both my father's holding my hands as they dried their
eyes. Johnny then whispered softly in my ear.

"*Absolutely divine Roxy, I am sure even the angels are
crying.*"

The vicar then composed himself; and looking directly to
me he said.

"Thank you Roxy, for those heart felt words, and it is such things we try and teach in the church. We try and teach how the love of God is spiritual and amongst us all; and where the love between two people is without prejudice or agenda. For it matters not that of your gender, but more of the love between two people, for it is that love that gives us our strength and our courage and our faith in one another. A love that is not just bound by heaven and earth, but one that is bound to us, by us; and that are both mentally and physically rewarding to us. A love shared only by your soul-mate, and a love that is ours for eternity."

I turned my hands over so that I now held both father's hands, where I looked at them both and told them thank you and that I loved them. Then the vicar stood up and announced the choir would sing the final song, it was Danni's favourite and meant so much to him.

"We will stay seated as the choir now performs Danni's favourite song 'I will always love you' by Whitney Houston."

The choir was just like heavenly cherubs, and it was a perfect end to a choral service.
Just before it had all finished the vicar gave us his blessing. To end the ceremony, the vicar called upon Rik, to read the final eulogy. Rik got out of his seat, as he stroked my hand. My dad then looked at me taking hold of me as he placed his arm around me, as Johnny moved up and placed his hand onto my hand.

Rik made his way to the pulpit as he addressed us all, where he then began his final words.

"They say that there is no love stronger, than that of a parent and child. Well, Danni has opened my eyes to a different kind of love, where he has shown me the meaning of true love. True love, between two very special people who knew how to embrace that love.
I am here to tell you a story, a story about a special man, about my son Danni Svenningsen
I was fortunate to have been given custody of my son, when his mother signed him over to me at the age of fourteen. I have always hoped that I had brought my son up on the right path, with respect and honour towards others. Just after he was sixteen, we moved to England, having brought our business across the pond. Danni ran the English side of the business, whilst I concentrated on the American side of business.
Danni was born in a small village in Norway; and spent many days out and about with his grandparents, which whom he loved. It was hard for him to leave his grandparents, but his mother decided that she wanted to go back to her homeland of America; and because of her uprooting Danni again, I feel he had it tough for a good many years living with her, that was until he came to live with me in New York.
In the late eighties I was introduced to Roxy, his partner; and after getting to know Roxy, it was then that I began to understand what love was; and what Danni and Roxy had which was so special. They had both fallen head over heels with each other, and like so many other relationships, they had good times and well as bad.

Sharing with all who were special to them, their good times and their bad, their funny times and serious and supported each other no matter what was thrown at them. I was so proud of my son Danni; and so privileged to have had him introduce me to Roxy.

Roxy was the best thing that had ever happened to my son, together teaching each other the true meaning of one's identity; the true meaning of sharing their love. Together they were strong, through all of life's obstacles, and they were never far from each other's sight. But I can tell you this now; one could not fully function without the other one besides them. They were both like lovesick teenagers, where I often had Danni phoning me for that fatherly chat.

We all knew that wherever Danni was, Roxy was never far behind; and together they have shown us, that they have one spirit, one heart and one soul.

I ask you, who is Danni Svenningsen?

He is a husband, a friend, and a proud businessman. He is a man who stood high above ignorance; and a man with a heart above all others, as he put others before himself. Danni is a peacemaker, a man of integrity; and his strength was his workplace, where his weakness was his love for his very dearest Roxy, for which he would do anything for.

Lastly, he was a son, and a true friend; and I am proud to say that Danni Svenningsen was MY son and my friend. You will be sadly missed son, and you will always hold a special place in the hearts of those you touched. Rest in peace Danni, rest in peace my son."

There was not a dry eye in the church, after Rik had finished his speech; and let everyone know just who his son was. My father held me so tight, as I could not stop crying, with Johnny still holding on to my hand, as Stuart, and Adam put their hands on each shoulder, from the row behind me. I think Rik's words hit my dad hard, as there was truth in his words; and I think my dad realised just how much he had missed out, sharing his time with me.

The vicar then cleared his throat, as he thanked Rik for the wonderful portrayal of his son, where he then told us that we would now place our son in the hands of heaven. We stood up, and as the bearers came to carry him out of the chapel, I placed my hand on the coffin and again told him that I loved him. With my father's holding me up, they placed me back on the arm of Johnny where I followed Danni out of the chapel, with everyone else following suit. As the crematorium was next door, they carried him out of the church and into the crematorium, taking him through the doors and placing him down; so that everyone could pay respects and say their final farewells, and then they left his close family to say their goodbyes. Forty minutes later, I stood up from my chair with my arm under Johnny's as I saw Danni go through the curtain and leave me for good. I turned to my father and sobbed on his shoulder, as he held me tight and told me he would always be there, and that Danni would always be with me. Rik then said that he would stay behind and collect the ashes, and then take them back to my home. It was arranged that we would have two urns, as Danni wanted to be placed in the grave of his Grandma and Grandpa; and the other urn given to me as

Danni always said he wanted to be with me too in beautiful Hove

Once everything was sorted, we then made our way to the Rainbow where it was closed for Danni's wake. Not everyone attended, but I knew most had other commitments, especially the celebrities. However, I was so thankful for their support and so thankful that they showed up. Danni was loved by a lot of people, and that day proved it.

I stayed in the bar until around 6pm, when I told Ellie I was going home. I told her not to waste a good spread, as she may as well open for the last four hours if she wanted. I asked her to let me know how much I owed her for the wake; and that I would pay her the next day, as I did not want any outstanding bills, in which I too thanked her for everything she had done.

Most of the family had now gone, with my father going back to Dover; and Rik heading back to the States, as he had a very early flight the next day. I looked at Johnny and then took his arm, looking him in the eye as I softly whispered to him to take me home, as I needed my bed.

"Come on then sweetie let's get you home, you do look tired and have had a very long day." He said, as he kissed his sister and told her he would call her.

I grabbed hold of Stuart and Adam; and thanked them for helping in all that they had done, as I told them I dearly loved them. They hugged me and told me to come down to Hove when I was ready, as they thought the break would do me good. I gave them both a kiss, as Johnny shook their hands, as he grabbed hold of my arm and gently got me outside to the awaiting cab. We then got in the cab and went home taking a bottle of champagne with us, much to the bafflement of Johnny as I had a cellar full of wines and champagnes.

"*I couldn't be bothered to go to the cellar honey, and Ellie didn't mind. Is that ok Johnny?*" I asked him.

"*Of course it is Roxy; I was just trying to make you smile. Come here, come and give me a hug.*" He replied.

We got inside the apartment, and I went straight to the couch where I slipped off my shoes. I told Johnny to get two glasses and to come and sit next to me, and chat to me even if it was nonsense chat.
We spent time chatting till about 11pm and catching up on stories, having the odd tear as well as a laugh. Johnny then got up and went into the kitchen where he fetched another bottle of champagne, took me by the hand and told me that it was best we go to bed. Johnny apologised to me, as he told me that he just presumed that he was to share my bedroom; and offer her comfort. I gave him a smile, telling him that it was ok; and that I would love his company. Getting into light conversation, I told him that if it were not for him and Stuart this last week, I do not know what I would have done. That having them both here made me feel safe, and it was nice having him stay with me; and how nice it is that he is still here.

"*So have I, I have enjoyed your company. This is the first time in all the years we have known each other that we*

have spent so much time together, and I am honoured."
He said, as he helped me up of the couch.
"I just hope Ruby is not mad at me for keeping you here, she must be anxious to have you home." I replied, still hurt that she did not come over. I thought we were friends; and one time I really needed her, she decided to pull a sicky of an excuse.
"Don't worry about Ruby, she has the business to keep her busy. She probably hasn't missed me anyway, what with being so busy." He replied, rather sarcastically.
"Is everything ok Johnny, I mean with you and Ruby." I asked, now wanting to find out if there were problems within their relationship.

He hesitated at first, then looked at me sheepishly and said.

"Ye,s everything is fine, just she has the apartments and I have the bar, and to be honest we hardly see each other lately. Well apart from when she comes over to the bar in the 'Yumbo Centre' to see me and have a drink or two."
"I think I can relate to that, when I was touring it was awful not seeing Danni. I was so glad when he took time off and was able to come up and see me, but without him I was a total loss. Oh, Johnny what am I going to do, he has gone; and you will be going soon." I said as I began crying.
"Hey Roxy, it is ok; I promise you that you will not be alone. You are coming back with me to the Canaries, aren't you?" He asked.

"I need to spend some time here first, and there is the reading of the will on Wednesday." I replied.
"I will phone back home; and see if my manager can look after the bar till the Thursday, and I will let Ruby know as I don't think she will be too pleased to look after it for me all on her own; what with her business as well." He said, in a voice that told me there was some concern within his relationship.

He poured me a drink as I sat on the bed, and then he sat next to me. I told him I would need to go for a shower as it had been a long day. He asked for one too, and I told him he could either use downstairs or get in after me. He said that he would wait, as he didn't want to really leave me alone for too long, just in case I got a little bit emotional again, and he wanted me to know that he was just in the other room should I need him.
I took my shower, and then left my make-up off as I placed a bathrobe around me. I towel dried my hair as I called into Johnny that he could now jump in, and not thinking twice that it was Johnny. He undressed in front of me, dropping his clothes to the floor, and then as I caught a glimpse of him in the bathroom mirror, I got embarrassed.

"I am sorry Johnny, please forgive me. I totally forgot myself and thought you were Danni. I am so sorry honey." I said as I ran out of the bathroom.

Johnny then put his head around the door as he shouted it was ok, then closing the door behind him.
Shortly afterwards he came into the bedroom, where he

told me everything was ok and that it was he, who should have apologised. I just could not get the thought out of my head about seeing him totally naked, as I looked into the mirror then realising it was not Danni. He sat on the bed and removed his towel, and I could see he had put on his boxer which was much to my relief. He reached for his glass, and then reached for my head. I was still very red and embarrassed, but I climbed into his arms, where we finished our drinks and fell asleep. We spent a few more days together, before we made our way to the solicitor's office; where it was time to hear the reading of Danni's will.

Prior to going to the solicitor's, I had said goodbye to my dad and Rik, Stuart and Adam; it was just now just me and Johnny; and having him as company helped me a lot during those day's I spent with him. Slowly he began to make me feel comfortable, as he brought out a few smiles here and there when I was feeling sad.
We sat in the garden as we chatted again about the past, and how I should take time out before thinking about my future. All the time he stayed with me, he only ever shared my bed when I was an emotional wreck, and he comforted me until I had fallen asleep.
Most times that I had woken up during the early hours of the morning, I awoke to find he was no longer in bed next to me; had he gone into the other bedroom.
He gained a lot of respect off me those weeks that he stayed with me, as I slowly got my act together.
Johnny was by my side each time we went into the Rainbow; and stayed by my side when I sat on the bar stool at the end of the bar, as the customers kept asking

when was Roxy Garcia going to come out of retirement and perform on the Rainbow stage again.

Johnny was able to stay with me until the reading of the will, which I was pleased about, as I did not want to put on everyone, or have anyone feel sorry for me.

Johnny made sure that he informed everyone of how I was doing; and told them that he would stay with me as long as I needed him there. This put the rest of my family at ease, as they still had lives to live; and needed to get on with their own lives and leave me to grieve.

Finally, it was time to leave to go to the solicitors; and Johnny made sure I had everything I needed before he escorted me out of the apartment; and drove me to our solicitors' office not knowing or having any clue what was in store for me.

I had taken my seat, oblivious to who else was in the room as our solicitor began reading Danni's will.

'*To my brother and sister Jake and Sophie, I leave the sum of two million dollars each, to be put in a fund in which my father will have full control over until they reach their twenty fifth birthday.*

To my father I leave my half of the Svenningsen business; and all of my shares that I lawfully purchased from our ventures that we shared together, with the knowledge that I am very proud to have been your son; and I am thankful for everything you have done for me in showing me what a father's love really meant.

To my mother I leave this message. Love has no bounds and no agendas. To love someone comes from the heart and not from a cheque book. A parent's love should always be unquestionable; and should always be above all others. If you thought about others and loved them first before thinking of yourself, then your heart would be the richest of all women; and of all who have the rights to be called a mother. For that which you have shown me, I leave you the sum of one dollar, for each year you allowed me to stay in your home, before selling me out; and that being the total sum of six dollars. It was my father who has brought me up, knowing I am loved and thankful for my future that he allowed me to live. I am a Svenningsen like my father; and like his father before him which you will never take away.

To my darling Roxy, I leave you my half of the business with Steve. I also leave to you my cars and my apartment; and all of my possessions. I leave to you my bank accounts, and in doing so I leave to you forty million pounds, which is my untouched earnings from my father's business, which is in that said bank account.

I would lastly like to say to my dear Roxy. Thank you for helping me to know love, to feel love, to understand love; and importantly for showing me what it is like being loved and to fall in love.

Thank you for allowing me into your life and into your world; and to have been allowed to have been a very special part of your life; and of course, for accepting me as your husband, now legal by law, as I know you are still a born worrier. Please know this, that I will always be with you Miss Roxy, as I am with you in our past, our present, and for eternity.

Your dearest husband and friend... Danni"

That brought a tear to my eye, where I reached for a handkerchief, as Johnny held me tight as he helped ease

my crying and shaking, as I heard Danni's words.
Once he had read everything out to those who attended, and then asked if anyone contested the will. A tallish man at the back stood up and approached him, saying he was the representative of Elizabeth Fontaine, formerly Elizabeth Svenningsen.

"Elizabeth Svenningsen, who on earth is that?" I asked Johnny, now looking puzzled.

Then it dawned on me, it was his money grabbing bitch of a mother, and just like her background, she was out to see what she could get out of her son's will. There were a few remarks made at the hearing; and as it had got out of hand it was then that it was decided that this would have to go to court, with it being for a judge to decide over, due to his mother contesting the will.
I was gutted as this was all I needed, what else could happen to me?
Once we were dismissed, I went up to her representative and said.

"Tell that bitch she will get fuck all from me, as she has not wanted to know her son all these years, so go and tell her to crawl under the rock from where she came from."
"Roxy! leave it, she is just a parasite, a typical gold digger, leave it to the courts. Remember you have a lot of friends in high places, she is nothing." Johnny said, trying to get me to calm down

Johnny escorted me out of the offices; and told me that we should go back to the apartment to pack a bag.

"Let's see what flights available Roxy are; and let us book up as soon as we can. You go into the bedroom and pack a case or two, and let's get out of here." He told me. *"Fuck the available flights Johnny, let me get in touch with Dominic, he has a private jet."* I replied *"Dominic, who is that?"* He asked. *"He is a friend from the fashion world, we stayed with him one month in Dubai in his villa before doing a fashion show for him."* I told him. *"Very nice, and do you think he will fly you over?"* He asked.

"Let me quickly call him; and see what he is up to." I replied, as I reached into my bag for my phone.

I called Dominic, and he said he would sort it out. He needed to book airtime and a route and would get back to me within the hour, and as true to his word he did do. He told me that it would have to be tomorrow morning or the following day, as that's the earliest he could get. I told Johnny and then packed a case or two, as well as sorting out passports and money. I also telephoned Ellie to see if she would look after my home; and any court letters that arrived she was too open and let me know what they say.
Ellie said she would come straight over and pick up the keys, and if possible, she and Di could stay overnight. That evening Ellie came over and I showed her the run of the house, and the codes for the alarms and security

doors, and told her she could stay here with Di if she wanted. We all had a natter and catch up, and I then made my way to bed, leaving Ellie and Johnny downstairs to catch up.

Johnny stayed downstairs, and it was not until he brought me up a cup of coffee that I realised he never came upstairs, which I was happy about, as I did not want people to think there was anything different going on, to what was the truth showed.

I knew there were people out there just waiting for a bit of juicy gossip; and would not think twice than to smear my good name with bitchy comments just to line their pockets for a good story. I put everything to the back of my mind, as I then showered and got myself ready to have a long deserved break away from England; and away from prying eyes and flashing camera's from the paparazzi.

I spent two months with Johnny and Ruby, but in the end, I needed to get back home. Ruby had started to change, as she was not as interested in the bars as she used to be. She was now putting all her efforts into her guest apartments and then she began separating herself from me and Johnny.

I think in the whole two months we spent one full week together; and even then, she coaxed me to go to the bar to see Johnny and have a good time.

It was then that I decided I have to come home, as I thought it was because of me that things were like this. I gave Ruby and hug and kiss and told her to keep in touch, but like a cold heartless bitch she just told me if she had time she would and then told me to have a safe flight. Johnny then drove me to the airport, where on the way he apologised for her attitude and how she was.

"She is going through a bad time Roxy; I am not sure if it is because of the change of hormones, but please be a little patient with her." He said, in her defence.

"Bollocks Johnny, she was absolutely rude towards me, and there was no need to be. If she did not want me there, then she should have said so and I would have booked into a hotel; and this is nothing to do with hormones. She really did not want me there with her, as I have felt it this last fortnight. And what about packing me off to the bar every night, what's that all about?" I asked, now infuriated with her, apologising for being rude by swearing
"Told you it's her Roxy, she is on strange grounds at the moment. She has been like it for a while, so give her time." He replied.
"Don't get me wrong Johnny; I was glad of your company, and stuff, because I had a wonderful time with you. It was fun wasn't it Johnny, me lending a hand at the bar, just like old times when we were sat at the end of the bar people watching? Then the two of us going for a meal together, whilst your manager took over for a few hours; with you keeping my head above water, as you constantly made me laugh" I replied, as I had flash backs at our time with each other, but still annoyed how he was backing her up, when it was obvious, she was being a mean old queen to him.
"It sure was sweetie, oh how I miss London. And it was so nice spending time with you here on the island; seeing

you laugh and joke was such a blessing. Even in your quieter moments, I saw that flash of Roxy sparkle in your eyes when another glass of champagne came your way."
He replied, as he smiled contently at me.

When we got to the airport, we sat around for a while and had a bite to eat. My phone rang and it was Dominic letting me know we had an hour turn around, so I had best to get my things checked in as soon as I could. Johnny took me to the private section of the airport to check in; and go through customs where Dominic was waiting. I hugged Johnny and thanked him for everything he had done for me both before Danni's passing; and whilst on holiday these last two months; and for his support through my hard time, and for helping me with Danni's affairs.
I then looked him in the eye; and said to him as he held me tighter.

"You are a very special guy Johnny; and I love you because you are just that. I do not know what I would have done without you these last few months; and for that I am forever grateful. You will always hold a special place in my heart, and please try not to make it too long before you come and visit me in London or Brighton."

As I kissed him on the lips, he held me tightly putting his head onto my shoulder.

"I love you to Roxy, so please always remember that. You are a very special person, with an incredibly very special heart. Be safe and have a nice flight, I will call

you later this evening if that's ok?" He replied, not wanting to let go of me.

"Sure honey, you take care, and please do not be a stranger to London." I said, as I brushed his face with my hand before landing him a kiss on the cheek.

He looked at me and just smiled, as he again hugged me never wanting to let me go. I then told him again that I loved him, and I then heard him say I love you back, as I was also sure I just about heard him say more than you will ever know. I was not completely sure as the airport announcements were going off. I looked around and waved him goodbye; and I had never seen such a lonely looking man in my life. I am sure if he had had the energy, he would not have let me go, and I am sure if I had asked him to come back with me, he would have done so as quick as a flash.

My bags were taken from me, as I was driven to the plane, where Dominic greeted me and said that as soon as I was settled and checks had been done, we would be on our way to queue up for departure. I just sat there in my seat, reminiscing about the past few months; and how much of a bitch Ruby was and how much an angel Johnny was for helping me to cope, and for making me remember all the good times, and how I should laugh more often.

Dominic then came into the cabin, where he told me we were about to taxi and head back home.

Within a few hours I had landed at Gatwick, where I then had a private car waiting for me, I told Dominic that I would post him a cheque that very evening, once I had sorted myself out.

I was finally home and as I dropped my bags, I just looked around and thought how quiet it was.

Ellie had left me a note telling me everything had been ok, and she had gone back to her own home the night before. The keys would be at the bar and I could pick them up when I went in to visit them; and they couldn't wait to see me again. I then noticed the picture of Danni next to my side lamp table; and as I picked it up I fell to my knees as I held the picture close to my heart, as I embraced the photograph I slowly began crying as I called out his name.

As I began to get myself together, I picked myself up as I sat down and put my feet up, when the reality took over. I sat there crying my eyes out to the silence, knowing my Danni would no longer be coming home.

Noticing that the telephone answer machine was still flashing, I got up and walked over to the dresser as I then pressed the play button to hear if there were any important messages.

Listening to all of the phone messages started to bring memories flooding back, so I then picked up the mail that was piled up on the coffee table.

I must have sat there for at least thirty minutes or more crying, holding a picture of Danni close to me.

I did not go out that evening, I just ran myself a bath, listened to a bit of music as I had a glass of wine on the patio watching and listing to the sounds of London.

I then made my way to the bedroom, climbed into bed and just cried, as I then caught an odour of Danni's cologne come sweeping into the room, as I then cried on his pillow.

Around 11pm the phone rang, and as promised it was

Johnny. Again, I just burst into tears, as I told him this was the first night I had been alone, and I knew Danni would not be coming through the door.

He comforted me and told me that things would get better, and how it will feel very strange at first, but things would really get better as the days go by.

He was on the phone for about an hour comforting me, telling me he wished he had not let me go; wishing he was here with me now, as he didn't think I was ready to leave. But after yet more crying and a bottle of wine, I soon found myself dropping off, so I wished him a very good evening and thanked him again for keeping his promise in calling me to check on me.

We always ended up telling each other we loved one another, as it made me feel better to know that I did have people who cared, as Ellie was always there for me as was Stuart and Adam.

The next day I text Pip to see if he could come around and help me clean, as I could not face picking up the washing out of the laundry bin as there were a lot of Danni's clothes there. Like a trooper Pip got to me within the hour; and he told me to just sit down as he would deal with it. He made me a pot of coffee, as we first of all spend a few moments chatting, when he then picked up the laundry and began washing Danni's clothes.

Over the next few weeks, I went to the bar; and I was embraced by my little family in the royal circle.

I slowly began to live a life of a single woman; and my shopping trips were few and far between now, as I had no desire to want to go out and buy a new dress, or even a new pair of shoes, as I slummed around in guy mode around the house; and on the few times I went out it was with mixed feelings. Sometimes I would go out as Bobby; and on the days I was feeling a little better I would go out as Roxy. I had a few more television interviews; and one or two fashion shows, but I was now thinking of a life of retirement from the circuit. I needed to find out what I would like to do with my life, as I know Danni and I were thinking of opening a bar in our beloved Brighton and Hove.

I continued with the Wednesday nights; and called in Dixie to help, as Ellie had said she would continue with them so long as I was around. Wednesday was also the day in the week in which Ellie had off, due to the place still not being that busy, so I did not have to reschedule to another day. Dixie was a hit with the crowd and made lots of money, as well as having made a few acquaintances that started to fill up her little black book. I just thought why not, she lives in a house in a very good neighbourhood and she deserves it.

Then a few months after being home I received a letter from the courts regarding the will, I sat down and trembled as the date was in less than two weeks.

I really could not be bothered with this; and thought if she wins then good luck to her, as all I wanted was my home as it had happy memories; and I knew his mother would be demanding the whole lot. She was also fighting this, and she was using her wild card as the relationship between Danni and I being immoral, and perverse; and I told Ellie and Di about it and what it was doing to me; and it was Di who suggested I go and see Russell her lawyer, who helped her with her mom's will.

I did just that a few days later; and I presented him with all the information he needed. He told me that although we were a couple, but not to some people; and we had done things correctly, he did not see much of a problem. He then informed me that the wedding issue may be a big thing though, as the courts would not recognise the certificate from another country, but again not to worry about it as we were over the age of 21; and we were consenting adults.

It was then that I presented him with a certificate of a civil partnership, in which we took out privately back in the early part of May 2000 to legally bond our relationship, as well as provide bank statements for the last five years of our comings and goings proving we were a couple; and that both of our wages went into that account. I did have a separate account, which was for my drag shows; and that of my work at the rainbow in general. My television and modelling work salaries went into our joint account. This was good news as no one had heard about this, as Danni and I kept it to ourselves, having just a few people from our circle present.

When it was the day of the hearing, I looked around to see familiar faces. I recognised both the judge and the barristers; and I was put at ease knowing I would have a fair representation of character. It was not until I saw her lawyer that I worried, as it was the same guy, I had a go at when the will was being read.

The hearing took just under an hour with all evidence provided to the court; and when my lawyer presented my civil partnership, her heart nearly dropped to the floor. After much deliberation the judge came back and addressed us all, he told us he found no just cause in denying me to be the sole heir to Danni's will.

There was nothing out of place, and I had all the right legitimate documentation at hand, plus the fact Danni was an adult; and that his will was written and presented in the proper manner and whilst he was of sound mind. The judge then looked at his mother and called her all sorts of horrible names, all within the courts jargon which I did not understand. Telling her she had no rights under British law, or any other law to get her hands on what was not rightfully hers. Telling her what an awful mother she was, as she sold her son to her father for monetary gain, whilst he was still a child and how despicable that was.

He then ended up saying, that the court favours me and that the case was now dismissed.

She shouted abuse at both the judge and her lawyer; and then as we left the court room, she then looked at me and came for me as she shouted all manner of obscenities towards me. I just stood there; and as Russell held my arm I turned around and told him it would be ok, as again I looked at her and shouted.

"Do not you ever cross this bitch honey, if you had been half the mother you should have been, then do you not think, that Danni would have left you something?"

"You have not won yet, you perverted little freak." She cried.

"Get your fuckin face out of my space, before I rip your head off; and let me tell you something madam. You tried to steal your younger children's inheritance and

that did not work; and now you try to steal my inheritance given to me from my husband Danni, your lost son. You are just a sad twisted gold digger; and you will not win I assure you. Now get off that pedestal we call a tampon; and get the fuck out of my life, because I forewarn you, I will have the last laugh I promise you." I replied, now in a fit of dignified rage

"*Oh, sad am I; and what have you done for my son.*" She yelled.

"*How dare you. I gave him a home, a life, happiness and love. I gave him everything that he never got from you. I gave him a reason to live and be happy, now fuck off and leave me alone, or I will have you charged with harassment.*" I said, as I pushed my face into hers

I heard her lawyer tell her to calm down, as there was nothing she could do, everything was legal and above board; and the judge saw that; and that is why he made his judgment.

"*You could have at least had the decency to make sure I was ok; I am at least his mother.*" She cried, looking at me and using a handkerchief to wipe away her crocodile tears.

"*Wrong you were his mother, and you gave those rights up nearly thirty years ago. If I thought a facelift and a personality transplant would have helped, I would have readily paid for it madam. So instead of standing there in your fake Gucci shoes and a plastic face that has been*

278

done cheaply, why don't you crawl under the rock from which you came?" I shouted, now being held back my solicitor, as he told me to be calm and to walk away.

We were now getting a bit of a crowd watching us; and as the security asked us to leave, we were ushered outside by our lawyers. Then just on the top of the courts stairs she flared up again, so I just looked at her and shouted.

"I am more of a woman you will ever be; and more of a man you will ever get madam. Here take that, as this represents a symbol of each time you were his mother." I said, as I went into my purse and threw six pounds at her. *"What's this, you crazy bitch?"* She shouted, bending down to pick up the money
"It's a pound for every year you were his mother, sorry but I have no dollars and besides it's the weaker currency." I said, as by now Russell had got my arm and escorted me out of the courts.
"I have not finished with you yet, let me tell you that. I will have my day I promise you." She shouted.
"Be careful you do not burst a vessel, or you will need another face lift. And if you have any more facelifts, they will be transplanting your tongue to your vagina, so you have something decent to talk out of." I said, now having applause from some of the crowd.

As I was now being escorted down the steps by Russell, as she was still hurling abuse at me. I turned around and looked at her and told her to wind her neck in and to go to hell, as there was nothing more to say. I then left the

279

courts where Russell took me around the corner to have a coffee to calm down.

"Christ Roxy; I definitely would hate to be on the wrong side of you in an argument." He laughed.
"I am sorry Russell; she really wound me up. Thing is, if she had been nice, I would have possibly considered giving her something, but not as she was damn right rude. And living a life of cabaret and heckler's, certainly helped me in that one." I replied, as I smiled at him

"Really Roxy, you would have actually given her some of your inheritance?" He asked

"No honey, just joking. I owe her nothing and neither does Danni. She has not wanted to know Danni since he was about eight, as Rik looked after him whilst she swanned off sleeping with other guys to find a richer husband. She would get nothing off me, not even if she came to me on bended knees." I told him.

Russell then brought me a coffee; and asked me what I would do next. I didn't know as such and I told him so, but I had all the time in the world. It was then that her lawyer came in and spoke to Russell, when he asked if he could sit down with us. I asked him if that was wise, after all he was still her representing lawyer

"The case is closed, she has lost and she needs to deal with it. The law was on your side for more than one reason; and you had supporting evidence that supported your claim. Congratulations, I would now forget all that

has happened Mrs Svenningsen, but I will say you played a blinder in there; and I would hate to be on the wrong side of you Mrs Svenningsen." He said, now pleased he was free of such a bitching match.
"*Oh don't I know it, my mouth will get me into trouble one of these days, you mark my words. Think it is the quiet life for me now, get out of the limelight for a while.*" I laughed.

It was about six months I waited, before I heard anything from my solicitor and from probate; and in the letter alongside the will, it listed all that I was entitled too.
I got to keep my home and the monies that were in Danni's bank account; and our joint account was now freed; and I could now get all monies transferred to my own bank account when I was ready to do so.
I just needed to sit down before I collapsed, as Russell listed everything in a monetary value alongside each item that was left to me.
I was left a staggering £47.5million, and all I needed to do now was take all the information and court letters to the bank to have Danni's name removed and to have those accounts transferred to just my account.
I could then use the account, as for the last six months or so I had been using my own account. I sat down and cried; and for the first time I got religious as I said.

"*Oh dear lord, I would gladly give every penny of this away, if only you gave me my Danni back. What am I going to do with all this fucking money, with no Danni to help me spend it? If at all you are the true god, then please send my Danni back to me; and you can have everything I own."*

I could not believe that his mother even questioned my Hove apartment, stating that it was purchased through ill gains and prostitution.
Of course, she had no proof, except that of being a sad twisted bitch, and what a battle she gave, because at one point I thought I was going to end up losing everything. It was only when she marked my own property as being that of her son's; and of course, blackening my name, that the judge and the court could see how desperate she was to have control of money, which was her only concern, as she never once painted a good picture of her so called son Danni. No, she was money orientated, and thought that she had the sole rights to Danni's estate; and that she was above the laws of England, even calling the judge a few nasty names; and being so close for the judge to rule a ruling of contempt against her.
I put all the letters and deeds to the house in the safe in our bedroom, which included my diamond jewellery and my other bits from Hove. Then once I had put everything away, I climbed onto the bed and wrapped the quilt around me with Danni's picture held closely by my heart; and I just cried continuously until I could cry no more. I was still able to smell his cologne in the bedroom and on his clothes in the wardrobe.
I called his name so many times until I ended up not having a voice, or a dry side to my own pillow.
I stayed in our bedroom for five days, not answering the phone or replying to messages. It was only when I decided to get up to make a cup of coffee, that when the

phone began to ring, that I looked to see who it was and from that I answered. It came up on caller display as '*Danni's work*', so not thinking twice I answered it.

"*Danni is that you honey?*" I cried
"*Roxy it is Steve; I need to see you. Is there any chance I can call in and see you later this afternoon?*" He asked, not quite getting to grips who Steve was.
"*Steve, Ermm Steve from the office?*" I answered

"*Danni's business partner Roxy, it is important can I please come and visit you this afternoon?*" He again asked.
"*Oh yes, I am sorry Steve my mind is all over the place, sure you can call in just phone me when you get here.*" I replied

I then put the phone down, and as I stood up, I looked into the mirror above the fireplace and what I saw was not a pretty sight. I thought I had best take a bath and a shave, as I looked very rough and nothing like my old self. I dithered around the apartment tidying up as I went along, and soon got myself back into ship shape.
That afternoon Steve came to see me, in which he asked what my interest in the business was; and what I would be doing with my share, as I looked over the shares and ongoing contracts. Not really remembering, all that was contained in the will, Steve reminded me that they had equal shares, as they always got on well together; and Danni always stated that he did not need one, to have a smaller percentage than he did. Looking further into the contracts, and shares, Steve had tallied everything up and

according to his records, Danni's share was worth around £10 million. Steve then said that on paper it was correct, but in theory it was not, which made me slightly confused. He told me that on the day that Danni left the office to go home, that fatal night he had wished he could have persuaded him to stay, just so they could go over the future contracts that needed completing, they had put in a contract to the Dutch, with a value of around £25 million. After the funeral, the contracts were signed and their company was successful in the bids; and that opening amount of £25 million which was agreed, could now exceed the original figure and easily end up netting them four or five times the price in profit alone, as he then removed those contracts from his briefcase for me to see. Not being that savvy with regards their business, I asked Steve, that before they both put in their offer, as I scratched my head with the pen, and then wrote some figures down. I then asked him, that before they clinched the deal, his share was only worth £10 million, in which Steve told me that I was correct, that Danni had put in £10 million, of his own money into the business, alongside him, with his wife putting in the other £5 million. He told me that in theory, I also had an entitlement to fifty percent of the deal, when contracts had completed, and properties had been sold, then asking me what plans if any do I have, and what can he do to help me with these plans.

"In theory the business owes Danni £10 million, because that is the money that was taken from his account, to be placed into the business and towards the Dutch contract. The work that you and Danni achieved on that day was

284

only the signing of contracts, as no work had yet been started. You yourself went along with this business deal without any of Danni's other monies. You yourself put up the collateral for this investment, because Danni obviously could not sign anything due to unforeseen circumstances. So, I therefore put to you a plan to buy me out; and to buy me out for the amount that will be set in my letter from the solicitor. I will settle for the amount of £10 million and no more Steve. This is now your venture; and I hope you have a success at it without Danni. I have no reason to profit from the hard work you and your team will do in the future, so will get my lawyer to make a note of that, which by the way is for your own protection, not that I will change my mind. I just want everything done right, and by wavering my rights to future work, tells you I am not after something, that in theory is not mine to begin with." I replied, as I then sat back and placed the documents on the coffee table. "*Christ Roxy, are you sure? You are throwing away your rights to the contract to your fifty percent, are you really sure about this? You would be a very wealthy person, something that should be thought of hard and long.*" He asked, looking quite bewildered.

"*The way I see it Steve, is I am not throwing away any rights. Danni only signed the deal with you; and as far as I am to believe, the work does not go ahead till just after Christmas of this year. Therefore, I waiver any rights, as this is solely your responsibility. I do not know anything about property and business development like you; I can only cope with decorating. I am more a celebrity and stiletto heel kind of girl, than that of a business and steel toe cap boots kind of girl, as I left all*

285

these matters to Danni. And just for the record, I am already very wealthy, all I want to know is do you have the money to buy me out; and more importantly do you want to buy my shares?" I told him, now putting my point across, with the knowledge I was not and would not scam him.

"Yes, Christ yes Roxy, I do want to buy you out; and I can get you the whole amount you ask for in around twelve months' time, once we have finished the Dutch programme if that is ok?" He replied, still amazed at what I had proposed.

"Right let us shake on it then Steve; and let us make a deal today and finalise matters. I will inform my lawyers of our meeting today, and of my proposals; and we will arrange a meeting very soon." I replied, glad that we had come to a fair and just arrangement.

We both shook on the deal, and then he told me I should be a businesswoman, as I think logically; and I am not out to fleece anyone. We then spoke for a while as he asked how I was coping; and I told him it was very hard that I had good days as well as bad. He told me that if I ever needed anything I knew where he was, and that he and wife were only a phone call away. I thanked him for that, and told him also not to be a stranger, as I classed them as family. He stood up and made his way to the door, hugging me before he left and telling me to be strong. I closed the door behind him and lay against it, shaking as I had just realised what I had done. I had never been so patient and calm like that in a while, and the aftershock just got to me. I knew Danni would not have been annoyed with me about what I had done, he knew I had no clue about property management or indeed renovation; and he knew I would have done the best thing for myself. I quickly picked up the phone and called Russell on his private line, asking him to make an emergency appointment for me.

It was arranged that I see him the next day at lunchtime, in the bistro we had that coffee together on that day of the court hearing.

I then decided I needed to eat properly, as not having anything but toast this past month was not enough; and it was now taking its toll on my body. I chilled out for a while before getting changed again to get ready to go out; and I thought about going to my favourite Italian restaurant. Having arrived I was given my usual table, where I sat there thinking back to when Danni and I used to call in; and the things we said to each other and the laughter we made. I pictured him sitting there looking over at me, and some of the faces he used to pull to make me laugh; and how very well-groomed he always was, and how he never ever let me down once.

Once my meal had arrived, I struggled to get through it, so I called for the bill and asked them if they would get me a cab. I made my way to the Rainbow, where upon getting there I looked at Ellie and she just knew.

She came over to me and told me not to worry, as she put her arm underneath mine and walked me to the end of the bar. I told her I tried to eat, but it was no good on my own, so I had to come here. I told her that I felt safe and contented here; and hope she did not mind, then promising her, that I would not get drunk or emotional, that all I really wanted was a little bit of company.

Ellie was such a sweet girl, a diamond she was, as she told me that I do not need a reason, as the doors were always open for me; and that I could go there anytime, even if it is to sit at the end of the bar and gaze into space, as I was still family and the rainbow was still my home from home. She knew I was having a bad day, so she put me at ease.

I stayed at the pub until closing time, and then ordered a cab to take me back home. Ellie asked me if I wanted her to come and stay with me, but I told her it would be fine. I got back home; and went straight to bed going through my usual routine of locking up and saying goodnight to Danni. The next morning, I was bright and cheerful, as I saw the sun coming through the window. I got myself ready and after doing a few things, I drove into the city. Once I had been met by Russell, I explained what Steve had said to me; and I then asked him to contact him to make an appointment for a meeting between us and Steve and his lawyer, when he told me he would do this straight away that afternoon; and then asked me what I was up to. I informed him that I had nothing planned, that I am getting by; and that I may contact my friends Adam and Stuart and go to Hove for a while.

He thought this was a good idea, and then told me that it had been nearly twelve months to the day, that I had lost the love of my life, asking me how I was doing in the process. He told me that I seemed to have managed but had lost my sparkle that he so loved to see. Then telling me that if there was anything he could do, then I only need ask him. I thought him rather sweet, when he told me that he thought both Danni and I were fine people; and very special friends to himself.

"Best friends and better clients don't you mean? I am ok, it is a slow road, but each day gets better. I just have to learn to be on my own; and I do have Margaret as well as the Rainbow and my family." I told him, with just the slightest of sarcasm.

"That's more like it Roxy, however, I mean it as I am here for you if things get too much." He replied.

"Thank you, Russell, thank you so much. Now do not forget to call me when you can set up a meeting, I want this done and dusted as soon as possible." I told him.

He assured me he would get on with it as soon as he got back to the office; and I should go away for a few days and chill. So, once he had left, I decided to text Stuart, and asked if it was ok to spend a few days with them. Surprisingly enough I had a text right back; and he told me that our room had never been slept in and that it would be made up ready for when I arrived.

Those few months before the anniversary of losing Danni, I spent it in my London home and in Hove with the boys. Johnny's calls were getting less and less; and I hardly heard from Ruby anymore. I no longer hosted the Wednesday nights, as I now passed it over to Dixie.

I had now hung my hat up on the cabaret circuit, but I did every now and then, contribute in appearing in the charity shows that the Rainbow and the cabaret circuit held. I was becoming more of a lady of leisure, where I was now spending fifty percent of my time as Bobby, only dressing as Roxy when I was going to the Rainbow or somewhere else that was special.

I had the meeting with Russell and Steve; and we drew up contracts stating that I would be paid the sum I asked for in the conversation I had with Steve, where it was agreed to be paid in full within the end of the notified twelve months that was stated in the contracts

That year had gone by very quickly; and it was the first year I had missed Christmas, as being on my own it did not feel right to celebrate something that you had such fun with when you were with someone you loved.

I never put up the tree, although I still had lots of cards and presents. I locked myself away; and wished for it to be over very quickly. I also had not scattered Danni's ashes; and though the nicest thing to do would be to scatter them on the anniversary of our wedding.

I replied to Stuart's text and told him that I would be down to Hove that Saturday. I let Ellie know that I was going away for a few days which she thought it was also a good idea. I made my way down to Hove, putting everything I could in the new Mercedes we had brought the year before the tragedy struck; and then I carefully packed his urn in the corner, with my cases surrounding it to protect it through the journey.

Upon arriving at my home, I let myself in to what was a very quiet home. It brought back memories of those days we both shared there, as I looked out of the window to the spot that we so loved. I was certain that I caught a glimpse of Danni on the lover's seat, waving to me to come and join him, which brought a smile to my face and a tear to my eye, but knew it was just another living memory that had washed amongst the memories that I held. I text Stuart and Adam to let them know I had arrived, and I would see them when they got home.

Adam text me back and told me that he would be home around six, as the shop closed at five thirty.

Shortly after Adam's text, Stuart text me to let me know he would be home between ten and eleven in the evening. I then made my way outside and sat in the garden, as I looked how well the boys had looked after the apartment and garden. I knew I had made a good choice by letting them use my home, as I knew it was in good hands. When Adam got home, he came into the lounge and saw me just sitting there in a little spot in the garden, as I had left the patio doors open. He came up to me and threw his arms around me in an instant, as he began to get emotional, telling me that he had missed me and that he was very worried. He too told me that I had lost my sparkle, that he knew I loved Danni, but he thought that it was time to let go now; and there was a time where I stopped wearing black; and put a bit of colour into my life. He was right I was still in the woe is me mode, but it was easier to hide away, than to confront it; and meet people. I was not ready for that sort of life yet, as he then told me that Danni would hate me being the way I was, and he would worry just as much as he was

"In my own time Adam, I still cannot let him go yet. I know it will just happen, so please forgive me if I am not myself, as I still need time. I am getting there slowly honey trust me." I replied.

He then sat with me for a while as he took a trip down memory lane with him. Then he told me he was going to prepare dinner; and that Stuart would eat when he got home. So off he went into the kitchen to prepare dinner,

as I went back indoors and started chatting to him.
He knew I only ate light, so he made me a nice chicken
and pasta meal, with my favourite green salad, then he
put a plate by for Stuart. When Stuart had got home, I
think I had gone through my second bottle of wine; and I
knew by now I should have been tipsy but it had no
effect. Stuart popped his head around the corner, and this
was the first time I had seen him all official and in his
uniform.
He looked so sexy, and very horny.
He asked me how I was, referring me to is favourite girl.
I then stood up and ran into his arms, holding him tight
as I rested my head on his chest, as I told him he had
caught him off guard, as I did not have my heels on.

*"You still look beautiful Roxy; come here I have missed
you."* He told me.
*"And I have missed you two as well, I always miss my
boys."* I told him, as my head was fixed firmly on his
chest.

I let him go, so that he could get changed, and then let
him have his supper. Once he had finished, we chatted
some more, and then I told them I was going to go to bed.
Looking at me, and having a cheeky grin about himself,
he told me that I was more than welcome to jump into
bed with them, if I was feeling lonely; and that I should
not go to bed thinking I have no-one. I thanked them,
telling them that I am quite happy to just crash out on my
own for a while. I then got up and gave Adam a kiss on
the lips and a big hug, then I made my way over to Stuart,
looking at him I had a tear in my eye as I gave him a kiss,

292

as I hugged him and bid them both a safe and loving goodnight.

Shortly after I had gone to bed, I heard them retire too; and before turning to go to their room, my door opened, as Stuart asked me if I was ok, as they were both very worried about you me. looking at me, in a way that only Stuart could look at me, which made me feel warm.

"Yes honey I am fine, I think I just need time to adjust. Being in this bed does not help, as I keep getting old memories coming back; and I have a constant smell of Danni's cologne in the room." I replied, as I lay my head down one more time.

He then came and sat on the bed next to me, now just with his t-shirt and boxers on. He chatted with me for a while as he made sure I was ok, then kissed me on the forehead and told me he loved me. I placed my hand on his chest and my other hand on his cheek, as I gave him a slow kiss back and thanked him for looking out for me. I then told him to go to bed; and that tomorrow we needed to have a chat and to consider changing things round. Not quite understanding what he meant, he asked me what I had in mind. I thought that it was pointless having the master bedroom, now that I was on my own, so I told Stuart, that he and Adam need to move into my room, as I did not think I would be able to get through the many thoughts I had of Danni, it was still too soon for me. And that he needs to tell Adam, that he needs to help me sort out the rooms, which will give them a little more room for their clothes and storage. Their room was adequate for me, still being a large room, and I just thought that they could do with the extra space, as I did notice, they had clothes hanging from the curtain rail, that could not fit into their wardrobes. Stuart then told me that he would sort it; and that I now needed to get some sleep.

This time as he kissed me my hand slipped, and as it did it landed on his groin feeling his now rather large bulge. I quickly pulled away apologising, where Stuart once again reminded me where they were, should I need a friendly shoulder or company.

It was not long before I fell asleep, which I think the wine also helped now taking affect.

The next morning Stuart woke me up with a cup of coffee; and told me he would be in the garden should I wish to join him, as Adam had already left and gone to work. He worked three weekends out of every four, so I was able to call upon Stuarts services when I needed to. I slowly drank my coffee and then got out of bed, went into the bathroom and washed all the make-up off my face and became Bobby. As I headed outside Stuart was sitting underneath the jasmine bush on the lover's seat, with just his boxers on as he was reading a paper, just like Danni used to. He bid me a good morning, and hoped I had a good night's sleep, in which I told him it was strange; and that I kept on tossing and turning; and that I still had not got used to sleeping alone. He then told me to give it time, as it took him two years to get over his grandma's passing, even though it was a different situation to my own. Then telling me that he still has his quiet moments and thinks of her brushing his hair. That he still can smell her perfume; and hear her soft voice. I thanked him for those kind words and memories; and told him that I am almost there, as I know I have to let go and start living my life. That at the moment, Danni is still at the fore front of my mind.

He then told me that there was more coffee in the pot should I want another, and there was some toast there too, a little cold but I should eat, as breakfast is the most important meal of the day. Now coming round a little, as the fuzzy head was going away, I asked him to pour me a coffee; and that I loved cold toast, as I sat down next to him. He told me that he thought I had lost weight, but he also knew it was expected due to my situation. I sat next to him, as he poured me a coffee and I buttered a slice of toast. Then as I sat back, he asked me to look at him, where again he asked if I was ok.

I told him I just felt drained and lost, that Johnny and Ruby are in the Canaries and I no longer hear from them; and he and Adam are down here in Hove. All I had left now of my family was Ellie; and that it is now pretty lonely back in London, as I hardly see anyone like I used to. He then put his arm around me and pulled me towards him, where I lay my head on his chest, and put my arm around his waist. As I looked up at him, I gave him a gentle kiss on the lips; and only a short one as I thought those days had since passed where we became intimate; and I knew it was wrong knowing he was settled with Adam.

We sat there for a while just holding each other, when Stuart asked me about the things I had got on my mind; and if I am that lonely in London why don't I move back down to Hove. As we were chatting, I mentioned to him that I was thinking of buying a bar, as it was something Danni and I spoke about before the accident, now thinking maybe Stuart had hit on the right note with moving. He thought that it was a great idea, and did I have any thoughts about when and where that would happen. It was still but a thought, when his idea seemed to touch a nerve, but as strange as it seemed, I could not get myself to live back here, as the memories are too much for me to cope with, so I would have to look for somewhere else, where I could make my own memories. Well, that is how I feel now as I don't know what I will be feeling in a months' time or two at that. I told him not to worry, as I was not the kind of person to ask him or Adam to leave, and I hoped he know that. I just needed a new adventure; and with the plans and ideas in my mind, I knew I would have a lot to think about. I then asked Stuart if he would like to accompany me to Danni and my favourite spot on The Downs, so that I could spread Danni's ashes, as it was about time it was done. He told me that he had no problem and that I could ask him for anything today, as he was there just for me. He also told me how nice it was to see me as Bobby, as it was a rare thing, but how nice it was and how I still had kept my looks. I turned around and lay on Stuarts lap, as I brought my legs up and rested them on the seat.

Stuart placed his hand on my knee as again we just lay and sat there chatting. My hand would often sweep against his face, as I told him how sweet he was, and I would often feel something stirring in his pants, which was never really anything new, as that was what my boys were like anyway. Nothing happened though, and it was just nice to flirt without the innuendo of sex; and it was just nice being able to chat and be held by one of my boys, who still watched out for me.

About an hour or so later we both decided to shower and get dressed, and then we headed out to the South Downs. The urn was still in the car, and so I drove to our favourite spot at Devils Dyke, where I told Stuart that I just needed a minute; and then as I was standing alone I opened the urn sprinkling Danni's ashes to the four corners. As I done this, I spoke to Danni and I told him stories about our past; and our happy times when I let my thoughts get the best of me, I went into a lovely trance as I imagined my Danni being here next to me, looking towards the horizon.

It was then that I felt a warm breath on my neck and a tingle down my spine and a strong small of Calvin Klein Eternity.

"*Danni is that you honey. You are home now Danni you are home my darling.*" I said, as I began looking around
"*Roxy are you ok, who are you talking to?*" Stuart asked.
"*It is ok honey; and please do not think I am crazy, but I think Danni is here.*" I told him, as my thoughts were now in the moment, of feeling Danni next to me.
"*Did you feel it as well then Roxy, the hairs on my neck stood up just as you scattered his ashes.*" He replied
"*Yes, I felt it honey, he is here with us; and he is home. My Danni is finally home.*" I said, as I ran into Stuart's arms and just let go of my emotions.

The strangest thing was, once I had scattered his ashes and cried, I felt ok. I had finally let go; and I knew that I would always have Danni's presence with me. I too was finally at peace in the knowing he was free; and he was safe. Stuart put his arms around me, where I sank into

297

them with my head on his chest. I then told him that I
wanted to go back home.

"Home Roxy, and which one is that?" He asked.
*"Home Stuart, my home and your home. You know the
Hove apartment."* I replied.

He took my hand; and then we made our way back to the
car, where we drove back home. Once we got back home,
I walked straight into the garden towards the end where
we used to nudie sunbathe; and just lay down on the
grass deep with my thoughts of what had just happened.
Stuart brought out a pot of coffee, and sat next to me;
and again, we chatted about the past, and this time I had
no tears as they were just happy thoughts. I lay on my
side looking at Stuart who then lay on his; and would
often take his finger and brush my nose.
We were like school children laying there chatting, and
being silly with each other, as Stuart began to make me
smile. We began talking about Adam, and both were
puzzled about his behaviour; because I thought he was
so much in love with Stuart. I kept telling Stuart that he
has made me feel a little bit uncomfortable in my own
home; and I did not know what to do for the better. I told
him there and then I wanted to go back to London, but
Stuart persuaded me to stay.
After another hour in the garden, Stuart told me that he
would have to get ready and shower, as he had to go to
work. We both went indoors, where I put on the
television, and Stuart jumped in the shower. Shortly after
he had gone into the bathroom; and as bold as brass he
just walked into the lounge with a short towel around his

waist. I asked him if he wanted me to fix him any supper, which he declined as they often went to the kebab house. He told me he would love a cup of tea though, so I went into the kitchen to make him a pot before he started his duty.

That weekend I stayed as Bobby; and it made a change just chilling out and tinkering in the garden. Stuart then came back in just in his boxers and sat down next to me, as I played mother and poured the tea.

He stayed like that for a further twenty minutes, before going back into the bedroom to put his uniform on.

When he was ready to go, I walked down the hall with him and then at the door he reached down towards me and kissed me on the lips. He told me he would see me in the morning; and not to wait up for Adam as he most likely would go to the club after work.

I found out from Stuart, that not only did Adam work in the menswear shop '*Tailored to Suit*' in Churchill Square, but he also took part time work in one of the bars. I just thought now wonder he is always shattered, but still thought he was avoiding me. Stuart then came back and said he had forgotten his keys; and blamed me for his lack of concentration which brought a smile to my face.

"*It is only because you wanted another kiss Stuart, you horny devil.*" I said, as I gave him a wink and a smile.
"*Well of course it was Roxy, now you be good otherwise I will have to come back and handcuff you.*" He laughed.

I again held him as he gave me a kiss and told me that he had to go. I waved him off and went back into the lounge, where it was champers and 'corrie'.

I did not wait up for Adam, but thought I am going to have to have a word with him, because he was supposed to have helped me move the rooms around.

Before going to bed, I quickly phoned Margaret and told her I would be over Tuesday afternoon to see her; and we could both go for lunch if she felt up to it.

She asked me if Stuart was ok, as she had not heard from him that week, in which I informed her he was on late shifts. She then bid me goodnight, and looked forward to Tuesday, in which I then went to bed.

I never heard Adam come home; and by the time I had woke up the next morning he had already left. I then went back to bed with a coffee, before again being woken up by Stuart who brought another one in for me. He sat on the edge of the bed and wished me a good morning, hoping I had managed to have a good sleep. Then Stuart made a move which surprised me, and I did not care as I did not stop him. He placed his arm around me and pushed me onto my back, when he then lay on top of me. As he started to kiss me, I placed my hands onto his chest as I slowly caressed it. I then felt Stuart get erect, as he pressed his cock firmly against me, kissing me passionately as he now pushed his hard cock on top of mine. With his legs straddling me, he slowly lifted up my t-shirt revealing my soft muscly breasts, as he put his hands inside to feel them

"You are getting a nice pair of boobs Roxy, are you sure you are not on hormones?" He asked.

"It's the white wine and the champagne honey, they do wonders for your boobs, but I really must try and stop, as I do not want people thinking I am on hormones, as

you already thought I was. So, I think I may have to consider working out, or something like that." I replied. "*Well, you look gorgeous and sexy Roxy; oh my God I have missed this.*" He told me, now rubbing my chest.

"*Then shut up and do what you are supposed to do.*" I told him.

He then started to kiss my breasts as I put my hands on his head and stroked it. With his hands he caressed my tummy as he slowly placed his hands into my boxers. He then sat up and began to undo his shirt, when I took over, as I was not going to miss the chance to undress a copper. As soon as I undone his shirt, I removed it to reveal his soft hairy chest. I was quite taken back, as I never realised that Stuart had a hairy chest, especially in light of past events, as I thought he had just a little or none at all. He then put me out of my misery; and told me that he used to clip or shave his chest; and that he no longer did that anymore; and by not clipping, his chest hair seemed to have grown back thicker, now teasing me as he brushed his hand through his chest. I was also in a joking mood, as I told him that something was growing thicker; and it was not chest hair. I then placed my hand by his trousers, and undone his belt, but as usual I could not undo the top buttons, so Stuart took over and undone them for me. He then lay on his side as he removed his trousers, leaving him with just his boxers and a rather thick erection bulging out of it.
I decided to take over, where I laid him on his back, where I then straddled him and started to massage his chest and play with his nipples. I gently moved my

301

hands down his body following the line of hair to his cock, as I began finding his weak spots as I brushed him with my nails which I had not clipped short.

As I sat on his groin and felt his cock under my ass through his boxers, he put his arms out towards my waist and held me, stroking my waist until he got to my chest. He was in complete heaven as he moved from my breasts to my waist, and finally to my ass. He placed his hand into the back of my boxers stroking my ass, as he gently inserted a finger into me. I then lifted myself up as I told him to remove his boxers; and as he did so I removed mine now revealing my hard wet cock.

Stuart then grabbed hold of my cock, as I gentle straddled him taking him into my ass inch by inch.

My cock was getting wetter and wetter as I rode his cock; and felt him deep inside me. Stuart was now cupping his hands as he held onto my ass, to help me ride him faster and harder as his breathing got deeper.

"This is so damn good Roxy; you still have not changed in the slightest. You are one very hot sexy lady; and I never thought this would happen again. Oh God I love you Roxy." He said, as he stroked my body and kissed me

"I did not expect this either Stuart, as it has been such a long time, and you are so big honey." I replied.

"Not that much bigger than you Roxy, more like you are very tight; and it shows as I am going to cum soon." He said, as he held on to me tightly.

I lay back slightly feeling him stretch inside me, but this was too much; and he sat up. He told me he couldn't do it like that as he was beginning to get cramp, so he threw my arms around him and with me in them he got up and laid me on my back. As I was on my back, he got my legs over his shoulders, as he played with my breasts and again entered my ass with his thick wet cock.

"Oh Roxy I am going to cum, oh shit I am fucking cumming." He said, as his grip on my waist got tighter.

I held onto his ass cheeks as I felt him thrust until he thrusted to completion, holding onto my legs as he pushed and withdrew, letting some cum drip onto my balls as he thrust back inside me again and again.
He could not control himself, and I did not think he was going to stop. He just kept going and going, until he told me I had completely drained him.

"Christ honey, is there no stopping you? I did not think you were going to stop. You have almost worn me out with all that thrusting. When was the last time you and Adam made out, as I am sure I have had a few months' worth there, honey?" I asked, as I no longer worried about making out with him, and with Adam not being there also.
"It's been about six months now Roxy, not sure what is going on with him. He is working nearly all the time now, and I am still on split shifts." He replied.
"Well, I hope things are ok honey, and I am not complaining as you did me good and proper." I told him.

He went bright red; and then I told him it was not finished as it was now my turn. I then got him to lay on his back, as I gently inserted my wet cock into his ass. Once inside him, I noticed it was not long before he got erect again, so I thrust myself into him harder than usual. I had his legs opened wide as I held onto them, and I worked his tight hole deeper and harder.

At some point I knew it was a little too hard, as he made a yelping noise, but still enjoyed it.

Each time I pulled out of him, and then thrust back inside him, he was in heaven as he jerked his cock again. I would then stop as I rested his legs against my breast, and then just took hold of his cock.

With all of the wetness I felt between his ass; I slid my hand there and soaked up some of the juices, then place it on his cock and just rubbed the head of his cock.

He got so excited and many times told me to stop as he would certainly not be able to stop as he was going to cum. I did this off and on, bringing him almost to completion; and then just stopped as he begged me for more. I could also feel him clench his ass, which felt so nice against my cock, but after such a long time I told him I could not hold on anymore. I told him to hold onto my waist, as I thrusted a few more times until I emptied my load into his hot ass; and then with his legs now off my shoulders, and firmly by the side of my waist. I placed my hand over his cock; and again, I rubbed the head of it until he could not hold on any longer.

With his breathing getting heavier which told me he was close to shooting; and the moans he made begging me to go faster, I grabbed tightly onto his cock as he then shot his second load into my hand, with his legs now trembling as he went into a muscle spasm.

We then just lay there for a while as I was still stroking

his cock, draining his entire load. I then lay by him and kissed me on the lips, holding me towards him as he straddled my waist, as his load dripped onto me; as he then leaned forward as he thanked me for a wonderful time, and he hoped that I also enjoyed it too.

That weekend when we were alone, we made love when we could. Adam seemed to be coming home later and later, and although he texted me to say he was ok and running late, I was slowly distancing myself from him. I felt he was changing, and he no longer wanted to be here when I was. But that did not stop what Stuart and I had; and in the back of my mind, I knew either Adam was cheating on Stuart, or he was just avoiding me.

Sunday night I decided that I would go back home Monday morning, I text both of them to tell them I would not be here when they got home; and I thanked Stuart for all he had done for me.

It was a further twenty minutes, before I got a text back from Adam just saying ok, but Stuart asked me to wait ten minutes as he was passing by; and he wanted to see me before I left, so I waited a little longer for Stuart; and when he arrived, I heard the door fling open as he came running into the lounge. Standing there in his police uniform, I could have ripped it off him straight away. He came towards me and gave me such a big hug, that I thought he was going to break all of my bones.

"Thank you Roxy, for such a wonderful weekend, I have really enjoyed myself; and have enjoyed having you stay over with me. Please come and visit soon, as it is a pleasure to always be in your company. I do apologise for Adam, I have no idea what the hell is going on with

him" He said, as he embraced me, picking me up so I could be at his level to kiss him.

"*Do not worry honey I will; and do me a favour… sort that bloody Adam out, as something is not right; and you can tell him from me, that I am not happy one bit with a one word text either.*" I replied, mad at the fact Adam did not have a care in the world, or the decency to come and see me to sort things out. Being furious was an understatement, as I could have bloody wrung his neck for what he was doing, not just to me but to Stuart as well.

"*Will do Roxy, but please do not go back to London tomorrow before I* come home. Let me please see you off, before I go to bed." He said, as he kissed me on the cheek, and gave me another hug.

I agreed that I would wait until he got back from his shift; and thanked him for wanting to see me off safely.

I quite often went down to Hove that first year, but each time I went I could sense there was something in the air that was not right. I just had a gut feeling; and I was not often wrong when I had those feelings.

Although I was still pondering over the thoughts about moving down, my gut feelings proved right, as Adam had been seeing someone else behind Stuarts back; and had since asked Stuart to move out. Not having the decency to ask me first, he just went ahead and gave Stuart notice; and as Stuart did not want to worry me with yet more drama, it was his mother who informed me of what had been going on.

I decided that I had to go down and sort out this mess; and I had decided that I would make this visit my last visit, before finalising things back in London, as I was now determined to move back to Hove and leave the bright lights of London to the other queens.

As I let myself in the apartment Adam was in the kitchen, where he looked at me and just said hello in a sharp cold manner, which was so unlike him.

Yes, Adam had indeed changed, as there was no more pleasantries or respect, as no longer did he think of calling me Miss Roxy, or even him running up to me to give me a hug. No, he was as cold as ice, which was what I felt with Ruby a few years ago.

I greeted Adam, asking how he had been, when he just told me that he was fine; and that there were a few things he needed to ask me. Now intrigued, I asked what it was he needed to ask, as I told him to sit down. Then looking at him before he got a word in, I told him that I thought I knew what he was going to say, that he was no longer with Stuart, or maybe it was a fact that he had been messing around with someone else.

"I don't love Stuart like I used to Roxy, I need someone here with me all the time. To be able to go to the cinema, or for a meal, just like you and Danni did." He said, as bold as brass.

"Don't you dare bring Danni into this Adam, he worked through the day; and sometimes through the fuckin evening, so don't bring him into it, because he never cheated on me. And when I was on the road, he was left alone, but it gave him no reason or excuse to sleep around behind my back. You talk things through Adam, not just jump into the nearest bed that has an active cock

waiting for you, like a cheap slut." I said, now vexing some anger to him using Danni as a scapegoat.

"*I don't believe you have said that Roxy, it just happened; and I fell in love with this guy.*" He told me.

"*You should have finished with Stuart first then, before getting involved with someone else. I knew there was something wrong with you, as you were distant each time I came down. You were not the boy I once knew, and whatever happened to texts and chatting?*" I told him, still very angry at the backstabbing nature that had occurred.

"*Well, Stuart worked most nights; and I got lonely all on my own Roxy. I decided to go out as I did not want to just sit at home doing nothing; and it was there I met this guy. We have been seeing each other for over a year now; and it has got serious. I was going to ask you if he could move in here with me; and ask Stuart to leave.*" He said, as though he had no care in the world.

"*Really Adam, well here is my answer. 'Fuck off.' I let you have this place rent free because you were with Stuart; and that was the only reason. This is not a brothel for you to bring back your shags when you please, so the answer is no. If you are serious about this guy, then move in with him, because I am not turfing Stuart out just because you no longer want him, as you have a new fuck buddy. You move out, as it is the least you can do. And do not think I will not know because next week, I shall move back in here.*" I said to him, now very irate...

Adam was dumbstruck at what I had said, and then got on his phone to call I guess his shag. I heard him cry a little and then he ran back into the lounge, where he went to the bedroom and collected a few things.

"*I fuckin hate you Roxy, you could have easily let my boyfriend move in with me; and you could have found somewhere else for Stuart to live, what with all your money. You have turned into a rich sad cow since Danni died, as he would be turning in his grave by now seeing you as you are*." He said, now crying
"*How dare you... How dare you bring Danni into this you fuckin spineless queen. No Adam, you have money and a lot of it, as I recall you did very well from those parties back in London. This is my home and not yours; and it would be ideal if you remembered that. I say who stays here and who doesn't. I suggest you go to your new boyfriend and ask him to let you stay there. And don't you ever assume I would think otherwise, or indeed side with you because we have history. This is my fuckin home Adam, now deal with it, or sling your fucking hook*." I shouted to him, now pointing towards the front door, fuming with what he wanted me to do.

Adam then left the apartment slamming the door behind him; and then posting the keys through the door.
I stayed there until Stuart got home; and told him of the big argument we had both had. I told him that Adam asked me to kick him out so that he and his new shag could stay here, but I would not do that. I told Stuart that my home was now his; and that tomorrow I would contact a locksmith and get all the window and door

locks changed, just in case he had a spare set of keys somewhere; and he tried it on. I told him that I was sorry that it had come to this; and that I just did not know what has got into that silly little queen, as I held onto Stuart's hand, letting him know that all was well.

"Thank you Roxy, he has been like this for over twelve months now. I have got over the stage of crying now, as I have put all of my concentration into my work. I still love him, but I also hate him if that makes any sense? I am also sorry that you have had to have a confrontation with him, because I know how special he was too you Roxy" He said, now looking relieved but also looking deflated.

"Yes honey it does, and please do not think you will be on your own long as you are a very handsome young man if I say so myself. I think the confrontation was only a matter of time; and to think he thought I should have found you somewhere else to live, what with all my money just sitting there. The cheek of it." I replied, as he blushed, and again apologised for Adam's behaviour.

"Well, I am not interested in love, boyfriends, one night stands etc. At the moment Roxy. I can wait as I am not going anywhere." He said, so glad that he did not have to encounter a bitching match with Adam, or indeed him and his new shag.

"That's good honey, besides we have a pretty good friendship anyway; and I will still like you to escort me out on a dinner date." I said with a smile.

"Of course Roxy, you know I would like that. And yes, we do have a pretty special relationship." He answered, smiling at me just like a little boy.

I told him that I would be moving back down to Hove within a month or so, when his eyes just lit up. We just looked at each other and smiled, as he gave me a hug. That day brought us both together closer; and I think it bonded our friendship even more, for the fact I stood up to Adam and told him what I thought of him; and in some way fought Stuart's corner for him. He knew I was not one for taking sides, as I had always shown to be fair in anything I did, but he was so relieved that he did not have to move out, as it would have not only caused him stress in finding somewhere else, it would have also had an effect on his working life too.

We spent the rest of the night together, watching old tired videos, as we cuddled up on the sofa with some munchies and drinks. Even when we went to bed together, it was not about sex, as he gladly just held me and fell asleep with me, just as much as us going to our separate bedrooms when we wanted time alone.

We became each other's shoulder of support, even though a part of me wanted him to ask me out on a date; and maybe take it a step further than friends with benefits.

That morning I waited in for the locksmith who had spent a good few hours changing all the locks; and of course me being the little maid by serving him tea and biscuits. As it got hot I noticed he took off his shirt, all I saw was this gorgeous man with a few pounds that he could shed in a gym; and it did not help, that he had such a gorgeous colour to his skin, which you could tell he had been in the sun; and a nice pair of legs in a ripped pair of jeans, which were covered in hair which sent my pulse racing as I could not help but gaze at him, when he then flirtatiously placed his hand over his groin, now sending my pulse into over-drive as I saw him touch himself, in a way that got him aroused that you could not help but notice in his shorts, which I am sure the tip of his manhood, just peered through the opening of one of the many cuts that exposed his flesh; and yes I had begun to realise that he had gone commando.

I was sure he was flirting with me, because each time I looked at him he seemed to adjust something in his shorts, but to be honest I was not the slightest bit interested in a one-nighter, so I just ogled at him, as I sat there, window shopping, hoping not to get caught by looking at his now rather swelling groin area.

He was there to do a job, and my job was looking at him; and when he stretched a little, I lusted at the thought of seeing the outline of his pubic hair. I so wanted to tease him and gently stroke him, but I declined the thought of getting myself into trouble. Like Stuart, I knew that my time would come when it was ready to, so in the meantime I just got on with things, as in the back of my mind I did keep willing that Stuart and I would become a couple, as we both knew each other so well.

I waited for the locksmith to finish, then I text Stuart to let him know I was leaving. Before the locksmith left, he handed me his card and then told me, should I need him for anything then to call him anytime. He told me that I was a very beautiful young lady; and when I was about to tell him I was a man, he said that he knew who I was; and he still thought I was a very beautiful young lady. He made my day, but I could not indulge as he must have been about twenty years old if that, no matter how tempted I was. Within thirty minutes Stuart had turned up to say his goodbyes, as he kissed me and held me tight. He carried my cases to the car, as I had left most of my clothes there to save time later. When I got outside, I noticed the police car just by the drive, with a young police officer still sitting inside. Just before I was about to leave, I changed my heels to a more suitable pair for driving, as Stuart then held me as he gave me another kiss, despite his colleague seeing him.

I got in the car, then turned around and waved him goodbye, also noticing his colleague glare at me, so looking at him I blew a kiss towards him which made him go bright red, as Stuart burst out laughing hysterically, as he waved his finger at me in a gesture that told me I was naughty; and then spoke a few words to a rather embarrassed young police officer.

A few hours later I arrived back in London, where I text Stuart to let him know I had arrived back safely.

I dropped my bags and made my way to the couch; and just dropped onto the couch gathering my thoughts, as I looked at Danni's photograph and asked him to help guide me, as I was unsure what to do.

I walked into the kitchen where I put the kettle on to make a coffee; and then sat back down as I chilled out where again I began thinking about all that had happened through my life, as I took a trip down memory lane alone. Having looked back at a long harrowing year, a week or so later I decided that I would move back to Hove, but still keep my London home.

I had just celebrated my fortieth birthday; and had come to the decision that it was now time for me to live my dream. Danni and I always said we would retire to Hove; and together we would open up a bar in the gay district of Brighton. I said my farewells to everyone, throwing one final big bash at the Rainbow.

I gave Ellie my forwarding address and told her I would still come and visit; and I wished her and Di all the happiness and success in the world. The settlement from Danni's business had gone through, and once I had paid all the fees, I was finally free of any debt from the will. I locked up my London apartment; and secured the cars that were parked there, as I made my way back to Hove. I had already asked Stuart if he minded me moving in with him; and if he would help me look for a business. Everything was cleared and I stayed with him; and in return for my company and friendship he helped me look for a business; and it did not matter about the state the bar may be in as I still had some connections.

A few weeks into me moving to Hove, we then had a little bit more good news, as Margaret had got a little bit lonely on her own in Chelsea, that she decided to sell up and move to Hove where she and Start looked at renting a flat in Kemptown. She had previously asked Stuart if he would move in with her; and Stuart asked my permission to leave my home to live with his mother. I was very happy for them both; and I was happy to know that I would have my friend back with me, as I only got to see her now every other weekend.

I did understand that Margaret wanted her own place; and did not want to be pressured with the two of them living with me, although I would not have minded, even though it would have been a little cramped, meaning one of us would have had to use the couch.

It was the June of 2002 when I found the right place, a nice big sized bar overlooking the beach. It needed a lot of work doing to it, but with the right people we had it completed by the New Year of 2003.

It was so nice seeing the name of the bar go up, and in blue neon lights flashed 'Danni's Bar.' Above the bar was a two floor apartment, with a very large lounge, dining room and kitchen on the first floor, followed by a bathroom and three bedrooms with en-suite on the second floor. I also had that renovated to the highest standard; and as I did not know much about the trade, I got in touch with Steve who got the word around and sorted a team out for me.

Stuart then asked if he and his mother could rent the upstairs flat, as they did not like it where they were, as quite often the lifts were out of order; and Margaret was having trouble with the stairs. It was then that I put a proposition to him; and I asked him if he would be my manager, then he could have the apartment rent free.

Stuart jumped at the idea, but he was also undecided as he had a love for the police force. I just told him that it was ok, so long as he thought it over, and the flat would still be thrown in.

I told him he did not have to leave the force, as he could still be the manager and help me out a few times; and that he could help me with the books as I knew he was good at things like that. It was not as though he was moonlighting, as he had his job with the force; and I

would not be paying him for working with me, as that is why he would have the apartment upstairs rent free.
He just looked at me and then he smiled, as he knew I still had time for him; and that I still looked out for him.
It was then I asked around my fellow landlords about getting some decent staff, which in turn they put the message about again.
I know I could have gone to a job centre, but I wanted gay staff and this way I would not be seen to be prejudice if I recruited within the gay circle.
A few weeks before the big opening, I started to interview candidates; and had about eight hopefuls.
A few candidates were still at college and were looking for a bit of casual, but I never worked like that, I would only employ part time and full time; and everything had to be legal. I also knew that pretty boys always pulled in the customers, so I wanted to make sure I had a pretty boy working each night to ensure we pulled in a crowd.
With each person I saw, I told them at all times they would have to call me Miss Roxy, but if we ever were in private, or away from work then they could just call me Roxy if they so wanted too.
There was this one boy who stood out, and he was slightly feminine and was a little bit like me when I moved to Brighton.

"Excuse me for staring honey; I hope you do not mind me asking. Do you dress at all, like in cabaret?" I asked.
"Cabaret! Do you mean like a drag queen?" He answered.
"Well not like a drag queen as you have such a pretty face; and cross dressing or trannie are too harsh for you.

316

I was thinking more in the lines of showgirl." I replied, with a smile
"Well to be honest I used to dress when I was young, and I have always wanted to work as a woman, so I guess the answer is yes." He replied, in a sweet soft voice.

I looked at the application form; and read a few things that he had wrote in the hobbies section; and it seemed like he was very artistic, as he had also got a fashion and design diploma.

"Well, Michael, what I am looking for is a transgirl to work here, as I know I will have a very big following from the transgender community. Would you be up to work for me as your female self?" I asked.
"Yes Miss Roxy I would, but I will also need to sort out my wardrobe; and god knows what I would call myself as I have not yet thought of a name." He replied, now excited at the fact he was given a job.
"I will think of a name for you do not worry; and I would like to see you dressed femme. Would you do that for me please Michael?" I asked.
"Yes Miss Roxy, when is it that you would you like to see me dressed?" He asked.

"I will be back here tomorrow, so if you could pop in around 2pm you can go upstairs and get changed. I will officially interview you then." I replied, as I gathered his application together and put it in my briefcase

He thanked me and told me that he was looking forward to his next interview tomorrow; and hoped he wouldn't

let me down. I stood up to let him out, when he held out
his hand to give me a handshake. I smiled at him, and
then with a little laugh I just told him that it's never a
handshake between girls, that we give each other a drag
kiss. It is just a pretend kiss done on each cheek and I
mean on the face honey, but not actually touching skin,
which made him blush.

He then drag kissed me, as he left the bar, looking back
and then waving to me. I put all the other applications on
the counter to sift through, later as I needed to have a
cup of coffee and chill for a while.

The workmen were still in the bar finishing off, as were
the decorators; and by now the upstairs had another
week to go before completion. The workmen were very
friendly, and if truth be known they were very naughty
and flirtatious; but they knew when I said back to work
that I meant it. I did not mind a bit of boyish behaviour,
and I reminded them of that, also reminding them that
they had a job to do; and of course it was only natural for
me to be flirtatious too; after all who wouldn't with a
dozen hunky strapping men around you?

Steve had sorted me out a top team, and I could not be
happier than with the workmanship they all portrayed.
Quite often when it was lunchtime, we all sat together as
I cracked a few jokes, and became a bit of a lad; and I
also helped out as I was not afraid to lend a hand when it
was needed.

They had no qualms, about seeing me in Roxy mode;
and a few times they told me that they had to have a
second look, as they thought I was a real woman which I
thought was so sweet of them. We may have had some
flirtatious moments, especially me when seeing these

hunky men all hot and sweaty, with packages set tight in their jeans which got the pulse racing even more, but I still got respect from them. The nicest thing was, I think the site manager must have had a crush on me, as everytime I made my way towards the kitchen, he would himself come in and then ask if I was making everyone a cuppa. He would stand next to me, as I got a whiff of his aroma of sweat and paint, and where he would tell me that I smelt absolutely beautiful.

There were times that we would spend sitting in the kitchen, him opposite to me, just staring in my eyes, as he told he that I was a beautiful gay woman. How he wishes he could have met someone like me a long time ago, then he knew he would have not got married to his wife. It then dawned on me that as much as this guy was gorgeous; and God I could have taken him to bed.

The fact was he was married, he was someone else's husband; and I would never impose on someone's husband, even though Adam and Stuart had once shared my bed. It was at that moment that I looked at his hand, where there was no wedding ring, however, there was a white mark where one had since been. He told me that he and his wife were having difficulties; and there was a chance they would divorce. That he loved his wife, but he was not in love with her; and thankfully that had not had children as she was a person who wanted a career first and hoped children would follow.

This one day that we were in the kitchen alone together, he told me that he had considered himself to be bi-sexual; however, with the right person he would consider a full-on gay relationship. That he had engaged in gay sex with a few guys from the scene; and even when he had a private job on, that somehow, he always seemed to find his way into the bed of the man of the house at some point. Then looking at me, he surprised me, as he told me that he would definitely choose to be gay if he had someone like me to come home to.

I looked at him; and then told him that being like me was not a choice, that I was born gay; and that it was not something you can switch on and off when it pleases.

I told him that you are either gay or straight; and there is no compromising your gender.

He then asked me what my thoughts were about bi-sexual people, where I told him that we were all part of the LGBT community; and the first point of accepting, should be that of accepting ourselves for who we were.

I think that afternoon he got to know who the real Roxy was; and he never again came onto me in a way that he did before. We had many discussions about his gender, where I told him to embrace it and be proud of who he is. However, he would still tell me that I was beautiful; and he would love to have met me before he met his wife. I just smiled at him and gave him a peck on the cheek, as I told him there were lots of girls like me; and in time he may even find his own Roxy somewhere in London.

That afternoon, I was sitting in the office, as I sorted through the applications, putting them into two piles for yes and no. After much deliberation, I had managed to sort out twelve that I thought had potential and then I got it down to five, putting the others aside as a backup.

I had decided on my five staff, and if I liked Michael when he was dressed then he would have got through the first interview stage, even though I had no doubt in my mind that he would sail through from the get-go.

The pretty boys I had chosen had second interviews in two days' time, as I needed to see what they were like behind the bar first, as it was no good hiring anyone if they could not pull a pint or become flustered when using the cash register. I also decided to put them a further test should the cash register go haywire, so they had to show competency in being able to add up without the help of computers. It was at that time, being lost in thoughts that my phone rang and startled me; and as I answered it, I found out it was Stuart. He was asking me where I was, so I told him; and invited him to come to the bar. When he arrived, I showed him the hopefuls I would be employing; and then mentioned to him that I was also going to be interviewing a transgirl tomorrow. His face lit up when I said that; and he told me it was a very good idea because it is good to be diverse with staff, as having a transgirl would also put the message across to the transgender community that they were welcome in the bar.

I had decided to go with six staff to start with, having two who were to be full time, giving them alternative weekends off. Once I had sorted the paperwork out and saw what else needed to be done, I asked Stuart to take me to our favourite gay bar and then we would go home. Margaret had not yet fully moved down to Hove, as she was waiting for her home to be sold, so she would come down every few weekends or so; and it made me giggle when Stuart said she feels like she has two homes just like Roxy; and soon she knew she would move to Brighton & Hove very soon.

Stuart would still spend a few nights with me, just to keep an eye on me which was nice, as I always had company; and it made it even special, when we stayed in and watched a movie together. Stuart and I were no longer intimate, as we decided our friendship was more important than sex, even though he would always have a special place in my heart and a part of me still wished he would ask me out. We had the occasional hug and peck now and then, but we never were intimate as lovers or potential partners. I think this was more because of putting all of my efforts and time into the bar, as Stuart concentrated more on his job as well as his mother's welfare and relocation plans.

The next day as planned Michael came into the bar, and once he had caught my attention, I showed him upstairs. Although it was finished, there were still a few more things to just tweak, but it was safe for people to go up and not worry about any health and safety issues.
I was waiting for Stuart to take a week off work, so that we could go and buy furniture for the apartment, as it would be really to his taste rather than mine.
After about an hour Michael came down in a lovely tight fitted short dress, and he looked fabulous.
His make-up was simply stunning, and not a hair was out of place.

"You are very much my kind of girl honey, as you look absolutely stunning. And please do not worry, I do not pounce on fellow girls." I said, as I admired her

"So, everything is fine then Miss Roxy, do I meet to your needs and standards?" She asked, a little nervous as she looked in the mirrors along the bar.

"Yes, you do honey, and I think I am going to call you Michelle. Now will you please go to the bar and do these tasks for me?" I asked, as I held out a piece of paper on a board, just like an inspector.

She told me that she liked the name Michelle; and she thanked me for naming her. Being cheeky she picked up the list and looked at what I asked of her, the trickiest one being how to pour a pint of bitter shandy without spilling too much, which made me like her more seeing that side of her. I had no worries at all, although a little shaky she managed to do all I asked of her; and added up correctly, even though there was an itemised tab on the till which I told her she would have to get used to. I also had a test where should the till throw a hissy fit and you had to manually do it, I needed to see her maths skills which she had shown me both by working it out in her head, as well as writing it down on a note pad by the side of the cash register.

"So Michelle, would you like the job as bar attendant here at Danni's bar?" I asked, as I stared at her in anticipation.

"Yes Miss Roxy, I would love to work for you. When do I start?" She replied, now very excited.

"Officially, in a few weeks' time honey." I told her, as I gave her a hug and welcomed her as my first member of staff, and welcomed her to the family.

Having found out she had no job at present, I told her to call in tomorrow and she could help me with a few things in the bar, also asking if she wanted to work for me full or part time. She snapped my hand off for the full time, which I was very happy about.

Those few weeks before opening she was a diamond; and she did all I asked of her including sweeping up and cleaning. It was then I thought to myself how nice it was to have a sister back, even though he came to work as a man, he assured me he would come on duty as Michelle. She told me that she did not have that many clothes for Michelle, as this was still very new to her; and she only went out dressed a few times in the evenings.

I then suggested to her that she come over to my home at some point; and I would sort her a few things out as some of my clothes were now too tight for me.

I also explained that I did not mind her working as a guy, but in the evenings, I would like her dressed as Michelle. We had a few long chats; and she got to know my story regarding Danni. It was nice talking to someone who did not know the situation; and who could listen without saying remember this or remember that. She told me that it could not be easy; and how proud he must be of me now. Michelle was also a little spiritual; and she often told me that he would be looking out for me and looking over me, that he would always make sure I was fine as our loved ones do that. Each day she came into the bar we got closer and closer, and she started coming in the bar in the morning as Michelle to please me, as she herself got used to the idea of dressing in the daytime. She again told me that at the moment she was not a transgirl 24/7, as she only had a limited wardrobe of clothes and lack of practice with regards day make-up.

"I know honey, you told me, you look about the same size as me honey, a 12/14, would I be correct?" I asked, looking her up and down.

"Yes Miss Roxy, but would like to drop the 14, but I am afraid it is because of too many takeaways and the dreaded white wine." She answered, as she pointed to a bit of a swelled tummy.

"Oh, a girl after my own heart, we are going to get along fine. By the way honey, do you know where this address is?" I asked her, as I gave her a slip of paper with my address on it.

"Yes Miss Roxy, I have a bedsit two streets away, but not with such a lovely view as yours." She replied, as she said it did her for now, that was until she could afford to change things.

"Right then, I will let you get changed back into your drab clothes, so come over tonight to see me. Call in around 7pm." I told her.

"I will be there Miss Roxy, should I bring some wine so we can have a natter?" She replied.

"Don't be silly, I have a rack full of the stuff, just pop in and we will chat." I said, as I gave her a hug and got back on with some work as she got changed.

Before she left, she came over towards me and told me that she would be over later tonight. I gave her my number should she have any problems, then I decided to finish up and get a cab myself, even though I would have gone with Michelle, but I had another few hours work to do and did not want to put it off. When I got home, I ran a bath and took off my make-up and just chilled out as I thought about Danni; and wondered if he would be proud of me like Michelle had told me. I was very excited about my new venture; and also, very scared, as I had never been in this situation before; and now not having Danni to help with the paperwork, but I knew I would learn by my mistakes.

Having taken a bath, I sat on the bed and just chilled out for a while, before once again preparing my face. I then picked out a more casual outfit for the evening. Not realising the time, I had nodded off slightly when I heard the doorbell ring; so staggering to the door, I opened it to find Michelle on my doorstep. I told her that this was the first time she would have seen me without make-up. I laughed as I told her that I was about to get ready, but this old queen fell asleep, as I let her in and pointed towards the lounge. She told me not to worry about it, as she does it all the time, then asking me if I dress at home as well, or did I leave it to just when I went out.

"Oh yes, I do sometimes have one day or night as my male self, just so I can moisturise and let my skin breath." I told her. *"Anyway, go into the lounge, no good chatting in the hallway.* I will be in shortly, let me just put on my dressing gown."*

Michelle went into the lounge, where I told her to fix herself a drink. She shouted out to me to see if I wanted one, and I shouted back to her that I would have a glass of champagne. Once I got back into the lounge, we started chatting again, and it was then that I knew we would become very close friends; and I really was so pleased, as it was as though we had known each other our whole life. I also told her that I would call her Michelle at all times, unless she disagreed with it as I had to consider her thoughts too; and not just those of my own for which she did not object too.

"Right honey; come with me as I want to show you something." I said, as I asked her to follow me into the bedroom.
"Oh really, I am intrigued." She replied.

When we had got into my bedroom, her mouth just stayed wide open with the magnitude of the bedroom.

"Close your mouth dear, I think the tide is about to come in." I said, as I had a little giggle.
"This is a beautiful bedroom Roxy; it is so large." She said, as she looked around taking every little detail in.
"Yes, I think it is too as it used to be two double rooms; and I had Danni knocked through to make it into just the one many years ago." I replied.
"Well, it's beautiful Roxy; and it is very classy, you really miss him, don't you?" She said, as she noticed the photographs of him and us all around the bedroom.
"Thank you honey, that is really sweet; and there is not a day that goes by where I do not think of my Danni, but what is that saying? Life goes on and you have to accept it." I replied, as I opened one of the wardrobes that I put the clothes in that I no longer wanted.

"He is, sorry, he was a very handsome man Roxy. I am sure he is here with you." She replied, as she put her hand onto mine and just squeezed it.

"Right if you are not afraid to change in front of me, you can then try these on. Remember you do not have to strip, as you can put them on over your pants. And yes honey, I am sure he is with me, as he still holds a place in my heart." I told her.

She then told me that she doesn't wear men's pants, that she never has done. That the only time she wore underwear, was when she is a girl. That she goes commando 99% of the time. I smiled and giggled slightly, as I told her that I would leave her to it; and that I promised that I would not look. Then telling her that I needed to put my face on, so I looked beautiful again.

"It doesn't bother me Roxy, we are both girls at the end of the day and I know I am safe with you. Besides like you, I too am not into girls." She replied, now beginning to remove her clothes.

"That's good then honey, you can search through that wardrobe and try anything on you want. However, the first triple wardrobe is out of bounds, as they are my latest collections." I said, as I looked at her and gestured, that she would get a slapped bum.

Like a typical girl she checked the clothes, and then checked the labels and went into tranny heaven.

"OMG Roxy, these are designer, they must have cost you a small fortune?" She asked, now in awe at all the designer labels; and the vast number of dresses I had. *"Maybe, but do you like them? I must admit that tailored dress suits you. If you look closer you will see a few evening dresses too, and that long gold one I thought about you wearing it on the opening night?"* I said, as I picked it up and draped it over the bed.
"OMG, I would love to Roxy. Are you sure, as this is way too kind?" She replied, now ecstatic.

"Yes, I am sure, and please take whatever you like from there as they are yours." I told her, knowing that they would go to a good cause.

I do not know what it was about her, but I had a very good feeling. I don't just give all of my unwanted clothes to anyone. Even Adam had to wait a while before I gave him my men's clothes. She then told me that she would prefer to keep them here, as she really did not have the room back home. I agreed and told her that before going to Danni's Bar, she could come here to get changed if she wanted too.
I also understood if she did not want to dress every night, as I knew she was not like me, as any chance I had to dress all glam I revelled in it. She told me that for now she would like to dress just at the weekends until she got more confident. Like me, the queens in Brighton also snubbed her, and was very cruel to her, as quite often she sat in the corner on her own, whether dressed as a guy or a girl; and she found it so hard to be accepted into the clicky circles if your face did not fit.

I then told her that things will now change as she is part of my family; and we will have an elite circle of our own, and we would be in a position to snub those bitchy queens who did the same to us, that they would soon beg her to be their friends, as now we were in a position to ply at pay back.

We had a lovely few hours, trying on dresses and suits, as well as the more glamorous evening wear, even if I did laugh a few times when she picked a tighter dress; and her cock was protruding out somewhat, where we both just began laughing.

With each chat we got closer and closer; and she started to bring me out of my shell. Just before 11pm, she told me that she had to call it a night and go back home, as she needed to see her mother early the next day, because she was going on holiday with some friends. I kissed her goodnight; and told her that she must call in again whenever she wanted. I never did put my face on that night, as I had so much fun with Michelle, seeing her excited with everything she tried on; and with her face lightening up when she saw the costume jewellery to match the outfit. It was also now so very strange, with having the place to myself now that Stuart had moved into the apartment over the bar with his mother. He never ever forgot me, as he did quite often come and visit me when he had time off from work, as well as popping in if he were in the area.

In some way though I now liked the solitude, as away from my home it was busy and noisy, so I relished a bit of peace and quiet time.

Over the next few days Michelle did as she said she would, texting me before she come over. We both chatted and had lunch together, with her bringing cake and sweet things to eat; and she even dressed in the daytime so I could have my sister just as she was meant to be, a very pretty girl whose confidence was growing even though she put her make on at my home.

We would sit in the garden with a pot of coffee, or champagne, depending on our mood; and just talked about girly things, oh and men. She so wanted to find a nice man, as she had been messed about herself a few times. I told her it would happen when she least expected it, and not to rush into things.

It was then time for the big opening, when Stuart told me he would be in later that evening as he was still on duty, when he also asked if he minded if he was in uniform, in which he knew I would never object.

Michelle wore the long gold evening dress; and had a beautiful pair of six inch heels on, which complemented the gown. I knew that I could not wear them, as I was more comfortable in a five-inch pair; and a six-inch pair was pushing it, so I wore a long black sequin and rhinestone evening dress with a fishtail skirt, one I had brought from America. We both got into the cab and made our way to the bar; and then waited for my staff to arrive as well as the cabaret.

Opening night was a success, with having the top cabaret perform from London, my top acts being Totty and Dixie. I was still mad at the Brighton queens; and I never passed any invites out, as it was I who now commanded an audience; and it was I who now invited people into my circle. Strangely though I no longer got snubbed by them like I did when I was younger; and it was lovely, but bitchy of me to be revelling in how those who once snubbed me, now began grovelling towards me for favours. I knew I was a little like them by doing to them as they did to me, but I guess I was trying to teach them a lesson. I never let anyone sit alone; and if I did see someone on their own in the bar, I would quite often go over to them and introduce myself to them, as well as introduce them to the regulars in the bar. I had always sworn that I would never see anyone sit alone; and would show them that we were a friendly bar, as I so detested clicky queens and bars who only attitude was that they wanted money in the cash register.

Towards the end of the evening, I asked Michelle to sit down with me in my royal box, where we chatted about the evening that had been unfolding quite nicely.

Just then Stuart walked in; and it was not until Michelle told me we have the police in the bar that I looked.

"Oh do not worry too much honey, I do have friends in uniform. Here let me introduce you to him." I said, getting up; and then reaching for her hand so she could be introduced to my sexy Stuart.

Standing up, I called Stuart over; and as he was in uniform, I knew he could not drink, because I knew he was only there for support before taking me home.

"Stuart, this is my new sister Michelle. You know the one I have been telling you about." I told him, as I introduced her to him.

"Michelle, this is the lovely Stuart. And yes, he is a real policeman and not a stripogram, that he was the one

who used to live with me." I said, as I raised my
eyebrows, and then pushed her basically towards him.
"*Nice to meet you Michelle; and if I may say so you look
absolutely beautiful, as do you Miss Roxy.*" He replied.
"*Nice to meet you too Stuart; and Miss Roxy has told me
so much about you.*" She replied.
"*Stuart, have you forgot your manners. Where is my kiss,
you sexy policeman you?*" I said, as I put a finger to my
cheek, telling Michelle that he must have had a busy
night as he never forgets to give me a kiss on the cheek.

"*Sorry Miss Roxy, I do apologise, I did not mean to be
rude.*" He said, as he placed a kiss onto my cheek and
then gave me a hug, as I told him that I forgive him; and
not to let it happen again.

He then asked if we wanted a drink; and as I was about
to go to the bar myself to fix them, Michelle took over.
She told me that she would get the order, which was the
usual for us, as she then asked Stuart what he wanted to
drink.
Knowing Stuart could not drink, I declined asking for
another glass of wine and lemonade, because it would be
his job that would be in jeopardy, she he be caught.
She then caught my eye as she called me over, only to
tell me that she thought he was simply gorgeous; and it
was not just the uniform that was appealing. She also
told me that I do have a way with men, as she could see
why I had such an aura about me as I made people feel
comfortable; and she told me she could see that they
respected that. When she told me what she felt about
Stuart, I had lots of things buzzing in my head, so I

turned around and sat back down where I chatted to
Stuart. He whispered into my ear, that he thought her
absolutely beautiful, like you me, who was indeed
another stunner.
I was a little naughty, as I began to tease him, then
becoming serious when I asked him if he really liked her,
now with my arm under his as we began to chat.

"Oh god yeah, she is lovely." He whispered.

I then told him, that she really liked him too; and that she
was only twenty five; and such a beautiful young lady.
At that moment his heart sank, as he told me that he was
most likely too old for her, as well as him being out of
her league, because he was certain there were scores of
men seeking her attention. I told him that she has had
some interest, but she showed no promise towards them.
That she was an old-fashioned girl, with a young head on
her shoulders; and that maybe he should ask her out on a
date. That she too is like me, where she is not dressed as
a girl all the time, something in which he liked me for
from the moment he saw me.
Michelle then came over, and she sat next to me, where
we all started to chat, but I could see Stuart's mind was
not on things as he was certainly tripping about Michelle.
He looked at me and then looked over to Michelle; and
could not concentrate properly.

*"Right Stuart, I need to get up and mingle a little more,
see how the customers are doing, so I will leave you in
the hands of the lovely Michelle."* I said, as I kissed them

both on the cheek and walked amongst the crowd, also keeping an eye on the bar staff and the running of the bar.

I then got up and walked around the bar, asking everyone if they were fine. I would often turn my head and see Michelle and Stuart in conversation.
It did make me feel happy that Stuart may have found himself another partner, as I know he longed to come home and do those boyfriend things. We had a very good understanding; and we knew we were the best of friends as we had a history together, as well as a very close bond. Even though, sometimes I wished that Stuart had asked me to be his girl. I knew Stuart would always be there for me no matter what; and I knew I could rely on him, besides, we still went out with each other, so I still got to be alone with him. I then walked out of the bar to see how my door staff are doing and if there had been any altercations. They told me that everything had been going smoothly; and only had to move a few drunken souls away from trying to get into the bar, much to my delight, as I did not want a repeat performance from that incident in London.

Over the coming months Michelle and Stuart got closer and closer; and one day Stuart approached me where he then popped the question. He asked me if I would not object to Michelle moving in with him, in the flat above the bar. That they had decided that they wanted to be together; and this was something they really both wanted. Now telling me that they were officially a couple. I told him that I did not mind; and that I was very happy for them both. That they had my blessing, and Michelle had no excuse now to be late for work, now relieved he had someone, but deep inside a little sad, as I hoped that we would have rekindled our emotions.

"You know you are very special to me Roxy, you will always be my best friend and my sister. We have gone through a lot together; and you will always have me and my heart. Please remember that Roxy, I will always be there for you come rain or shine. Alongside my mother, you too will be my priority for sure. Michelle and I get on so well; and I would kick myself if I did not give it a try. I have to do this Roxy, because if I do not, then I will forever be wondering what if…." He said, as he held me tight and kissed me on the forehead.
"Yes I know honey, it works both ways; and I will be here for you, for you also have my heart. I can see you get on, so go with it; and please just be happy." I replied, as I knew I had to let him go of him; and just accept what we had was now just friendship.

Michelle moved in with Stuart and his mother; and things seemed to be going well for them all. I still had my shopping days with Margaret; and we would still have days where she would come over and sit with me. She told me on a few occasions, that she thought Stuart and me would have got together, as she saw how close we were; and it was then that I thought that maybe I should have asked Stuart out; and not waited for him to ask me. I told her that it was a nice thought, but we made better friends, as I bit my tongue and did not show my disappointment.
Stuart helped at the bar when he could, but I was lucky

that Michelle now had taken some of the strain off me, so that it gave me time by myself to have some chill out time, as I had been working seven days a week for the last six months.

It was now a Tuesday morning; and I had taken the day off work which was needed. I was in the kitchen just finishing breakfast when my mobile phone rang. Not recognising the number, I picked it up and in a soft voice just asked who it was. Just then I sat down on the couch and began to cry, as the person on the other end of the phone told me who he was.

"Rik, is that really you? Where on earth have you been? It has been so long." I cried.

He told me that it had been hard on him after losing Danni, that he just locked himself away with work.
He then told me that he was in London, as he had a few meetings; and he would be there all week. I explained to him that I was now in Brighton, even though I still had my London apartment which I still used from time to time. He asked me if he could see me; and could I come up to London, where I then told him I would see if I could get someone to cover the bar; and I would get back to him as soon as I could.
Luckily enough, I knew I had a few people who would look after the bar for me, so I arranged a few days away and told them to call me should there be any problems.
I then packed a bag; and made my way to London.
I arrived at my apartment which did feel strange, as this was the first time in six months that I had been here.

I dropped my case and my bag, as I then text Rik to let him know that I was now at Victoria Embankment.
He texted me back and told me he would be with me around 4pm, as he was just finishing up in a meeting.
I began tottering around the place, noticing that Pip had kept the apartment spic and span; and I was so pleased that I had kept him on as he never let me down.
Once I had gathered my thoughts and made myself a cup of coffee, I thought I had best get changed and spruced up, as I did not want Rik to see me in what I called everyday clothes. I had a quick shower, as I then sorted out a nicer dress and just waited for him to arrive.
It seemed like hours that I waited, as I sat on the balcony looking over at the Thames. I had a coat over my shoulders because of the coldness of the late summer's night, sitting there watching people scurry by as the traffic backed up because of the rush hour congestion of people wanting to get home. Suddenly the intercom sounded, as I rushed to the door and pressed the release button, letting Rik into the building. I then had the door open as I heard the elevator come to the floor, as it opened Rik just standing there, as I then ran towards him.

"Oh Rik, I have so missed you." I said, now with my arms entwined around his neck.
"I have missed you too Roxy; and I sincerely apologise for not contacting you sooner. Life has been pretty busy and hectic I am afraid." He said, as we walked down the hallway into the lounge, then giving me a beautiful bouquet of roses and orchids and of course a bottle of the finest champagne.

I asked if I could get him a drink, when déjà vu set in, when he asked for bourbon on the rocks. I walked into the dining room where I poured him a drink; and then came back into the lounge where I sat next to him as we caught up on the past year that had gone by. He told me that he just threw himself into work, after having a minor breakdown because of losing his Danni, which Jake and Sophie were his rock as they finally brought him back to reality. I placed my hand onto his as I told him it has been hard all around, but that we all have to deal with these things the best way we can.

We spent a good four hours talking, before he told me he would have to go, as he had to sort out papers for tomorrow's meeting. Then he asked me if he could see me again, and would I like to go out for a meal.

"Oh Rik, that would be wonderful. I have not been out for a meal in such a long time, what with getting the bar sorted ready for the grand opening. I have had no reason to get dressed up so fancy; and this would be a lovely reason. I would love to go out with you for a meal." I told him, as I put my arms around him.

Just before he left, I stood at the door where again I gave him a hug, as he held me close to him, kissing me on the cheek just as gentle as Danni used to. He told me that he would come over straight from his meeting, which he hoped would be around 3pm; and for me to get a good night's sleep, so looking towards the side of the dresser, I noticed Danni's keys were still in the silver pin dish next to the 19th century Bohemian vase he brought me for my 2nd Christmas present, so I gave them to him and told him to let himself in, not realising he had his own keys, but out of respect for me he did not want to just let himself in as he was a gentleman.

Again, I gave him a hug as he pulled me close to him, and he then bid me goodnight.

After he left, I was floating on air, as I thought how he had not changed at all, apart from the now white hair that he had, but how dashing he looked. I was so pleased that he had come over, as I had been meaning to phone him, but with the bar I got side tracked; and well, things go by and you keep saying I will do it tomorrow.

That night I could hardly sleep, as I was like a little excited girl, going on a date for the first time. I kept looking over at Danni's photograph, as I thanked him for sending his father over as it brightened me up; and it pulled me out of a dark place that I often saw myself retreat into. I got up that morning after I finally had gone to sleep, all refreshed with a nice feeling hanging over me. I opened the wardrobe and looked through the many dresses that I had massed over the years; and just put to one side. I decided to wear the Oscar de la Renta 60s style pencil dress suit styled for Jackie Kennedy, which was brought for me by Danni when we were shopping in Milan. It was a cream colour; and I had a lovely pair of Salvatori shoes and matching handbag to go with it.

Rik text me throughout the morning, also asking if I would like to go to the opera on the Friday night, as well as a charity cocktail party on the Saturday night, which would be with his banking associates.

Usually, he would go and he would be the one on his own, as he made up the numbers and did not stay long. He thought that I would enjoy the party, as he knew how

much I loved the glamour; and the excuse to dress up.
I text him back to tell him that I would love to go to both
of them; and that I would be honoured to be his guest.
I scurried around and found two more dresses for the
other occasions, which I knew I would change my mind,
as I am like that never being able to choose one dress on
impulse. I had by now had my bath, and I had put on my
make-up, as I then heard the elevator arrive. I walked
into the dining room, where I opened the drinks cabinet
and got Rik a bourbon ready. I myself had my usual
glass of champagne, and as he walked through the door,
he looked at me and told me how beautiful I looked, and
that I never ever gave reason for disappointment, as I
always maintained that classy look, and a look that any
man would move mountains to have just a piece of me. I
of course, thanked him, telling him that I was not dressed
in the outfit that I was going out in. That I would change
just before we were ready to leave.

*"Oh I see, I was going to say that I thought you were
dressed a little too early."* He replied, as he gave me a
peck on the cheek.
*"I did not want to be sitting here in just a dressing gown,
so thought it would be best to put something on."* I told
him, as I had a little laugh.

He then told me that he would need to freshen up, and
could he take a shower. He did have a small case with
him, that I believe had another suit in it; or at least I
hoped it did. We just sat there for an hour as we caught
up on the old times, as well as Rik filling me up on
pastures new. I asked him about Jake and Sophie; and he

told me they were growing up quickly now.

I told him that I still get my letters from them, and I look forward to reading about all they have done; and that I still miss them very much; and that he must send them my love when he returns back to New York.

After a trip down memory lane, Rik asked me to excuse him as he made his way to the spare room to get showered and changed. I then went into the bedroom to put on my outfit for the evening.

It was around thirty minutes by the time I had preened myself; and changed into my suit. When I walked down the stairs to the lounge, Rik was already there with drink in hand.

"Stunning Roxy; absolutely stunning." He said, as he passed me a glass of champagne.

"Thank you Rik. It feels so nice getting all glammed up again, as it has been a while." I replied.

"You never cease to amaze me Roxy, as you always look so divine. You always look so feminine and ladylike; and how you remain so beautiful is beyond me." He told me, as he then gave me a kiss on the cheek.

I then walked over to the window, as I noticed the traffic building up with the congestion of the rush hour.

Rik then came over towards me as he admired the view, saying how wonderful it was to see the lights of the city, and the lights of the boats on the Thames.

Shortly before 6pm he had a phone call, in which he then told me that the car was waiting for us downstairs.

I picked up my handbag, as Rik held open my faux fur coat as I slipped into it. Leaving the hallway light on, we walked down to the elevator as we made our way downstairs. When we had got to the basement, the car was already there; and as the chauffer opened the door, I noticed it was not Marcus.

"*Good Evening Sir, Madam.*" He spoke in a strong European accent.

"*Good evening Kristian.*" Rik replied, as he waited for me to get in the limo.

Once I had got in the limo; and sorted myself out. I looked at Rik and then asked where Marcus was. He told me that he had moved back to the US, after the funeral. That there was no need for him to stay he in London anymore, as he had better use for him and his wife back in New York. I asked him to give them my regards when he next saw them, as I did like those short chats we had when Danni and I went out and he came to pick us up.

"*Where to sir?*" Kristian asked Rik.
"*Mayfair please Kristian, to La Gauroche.*" He told him.
"*La Gauroche? Wonderful Rik, I have not been there since Danni took me on the anniversary of us getting together.*" I told him, now placing my arm under his.

We finally arrived at the restaurant, when Kristian opened the doors for us, as we then were bombarded with photographers flashing their camera's. although I was not doing the shows on a regular basis, I was still an 'A' lister, when it came to celebrity status.

"*Welcome to my world Rik.*" I told him, as we hurried into the restaurant, wondering how on earth did they know I would be at this venue, or indeed in London.

The meal went very well, and we both caught up on a few things from our past. The waiters and maître de recognised me; and without hesitation they came up to make sure that everything was fine.
Rik so reminding me of Danni by ordering in French, as he told me that this was his and Danni's favourite French restaurant in London.
Yes, that night it was so nice being back in the limelight, but more so going back out on the London scene that I had so come accustomed too.
The next night whilst going to the opera, the cameras were there again, as reporters bombarded me with questions asking me if I was going back into runway; and was Rik my new husband.
Again, I welcomed Rik to my world; and he did not seem to mind replying that he felt like a celebrity; and he thought he was walking in his son's shoes. I told him that I was glad I had the bar in Brighton, as that brought me down to reality from all the photographers and reporters, as it was my own little world of safety and security.
The charity ball went to plan, with Rik introducing me to his colleagues, as I had dance after dance with the group, gracing the dancefloor like royalty. I had a wonderful evening; and finally, Rik had helped bring that sparkle to my eyes that I had so lost some time ago.
It was whilst I was sat at our table, in a gorgeous red Versace evening gown encrusted in diamantes and beads,

that his colleagues thought I was his wife.

Rik introduced me as Mrs Svenningsen; and then had to explain that I was his late son's wife. They then realised that I was formally known as Roxy Garcia; and once I had been pressed with questions about my television contributions I explained to them that I had since mellowed as I can now argue without such vulgarities. It still did not make any reason for issue, as to his work colleagues the fact was that I was a Svenningsen; and I was given the utmost respect. Or was it because they were a lot older, and seeing a beautiful woman was all they saw without trying to understand the logic of a man dressed as a woman?

It still did not stop them asking me to dance, as they held me close to them and engaged in conversation.

After the evening's event, Rik once again dropped me home, then as I made my way to the elevator, he gave me a kiss on the cheek as he thanked me for a wonderful night, then sadly he left to go back to his own apartment. On the Sunday afternoon, he phoned me and told me that he was staying a further two weeks in London, and could he spend time with me. I was overwhelmed; and thought that it was a lovely idea that I suggested he come and stay with me, rather than stay on his own in his Knightsbridge apartment, as it seemed pointless going from one apartment to the other all the time. He agreed, and on the Sunday evening he brought his cases, where I then showed him to the spare bedroom.

I contacted Stuart and told him I was staying a further two weeks in London; and asked him to email me over the work rota and time sheets. As I had placed all that in order, I just chilled out and talked and talked to Rik.

It was so nice having a man around the house again, and although I did cook a meal, most nights it was dress up and eat out.

Those two weeks went by so quickly; and on the last day we decided to make the most of it. Rik suggested we go for a walk along St James Park; and then go for some lunch. He made sure that Kristian was available, so that I could be driven around in style; and to be able to see all the sights in which I had not seen for such a long time. Kristian came to pick us up at around 11am, where we made our way to St James Park, whilst Kristian waited for us to finish our walk. I had my arm under Rik's all the time we walked around the park, oblivious to all who were around.

We did have a spate of photographers, but they soon dispersed once they had taken what they wanted picture wise; and they then left us alone. After about an hour and a half we made our way back to the Limo, when Rik informed Kristian to drive us slowly towards The Ritz, where we had lunch before going back home.

Once we were indoors, I made us both a coffee, as we just chilled out on the couch, before Rik suggested that our last night together, we could spend having a meal out, as he then phoned The Grosvenor to make a reservation. Once again, I was told that I did not disappoint Rik, as he told me how beautiful I was; and again, arm in arm I was escorted downstairs and to the Grosvenor. Rik had been a gentleman for the three weeks we had been together, kissing me on the cheek before we retired to bed.

I thought that this evening was a wonderful evening to finish off our three weeks together, as I had the finest of champagne and food, to the finest conversation of old and new memories. The night was finished off with Kristian dropping us off home, as Rik told him that he could now retire for the night as he was no longer needed. We entered the elevator and as we made our way upstairs, again Rik complimented me on a wonderful night. I placed my keys in the sliver pin dish on the dresser as you walked through the door, then asked Rik if he wanted to finish the evening with his usual bourbon. Rik helped me out of my coat, as he placed it in the coat room; and then I made my way to the dining room.

I had poured Rik's drink, when I opened a fresh bottle of champagne from the chiller, when all of a sudden Rik stood behind me. I first of all jumped as I was startled, then the next thing I knew Rik had placed his hands around my waist. He then gently kissed me on my neck, as he held my waist tightly close to him, my body began to tingle as I felt the soft warm kiss of his lips, just brush lightly against the skin of my neck. With my head now slightly tilted sideward, he began kissing my upper neck towards my ears, I felt his warm breath invigorate my senses. The hairs of my neck standing on end, as I stood there and savoured the intoxicating aroma of his cologne, tingling as his hands gripped my waist as he pulled me towards him.

As he kissed me more seductively, my hands then moved towards his hands as I held them and gave myself to him, feeling the arousal in his groins stimulate the very senses in my lower body. He turned me around, as our eyes met; and I saw that look of ecstasy as he then placed his lips over my lips. With my arms now around his neck, as he had his hands stroking my back; he then started to unfasten the zip of my dress. Holding him tighter, he kissed me with passion as he moved his hands up and down my back, my dress now falling to the floor, as once again our eyes meet as he wrapped his arms around my body, pulling me closer towards him as I felt the excitement of his loins now pressing firmly into me. As I loosened from his grip, I cupped my hands and placed them on his face, where I kissed him on the lips gently. I then started to remove his tie, I started to undo his shirt button by button until it opened out to reveal a gorgeous mass of white hair. Stroking his chest hair, he again pulled me towards him as he held me there with his hands stroking my back, until he reached the panty line where he inserted his hand. With an intake of breath, I felt his hand caress my buttocks, so I placed my hands towards his trouser line where I placed my hand over his now protruding bulge of erotic delight. With a deep gasp he placed his mouth over my mouth, as he kissed me with forceful intentions, I felt his hand now hold my buttocks firmly.

My hand now slowly moving towards his belt as I slowly felt for the fastening. I then placed my hand inside, as I undone his clasp and zip, making way inside his underwear as I held him softly in my hands.

"Oh Roxy, that is sheer bliss. Please do not stop, I am all yours." He told me, now with my hand firmly around his hard bulging erection.

With his trousers now dropping to the floor, I stepped out of my dress, as Rick removed his shoes and stepped out of his trousers. Standing there in front of me was this

mature man, who was as fit as any young man I have seen, with white hair shimmering throughout his body, with the line of hair from his chest, followed his body towards his navel disappearing into his white briefs.
He pulled me towards him again, as we embraced and we kissed. Slowly I removed myself from him, as I started to move down his body kissing him on his chest; and then kissing his tummy until I was on my knees with his bulging underwear staring me in the face.
I placed my mouth over his bulge, taking his underwear into my mouth, as again he took a sharp intake of breath. His hands firmly on my shoulders, as he savoured the moment that I indulged in to taking him into my mouth. With my hands I placed them along the waistband of his briefs, I slowly removed them to reveal a very wet and large manhood standing before me. Standing at nine to ten inches, I placed my hands over his bulging manhood; and gently took him inside my mouth, his breathing now becoming erratic as I took him deeper inside me; and whilst he held firmly onto my head, he helped guide himself into me.

"*Oh Roxy; oh, my goodness, that is simply wonderful.*" He said, now holding onto me as he thrust a little deeper into me.

Now placing his hands onto my shoulders, he lifted me up and held me close to him. His throbbing manhood sticking into my tummy, as he passionately kissed me and held me close to him. He then turned me around, as I now felt him pressing himself firmly into my ass, as he placed his hands over my breasts, as he kissed me on the neck. Slowly he moved his hands lower over my basque, until his hands were in reach of my panties, where he placed them inside to discover its hidden jewel. He then bent me over towards the dining table, removed my panties and placed his throbbing wet erection inside my ass cheeks, gently finding my love hole as he pressed himself further into me, as I took him inch by inch. Now with my torso held firmly down onto the dining room table, he spread my legs and thrust his hard wet cock inside me, reaching down to kiss me on the neck as his other hand reached for my front, as he took my cock now in his hands.

*"Oh Roxy, you are simply gorgeous. I have been wanting to do this for such a long time. You turn me on so much my dear Roxy. Thank you so mu*ch." He said, as he pushed deeper inside me.
"Rik! I never ever thought this would happen, not in a million years, but I am so glad it has been such a long time that any man has been near me." I replied, as I looked back towards him to see the sweat pour off his brow as he filled my ass up with his cock.

For twenty minutes he penetrated me, giving me all that he had, until he could no longer hold on. As he was about to shoot his load, he withdrew and spilt his juices all over my back and ass; and I felt it trickle down towards my balls. He then stopped for a while, before turning me around and placing me on my back on the dining room table, where he then reached down to take me in his mouth. Feeling my own cock grow inside his warm mouth, he held my legs apart; and then took all of me including my balls inside him, as his goatee tickled my sensitive spots, was a simple dose of heaven.

Then standing up he placed my legs over his shoulders and again he thrust himself deep into me; and with his other hand he began jerking my cock until I climaxed and shot my juices over my tummy, at the same time that Rik again shot his juices, only this time he exploded inside my ass.

We then got up and made out way to the shower, as he took me to bed and made love to me for a further time, before we ended up falling asleep.

The next morning when I got up, I noticed that Rik had already got up. I put on my dressing gown and walked down the stairs still floating on air from the night before, when I then noticed Rik was no longer in the apartment. I thought that he must have left to go to the office, but it was not until I went into the lounge when I was now more awake, that I noticed there was a note on the coffee table. I picked the note up and began to read it, as I then sat on the couch and cried my eyes out.

'To my dearest sweet Roxy. Firstly, let me apologize for not being here when you got up from your sweetest of dreams. You looked so beautiful just lying there, that I did not want to disturb you. I do apologize for last night, as what happened between us was not supposed to happen; and I apologise if I may have led you on.
I find you a very incredibly beautiful woman, who has a heart of gold; and a body that stirred all of my senses that I thought I had lost so long ago.
I have had a wonderful three weeks with you, but alas I

351

have had to go back to the States. This I think my dear Roxy is for the best, as I find myself so attracted to you; and I find that I am falling in love with you, which is wrong, because it has left me confused. I need time to think, so again please forgive me for not being able to tell you this face to face, for fear of seeing you upset because of my selfish way, that I fear this is the right way to say goodbye.

If I had waited for you to wake up, I know I would never have been able to pick up the courage to look you in the eye to tell you how I feel; and that is why I must leave without being a man to say goodbye properly.

I will always love you Roxy, please believe me when I say that. Yours Always Rik'

The message that Rik left really crushed me; and I felt cheap and dirty. I did not expect anything to happen with us, but when it unfolded like it did, I thought Rik wanted me just as much as I wanted him. It felt right; and he made me feel like the Roxy I once was, the Roxy that was so much part of Rik and Danni's world.

It took me such a long time to get over the guilt and betrayal, but in time it became a memory, where I soon brushed it to one side. I had happy memories of Rik; and I was not going to let a bit of flirtatious fun and intimacy get to me, even though he really broke my heart. I was strong enough to let it go, where I still maintained my routine of phoning now and then; and still sending letters to Jake and Sophie.

Normally I would have gone into a world of what if; however, this time it was easy for me to accept that Rik was a full-blooded male, who got hypnotised by the beauty of Roxy, when in all fairness, he really did not know who he was which was confusing for him. I would never have stood a chance with him and his curiosity, because I felt he was neither gay nor straight; and that he just tested the water. He was a man who was brave enough to taste the forbidden fruit; and I was thankful that I was his first, knowing that somewhere down the road I was sure he would taste it again somewhere else, with someone new.

It had now been another year that I had spent in Brighton; and another year that I had been on my own.
The time was now approaching where I would soon be celebrating my forty second birthday; and I had invited Ellie and Di, as well as Russell and his wife to come down to Brighton to celebrate with me.
The others, that I had invited could not make it, however, they promised they would celebrate with me when I got back to London.
Well, my night went well, and by now I had got used to living on my own once more. Danni was still in my heart and always would be, and I still had my moments where I would sit on my bed and talk to him. I knew he was with me, as every now and then I smelt his cologne in the house, or sensed he was watching over me as I slept, making sure I was alright.
I had got yet another lonely Christmas out of the way, spending most it with some new friends I had found being in the trade, as well as spending time over the Christmas period with Margaret and Stuart. Things did not work out that well with Michelle and Stuart, as the novelty of being with a policeman had worn off; and she

was forever arguing with his mother over trivial things, so they called it a day. She still worked at bar, but I knew she wanted to fly the nest sometime soon, as she wanted to find her way amongst the bright lights of London, and its fabulous drag circuit. I was busy at Christmas, and I was so thankful for all of my staff and my friends for helping me make it a special one.

I had a growing circle of family, as well as respect from the other bars; and it was a very nice family circle of bar owners, looking out for each other.

Just as we were closing up, I went to lock the doors and over the road I saw a man's figure in the distance by the seafront. It was not so uncanny to see lonesome figures of men looking out to sea, but this felt a lot different. This was not the first time I had seen this manly figure, as he had been standing there for the last two weeks, with what seemed to me, was that of him giving a backward glance up towards the bar.

I thought nothing more of it at first, as I locked the door, thinking he must be a tourist and he was just admiring the view, as I had one last drink with Stuart, Margaret and my bar boys before going home.

I did however mention this to Stuart, but by the time he had gone outside to investigate, the person in question had disappeared. Stuart told me that he would keep a watch out over the next few days, but it may be just what I first thought; a tourist just taking in the views of the seafront, and the many old buildings that lined the Brighton coastline.

The next night I saw the figure again; and as the moon shimmered down over him, I caught a glimpse of a man with light hair and a goatee, that under the moonlight looked white. I just thought it was Rik, so I asked Michelle to look after the bar whilst I got my jacket and proceeded to the seafront. By the time I had walked out of the bar; and got over the road to the railings over-looking the promenade, the mystery man had gone yet again; and as I walked towards the pier and seafront, I shouted out Rik's name, but to no avail.

Having got back to the bar, I again told Stuart when he came in later that evening. I told him that it was strange, as all I could see was a tall figure of a man, much like the man I had been seeing for a while; and as the moon shone down over him; I noticed his white hair. I told him that was all I could see, so I would be no good at recognising the person although it resembles Rik in stature and hair colour, even though I knew the moonlight could play tricks on you.

Again, Stuart told me he would keep a watch out, as he escorted me into the taxi to go home; and again he reminded me that he would keep an eye out over the next few nights as he was on night duty. He also told me that I had been working too hard; and he thought that my imagination was playing tricks on me, as he cheekily told me that it must be my age.

Well, that made me smile, as I gave him a little slap across the bum, when he told me he would drive past the house every hour or so to check all is ok before heading back to the station to check in.

By now I had also brought the apartments above mine; and had been successful by obtaining planning permission to revert it back to the grand Georgian house that it once was. It was more difficult than it was in

London, but I still had enough high powered friends in Brighton to pull a few strings; and Stuart was right, as I had been working non-stop for such a long time, sometimes working up to eighteen hours in one day, that I thought my mind must be playing silly tricks on me.

I had the upstairs of the apartments completely knocked out, making it into a large sitting room and beautiful open plan kitchen diner, keeping the downstairs almost the same, except for the kitchen which became a summer room and the bathroom, which was made into a smaller shoe room, whilst the downstairs bedrooms were stripped and re-plastered; and had the added bonus of both being fitted with en-suites.

The entrance to the lower level I had now had an iron gate put on for security; and still left the door there as it was acting as a lower ground back door, as now the main door was up the six steps to the beautiful front door that I had had restored to its original colour and feature.

I had also gained even more gardens, as the land above my little garden, was enough to build a further four houses, as it uncovered not only a walled garden, but also a secret garden. I had since had interest in the land, and had offers, but I had no intention of selling, because it was so lovely having all the gardens to walk through and to get lost in them, knowing you had no houses or apartments looking over at you. Steve again gave me the crew who had renovated the bar; and it was there that I found out that the site manager had since divorced.

This time we were on first name terms, and he introduced himself as Nigel. I stayed in the ground floor apartment whilst the work was carried out above me. The crew also stayed upstairs in the rooms that had not been converted, whilst Nigel stayed with me downstairs; and there were talks from the crew that we were having a liaison of affairs, which got us both laughing.

I know a few times Nigel used to comment to the boys, that he so wished we were, as who could not turn down such forbidden fruit as Roxy Svenningsen.

I also have to admit that we came close, as one night that I was going to treat the boys to a meal; and then of course a glamorous evening at Danni's bar.

I was getting myself ready, and I thought that the bathroom was empty, that I just walked in.

To my surprise there was Nigel standing in front of the mirror shaving, completely naked. He had the thickest of chest hair that I had seen; and you could tell he was a straight bloke, as he did not trim his bush. He had a bit of a beer belly, but still had a six pack, if not a bit flabby by now. His cock was about six inches; more if he trimmed his pubic area; and he had a cute bum, as well as being hairy from head to toe. He was a typical beefy construction worker, who had sex appeal.

Me walking in did not faze him in the slightest, as he stood there and continued to shave, showing me all that he had to offer. Now red faced, I turned around and left the bathroom, as my thoughts still were towards his gorgeous body; and a part of me was very tempted to go back into the bathroom and kiss him. That was the first time; and was certainly not the last time I saw Nigel butt naked in front of me; and I think he did it just to tease me, so much so on one occasion I did indeed slap his ass, however, we only got as far as a good old fashioned kiss with each other, because Nigel again discovered Brighton; and there was too much eye candy for him to be faithful to one person.

I did though have a very good friendship and understanding with him; and when the job was completed, he told me that he had since met a Brighton guy, a guy who was also in the trade; and he was taking him back to work for him in London, as well as to live together, as they had both fallen for each other. Like Nigel, he too was hairy; and it was then when I asked if I was going to be invited to a bear wedding, as it would be my first wedding in such a long time. He just smiled at me; and then said you never know.

As I got my cab from the bar, I let myself in and just closed the door behind me, where I threw off my shoes and looked at the clock. It was now one thirty in the morning; and I just said to myself I need a soak in the bath, so I made my way to the bathroom to run a bath, when I heard the doorbell and wondered who the hell that was at this time of morning. I was not expecting anyone; and I knew Stuart would not come over before texting first. Putting my slippers on, I made my way to the interior security door; and pressed my finger onto the intercom and said hello softly, being a little cautious.

"Hello, is that you Roxy?" A male voice replied
"Yes this is Roxy, who is that?" I replied
"It's me Roxy, please open the door. It's me sweetie." He said, as I heard a voice that was like someone desperate, or about to give up as the voice seemed distant and tearful.

At first, I could not think who it could be, as I never had any visitors at that time of morning. So again, I asked who it was; and although he never quite told me his name; all of a sudden it dawned on me as he kept saying sweetie.

"*Johnny, is that you Johnny?*" I shouted as I scrambled to the front door.

I opened the door; and there standing before me was Johnny. He looked like he had the world on his shoulders, looking all bedraggled and needing a shave.

"*Oh Johnny oh my dearest Johnny, where have you been? Why have you not you text or called, it must be how long now?*" I asked, as I ran into his arms.
"*I am sorry Roxy it has been too long, three years if I am not mistaken. Can I please come in sweetie?*" He asked, as he stood there shivering.
"*Oh yes sure forgive me, I am just shocked.*" I said, as I opened the door a little wider; and put my arms around him.

Standing on the doorstep with my arms around him, he asked me how I had been; and what had I had been up to? We had a brief catch up, before I told him to come in. I was just so shocked, that my manners had slipped slightly, and we just stood in the doorway embracing each other. I asked him to come in, as I helped him out of his wet coat. He followed me into the hallway; and as I closed the door behind us; not knowing where to go I pointed towards the lounge, where he made his way as he then slipped off his shoes.

As I locked up again and like routine, I made all the security checks of locking up which was a force of habit being on my own, I made my way to the lounge where Johnny was standing up admiring the room, as again I ran into his arms. Just then before Johnny could speak, I remembered I still had the bath running.

"Oh damn my bath, excuse me Johnny I have left my bath running. What a dizzy queen I am." I said, as I hurried into the bathroom.

I had got there just in time, but would not be able to jump in the bath for a while as it was scalding hot, so I went back downstairs and into the lounge where I sat next to Johnny. I asked him how long he had been back in the UK; and where the hell was Ruby, now sitting next to him as I placed my arm under his. He then told me that he had been in the UK for the last two months; and that he had been staying with Ellie, thinking things over. That Ruby and he had split up about a year ago, saying that she did not want to be reminded about anything or anyone from her past. Feeling drained and unkempt, he continued to say that she was so swallowed up in her new life, that she eventually shut him out.

"Johnny it is ok honey, I am here. Come on spill the beans Johnny, and please stop those tears." I said, now handing him a tissue

"She started seeing someone on the island, became quite the celebrity too. She was able to shut her past life out; and start a new one. We very rarely saw each other; and

a few months after she was dating this guy, she asked me to leave. We had an almighty argument; and rather than just put up with her lies I grabbed what things I had and rented for a while, that was until I got everything out of the house. I was lost and lonely and often thought about you, but I could not get around to telling you what was going on. I thought it best if I just disappeared, that's why I never called, as I knew you had lots to cope with and I still feel that I have let you and Danni down. I then realised this was wrong and well, well here I am. Please forgive me Roxy, please forgive me." He said, as he broke down in a flood of tears.

"*There is nothing to forgive Johnny, but you should have phoned me or text me even if it were a lie by saying all was ok. I have spent the last couple of years wondering what on earth I had done wrong; and were you both were or what you were up to. I even contemplated on coming over to see you, but too many things were going on this end.*" I replied, as I placed my hand on his and then kissed him on the cheek.

"*I am so sorry Roxy, I have let you down and I have let Dannie down as well.*" He cried

"*How Johnny, how have you let us down?*" I asked, as I looked him in the eye

"*A while before Danni's accident, he asked me that if anything were to happen to him, would I promise him that I would take care of you. I didn't Roxy I went back to the island and tried to sort out my mess, but I so wanted to stay with you, as I somehow knew Ruby and I were heading for disaster. I let Danni down and I broke my promise.*" He said, again beginning to cry.

"Hey do not be bloody stupid, you are here now and that is all that matters. Now sit there and let me fix you a drink; and for goodness sake take off your jacket." I said, as I got up to go to the drink's cabinet
"Yes Miss Roxy and thank you Miss Roxy." He said, as he slowly began to tear up.

I went up to him and bent over; and as I kissed him on the forehead. Feeling so happy that I had got my dearest Johnny back, that I told him that he was not going anywhere. And that he will stay with me for as long as he wished.

"Please believe me when I say that; and trust me when I say you are going nowhere, because I am going to look after you."

He then began to cry once more, as he grabbed hold of my hand and smiled at me, as I began wiping away his tears. I then went into the drinks cabinet and poured him a large scotch. On the way back I noticed him looking around the house; and looking rather bewildered, as he told me he had tried to use the apartment entrance, only to find that there was now a rather large iron gate to get through which was also locked, telling me that it was so different to the photo's that I had sent him, now looking grander than just apartments.

"Oh, I have had a big change around honey, buying these apartments and knocking it to one house. As you can see the lounge is now upstairs which I call my sea view lounge, followed by my open plan kitchen and

dining room. I have since changed one of the bedrooms here into a mini shoe room. I will give you a tour later, as there is quite a lot to see Johnny" I said, now pleased that finally I got to find out what had been going on. *"It is wonderful Roxy; Danni would be very impressed with you."* He replied, also being impressed with my design skills.

We then both sat down again chatting, as we spoke more of Ruby and what had gone on. Johnny had since sold his bar/club; and decided to move back to London, as it was pointless him staying on the island if he and Ruby were no longer together. He sold it at a loss, because he no longer wanted to be on the island, as there was nothing more for him there. He told me that there were quite a few drag queens there that were lovely, but they just never did anything for him; and they never possessed the quality that he was used to with myself. I thought that was such a sweet thing to say, as I then asked him to forgive me, but what had he done to his hair. I remembered him as a man who had the most gorgeous black hair, that was so distinguished and sexy looking. And how now it had changed to a silvery grey, which by the way was still distinguished. Looking at me as though I did not approve, he told me that it had been like that for the last few years. He put it down to stress, but I could read between the lines that it was that bitch of a partner, Ruby. I thought it really suited him, as did the goatee that he had since grown. He may have got older, but he certainly had matured very well indeed, and he seemed so mellow now, not having the stress of the rainbow and of Ruby; and he had still kept his good looks, even though at present he looked so tired. Bless him, he thanked me for my kind words, but thing was, I meant what I said, as I was never known to butter things up, as I spoke as I found. He then put me on the spot, as he just came out with that awkward question, by asking me if there was a man in my life. As I was stuck for words, I playfully told him that there were a few men in my life, referring to Stuart, as he really had been looking after me these past year's; and that we were now better friends than before, even though I thought that we may have got together. I told him that he had split up with Adam; and then he began seeing a girl from the bar, which was a long story, and he was now single. I told him that I had my boys in the bar; and a few regulars who are now in my circle of trusted friends.

"That's nice, you have always had a way with presenting yourself; and for people liking you for showing yourself as being genuine. I think it is your nice kind feminine nature, but what I meant was, is there a special man in your life?" He asked, as that little boy came out.
"Not at all Johnny, I have not had time for that kind of love, or indeed romance. I have put my strength into Danni's bar; and had my quiet walks along the seafront and the downs. I am afraid I am a bit of a stay at home girl now, apart from working at the bar; and I have not got all glammed up in years like I used to, when times were so that I dined out in style. And may I truthfully say; I have certainly not come close to finding a man to share my life, even though I thought a few times I would have done. What about you Johnny, are you seeing anyone?" I

364

replied, now feeling inquisitive; and wondering if he had someone in his life, now that Ruby was out of the picture.

He told me that there was no one special in his life, that he needed to get over Ruby first, which he had almost done; and that he would be no good to anyone in his present state anyway, as he really did need to sort head out. He continued to tell me that Ruby was such a bitch; and she really had fucked with his head, calling him a sad old gay man and other harsh names.

"I have to admit, I loved it when she was Ruby and had a cock, but she would never let me touch it that often. I put up with everything because I loved her, and I never thought she would ever change. Thing is I am not straight, I am a gay man who likes cock, tits and ass on his girl. Does that sound strange to you Roxy?" He said, as he then took a sip out of his drink
"No, it does not sound strange honey, some guys like women who have everything, others like us women with a dangly bit and boobs, whilst others will make do with a gay guy who lives as a woman with everything a guy has on the underneath. And I do not feel you should be labelled for what you like sexually, or even mentally and physically, labels are best kept for clothing and food." I replied, feeling for him, as Danni was exactly the same
"Exactly Roxy, exactly; and still the same Roxy I have always known, wise and very beautiful." He replied, now with a smile on his face.
"Right, it is time I took my bath Johnny, you are welcome to come and say hello if you want to talk." I told him, as I got up and made my way to the bathroom.

I went into the bathroom and slowly undressed, then climbed into my nice hot bath. Not as hot as usual but was still pretty hot to make me go like the colour of a lobster, as I played with the bubbles and reflected on the evening. Just then, Johnny poked his head around the door to see if I were ok, then asking me if he could join me. I told him that it would be nice to talk to him, so long as he did not mind me being in the bath, as I then asked him to bring my glass of wine in with him, as I had just covered my dignity up with the bubbles. I don't know why I did cover myself up, because it did not bother me too much in the past; and this was Johnny, and I am sure he had seen lots of naked men before. He then went out and fetched my wine; and came back into the bathroom. We were chatting nicely when I noticed him staring at me, so I looked at him and asked him what was wrong; and why the stare?

"You are so beautiful Roxy; I have always thought that of you. I am proud of you for all the shit you have gone through; and how you have coped with it, and all that you have done to make your dreams happen; and to make true a dream you and Danni thought of long ago; and how you manage to still look as beautiful as the Roxy I knew all those years ago." He said, as he poured his heart out.
"Aawww stop it Johnny, you will make me cry in a moment." I replied, as I picked up my hand and threw some bubbles at him.
"You naughty girl Roxy, playtime is it?" He said, as he got up off the chair and came over to me.

He knelt by the bath, and with his hand he pushed my head under the water. Once under he released his hand as I jumped up coughing and spluttering, as again I threw the bubbles over him in a playful gesture. Then our eyes met; and it was at that instance that I threw my arms around his neck and kissed him on the lips.

He pulled me towards him; and he held me tightly, with his arms around me he kissed me with so much passion I thought he was on heat. The next thing I knew he had climbed into the bath; and I just screamed and laughed at the same time, as I said. "*Johnny you daft blighter, you still have your clothes on.*"

Now completely soaked, he told me that they were only old clothes, and that he had been waiting years to kiss me. Not even thinking about the situation, I told him to get out of his wet clothes; and to come and join me in the bath. I don't know what it was, or why I said it, but it just seemed the right thing to do. I told him that I would get his clothes dry cleaned tomorrow; and I was certain there was some of Danni's clothes still in the wardrobe for him to change into. He climbed out of the bath and removed his clothes, dropping them into the shower before climbing back in the bath with me.

That was the very first time I had seen Johnny stark naked; and I can tell you I was not disappointed in the slightest. He still had his lovely dark hair on his chest although greying slightly; and he was still very fit and muscly, with just the right amount of love handles to hold onto.

He was very modest; and before climbing into the bath,

he placed his hands over his manhood so that I could not see. It just made me smile, as this was the very first time I had seen my Johnny show his shyness. He sat at one end of the bath and then asked me to turn around and join him, as he opened his legs and held out his arms. I turned around and done just that, feeling his arms wrapped around me. For the first time in three years I again truly felt safe, I felt protected and safe at last as this was so very different to being with Stuart or any of my boys. Johnny gently kissed me on the neck as he held me in his arms, with him placing my hands over his as he told me that it was so nice to see me; and he did not know how I would react to his absence. I then held onto his arms, as they were tightly holding me, and told him that I was so glad he had come to find me. I told him that he was never out of my mind; and that I had missed him so much. He then kissed me on the head, as he told me that he will never leave me again.

Just before the water went cold, we finished bathing as Johnny got out of the bath first. He reached for the towel and wrapped it around himself, as he reached for one for me and held it open, but not before I caught a glimpse of his cock. He was about seven to eight inches, and it was quite thick. He had a nice trimmed bush, which told me that he still maintains his look down below; and smooth shaved balls, which was a thing for gay men to do. Wrapping the towel around me, he picked me up and carried me over the bath, giving me a kiss on the lips as he told me it would be a nice gesture to have a nightcap and go to bed. He let me dry off, as I then removed my makeup and placed a towel over my head wrapping my hair in it. I thought this would have shocked Johnny, as he rarely saw me as a guy, but in fact he did not flinch, seeing me come into the lounge he looked at me and said.

"I have poured you a glass of wine Roxy, would you like to chat some more, or would you prefer to go to bed? And may I kindly ask where the spare room is."

"Too many questions Johnny, just relax for me please. Let's go to bed Johnny, it has been quite a day; and are you sure you are happy with me like this?" I asked
"Sweetie you are you, and I like you for who you are. You are still Roxy to me, whether you have a dress and make up on, or lingerie, or as you were born and just in guy mode. You are still my Roxy." He replied, as again he asked where the spare room was.
"And you are my sweet handsome Johnny; and I never thought I would ever be in this situation, never in a million years." I replied, as I held him as I pulled his head towards me and kissed him on the cheek.
"What about Danni, I wonder if he is watching us?" He asked.
"I always feel Danni with me; and twice I have felt his presence Johnny. The first time was when he was laid out in the hospital, I knew Danni was waiting for you. The moment you came into the room where we were, and you held his hand, I also was holding his hand at the same time if you remember. It was then that I told him I loved him as you told him that you were there, I then saw a tear fall from the corner of his eye; and I felt him squeeze my hand, then all hell broke loose. I now know he could not hold on any longer Johnny, his body was too damaged and he could not get back to me, back to us.

He waited until you were with me, because then and only then did he know I would be safe." I told him, as he embraced me and held me tight.
"Oh Roxy, my beautiful Roxy do you really think so?" He replied, as he just held me close to him.

"Yes Johnny, I felt him. And the second time was when I brought his ashes down here back in 2002. I was with Stuart and we stood on the downs; and as I opened the urn, I scattered his ashes. It was whilst I was scattering them that I felt a warm breath on my neck; and a tingle down my spine as I caught a smell of his cologne. It was then that I knew he was finally free and in a place we both loved; and I also knew he was home and that he would always be with me to protect me." I told him, letting him know that everything was ok; and there was no longer a reason to cry

Johnny then put his head on my shoulder and cried his eyes out, as he began to tell me just how much he has missed him; and that every day he wished he was still alive. That he had never found anyone who came even close to the friendship that he and Danni had; and how hard it was when he had problems and no one to talk to. I put my hand onto his cheek, as I kissed him on the lips and told him that it was best that we go to bed, telling him that he will be in no spare room; and that he would be sharing my bed if he wanted too.
He held me all night as we fell asleep in each other's arms, comforting each other from our tears and pain. That morning, Johnny got up before me where I had a lovely aroma of bacon wafting up into the bedroom.

I just thought I have not had bacon for such a long time, even though I always kept a pack in the fridge; and it was such pleasant to smell to entice me downstairs.
I then got up and made my way to the kitchen, where Johnny had set the table and almost finished breakfast.

"Morning Johnny." I said, almost scaring the life out of him.
"Morning Roxy, thought you may have stayed in bed a little longer; you have spoilt my surprise." He replied.
"I am sorry honey, but the smell of bacon woke me up; and it has been such a long time since I have had such a lovely smell wake me up." I replied, as I went up behind him and placed my arms around him just hugging him.

He then told me to go and sit at the table, as he did not want me to get burnt. I made my way to the dining table; and poured myself some of the orange juice that was already there. We started chatting again; and I could see that he was a lot better than he was earlier that morning.
I could not believe that it was ten o'clock, as I am always out of bed by 7am, come rain or shine, but had no concerns as Stuart was going to open the bar for me as he was on a late shift that evening.
Johnny had made me a full breakfast; and I knew I would not manage it all not being a big eater, but I did not have the heart to tell him. It was so sweet that he had gone to all the hassle, so I was not going to ruin it by just having bacon. I did eat half of it; and then made my excuses that I rarely eat breakfast nowadays.
He was a very old fashioned guy; and then he told me that breakfast was the most important meal of the day.

I just looked at him and told him that it was not for me, as mine was more the evening meal, especially with champagne.

"You and your champagne, I am surprised you do not have shares in the vineyards with the vast number of bottles you buy. That is if you still do." He replied, now rather perky, and getting back to the Johnny I so knew.

I told him I still buy champagne, as a girl always needs a bottle or six in the fridge. I also told him that my London home has a walk-in chiller with wine stacked up high.

"You never change Roxy; and that is why I like you so much. You are still the same Roxy that I met all those years ago back at the Rainbow." He said, as he gave me a smile and a wink.

At the table we began chatting again, and it was as though we had never ever been away from each other, this time though I was not expecting Danni to come through the door, or even Ruby come to that.
I then mentioned to him how scared I had got over the last few weeks, as every time I came to lock up the bar, I often saw a figure of a guy over the road looking over.
I was hoping that I was not becoming paranoid, but it did seem as though he was staring right over at me.

"Roxy it was me. I never had the courage to come over to see you; and just watched you from a distance. I saw a few times that you were with another guy; and thought he may be your new partner. I still needed to see if you

were ok, and like I said, I just did not have the courage to come over to you." He explained, as he again apologised. "*You should have come over Johnny, I would never have turned you away, you know that. As for the guy, you now know it was Stuart; and yes, there were times even I thought we would be together, but our friendship was far more important than a stab at a romance that may not have worked.*" I replied, now placing my hand on his hand.

"*I am sorry if I made you a little paranoid, it was not intended. Ellie was the one who told me to come down to see you, so I booked into a hotel around the corner; and tried to muscle up the courage. When I first saw you, my heart skipped a beat and then I saw Stuart, so I backed off, but still continued to see if everything was ok. I phoned Ellie last night to tell her that I was coming back to London; and it was Ellie who again told me to get off my stubborn ass and see you, knowing that I still had not done so. I still did not have the courage to come to the bar, so I decided to walk along the seafront, and before I knew it, I was in Hove, so decided there and then that it was now or never. The rest is history sweetie.*" He said, almost sobbing again.

"*I am so glad you did Johnny, and I was a little paranoid, however, I knew I had my boys who would look out for me and make sure that I am ok. I am very fortunate Johnny to have such people look out for me; and as for Stuart, I really do not know what I would have done without him.*" I told him, as I placed my hand over his and looked him in the eyes.

Johnny told me that he always liked Stuart; and way back when he had the Rainbow, he knew Stuart was of good stock; and he was so grateful that he had maintained his friendship with me; and had continued to look out for me. We then finished up in the dining room, and as Johnny was about to do the washing up, I cleared my voice, then standing next to him I opened a cupboard. I told him that I now have a dishwasher so no more going in the sink. No more having hands that prune up, even if I do use fairy, then calling myself a posh totty. Johnny smiled, as he said I was very posh indeed, thinking that I only had a rather large American fridge freezer in there, as he could not see anything else, as it was all cupboard doors. I went from cupboard to cupboard, showing him washing machine, dryer, spare fridge with just wine inside.

"Very posh indeed, and all out of the way; how genius you are." He said, now beginning to brighten up again as he joked.

I then told him that it was Steve who designed the kitchen for me, after I told him what I wanted. That it was nice having your white goods there, but clearly out of sight. I then just looked at him and told him that I did not want anyone robbing my champers, that they could have anything else but not that. It's my only weakness, as I do not smoke; and a girl needs a little pampering and luxury from time to time. He just told me that I get worse.

I we then continued to have a chat about present and future, I told him that I was grateful for Stuart being down here, as he was a diamond, that he helped me so much; and I would not have known what to do without him. That all my boys, and girls were my rock, with it being Stuart whom I leaned on more. We stayed indoors for a little while; and as I was not taking over the bar till this afternoon, I stayed as Bobby.

Realising that Johnny had no clean clothes with him, I walked into the spare room and got one of Danni's suits, as I forgot to remind him to go and help himself. I then placed it on the bed, as I told him I had put a set of clean clothes out for him. I never got rid of Danni's clothes, even though a few times I thought I had best do, but I also knew that if my boys were going to a party or posh dinner, that they were there for them should they need to ask for one. He was thankful for the clothes, as he thought he may have had to spend the day in the nude; much to the approval of the smile I had on my face. I told him that there was underwear in the cupboards too, but he would need to take some scissors with him, as they still had the labels attached.

We went into town to do a little shopping, as we then headed towards the bar. When we arrived, Stuart was a little startled with me coming in with a man; and then the penny dropped as he recognised him to be Johnny.

He left the bar and came up to us both, shaking Johnny's hand, as he then gave him a man hug and told him it was so lovely to see him again. He asked where Ruby was, as Johnny then just told him long story, whilst I went to the office to sort a few things out, as I left the boys talking, as I saw the relief on Johnny's face as he had a friendly male face he could chat with; and being Stuart, it was as though nothing had changed. I walked into the office as I wanted to see who was working with me that afternoon and evening; and to put a few things in the safe.

When I got back to the bar, the boys were engrossed in chat as they stood at the end of the bar together.

This so reminded me of the times Johnny and Danni were in chat at the Rainbow; and it was lovely to see Johnny slowly getting back to his old self, as he looked handsome standing at the end of the bar and tottering around like he once used to.

Stuart then asked me if I would like a drink, so I told him that a soda and lime would be enough, as I did not want to get tipsy before the evening, otherwise it would mean a night off which I did not want to happen.

I had my Scottish Allen working from 4pm, as well as my lovely Brighton boy Tim, who would be coming in at 8pm, then alongside Michelle were my full timers, who were also very much a big part of my family. Tim was a lovely little queen, so helpful and caring; and he would do anything for you. I was also sure he liked Stuart as well as Allen, as he was a little bit of a flirt when they were both in the bar.

Johnny and I spent the next few months getting to know each other; and I began getting a spring back in my step. I had only ever seen the business side of Johnny, with the few times that he managed to relax when we had dinner or threw a party back in the day. Now however, I was beginning to find out what Johnny was like as a person away from the business side of life. Closer and closer we got involved with each other as we went out for meals, where we laughed and cried and took our romantic strolls along the beach, but as of yet, he had not made any attempt to make love to me fully.

We kissed and hugged, but there was no contact between us in a more intimate sexual sort of way, not even with the number of times I felt Johnny's bulge press firmly in the arc of my back when we were cuddling. However, likewise, I never did anything to him accept for the times I were cuddling and during the night whilst asleep my hand resting on his bulge.

He was also my hero when it came to the bar, as he asked if he could help me out and sort out the financial side of things, as he knew I was getting frustrated with work that had piled up, now Stuart could not do it for me regular as he had been doing; and how expensive it had become by getting an accountant to sort out my monthly goings on. I accepted his kindness; and in doing so I no longer needed to pay my accountant every month for a service that Johnny was exceptional in. I only needed my accountant on a once yearly basis, which I think he did not like now not having that extra bit of money coming in.

In the autumn of 2004 Johnny had booked a table for me in my favourite Italian Restaurant in Brighton which was near The Lanes. As we got there, everything was fine at first as we made conversation like we always did.

Then he just surprised me, when he just came out with something that stopped me in my tracks.

"We have spent all these months together Roxy; and I cannot think of a day in my life without you. You make me laugh and cry, and you are never far from my

377

thoughts or from my side. I wondered if you would do the honours of being my girl." He asked, as he held my hand. "*Oh Johnny that would be lovely, I would love to be your girl thank you.*" I replied, as I held his hand, and pulled him towards me kissing him on the lips.

"*There is also one thing I would like to do Roxy, if you will agree, as I need to do this properly.*" He asked. "*Sure what is it honey?*" I asked, rather confused. "*Do you think we can go to The Downs and ask Danni if it is alright, as I have not yet been to his final place of peace? I am very old fashioned, and I would just like to have a moment and ask him.*" He said, as he welled up. "*Johnny that is such a wonderful thought, we will go there tomorrow before popping into the bar if that is alright with you honey.*" I said, appreciating his concerns and his loyalty to Danni.

That next morning, it was very bleak with thick black cloud over the horizon. I looked at Johnny and asked if he still wanted to do this, what with the weather being so cruel as it was. He had not changed his mind and said that he would still like to go to where Danni's ashes were scattered, as he did not want to wait any longer. Only then would he know it was right, once he had asked Danni, he would then know if I could be his. I now got Johnny; and what he was about. My barriers were still up, because I thought that he may be like the others, and just leave. I thought he may change his mind, as he would have been attracted to Michelle, so that was why my barriers were up, because no matter how close I get to someone, they end up leaving me. I asked him what that the reason he had been putting off being intimate with me, I mean we did sleep together, but we had only ever kissed and cuddled, which was fine in someway, but I was beginning to wonder if he had feelings for me. He was honest and open with me, telling me that I had the business that I concentrated on, and he wanted to take it slow until he was or felt ready. He spoke about the old times, and now he told me he has enjoyed our times together, but he could not come to terms with making love to me until he had sorted out his past.

"That is fine Johnny; I was beginning to think we were just buddies, even though I too did not want to rush into things. But how slow did you want to go, I mean it has been nearly a year; and I guess you did consider my age." I replied, with a bit of a wicked laugh.
"You never change Roxy; and I am so grateful for that. I too have wanted so badly to make love to you, but it just didn't seem right. I did not want to rush you for fear of losing you, so let's get this sorted and we can then start properly." He said, as he brushed my hand with his fingers.

We then got ready and drove to The Downs, Johnny parked up, as I then showed him the spot in which I stood all those years ago, when I felt Danni's presence. Johnny wrapped his arms around me as we felt the autumn chill; and saw the blackness out towards the horizon. He then began saying a few words, telling Danni how much he had missed him; and how much of a loss it is still in his heart. How he was sorry that he betrayed him by not looking after me; and how he would like to make it up to him, now with tears streaming down his face. Just then, at the moment that Johnny asked Danni if he could have my hand, I felt a shiver down my spine and a warmth on my neck, which Johnny also felt. Then for a split second, the sun came out and shone on the ground in which we stood, as the smell of his cologne hit the air and came flooding through the senses of our nostrils.

"Danni, my sweet Danni." I said, as I grabbed hold of Johnny's hand and held it so tight.
"I hear you Danni. I will take care of Roxy for you, I promise you that Danni. I will take care of our Roxy if you will allow me too, as I have really fallen for her; and I promise you that I will never let either of you down." Johnny said, as the tears again came flooding to his face.

Johnny then held me tight, placing his arm around my waist. He then pulled me towards him and gave me a kiss, pulling away to say thank you.
We stayed there for a few moments, savouring the moment in which we had both experienced, as we saw the sunlight slowly fade away, and the black cloud taking over once more. We both felt warmth in our hearts; and peace in our minds, but always knew that this would be our special place to go and spend time with our thoughts, our new love, and our Danni.
It was then that I asked him to give Ellie a call, as I knew she would want to know what had been going on. I also knew she had not heard from him in a while, so he could let her know that he was ok.
Johnny then asked me to phone Allen and to tell him that

I would be late coming in, as there was something he needed to do. So being intrigued I called Allen; and gave him the message which Johnny had told me to say.

We then got back into my car as Johnny drove us back home; and when we got to the front door Johnny picked me up and carried me indoors. Once indoors, Johnny embraced me as he kissed me gently on the neck. Although it had been a few months since Johnny came into my life, and we had hugs, this was so different. It had been so long since I had been in the embrace of a man, having his arms around me to strengthen me, to feel me, to protect me. The embrace that told you it was more than a friend; and even more than just a night of unadulterated love that had no other meaning that that of just sex filled with alcohol and orgasms. This embrace was the embrace that made you go weak at the knees as you know you were in the arms of a man that you strangely loved once for a different reason, that with a hand that simply caresses your skin sends shivers down your spine filling your senses with all manner of nice thoughts. And the warmth of his breath on your face keeps you wanting for more as you direct your lips to his now hot moist lips, that invites your tongue to mingle with his. This is the embrace that is special to just two people, two people who are falling in love.

And yes, I had now come to realise, that I had fallen in love with Johnny, my Johnny from the rainbow, who was once a sincere friend, that now the man who had captured my heart for another reason; and I knew that we would be together for the rest of our lives.

These past few months I knew that I had feelings for Johnny, but I did not know just how much. Ruby was

still in the forefront of my mind, thinking that I was
intruding, but feeling pleased he was back in my life.

 I made my way into the kitchen, which I thought it was
a champagne kind of time. Johnny looked through my
vinyl collection and noticed my Julie London album,
which was also his favourite artiste from the sixties.
He placed the record on the deck and let it play as he
grabbed hold of my hand and got me to my feet.
The smell of his cologne tantalising my nose, as he held
me close to him. Our bodies in a warm loving embrace
with my head on his shoulder as we slowly smooched to
the song with his breath blowing warm across my ear.
I melted, as he held me gently, moving to the music, as
he told me that he loved me.
He then took me straight to the bedroom, where he asked
if he could make love to me; and as I said yes Johnny
slowly undressed me leaving me in just my lingerie, as
he himself, stripped completely and lay next to me on
the bed. I no longer felt embarrassed about looking at his
manhood, which whilst soft was still quite a handful; and
aroused was still well endowed and thick.
He always had a lovely head of hair nicely trimmed, but
alas with age he had matured well with the same grey
peering through which really did suit him; and I think I
preferred this new Johnny, from the man I knew many
years ago.
That afternoon Johnny made love to me for around two
hours, before I told him he had to stop as I needed to get
to the bar. It was the first time since being together, he
had penetrated me. He came very quickly the first time

as it was too intense for him, then a bit longer the second time, until it came to the third time in which he made me shoot my load whilst still inside me. Even when he made love to me, he never once took my cock in his hands or mouth, which I just put down to him still being that little bit more nervous than before.

When I finally got to the bar, Allen and Stuart was already there; and as I walked in, I told them I had an important announcement to make. I told them that Johnny and I were now a couple, but not to buy a hat yet as we wanted to spend more time together before making such announcements. By now I had made Allen my manager and he revelled in the role, as Stuart only looked after the bar when he could. Allen would even come into work on his days off to help, so what I did in return, was to give him the keys to my London apartment, so that he could have a break every now and then and get away from Brighton.

Stuart was the first to congratulate us; and I am not sure, but I got the feeling he was a little disappointed. He then brushed things aside, as he told Johnny that he was pleased for him; and that he knew we would both be good for each other. Looking at me, he told me that it was about time I settled down again, as I had spent too many lonely nights alone. Then to my shock, Stuart whispered in my ear that he should never have let me go all those years ago, but was afraid if he asked me out, I would have rejected him. I looked at him and smiled, as I reassured him that there was still a place in my heart for him; and it will not be long before he finds the man of his dreams. That I too wished he had asked me out, but I thought he was not interested.

I then reminded him that we have a far better relationship as friends, as I then jokingly told him that he would give me a heart attack, what with the thought of him being in uniform and handcuffing me if I were a naughty Roxy. This just made him smile, as again he said that he was pleased for us both. Allan in turn then came up to me and kissed me on the cheek, as he too congratulated us, then he whispered in my ear.

"Roxy it is quiet here if you wanted to go home; and I am sure that I will manage ok without you. Besides we have a new lad starting tonight, so it will give him a chance to find the ropes."
"Oh right, you want to see the back of me do you whilst a little chicken works here? I get it; get the old queen out so you can ogle and have fun." I laughed.
"No not at all Roxy, I just ..." Allen said, as I interrupted him.
"Chill out honey you are getting way too serious, I was joking; you daft queen." I replied, as I slapped his ass.

I looked at Johnny and asked if he wanted a drink first, before going home, because it was obvious, I was not welcome in my own bar. He agreed; and said whenever I was ready.

"Anyway Allen, I need to be here so that I can get him to sign a temporary contract. Then he is yours to do with him as you please." I laughed
"That's not fair Miss Roxy, I want one." Stuart asked.
"You will have to share honey, and sharing is so much fun is it not?" I said smiling.

Just then another familiar face from the past walked into the bar; and he was looking rather bedraggled.
He walked up to the bar rather sheepishly, looked at me and then just said.

"Miss Roxy nice to see you again, I hope you do not mind me coming in for a drink."
"Adam! Is that you Adam? Good God I thought you were dead. Where on earth have you been?" I asked, as I got off the bar stool.

"I moved in with Mike, after you and I had that big argument. He was not happy down here, so we moved to Didsbury, back to his hometown in Manchester. After a while he changed; and things were not as nice as I thought they would have been. He would take all my money and leave me with nothing; and he would stop out night after night and get drunk, as well as sometimes staying out all night and then not come home. I am so thankful he didn't know I had money in another bank account, as I am sure he would have bled me dry. The last straw came when he beat me up, so I packed a few things and then just left; and since then, I have been living up the road, and just wondering what on earth to do." He said, as he became upset; and was not able to talk properly anymore.
"You have been through a lot then Adam, but you were a silly lad. We all make the wrong choices sometimes, but it always has to be your choice. You know I would not say anything harshly, but sometimes honey, the grass is

not as green on the other side as we often think it is." I told him, as I held my arms out to him.

I then told Johnny to come down the bar towards me, then looking at Adam I asked him if he remembered Johnny. He told me that he did remember him; and how could he forget because he was so kind to him, as he ten asked where Ruby was. I then looked at Johnny, who came over to me and stood by me.

"Johnny you remember Adam, Adam Johnny and I are now a couple; Johnny is my husband." I replied.
"Nice seeing you again Adam, it has been a very long time." He said, as he gave him a manly hug.

Not trying to give Adam a lecture, I told him that what goes around comes around, it that is a well-known fact. I quietly told him that he was foolish with what he did, but sometimes love is blind; and we often mistake love from lust, and I should know because I have done the same a few times since Danni left us. That the best thing he could do, is to get over it and try and rebuild his life. Then telling him that the royal box is just behind me; and that he should make his way over and I would join him in a moment.
He started to make his way to the royal box, just as I said to him. *"Oh and Adam, welcome home honey."*

He then turned around and came running up to me, where he threw his arms around me, giving me a hug and saying thank you. He then went to the royal box, where Stuart was sitting; and then also hugged him and by what

I saw introduced him to Allen. They all sat down as Allen came back to the bar; and it was then that I thought to myself that my family was coming back home. Johnny put his arm around me, then putting his lips to my ear he said.

"Your boys are coming home sweetie; and did you mean it about me being your husband?"

"Yes, they are honey, my boys are coming home. I also did mean it as I do look upon you as my husband, but I also want it done properly. You know me, I am also a very old fashioned girl. Now enough of this as I need to see this young man that Allen has got lined up." I replied, as I smiled and raised my eyebrows at him.
"Oh I see, so you are also looking at the young ones?" He replied, as he grabbed hold of me and kissed me on the neck and laughed.
"Honey, there is nothing wrong in window shopping. It is always nice to see what is on display before buying, besides it is not like it is a pair of shoes." I said, as I told him some girls need to look at eye candy to realise what they already have is too precious to lose.

We stayed there for a little while, catching up on what Adam had got up to; and seeing that both Adam and Stuart were getting along fine, excepting that he embraced the fact Stuart just got on with his life, without him even though it was hard. I just sat there with my arm under Johnny's; and was content to see I have once again got a happy family, where soon after I decided I would go home and leave the bar in Allen's capable hands.

When we got back home, we sat in the garden with a bottle of champagne, as Johnny put on the garden lights. Johnny then put his jacket over my shoulders as we just sat there, watching the night sky growing darker and all the garden lights starting to come on as they glistened like stars. Johnny asked about having a take-away in which he ordered Chinese, where we ate it outside before going back indoors where Johnny took me to bed and made love to me all night.

All that week it was nonstop with Johnny, he made love to me whenever he could. Like the times with Danni, I would never take my shoes off as I so often explained. Johnny took over the accounts to Danni's bar full time, as I became a lady of leisure again. It now started to feel like old times, with Johnny being the head of the bar as I entertained in my little royal box, where my closest friends sat; and in which was out of bounds when we were not there.
I had finally taken the step forward to get in touch with Rik, who told me he was seeing someone in New York; and that he was pleased for me and Johnny. I had always been in contact with Jake and Sophie on a regular basis since Danni's death, with them calling me every week or so to make sure I was ok, either by telephone or letter, which over time did get a little few and far between. Once Danni's settlement of the business came through, I promised I would look after my family; and with that I wrote out two cheques for Jake and Sophie.
In the letter that was accompanied with the cheques was my reasoning that they were family, as Danni had given me a family with whom I loved so dearly; and they were

my blood family by marriage; and one I would have for the rest of my life. I explained that it was also what Danni would have wanted me to do; and I would have never forgotten them. I knew that they had also had a settlement, I just wanted to let them know I would never forget them; and that was why I sent them an extra cheque, which I asked Rik to put into a trust fund for when they were 21, to use for collage and luxuries, also knowing they would have been at the age, where their mother could not ask them to sign their inheritance over, because they would have been adults. I also wished them well; and prayed for the time I would see them all again.

It was now coming to the end of 2004, Johnny and I had established our relationship, and the bar was doing well. We had spent our first Christmas properly together as a couple in Brighton and Hove and would be spending New Year in London, with Ellie and Di coming over to visit us in our Victoria Embankment apartment.
I had not been to my London home in such a long time; and Ellie had done a good job looking after my apartment alongside Pip. When I went into the bedroom, it was then that I realised it was time to start clearing out a few things, so as I sorted through the wardrobes of clothes it dawned on me… Johnny, could he use Danni's clothes? Johnny had lost so much weight since splitting with Ruby and moving back home, that most of his clothes did not fit him properly. He moved into my Hove home with just one suitcase, so I looked at him and asked would he like the clothes for himself.

"Roxy that would be great, I will sort through them and see what fits, thank you sweetie." He said, as he thought I would have gotten rid of them by now.

"There are suits in there Johnny that have never been worn, as well as casual clothes. There are also shoes and boots, however underwear and socks, I will throw away, except those that still have tags on, but please you do not have to have them if you don't want to." I told him, now realising it was the better choice than sending them to the charity shop.

"No sweetie, that's really lovely of you to ask, and it would be a pleasure to finally put them back to good use; and I can leave some here, as well as have some back in Hove, as it saves me packing a bag all the time." He said, now feeling pleased that he did not have to go shopping.

During that day, whilst I was on the couch listening to music as I read through the mail that had piled up, Johnny spent the time in the bedroom going through numerous suits and other clothing.

"Right sweetie, I have gone through everything and all, but the shoes fit. I have never had such a wardrobe of clothes before." He said, now looking relieved that the task was over and done with.

"Then we need to go shoe shopping for you and it will be lovely because it means I can drag you into my shoe shops as well." I laughed, and happy that there was a shopping trip coming about.

"Oh, you and your shoes, I was always warned about you and your shoes sweetie. But I have to be honest, I

really hate shopping. Never liked it when Ruby took me round all those shops, where we were constantly stared at." He said smiling, but with dread.

"Well, my dearest Johnny, I am not Ruby, and I don't look like a bloke in drag." I told him, being a little catty.

"That was a bit cutting sweetie, but if I am to be honest, yes, she was, and that was my dread. I know you are fantastic as a woman, and my only concern is all the men who look at you and whistle." He replied.

"And know they are not in my league, because they will never get me, knowing that you are just as lucky to have me, as I am to have you." I told him, telling him that it comes with the territory, a handsome man, being with a beautiful woman.

I told Johnny that I would sort the shoes out another day, and may see if Stuart is a size ten, as his police boots always looked massive. If not, I was prepared to give them to one of the many charity shops in Brighton.
We then quickly went into the city where we went from one shop to another, buying him shoes like they were going out of fashion. We stopped for lunch, before doing yet more shopping for shoes, which Johnny was just as excited as I was, even though he had told me enough was enough on a few occasions.
I began to realise that maybe I was embarrassing him, as it was I who always got my card out before Johnny.
I looked at him and just told him that this was my special treat; and he can buy me dinner later. We then made our way back home; and as we got inside, I opened the door, and dropped my bags, as I held the door open for a fully loaded Johnny, as he had to watch where he was

stepping, as he could not see where he was going with the number of bags I had loaded him with.

That evening when we were ready to go out, I had my shower and again had a feeling of déjà vu, as Johnny climbed in next to me. Again, we made love in that shower, as Johnny sat down on the ledge and placed me on top of him sliding himself deep inside me.

Once we had made love, Johnny just held me and told me that he loved me more than he could ever utter the words, when we both decided it was time to get out of the shower and to get dressed. I chose my dress for the evening; and then began to put on my makeup whilst Johnny looked through the many suits that were in Danni's wardrobe, finding it hard which one to wear.

Sitting naked in the bedroom I started to get ready, when I saw Johnny sort a nice suit out to match a pair of dress shoes we had brought. He then disappeared and came back with a glass of champagne, as he came behind me and then started to kiss me on the neck. I turned around and put my arms around his waist, as I looked up and saw his naked body all but for his boxers, and his manhood starting to swell again.

It was then that I just touched the tip of his swelling bulge, as I told him that he would have to wait until later. I turned back around, as I told him I should be no longer than thirty minutes, and that I was so very happy.

Johnny kissed me and then placed my glass of champagne on the dresser. Being a little playful he thrust his bulging manhood into my back, where I told him to behave; and that I would deal with him later. He smiled at me and called me a tease, when I then placed my hand behind my back and grabbed hold of his balls and gently

squeezed them. Johnny told me to be careful of his
crown jewels, as there was no replacing them if I
damaged them. So again, I gave them a quick squeeze,
as I told him to hurry up and get dressed then.
He bent down towards me and kissed me on my neck,
with his tongue pressing against my ear. I had to tell him
to stop, as it was my weak spot; and it was turning me on.
Johnny then smiled at me, as he had himself found a
weak point which he could get his own back on me at a
later date. I turned around and then placed my arms
around him, gently stroking his ass, as he kissed me on
the lips, when he then placed his hand over his crotch;
and thrust himself towards me, telling me that it was all
mine when I got home. He left the bedroom and made
his way into the dressing room, where again he shouted
to me that he loved me very much; and that I had made
him a very happy man, and a man whom he considered
to be the luckiest one alive.
Once I had got dressed Johnny told me how beautiful I
looked, as I looked him over and approved. I then
noticed that the shirt he was wearing was in need of
some proper cuff links; and not the ones that came with
the shirt as they looked tacky. I made my way over
towards the bedside table that Danni used to have; and
inside I picked a pair of white gold cufflinks. I then went
into his wardrobe and into the safe where I picked out
one of his expensive Rolex watches; and holding it
closely in my hand I walked over to Johnny and said.

*"Johnny, Danni would have wanted you to have this
honey; it is his Rolex and I think it very fitting I give it to
you."*

"Oh wow Roxy, really? It is beautiful; I really don't know what to say." He replied, as he had a lump in his throat as he admired the watch.

Reaching for his lips I kissed him, and then told him it is how it should be. I then placed the watch on his wrist, and then got my bag, when we made our way to the Rainbow, where Ellie and Di were waiting for us.
I just thought I have my Johnny back, back as he once was looking so handsome and tall; and now with me rightfully on his arm. We walked into the Rainbow like royalty, with Ellie running up to us and telling us it was as though nothing had changed, as well as to the bombardment of some of the locals who had stayed loyal to the Rainbow, who were once again pleased to see Roxy and Johnny, back in the bar where they so belonged, as they asked us how we liked the changes that had since been made by Ellie.

"You both look absolutely gorgeous together; and Roxy you certainly know how to choose and handsome man. Johnny… it is a long time since I have seen my brother looking so classy and dapper; and it is great to see you with that same air in your step as you once had." Ellie said smiling.
"You know me honey, glamour, heels and a sexy handsome man is essential to keep me accustomed to my lifestyle." I replied, as I smiled at her.
"Well, I was not saying it because he is my brother, you really do look beautiful together; and Johnny, you really don't half scrub up nicely." She laughed, as she

reminded him how he looked when he came back from abroad.

We had a brilliant weekend in London catching up with old friends as well as new ones, getting Johnny to sort out the issues in the London home with the likes of the cars in the garage. I told him it was time we sold them and brought something that was now us, even though I did give him the option of having them for himself. He thought it was a good idea to sell them all, as it was time to put the past behind us and embrace our future. Johnny decided to stay in London that week to sort things out; and of course, to spend some time with Ellie. I gave him a kiss, as he saw me to my car as I had to get back to Brighton.

"*It's only for a week sweetie; I promise I will call you every night. Will you be fine, or would you prefer I come with you and let Ellie sort this?*" He asked.
"*Honey Ellie cannot sort it, not when you have buyers coming to look at the cars. Besides you are a man; and they will not try and pull one over you, so please call me even if it is a text saying you are off to the Rainbow to see the girls.*" I told him, knowing he would sort things out better than I could.
"*Sure thing, sweetie you know I will, now drive safely and I will call you tonight. Love you lots Roxy.*" He said, as he held me once again, not wanting to let me go.

I left the basement and drove out of the secure gates, as I made my way towards Hove waving to Johnny as I left. Once I got home, I showered and chilled out before getting ready to go to the bar. I only now went into the bar to see how the boys were and to sort any mail they had; and of course, to have a drink and entertain in the royal box.

Johnny sorted the finances and accounts for me; and of course made sure he had the wages up to date which was a great relief to me. I did however, wonder to myself why did I not stay up in London, as the bar was running like clockwork and I felt I was not needed there, so I decided that I would go to the bar and tell the boys that I would only be here for the night, as I was going back up to London to be with Johnny.

"We are selling the cars and closing the past, as we only have our future now to think of. You know how to do the stock don't you Allen; and go to cash and carry." I asked him.

"Yes Roxy, I have an order coming in tomorrow and I have the cash and carry card in the till. Don't you worry Roxy; besides I don't know why you worry so much you know we always look after you?" He said, knowing that I never ever questioned his running of things.

"I know honey, and I am thankful for having good friends in which I can trust. Anyway, I like coming in here and making a nuisance of myself, and I have to have my royal get together every weekend." I said smiling.

Allen poured me a glass of wine; and came over to me where we had a little chat. He told me the new lad was doing well, and that he had picked the job up quite fast. Allen thought that at the end of his trial I should consider taking him on full time, as he was a very good little worker. I told him that when I get back from London, to ask him to come in, and we will both take him in the office. Well Allen had a dirty mind, as he asked me to rephrase what I had said, although he wouldn't mind taking him in the office, or anywhere really. I told him to behave, as he had sex on the brain; and that he should control himself, as he was like a queen on heat. Then Stuart called over to me, telling me that he was always on heat

"*I meant take him in the office; and put it to him about working full time.*" I told him. "*What you do to him in the meantime, either by thought or by reality is up to you, but I am not getting involved even if he is a cutie.*"

We laughed and joked most of the night, talking about our past and the fun we had. How all our lives had changed; and how even Adam and Stuart did not think they would have spoken to each other again, as well as Stuart's job getting busier because he was working a lot of over-time, I was unsure when I would see him.
I had a real nice chat with Stuart and still called him my special policemen; and I was so glad we had maintained a very close friendship.
Stuart became like a brother too me, a brother in which I needed away from my gay family; and I made sure that everyone only called me Roxy and not the Miss Roxy of old. I told them that it was time for a change, and it would be better if we were on first name terms.
I had cabaret perform every weekend, but it was very rare for me now to tread the boards. I liked to see the

cabaret from a distance, although I would bring them onto the stage, taking the role of compare, I just never made the make up so heavy as I wanted to stay as natural as I could. Stuart then drove me home, as he was going to start yet another night shift, where he kept asking me if I was truly happy. I placed my hand on his knee telling him that I was, and how much I wished he would find a nice man. He then asked me if he could come and visit me sometime, as he wanted to have a chat, a chat like we used to have. I looked at him and as I grabbed his knee a little tighter, I just told him anytime, that I would always be there for him no matter what. He then pulled up at the house where he opened the door for me, I then kissed him on the cheek and told him to have a pleasant night at work, as I made my way inside the front door.

Once inside, I locked up as usual and made my way to the kitchen where I made myself a coffee.

Again, I had a trip down memory lane, now being able to freely talk about Danni without getting emotional; and I was able to talk about my new life with Johnny, and how there is not much difference between the two of them. Both Danni and Johnny made love to me in their own way, but the loving tenderness was always there, with the passion that made me feel like every time was my first time. Just then the home phone rang which broke the silence of my mind wandering; and right on queue it was Johnny checking on me. As I answered I told him I had been at the bar; and had a good old natter with the boys. He was pleased that I had had a good time; and told me that he loved me as I heard Ellie shout over that he was also missing me. I teased him by going on about how much had he missed me, that it would not be for long before I would be in his arms again. I thought no I am not going to say anything to him, I am just going to show up and surprise him. I then told him that I was going to go to bed once I had drunk my coffee, when I told him to give Ellie and Di my love and I would see then all soon. After about another forty minutes I went into the bedroom and went straight to bed, texting Johnny as I hit the pillow. He called me again on the home phone as I was charging my mobile, and we chatted for about another hour before I told him to get some sleep, as I was struggling to keep my eyes open. By my bedside table I had removed the picture of Danni; and replaced it with one of both Danni and Johnny, a picture showing them both in wedding attire; and one which I thought was the best out of all the ones I had of them both. My other pictures were placed upstairs in a display cabinet, as I would not completely delete Danni from my life. I looked at the photo and said goodnight my dear boys, as I placed a kiss on each picture.

The next day I awoke to a good morning text, as I started to get myself ready. I put on one of my suits in which I had not worn for a while; and filled up with petrol before I left. I then started my long journey from Hove back to London, to surprise Johnny.

I arrived back in London and parked my car out of view, where I then made my way upstairs. Just before getting to the front door I had text Johnny to find out where he was, and what he was up to. He then texted back telling me he was on a test drive, and the guy may be interested in all the cars and he would call me when he had finished. I made my way into the apartment and made myself a pot of tea, opening the balcony doors to sit outside and admire the view. Just as I was seated and I began looking over towards the Thames, I noticed the gates open. In came Johnny with one of the cars; and he drove straight into the underground parking area.

I thought that he was going to be coming straight up to the apartment, but he then went out again with another one of the cars, where I just thought either the guy is wasting his time or he was really interested, I did not see the reason why he wanted to test drive every one of the bloody cars.

An hour later I received a text from Johnny to say he would be home in about twenty minutes, and then once he had sorted the paperwork out it would be another few hours before he would call me. He went on to tell me that the guy had brought all the cars, but he was not going to let them go until he had received a banker's cheque. He then sent another text telling me that he loved me and that he could not wait to get back to Hove tonight, as he had missed me so much in just a short period of time. I made my way into the bedroom where I picked out a new set of lingerie, complimented it with a black and beige basque, I ran a bath and jumped in slowly soaking myself in the luxury of the bubbles, leaving my phone on the side of the chair.

I reapplied my entire make up, and then got dressed and lay on the bed. Johnny then texted me and said he was on his way up to the apartment and to give him ten minutes, where he would then call me.

I heard the door open, and a bit of fumbling in the lounge, then my phone rang. I let it ring until it went to answer phone. I could hear Johnny downstairs tinkering around a little, as he said I must be out, so he will make a drink and call back in a little while.

I was now very excited, and kept wishing he would hurry up and ring, as I could not contain myself anymore. Then all of a sudden, my phone began to ring again.

"What the hell, whose is that damn phone ringing?" I heard Johnny say.

He then came into the bedroom, and much to his surprise there I was laying on the bed, with my phone held up to my ear and a big smile on my face.

"What are you doing here? I thought you were still in Hove. You didn't half give me a shock, you little sweetie." He asked, as he jumped onto the bed and then lay on top of me, kissing me on the lips.

"Surprise darling, I could not see why I had to stay in Hove when you were up here. Hope you do not mind me surprising you?" I said, as I flashed my legs at him and fluttered my eyelashes.

"Not at all Roxy, just do not do it that often. I am not as young as I used to be." He laughed, as he kissed me again, telling me that he loved me.

He then took off his shirt and trousers and climbed into bed next to me, placing me in his arms as he kissed me gently. I placed my leg over his, revealing my stocking clad legs, with a lush black suede pair of heels.

He slid his hands in between my stockings and around the back into my panties reaching for my ass, now stroking my ass with his warm hands. Then gently he removed my panties now revealing my flesh; and as I turned round, he caught a glimpse of my cock. With his arm around my neck, he looked in my eyes and said.

"Roxy can I touch your cock, and do you think I will be able to play with it as well?"
"Sure you can honey; I did not think you were interested in that part of my body honey." I replied.
"Remember sweetie I haven't done this for such a long time, as I have only ever been allowed now and then to touch Ruby in that sort of way; and she didn't like me touching her there. I have waited so many years to do this, as I have not felt a proper man. I loved Ruby and put up with her changing moods, but I never really wanted her to get rid of her girly cock. I understood she was transsexual, but I could not bare to leave her, not with all the history we had. So please be patient with me Roxy, even though I am a quick learner." He said, as I felt he had to explain himself.
"Do not worry about it honey, take your time and I hope you enjoy what you see?" I replied.
"I want to make love to you properly Roxy, take all of you and make you feel special, and I would even like you to make love to me. But don't get used to it Roxy, after all I am the alpha male." He laughed.
"That is fine by me Johnny; we can take our time as we experience each other, and remember I am a woman with a cock, and alpha means nothing to me, because a woman has her ways of seduction." I replied, as I gave him a wink and a cheeky grin
"Great Roxy, that's great." He said, now relaxing, knowing that there was no pressure to do what he was not comfortable with.

"And I have said this once before Johnny; and I will only say it one more time. I am a bi gender male, who loves to be a Roxy; and I love my cock. I have no intention of either taking hormones or having the snip, as I am happy being a man dressed as a woman, with all my tackle in place. It will only be on a few occasions that you see me in guy mode, the rest of the time you will see me like this; and you must accept it." I told him.

"I understand Roxy and that's all I have ever wanted, and I do accept you for all you are trust me; as both male and that of a female, is very appealing to me; and you know that I find you simply exquisite." He replied.

He then gently took me into his mouth, as he tasted my cock for the first time. He was nervous at first, but he took me deep inside him, as he tasted my pre cum, telling me that I tasted so sweet; and that he could not believe what he had been missing. That it had stirred something in him, that had been missing for so long, reinstating his role as a gay man. He then raised my ass as he gently slid his cock inside me, as he took my cock for the very first time like a very excited man.

The other times we that we made love he still made me feel like a woman as the times before were still very intimate, but this time I was being made love to for the very first time properly both front and back.

Closer he pulled me towards him as I could hear him getting closer to shoot his load. He then took hold of my cock and started to jerk me off, and as he did, I could not hold myself in anymore as I shot over his hand and my tummy. He took hold of me and holding onto my waist he thrust deep into me, pulling me harder onto him until he just yelled out and collapsed on me.

"Oh god Roxy, that was divine. You are a wonderful lover and thank you so much. I love you sweetie; I love you so much." He said, as he just held onto me as he gathered strength to get his breath back.
"And I love you Johnny, I do hope that everything was ok as I will not rush you." I replied.
"We have a lot to learn together Roxy, as I would like to feel you deep inside me too if you would like that? And I want to taste you, as well as you taste me. I am still buzzing Roxy; God I want to go again." He said, like a man who had just discovered a second childhood.

That evening we got ready to go out, to celebrate not only making Johnny taking my cock in his sweet mouth for the very first time, but also because Johnny had sold all the cars which was a weight off my mind.
Once we had finished our meal we called in to the Rainbow, and like the gentleman he was he opened the door for me, then with his arm gently around my waist he escorted me to the bar where Ellie greeted us again, although being quite surprised that I had since returned to London, smiling he told me that he thought I was still in Brighton; and could I not bare the thought of being without him for just one night. I just answered plain and honestly, NO.

Whenever we were in London we would always go to the Rainbow; and when in Brighton we would go to

Danni's bar, and this was now definitely becoming like old times. As we entered the Rainbow, minus the bag search as David recognised who we were, he just told me that it was lovely to see me again as we kissed each other on the cheek. Recognising Johnny, he greeted him saying that it was great to see him again, as I then told him that Johnny was now my man. Much to the delight of the door staff. I then told Johnny that I thought it was pointless me being down in Brighton, when I had the boys who were capable of taking care of things for me, when I could be here in London with my man. Again, we stayed at the Rainbow until the end, getting a cab to take us home. That night we made love again and again, and what really surprised me, was that Johnny let me take his virgin ass for the very first time. We stayed in bed all night, and most of the next morning just making love with each other; and it was later that day when Johnny finally took me in his mouth and swallowed my load before offering me his manhood.

Two days later Johnny had a phone call from the guy who brought the cars, and as promised he had the banker's cheque with him. The guy must have asked who to make the cheque out to, because Johnny looked at me and asked what name I was now using. Not thinking in the slightest about a name change, I asked Johnny to give me the phone; and I would deal with things. Johnny gave me the phone, and then went to the kitchen to make coffee. I spoke to the guy on the other end and gave him the name to write on the cheque.

"Mr J Delaney, just write that on the cheque and we will meet you at my bank in an hour. Remember it is Delaney with one n." I replied.

Johnny then came back into the lounge and asked me if he heard correctly, that did I just tell the guy to make the cheque out in his name?

"Yes honey, I have enough money I do not need that cheque. You have sold the cars for me, so you can have the money. Please do not be mad at me Johnny, if I did not want you to have it, I would not have said so." I replied, now looking like I had been told off.
"I am not mad at you Roxy, but you should have spoken to me first. It is nice of you, but you have to stop this, speak to me first please sweetie ok." He said, as he looked at me and I dropped my head in shame.
"Ok Johnny." I said, as I made my way back to the bedroom.

I just lay on the bed and I then started to cry, when Johnny came in and saw me. He sat on the bed and told me he was sorry if he had upset me. He was not used to so much kindness, and I also think it was part of his pride as I had not quite realised just how proud and humble a man he was. He told me that he loved me for being me, not for my money. That he was just taken back that's all; and for me to stop crying. He then told me that he would accept the cheque; and he thank me from the bottom of his heart, then telling me that no one has ever shown him so much kindness before, now comforting me.

"Well, I have far too much money Johnny, I just wanted to give you some, something from Danni. I knew you were on the last of your own money from The Canaries, as it was not going to last forever, so please forgive me, but I accidently came across one of your bank statements a few weeks ago. I also wanted to give you some of my money because I will not use it all; and I want you to be able to go out and buy things without asking me. I am sorry I should have thought about your pride, and not thought about my ignorance." I answered, still crying.

Johnny then lay next to me and gave me a kiss on the head, and he put his arms around me.

"You are such a sweet beautiful kind person Roxy; I can now see why Danni fell for you. I can also see why I have also fallen for you and trust me it is not for the money; it is because you are one in a million. I gladly accept your gift from Danni, and understand you wanting me to be more independent. I just do not want you thinking I am taking advantage of you sweetie." He said, as he placed his arms around me and pulled me towards him as we embraced.
"What is mine is yours Johnny, and I want you to be as happy as I am. At the end of the day, it is only money, and it should not make you miserable." I told him, still sobbing slightly

"I agree Roxy, and if it makes you feel better, I will only allow you to make this one gift of money to me. I am 52

in a few weeks' time and this cheque can be that special gift. Is that a deal Roxy?" He asked.

"Yes, honey it is a deal, so long as you do not stay mad at me for very long." I replied, as I looked at him with eyes that had teared up.

"If I did you know it would not last for long Roxy; besides I have given my word. How could I stay mad at you my sweet Roxy? You are my world, the love of my life. I just don't want people thinking I am out to fleece you because of what money you have, that's all sweetie." He replied, as he held me close to him.

"Ok honey, we had best get going to meet this guy. Do not forget your bank book, and all the paperwork." I told him.

I got up off the bed, when Johnny again told me he loved me as he tapped me on the bum and got my coat, then we made our way to the bank where Johnny got his cheque, and the guy got his cars.

We stayed another week in London sorting yet more things out from the apartment before going back to Brighton, so that we could make sure the cars had gone from the car park safely, and we would no longer have the concern. When it was Johnny's birthday I kind of forgot about our deal we made, but also, he should know what I am like. By now, Stuart had moved out of the apartment above the bar and had moved into a lovely house with his mother in Peacehaven. I was so pleased that she was finally here in the south, so that again we could share our times together, to go shopping and to have lunch, catching up with things as we indulged on our times together. I looked around the bar and noticed that Michelle and Allen were coping without us; so, grabbing hold of Johnny, I escorted him through the security doors at the end of the bar up to the apartment upstairs. Now having my own special moment with him, I then held him as I said.

"I am so sorry Johnny, but I have kind of bent the rules to our deal. I have got you a little present."

He looked at me and was a little mad, but just held me and kissed me telling me I was naughty, as he then asked me what I had done; and what is he going to do with me. I had in fact gone to the bank; and asked about putting Johnny's name on the business account, especially as he was in charge of the finances and working in the bar almost seven days a week. I had also gone to the solicitors, to have them draft up the proper paperwork to include Johnny as my business partner; and to top it off, I brought him a special present in which I told him he could not open until everyone had left.
It was a large bottle of his favourite cologne, and some sexy underwear just for the bedroom.

"Oh Roxy my sweet Roxy, this is too much sweetie. Oh I love you so much Roxy, no one has ever given me such a gift like this before. As much as I loved Ruby, she never treated me like this." He told me, now embracing me as he kissed me on the lips, and as he held me close to him.

"Please do not take me wrong Johnny, but the thing is you loved Ruby too much and your love was blind." I said.

"Blind, what do you mean Roxy?" He replied.
"I never ever once saw you act like Danni and I; and Ruby did seem to be in control far too much. I did not even see you hold her hand that often, or even saw hers on your knee when we were at dinner. And that holiday in Lake Como was a waste, as it was such a romantic setting, but you acted like friends. Yes, we fooled around and had some fun in the pool, but that was short lived honey." I said, as I looked at him with reason

"Aahh, but love is a funny thing, and you do put up with a lot of things Roxy; and I did love her even with her mood swings sweetie. She was going through a lot, what with her transgression; and then wanting to move away. Then of course wind up the cabaret, and those blasted parties of hers." He replied, trying to make excuses for her again.
"Well, honey you will be loved by me that's for sure, and I can promise you that we will be equals, as love is for two people not one. And my only mood swings will be, shall I buy shoes or a dress, Roxy or Bobby. You can also be assured, that I will you're your hand in public, pinch a crafty kiss from time to time; even tap your ass, just to be cheeky. You must also promise me honey." I said, as Johnny interrupted.

"Of course, I will Roxy, you know that." He said, as I placed my finger on his lips, telling him I am on a roll; and then smiling cheekily at him

"You must promise me that if you are having a bad day, that you will speak to me. Do not take it out of me, just because you are having a bad time. And if for some reason you do not like me anymore; or no longer love me, then please talk to me and please do not hurt me." I said, as I grabbed his hand and brought it to my face where I kissed it.

He then told me that he could never fall out of love with me, because I was such a special and kind person, with whom he has given his heart to. As we began chatting more, we agreed that we would make changed together, and not have one do it without the other knowing. We then got on to the subject of Ruby, as I thought it time that the door was closed on her, as I told him that he may have loved her once, but she tried to change him for her own selfishness, when he asked me how did she try to change him, as he did not quite understand. I smiled at him and told him that it was a 'girl thing.' I then took a deep breath and tried to explain.

"You were and still are a gay man, you like cock and ass. Ruby tried to get you to like tits and a pussy; and change who you really were. No one should do that to anyone, you should accept who you are, and they should accept your choices. I am not a transsexual, I am a gay man like you, but I dress like a woman as it is my choice, as it is Roxy's choice. If you like and accept both my roles, then we will get along fine, but I will not change you, and I do not expect you to try and change me."
"You know I do Roxy, you are a beautiful gay man who is also an incredible woman who has an incredible

beautiful cock and ass. I can't wait to make love to you again and again." He replied, as he looked at me in the eye and then kissed me on the cheek.
"*I know, because you have a stiffy, you horny devil.*" I said jokingly.

Johnny then smiled at me, as we continued to chat. I was on a roll for sure, as I then told him that I gave him credit for sticking with his relationship, though a part of me thought that he should have left her a long time ago; and then looked elsewhere for someone else, someone who could give him what he was seeking.

"*Trust me Roxy, I did so many times want to leave, but I just could not pick up the courage and do it. So many times, I had spoken to Danni and he said the same as you, but I just could not leave her. Besides, I do not think I would have ever been that lucky, to find love again with someone who is special and loving. Although I know I am lucky now, I never thought it would ever happen to me sweetie.*" He said, as he held my hand and thanked me for all I had done.
"*Oh and why is that Johnny? Why do you say you would have never been that lucky? You only have to take a look in a mirror to see how incredibly handsome you are, even with your white hair you are simply gorgeous.*" I told him, as I brushed my hand across his face

"*You say the loveliest of things Roxy, which always make my heart flutter. I said what I said because my dear beautiful girl was already taken, and I would not have come in between Danni and yourself.*" He replied, as he hung his head into his lap.

"*You are such a sweetheart Johnny, but at least we are together now.*" I said, as I smiled at him and placed my hand on his knee.

"*Thank you Roxy, but I feel it is you who is the sweetheart. You have made this old man very happy, as you have shown me what love is all about, just by listening to my stories and not judging me. By showing me how to love; and how to show love; by seeing me as an equal; and being just as much a part of your life, as you are of mine. With you I feel I can be who I am, and I do not have to pretend otherwise. You have shown me so much Roxy, in just a short time; and you have made me feel like a man again.*" He said, as he placed a kiss on my lips

I told him that I should not have left him at the airport, the day I was coming home back to the UK. That I could not turn around to say that last farewell, because I knew I would never see him again. If I had turned around, I would have run back through the barriers, where I would not have let him go, that is until he agreed to come back to the UK with me. The feeling was mutual, as he did not want to let me go, as he had a wonderful few months with me; and the last few days were like being in heaven. There he told me that he looked at me differently, as he began to fall in love with me. He knew there was an atmosphere with Ruby and I; and he could not understand why, because he thought that we were the best of friends. Oh how wrong he was. The time I was there, the friendship we had soured, as she showed me her true colours. As fort an atmosphere, well tell me about it, as once she told me a few things, I knew I could no longer stay there, because I knew at that point that I was no longer welcome. Johnny begged me to say what she had said, letting me know that we were now a couple; and that there should be no secrets between us, when I realised, I had opened my mouth; and now I had to say what was the reason behind what I had just said.

I fell silent for a while as I thought I had said too much as it was. I was not a bitchy person, but Ruby did hurt my feelings those past few days, and I now know why she does not want to know me. I just thought of all the things we did together, the chats we had; and how close we were. She hurt me a lot, and I would never forgive her for that.

"Come on sweetie, don't go quiet on me. What did Ruby say to you?" He said, now with his hand under my chin and he lifted it up, so I looked him in the eyes.

"She did hurt me Johnny, with what she was saying. I did feel I was no longer welcome there, as she so often told me to fuck off to the bar and be with you." I replied, still debating whether I should be honest and just come out with it, but I was scared of hurting his feelings, as he had been hurt by her for so many years, he did not need me to follow suit.

"Is that it, she just made you feel uncomfortable." He asked.

"No Johnny, ok you want to hear the full story, so I will tell you; but please brace yourself." I said, as I now began to compose myself as Johnny held my hand.
"Ok sweetie, it is fine you know that." He replied, as he placed my hand into his and let me rest against him.
"So many times, she told me that she wanted me out of the house; as she had a friend coming over, and that her friend does not really like gay people. She also said on a few occasions that I should fuck off to the bar and be with you, as she knew I fancied you; and that you were a worthless gay man, who could not satisfy her; and in her own words she said, take him off my hands as I have no more use for him, he is a pathetic gay man like a lot of your kind. I have myself a real man now; and he is a top surgeon here on the island. So Roxy, fuck off to the bar please; and let me get on with my life; my life with my new man Brian." I said, shaking as Johnny held me.
"Brian!!! the fucking bitch, thank you Roxy, you have just confirmed something I had been wondering about for years. She has been having an affair with her doctor, all the time she was with me." He replied, as he then began to well up.

He put his hands towards his face and started to cry. I then turned towards him and placed his head on my shoulder and told him that I loved him, as I told him that I was sorry for what I had said. He looked at me with red eyes and told me that he was grateful of what I had said, as he thought he was going out of his mind with worry these past years, thinking it was something he had done, as he questioned himself.

"I have spent so many years wondering if I was just making false accusation towards her, as I had no real proof or evidence to support my theories, as many times she had extra appointments which I thought did not seem to lay right. Then when on the island, she often said she couldn't help in the bar as she had extra work to do at the apartments. Roxy you have just made me realise what a stupid man I have been, and you have made me realise that I was not going mad. And now, what with the cheque you have given me; and all this paperwork, it is all too much; and I am sorry for being upset Roxy, it is just too much." He said, now crying and shaking, as he kept calling Ruby a bitch; and a lying one at that, who made his life hell; and how he thought that it was all his fault.

I again placed my hand onto his hand, as I then told him that the cheque, I gave him, was not even a quarter of what I would love to give him. That this was something I could do so he could have some money of his own, and where he could treat me without feeling guilty of asking me for any money. The business account and Danni's bar, where I was waiting for his signatures were because we were now a couple and it would be our business. That I knew that he was a very proud humble man; and he would have never have suggested the joint business, or indeed ask me for money for helping in the bar, because he was just happy sharing his life with me. I also told him that I would need his signature on my other account, my personal account, as I had no secrets from him; and that I wanted him to be just as free with spending and treating me, other than using the business account, as I thought the business account should stay as business. He then again held me and cried as he told me thank you, as he lay me on the bed and made love to me, before going back down to the bar.

Having explained my reasons, I also told Johnny that if he felt a little better, the business would give him a wage and that wage would go into his own personal account. I then giggled slightly as I told him, that way I would not know the cost of things when he surprised me with gifts he may buy me.

He looked at me and called me a crafty minx.

It was agreed that he take a wage, as he told me that he did not want to take from my personal account, but would instead prefer to use his own money; and not for the cheeky reason I gave. He said it would be nice if we both had separate personal accounts, as well as a joint one; and of course the business one, should I agree. I did agree with him, as I told him it was a good idea, but should he need extra funds he should tell me as I would have more in my own personal account than he would in his, and I still wanted us to be equals.

After yet more conversations, we agreed that a large sum would be placed in the joint account for other spending other than that of our separate accounts, which again I thought was the best way to go, as it still gave us both independence from one another.

Johnny and I discussed a few times buying a home together, so we could make our own ventures and to put our own stamp on things. We looked around and ended up buying a property just up from the harbour, with a view across the sea and a beautiful back garden that had lots of land in which we could design ourselves, where we did end up putting our stamp on the property; and where we had lots of parties and summer BBQ's. it was a beautiful five six bedroomed six bathroom property, and it looked like a mansion, with palm trees that followed the shape of the driveway, with pillars that guarded the front of the house. I still kept the Hove property, and let Ellie and Di spend time there when they came down to visit us. We also visited London every two weeks or so for a long weekend, going through the usual routine of fine dining in our favourite restaurants, whereas per usual we would end up spending the last of the evening in the Rainbow.

Johnny had a different swagger about himself, and I think it was because he no longer had to ask me for anything, though he was grateful that he had now had sufficient funds in which he was able to spoil me, with the things I was so used to, without having to come to me to have to ask for money.

I would have my little moments where I would reminisce about my life, how I first started with just one pair of shoes and now accumulating over six hundred pairs. How my first time on stage was scary, but was well rewarding, smiling about my first encounter with Danni. I would often sit alone looking out of the window, looking back at my life of drag, sex and stiletto heels; and knew now that I was with Johnny, that now that other side of my life flitting from bed to bed had finished, and how I was happy sharing only myself with him, as we never took a third person or fourth person to our bed. I wanted a new life, and a new start; and knew Johnny was all I wanted, as I too knew he was not into that sort of thing.

I never lied to him, as I did mention to him once about the liaisons of mine and Danni's past, when he opened up to me and told me about a rendezvous that he and Ruby once had, which made me smile, knowing that he too had since joined in the forbidden fruits of lust.

We would run Danni's bar together more now, more than when I put Allen in charge; and let Allen and the boys take over through the week, when we decided we were going to take only a day off here and there.

Michelle ended up going up to London, where she became a big celebrity on the cabaret scene, ending up in getting her dream, as she ended up having her name in lights, lit up throughout the West End theatres.

Stuart came in every now and then, and we had that long awaited conversation. He had now met someone in the force who was a little shy, and where I was soon introduced to him. His name was James, and he was a little younger than Stuart. He got on with Stuart's mother very well, so much so he often referred to her as mom, as she in turn called him son; and he in turn moved in with Stuart and his mother, as she now often said she had her own family, and simply loved her boys.

Yes, Margaret simply loved James; and always spoke about him when we went out on our weekly shopping sprees, telling me how proud Stuart's father would be of his son and partner; and how after all the hurt she suffered she has finally found some happiness with her lads which she never thought she would ever see the day.

Johnny was so much the same man as he was when I first saw him in the Rainbow, being the proud bar owner that he once was, but with a more genuine smile than he had ever had before. I however, was always on a bar stool people watching, if not in the royal box making sure my boys were ok, as again I would spend hours laughing and talking about old times as well as new; and seeing a new family evolve around us in Danni's bar.

It was very much similar to the old days now, with Johnny and I taking the place of Johnny and Ruby, but where we were both equal. Ruby soon became a distant memory, which eventually faded.

How things had changed around for the better, for the better of both Johnnie and me, and how lovely it was as each day we bloomed more than the day before.

I would still go up to The Downs, where I would sit quietly and talk to Danni, telling him all that had been going on and what we were doing. And if I were not at the bar or at home, Johnny would know I would be with Danni, where he would call me to see if I was ok and would come and pick me up.

I did not go that often to speak to Danni, not like I did in the past, as I had a new life now, I just wanted my quiet moments with him here and there, to let him know that both Johnny and I were fine as I muttered away contently to myself sitting down on the grass admiring the view out to sea.

Johnny and I had just had a nice meal at home, and I had to give Johnny credit where it is due, he knew how to cook. After we had finished our meal, we started to get ready to go to the bar. Once we got to Danni's bar, we greeted the boys and asked how things were, when we both sat down in the royal box and was joined by Stuart. He started to tell us that he was considering taking up a promotion that he had been offered, when all of a sudden someone walked through the door which took my breath away, as I froze in my tracks, I began to turn as white as a sheet. As I stood up, I accidently knocked the table spilling the drinks. I stepped from the table holding Johnny's hand, as Johnny, Adam and Stuart just gazed in awe, as they too could not believe what they were seeing.

"DANNI, is that you Danni?" I said, as I had turned white in shock
"No Roxy it is me, do you not you recognise me?" He replied, as I was still in shock, not realising that the accent was different

In front of me stood a young man in his early twenties I would have said, with blonde hair and a blonde goatee, and standing about six feet tall. He was the spitting image of Danni; and it was as though I had just seen a ghost.

"It's Danni Johnny." I said, as I put my arm behind me awaiting Johnny's hand.
"It can't be Roxy; it just can't be. He died sweetie." Johnny said.
"Roxy; do you not know who I am? It is me Jake." He replied, now holding his arms out for me.

I ran over to him and just gave him a hug, as Allen looked at me and miming the words fuckin gorgeous, as he asked who the cutie was. I told him that it is Jake, my little prince; and that he had come home, as I became a frantic blubbering wreck with tears rolling down my face. I looked at Johnny and told him we need to go home right now; and with that he ordered a cab. I looked at Allen and Stuart and told them that we had to get home, that I had to find out where my boy has been; and what he has been up to.

Stuart was about to go home himself, when he told us that he would drive us home; and then would catch up with us the following day, as he told Jake it was really nice to see him again after so many years.

Johnny phoned the cab company and cancelled our ride, as Stuart escorted us to his car. I held onto Jake with all of my might, as I placed my hand onto his face and told him how grown-up he had become; and how handsome he was. How much like his brother he now looked; and how much of a fright he had given me, as I then told him that he should have phoned first, as I am no spring chicken anymore.

Once we got home Johnny asked if we wanted a drink, and after we told him yes Johnny made his way to the kitchen to get me a glass of wine. Jake so much like Danni and his father as he asked for bourbon, when Johnny obliged and then poured himself a scotch.

I then asked him where he was staying, in which Jake told me he was firstly staying in London at the Dorchester, as he had booked a suite; and that it was Ellie who told him where I was. He told her to be quiet and not say anything, as he wanted to surprise me, so he then caught a train, and with the directions that Ellie had given him, he made his way to Brighton.

He had since booked himself into The Grand Hotel on the seafront; and then decided to come and see if I was in the bar. I then told him that he is staying with Johnny and me; and that we will settle his bill later when we fetch his things.

We sat there talking for hours, as Jake told me all that had been happening in his life since I last saw him.

How his mother had done the same to him and Sophie, as she had done to Danni; selling them to her father and waiving her rights as a parent. He did not mind though what she had done, as his father loved them more than their mother did, so it was a big relief when his mother signed parentage over to him, as they knew they would be looked after much better.

Then there was a lot of trouble when they had reached the age of 20, their inheritance was now accessible as their father decided to let them have it a year earlier; and their mother tried to manipulate both Jake and Sophie into parting with a good portion of it.

Their father decided to release their inheritance early, as they wanted to clear their student loans, as well as any other debt they incurred whilst on campus; and still she tried to get her hands on what she thought she had the rights too as a parent, taking them to court in which she lost again. He then told me that they had one massive argument, where he and Sophie told her to sling her hook; and to go back to the bars in which she spent most of her like turning tricks like a two-bit whore. Then after that they never saw her again; and if truth be known he was glad to see the back of her, when he then looked at me and said.

"Remember when I was at your wedding, and I asked you to be my mother?"

"Yes honey I do, I remember that as if it were only yesterday. It was so lovely of you and Sophie, you nearly made me cry my eyes out" I replied, holding onto his hand

"Well both Sophie and I went through high school telling everyone that our mother was our stepmother, and that you were our real mother. It was you who kept us going; and you who gave us belief. I grew up believing that one day I would come home; and I would have you, my real mother with me. I tried so hard to make it in America that I was lost, as people only wanted to know me because I had money and my mother… well she only wanted all we had inherited. I do not want to come across as an ungrateful person, but both Sophie and I rejoiced when she had lost the court case, ending up with her losing her big house, her status, and of course Sophie and me. We both told her that we never wanted to see her as long as she lives, that she is nothing more than a gold digger and a parasite; and we were grateful for dad having us, as it was only then, did we understand the meaning of love and what a parent is." He said, as he held onto my hand so tight.

I told him that I had missed both of them so much; and I had missed the letters when they had stopped coming. I began asking him what he had been up to; and did he have a girlfriend. Just like a mother I bombarded him with questions, not coming up for air, when he then said.

"No Roxy, I do not have a girlfriend, although I do have a few girls as friends if you know what I mean? I have had a few boyfriends though, but again they only wanted

me because I lived in a big house with Sophie and dad; and had all the money to go with it. I then decided that I would come and look for you Roxy. I have come home Roxy; I have come home mother if you will have me?" He cried uncontrollably, as he opened his arms out to me *"Oh my poor little Jake, you are home. Your uncle Johnny and Roxy will never see you alone, remember that sweetheart."* I said, as I held him and placed his head in my shoulder.

"But will you be my mother Roxy? I have always dreamed of it; and have never had a mother who loved me as much as you loved me. I always knew you were special; and always knew that Danni saw something in you that no-one else saw, unless they had been in your company to understand who you are. It was not until Sophie and I received that money from you, that we both realised you were our true mother. You honoured Danni's wish, and you thought of us with the kindness you always showed us when we were in your company. You never showed us any ill harm or showed nastiness towards us, because you were always very kind and thoughtful. Please say you will be my mother, as I so long to call it you." He asked, as he continued to cry. *"Yes Jake, my beautiful little prince. I will be your mother, and I will be honoured for you to call me that."* I told him.

He then cried on my shoulders, holding me close to him as he said.

"I have waited all my life for this moment mother, so many nights have I cried going to sleep holding a secret

425

picture of you wishing you would just take us away and look after us. Only when Sophie and I moved in with father, was we allowed to have a picture of you by our bedside. My dreams have finally come true, and I have my true mother in my life at last. I love you Roxy, I love you so much." He cried.

"And I love you too Jake; now please excuse me whilst I go to the bedroom." I replied.

"Do you remember the time you visited us in America with Danni, for a whole month? Sophie and I ran into your arms not knowing someone had tried to kill you, as we were so excited to see you. That was the best month of our lives; and from that month I knew that you were meant to be our mother Roxy, I always held you in my heart and looked at the picture that the three of us had taken; and kept it with me all these years." He said, as his tears began to fade.

"Oh Jake, you sweet boy, I did not realise you had such a love for me, and to keep something like that close to you and not tell anyone must have been awful?" I replied, now with tears rolling down my face.

"I contemplated so many times about running away; and asked dad to see if he would let us live with him, or if he would bring us over here to England to be with you and Danni. I was really happy when dad paid her off and let us live with him, as we had some stability and love in our lives. And when she signed the rights of parentage over to him, both Sophie and I were jumping for joy. When we had lost Danni, I wanted so much to come and see you, but thought you would have soon forgot about us. I did though still know deep down inside that one day I would be with my true mother, my real mother and a mother

*who really loves m*e, *and here I am now.*
I love you so much." He said, as he cried into his hands.
"*I would have never turned my back on you my little*
prince, nor would I turn my back on Sophie. I would
have never forgotten you, as you were and still are my
*sweet prince and princ*ess." I replied, as I held him close
and wiped away his tears.

He then told me that he had some other news for me, and
that Sophie was going to call me later in the week, as he
had since told her that he had found you, and that she is
going to call his cell to speak to me. Not being able to
hold myself, I asked what the news was, because surely
it was more than Sophie calling me, when he told me
that Sophie had given birth to a baby boy, not four
months ago; and that she has named him Danni-Robert,
after her two favourite people. I just thought how
wonderful, as I had not heard the name Bobby for such a
long time, now stroking his head as I told him that it was
alright. He told me that she hoped I did not mind her
using her other name; because they are planning another
baby in the fall, and if it is a girl, they want to name her
Roxie, with a 'ie' and not a 'y.' And that I must not let
her know that he had told me. I thought it was so sweet
of her, and I would tell her so when she calls me to tell
me, now with a few more tears running down my face.

I went upstairs to the bedroom and opened the French
doors to the balcony where I walked out, I took in the
view of the distant sea looking at the horizon, where I
reached for some tissues and started to cry.

"I have finally got my family I have finally got my prince and princess, all these years I have waited and now my little prince has come home… Thank you Danni."

Just then Johnny came into the bedroom where he saw me crying, as he walked onto the balcony, he came over to me and held me tight.

"It has been a very long journey Roxy, but everything has worked out fine. I had to look twice to see if it were Danni as did Adam and Stuart. It kind of spooked us all. I know how much you love Jake and Sophie, and now you have then back; and Jake your little boy has come back sweetie. He has come home Roxy; you little boy is home." He said, as he held me tightly.
"He has Johnny; my little boy has come home. I really love you Johnny, even if I am a crying wreck. I love you." I replied
"Then do me one last favour Roxy." He asked
"What's that Johnny?" I asked, as he then looked at me and got down on one knee
"Marry me, will you please marry me?" He asked.
"Yes Johnny, I will marry you, I would really love to marry you. But you need to do it properly" I replied, as again I had tears running down my face.

As he did not have a ring for me yet, he took off his signet ring which was too big for me; and then placed it onto my finger. I then noticed Jake had now made his way from the balcony; and was in the doorway where again he was crying, but a happy sort of cry.

"*Mother, Danni would most certainly approve.*" He said, now crying his eyes out.

Johnny and I held out our arms to him, where we both said.

"*Jake, come here son. Come on, give us a hug.*"

Running into our arms now crying as much as I was, he placed his arms around the pair of us resting his head on our shoulders. Johnny then placed his arm around Jake's waist as I placed my hand on his head gently stroking him and comforting him as he cried, letting him know that he no longer had to run or have to wait for a mother's love. That at last, his waiting was over, and he had got what he had always wished for.
That at long last he was finally home.

"*Everything will be fine son, you no longer have to wish; and you no longer have to dream, and you certainly no longer have to hide. You are home my lovely beautiful Jake.*" I said as I hugged him so tightly; and as Johnny kissed him on the forehead

He then held us both tight, as we both gave him a kiss on the cheek, as Johnny then told us that he will go downstairs and get our drinks so that we can celebrate; as I began talking to Jake, holding him as I called him my prince once again.
Johnny then brought three glasses up with him; and a bottle of our finest champagne as he carefully poured it into our glasses, spilling some and sending the cork

shooting out over the balcony. Now with the three of us standing there holding each other, we again stepped out onto the balcony; as we looked over towards the distant sea; with Jake in the middle being comforted by Johnny and myself.

"To us Roxy, to my future wife, and to my future son; here is to our future." Johnny toasted.

Jake then looked at us, and in a tearful voice he said.

"Danni would so approve mother. He would be so happy for you and Johnny. To my new mother and father, to my new family. He would so approve *Roxy; Danni would so approve."*

We then raised our glasses; and toasted our future together. Jake stood in the middle, as Johnny and I were either side of him as we held him close to us, looking out at the distant horizon, as I finally knew I had got my family back and we were once again complete. Thinking to myself the last words I had with his birth mother; and how they had rung true, as it brought a flashback to my mind, as well as a rather somewhat smug but thankful look that I had my true family with me.
We chatted and laughed together, looking over at that spectacular view of the harbour; and towards the distant horizon with the lights of Brighton and Hove to the right of us. And it was at that point that all of a sudden, the sun peered through the darkening sky; and how the three of us caught a smell of Danni's cologne, as our lips all tingled at the same precise moment in time, letting us

know that Danni was there with us, giving us all a sense of peace as we raised our glasses and toasted our future, as we thanked Danni Svenningsen for bringing us all back together again once again.